MORE PRAISE FOR
ORDEAL

"A gripping, always unpredictable page-turner . . . Mills writes with authority and confidence . . . fraught with suspense."   *—Lubbock Avalanche-Journal*

"Adds an arresting new dimension to the concept of mother love."   *—Kirkus Reviews*

"A taut hardcover debut . . . a fast-moving plot, infusions of Cherokee culture and vivid characters help drive the action as Mills explores the sordid reality behind the Oklahoma bombing headlines."   *—Publishers Weekly*

"Mills's characters are vivid and her plot is all too believable. This book places her in the same high caliber as Ridley Pearson."   *—Lake Worth Herald*

"*Ordeal* is all too believable in today's world of violence and anti-government sentiment. That, coupled with Mills's superb storytelling skills, makes this one novel you won't want to put down."   *—Gazette Telegraph*

"Swift and unpredictable."   *—Bookman News*

TIGHTROPE

Deanie Francis Mills

A SIGNET BOOK

SIGNET
Published by the Penguin Group
Penguin Putnam Inc., 375 Hudson Street,
New York, New York 10014, U.S.A.
Penguin Books Ltd, 27 Wrights Lane,
London W8 5TZ, England
Penguin Books Australia Ltd, Ringwood,
Victoria, Australia
Penguin Books Canada Ltd, 10 Alcorn Avenue,
Toronto, Ontario, Canada M4V 3B2
Penguin Books (N.Z.) Ltd, 182–190 Wairau Road,
Auckland 10, New Zealand

Penguin Books Ltd, Registered Offices:
Harmondsworth, Middlesex, England

First published by Signet, an imprint of Dutton NAL,
a member of Penguin Putnam Inc.

First Printing, February, 1999
10 9 8 7 6 5 4 3 2 1

 REGISTERED TRADEMARK—MARCA REGISTRADA

Printed in the United States of America

PUBLISHER'S NOTE
This is a work of fiction. Names, characters, places, and incidents either are
the product of the author's imagination or are used fictitiously, and any resem-
blance to actual persons, living or dead, events, or locales is entirely
coincidental.

For my brother, Brad Henderson,
who has always been
my champion, hero, and friend,
and who had the uncommon good sense
to marry my college roommate
and sister of the soul,
Pam—
with love to you both.

poker: *originally a card game for unprinci-*
pled players only . . . the object is
to have a better hand than any other
player or to win by bluffing the other
players into believing that one has a
better hand and thus causing them
to drop out of the game.

It is only by risking our persons from one
hour to another that we live at all. And
often enough our faith beforehand in an
uncertified result is the only thing that
makes the result come true.

———William James

UNDER THE GUN

under the gun: *A situation where a
   player . . . must make his decision
   to bet, check, or fold before any other.*

Every good and excellent thing in the world
stands moment by moment on the razor-
edge of danger and must be fought for.

—Thornton Wilder
The Skin of Our Teeth

PART I
THE DEAL

Dealer's Choice: *A poker session in which the dealer has the right to select the form of poker to be played.*

There is therefore no escape from the choice that lies before us.

———Bertrand Russell

Chapter One

Game starts. March 1997.

Dominic Antonio had never been summoned to the penthouse suite by the Boss himself, and he couldn't decide whether he should be nervous or excited. Few of them had ever even seen the penthouse; fewer still had been extended an invitation for a private audience. Maybe he and the old man would have a drink, and he would get a promotion. Maybe they would have a drink, and he would be fired.

The elevator had stainless steel doors polished to a high sheen. It was impossible not to stare at himself as he got in alone and pushed the top button. His tie was crooked, and as the elevator swooshed soundlessly upward, he straightened it, then smoothed back his curly dark hair with a hand held steady only by years of practice. There was a cold little hole in the pit of his stomach that shivered as the digital numbers over the doors flew past.

The elevator swooped to a stop, and the doors automatically opened into a wide, opulent corridor. Sky-blue walls decorated with hand-painted murals depicting cherubs and other angelic figures entwined with garlands of flowers vaulted all the way up and over the ceiling. Sparkling crystal chandeliers hung from gold-leaf arches. Louis VI chairs graced either side of the elevator doors. Persian rugs in shades of cream, gold, robin's egg blue, and seashell pink covered gleaming rose-colored marble floors. The strains of a Chopin sonata wafted from some invisible source.

It was like stepping foot into a palace.

Or a whorehouse, he reflected wryly. A casual glance

in the direction of several angles did not reveal a camera's eye, though he knew it was there. Just as he reached the door to the apartment, but before he could press the bell, it was opened by the Boss.

"Come in, come in, Dom." (The Boss was the only person Dominic knew who called him Dom.) "You're right on time."

"Thank you for inviting me, sir," said Dominic with just the right amount of courtesy and deference. The Boss hated butt-kissers and grovelers. "You have a beautiful home."

"Thank you! Thank you!" the Boss said with what appeared to be genuine delight. Waving a hand toward the corridor as he shut the door behind Dominic, the Boss said, "I flew in this painter all the way from Italy to do those murals."

"I'm impressed," said Dominic truthfully.

He followed his smiling employer past a breathtaking wall of windows that showed off New York's ring of skyscrapers around Central Park like a nighttime movie set. There was no sign of the beefy bodyguards who often accompanied the Boss.

Dominic was a big man, standing six-four and weighing in at two hundred pounds, and the dainty French and English antique furnishings and objets d'art made him uncomfortable. It was inevitable that he caught an ankle on a rocking chair in passing and dragged it six inches behind him.

"Oh, uh, sorry," he mumbled, setting the rocking chair back in its place. As he did, he recognized it as one of the late president John F. Kennedy's rockers, which had sold at auction for a small fortune.

"No harm done," said his genial host, leading the way into a cozy library. The room was paneled in hand-carved mahogany and lined with shelves full of what appeared to be leather-bound first-edition volumes, exuding an aromatic, masculine scent of tobacco.

"Cigar?" asked the Boss, holding one out to Dominic, which of course he took, although he'd never been particularly fond of them.

"They're Cuban," added the Boss unnecessarily as he extended a pair of cigar snippers to Dominic. "The Cohiba Robusto, the cigar favored by Fidel Castro himself before he quit smoking."

Dominic gamely followed his employer's lead in snipping off the end of the cigar, puffing it into life, and discreetly disposing of the bits of tobacco that clung to his tongue.

Taking a seat behind a heavy mahogany desk, the Boss poured them each a glass of vintage port from a crystal decanter and motioned Dominic into a deep-seated burgundy leather chair opposite.

"They say the best cigars are rolled between the soft thighs of a Cuban peasant woman," he added, and as he poured the wine, the diamonds in the rings on his fingers flashed in the flickering firelight. "But I've never believed that." He chuckled.

Dominic guessed that a nearby Jacobean armoire disguised a sophisticated computer and modem setup. *A man could stay in a room like this happily for six months and never come out,* he thought.

He still had no idea why he'd been summoned. A dozen work-related comments flitted through his head, but he decided to keep quiet until he knew what the meeting was about.

"Dom, what would you say is the most important quality an employee should possess?"

Dominic blinked at the Boss. He knew a trick question when he heard one. What was the angle?

"In what way do you mean, sir?"

Through a wreath of cigar smoke, the Boss shrugged. "What do you think is the most important thing an employee should offer his or her company?" He fixed his sharp blue eyes on Dominic's face.

Little needles of anxiety prickled Dominic's underarms, and he could feel himself beginning to sweat beneath his suit coat, vest, and crisp white cotton shirt. The Boss wasn't interested in what Dominic thought, of course, but in what Dominic thought *the Boss* thought.

Without breaking eye contact, Dominic said, "Loyalty."

A smile of approval stretched across the Boss's lean, handsome face. "You're absolutely right, Dom. Nothing matters any more in these trying times than loyalty.

You've got to be able to trust the people who are working for you, that's all there is to it."

"Yes, sir."

"If you can't trust them . . ." He narrowed his eyes. "What's this about, Mr.—"

The Boss held up a hand to quiet Dominic. "Watch this."

From somewhere beneath the desk he pushed a button, and suddenly one of the bookshelves that lined the wall swung out and away, revealing a secret room within.

"I want to show you something," the Boss said. He got up from behind the desk and headed into the entranceway of the secret room behind the bookshelves. Dominic felt a sudden wave of panic and struggled to suppress it. What the hell was happening? Was he about to get his ass killed and sealed up in some macabre hidden chamber like some freaking Edgar Allan Poe story?

Following reluctantly, still holding the fragile wineglass because he didn't know what else to do with it, Dominic hung back close to the entryway, keeping the Boss in front of him, and peered into the brightly lit vault-like windowless concrete chamber measuring about twelve by twelve feet. Nestled within the room was a *second* room.

The entire inner room, all four sides, was constructed of Plexiglas, resting like some giant cube of ice within a gleaming copper-mesh wire cage that was elevated about six inches off the floor. Dominic's jaw dropped. "You've got a *Faraday cage*?" he cried.

His boss beamed at him like a little kid. "My own little bubble. Completely shielded from all RF transmissions," he boasted.

"I've read about these," said Dominic in awe, "but I've never seen one."

Unlatching a copper-mesh screen door that overlapped the wire-encased glass walls, the Boss pulled open a thick transparent Plexiglas door underneath. He tapped the glass. "Vacuum-sealed," he said.

Curiosity overpowered Dominic's doubts, and he couldn't help being drawn toward the astounding little room. Inside were two chairs and a small table—all constructed of clear plastic. The floors beneath were well lit. He had to stoop to enter the doorway and stand somewhat hunched over in the little space. With the transparent walls and furniture, it was like walking on air and gave him a weird, disconnected feeling.

The Boss pulled the door shut behind them. "Sit down, Dom, before you get a crick in your neck."

The moment the door clicked shut, Dominic felt a rush of claustrophobia. It made no difference that the walls were see-through. This was a vacuum-sealed room. That meant there was no outside source of air. What was already present inside when they shut the door was it. There was no background noise whatsoever. The silence was so absolute that Dominic could hear himself breathing. It gave him the creeps.

The Boss took a seat opposite Dominic, still grinning. "This room is absolutely, one hundred percent bug-proof," he said, his voice booming in the cramped space. "The Plexiglas has an inner layer of acrylic. You would be able to see any electronic surveillance device whatsoever, and the outer concrete walls are flooded with phase-shift noise generators."

"What about the power lines?" asked Dominic as he glanced around nervously. It was hot in the close little room, and he was beginning to sweat in earnest. "It's well lit."

"Isolation transformers."

Dominic nodded. He pointed to a book that had been placed incongruously on the clear acrylic table between the chairs. "Tape recorder detector?"

"Yup," said the Boss proudly.

He couldn't help but grin. "And the pen in your pocket?"

"Bug alert." It was all the Boss could do not to preen.

"I figured." Dominic shook his head.

"Plus, the Plexiglas/acrylic walls are absolutely sound-proof. You could murder somebody in here, and nobody would ever know a thing."

Dominic's breath caught in his throat, and he struggled mightily to keep the fear out of his eyes. It was creepy enough being sealed up in here like some kind of mummy in a sarcophagus, but he had no way of knowing what the hell was going on in his paranoid boss's little mind, or why he'd chosen to show the secret room to Dominic at all.

The Boss leaned forward conspiratorially. Sheer theatrics, considering where they were, but Dominic inclined his head.

"This is about Joe Dalton," said the Boss, his voice gone suddenly cold and dead.

Goose bumps crawled over Dominic's skin. Joe Dalton had worked for them for about a month and then disappeared. Nobody asked any questions, because questions such as those were discouraged in this line of work.

Oh, Jesus, he thought, *did this guy kill Joe?* And then, *Shit, did he bring Joe in here to do it?*

The knot at the pit of his stomach folded in on itself in a cramp. He stifled a grunt.

"Joe Dalton was not loyal," said the Boss. "And now he's gone." He leaned back, fixing ice-blue eyes on Dominic.

Beads of perspiration popped up on Dominic's upper lip, and he was grateful for the thick mustache that hid the sweat. He figured he could take the old man on, but how far would he get? The bodyguards, he was sure, were just as effectively hidden as the surveillance cameras.

He had to say something, but his mind was frozen. *Think.* Stretching his long legs out to the side of the little table and feigning an arrogant smile, Dominic said, "Well, good riddance. One thing I learned playing football was the importance of a team player. Dalton didn't want to play by team rules, he could get the hell out."

The Boss smiled back. "I figured you would feel that way, Dom. I thought it important to let you know what was going on with Dalton, just in case you were wondering."

Yeah right, thought Dominic. *And we had to come into your little spy-proof room to do it.*

It was bizarre, but then, so was everything else about this job. It took every ounce of his willpower to sit still in the stuffy little glass cage.

Scotty, beam me the fuck out of here, he thought.

The mornings were always the worst.
Watching prison life as portrayed on TV and in the

movies, Max had always imagined that the nights would be the hardest, when darkness smothered the sobs of other inmates and shrouded certain acts best kept secret by the shadows. She had expected lights out to serve notice of tense vigilance and sticky fear, especially after the time she'd spent in the county jail awaiting trial.

They all expected that at first. But the Federal Prison Camp in Bryan, Texas, was a minimum-security facility that operated more like a college campus than a prison, in surface appearances anyway. Days were filled with work (for which she was paid forty cents an hour), counseling sessions, team meetings, classes, and other activities designed to teach some of the women "life skills" and to prepare them all for the outside world. By the time Max fell into her cot—one of four bunks in a cell approximately ten by twelve feet—she was usually surprisingly tired. She seldom laid awake anymore

Sometimes Gaby came to Max in her dreams, her soft sweet little face flushed with pleasure, blue eyes dancing, blond hair flying behind her as she flung herself into her mother's arms. The hug was so physical, so real, that Max would often think to herself, "This isn't a dream after all. It's really happening," and the joy would almost burst her heart.

Then she would wake up.

Insomnia, for Max, took shape as sudden predawn awakenings, long before the prison—even the boot campers—began to stir. She could never seem to go back to sleep. And there was never any doubt as to where she was.

She could almost forget, sometimes, while working outdoors in the greenhouse or mowing the smooth, manicured lawns around the prison compound. Originally an academy for boys until the federal government bought it seven years before—a year before Max had come—the buildings that housed the eight hundred or so women prisoners were cream-colored adobe blocks with neat brown trim around the windows and roofs. Tidy flower beds adorned the spacious lawns along with shaggy trees, gazebos where the women liked to gather to smoke, and colorful playground and picnic equipment for family visiting days.

Even the prison clothes they all had to wear didn't look like prison garb so much as work uniforms, with khaki-colored cotton pants and work shirts, and lace-up work boots. Prison officials often buzzed down the pathways between the buildings in electric carts. Most inmates moved freely on the compound, going about their business. Nonviolent offenders who had proven themselves trustworthy sometimes even worked in town.

The cafeteria food was so good that many of the women gained weight while inside. Chapel walls were ringed with gorgeous handmade quilts done by inmates, each with another inspirational quote or proverb stitched across. The corridors of the classroom areas were adorned with paintings done by some of the women in their art classes.

Sometimes Max could focus on these things and make herself forget that she was in prison.

Until the morning.

The living quarters for the women were cavernous two-story cement-block buildings with bare concrete floors opening into a large central area that contained a few metal tables. None of the cells had doors of any kind, just rectangular openings that revealed stark cement block walls barren of any personal effects, two bunks (top and bottom) on each side of the room and a row of metal lockers, one for each of the four women who shared the cell. Family snapshots and the like were tucked away in the lockers, along with one change of clothes, grooming items, and a limited number of personal effects. One small desk and a chair faced the single window between the cots, which was covered with wire mesh.

There were no TVs or radios or books or any other homey things that could soften their cells or make them tolerable. It was a prison, and anyone who doubted that had only to walk out of the Texas sunshine and into the comparative gloom of the cell block and endure the prying eyes of the guards, counselors, and other keepers to know that.

When Max opened her eyes before the six o'clock a.m. call, and before the five-thirty a.m. awakening of the Boot Camp inmates, the first thing she always saw was the cot an arm's reach away and the one hanging right over her head; the first thing she heard was the strangled snoring of one of her cell mates and the steady breathing of the others.

As the pearly luminescence of dawn crept through the metal blinds covering the window and striped the floor beside Max's cot, the familiar depression—held at bay only by a few pitiful dreams of the child she hadn't seen in almost seven years—always settled heavy on her chest like a feral beast who wanted nothing but to squeeze the life out of her.

And though she would always take a big gulp or two, she could never seem to get enough air in her lungs. Her chest would ache, her eyes would burn, and she would wonder, every single morning of her life . . . she would wonder how in the name of heaven she was going to survive another day.

Loneliness was the only real companion Max had, for the most part. In prison, which contained inmates from forty-six different states, people didn't indulge in all that much small talk anyway. Their lives always seemed so crisis-driven. Most of them were mothers, many of whom were separated from their families by hundreds or even thousands of miles, or by vindictive spouses, or by the courts; and every time they called home—which was several times a week usually—there was some new crisis to upset them. A son in jail. A daughter in the hospital. A cheating man. A wedding or some other milestone taking place that they were missing. Just not being able to be there was terrible punishment to many of them.

Some of the women lied to their small children, telling them that Mommy had gone away to college. No matter what they told the children, the kids often cried over the phone and begged their mothers to come home—or worse, refused to speak to them at all.

So many of the women's stories were sad recitations of their failures. More than a few of them wound up in prison because they'd gotten mixed up with bad men, but the majority of them were there due to drug addiction or drug peddling or both. There were a few embezzlers and tax cheats among them, but for the most part, they were women who, for one reason or another, seemed unfit for or incapable of handling daily life.

Max always felt set apart from most everyone else in

one way or another. The same education, job experience, and life background that separated her from the general prison population actually put her more in the same league as the prison staff—but of course she could never be close friends with any of them. For the most part, she tended to keep to herself, lending a sympathetic ear to a distraught cell mate when necessary, sharing a lunch table with coworkers, but never really being a part of anything.

So Max was surprised the day she looked up to find Trudy Barkowski striding urgently across the prison grounds toward her as she kneeled beside one of the flower beds, patiently transplanting bluebonnet seeds she'd carefully split open and soaked in water overnight.

On that day, her life changed forever. There was no warning, of course—but then, there never was, was there?

There'd been no warning the day her dad was killed or the day they lost her cherished big brother, Brand. She'd had no warning the day she'd found blood on the panties of her two-year-old child . . . no warning at all that the handsome, distinguished, intelligent federal judge who was her husband was also a child molester.

So Max was no more prepared to have her life changed on this deceptively warm March day on her knees by a flower bed, fresh new seeds of life resting in the palm of her hand, than she had been on any of the others.

Trudy had been at the camp almost as long as Max herself. Like seventy percent of the inmate population, Trudy was in for drug-related charges. By the time her shadow fell across Max, she was panting, which made her sound even more excited than she already was.

"Max!" she cried between breaths. "You got a visitor."

Max sat back on her heels and squinted up at Trudy, shielding her eyes from the bright early-morning sun. Like so many of the women incarcerated here, Trudy had that hard-eyed barfly look of somebody who never had much choice in life but to make all the wrong choices. As always, she fidgeted as she stood by Max.

Trudy, her eyes alight with curiosity, said, "This came down *all the way from the warden's office.*"

Sudden fear sliced through Max's jacket and laid a cold blade against her heart. *Gaby.*

Dumping the seeds onto the dirt, Max sprang to her feet and began striding toward the front offices. She wasn't sure where to go. Her mother nearly always met her at the picnic tables on visiting day.

Something must be wrong with Gaby. Something terrible. A car wreck or . . . Gabe? Had he found her after all? At the mere thought of her ex-husband getting his hands on their daughter again, Max's heart tumbled.

Calm down, she thought. *She's not a baby anymore. She's almost ten years old now.* Still, if he found her . . .

Or her mom! Something could have happened to her mom!

Max broke into a sprint, ignoring paths and cutting straight across the grass. She could not imagine life without her mom, who had visited her faithfully every single weekend of her incarceration and sent her goofy little cards and notes during the endless weeks. If it wasn't for her mom, Max didn't think she could have made it.

"Hey, hey, hey! Whoa! Slow down there." Mike Jackson, one of the prison officials who assisted the warden, appeared at her elbow and put a gently restraining hand on her arm. He was tall and good-looking and dressed, as always, in a suit and tie. Some of the women tried to flirt with him, but he was impervious to their sidelong glances and giggles. To Max, he was always unfailingly polite.

"Trudy said there's somebody here to see me." Max, panting from the run and panic, couldn't keep the anxiety from her voice. "Is something wrong with my mom? Or . . ."

"No, no. Nothing like that."

Max stumbled to a halt. "Then, who . . . what . . . ?"

He smiled at her. He really did have such nice brown eyes. "Well, I realize this is highly irregular, allowing you a visitor in the middle of the week, but he's flown down from New York and is only going to be here one day."

Frowning, Max said, "New York? I don't know anybody in New York, Mr. Jackson."

He opened the door for her, like a gentleman would any lady, and Max felt pitifully grateful. She smiled her thanks and walked into the building ahead of him, trying for once to hold her head up instead of schlepping along like she usually did.

As the door eased close behind them, Jackson hesitated. "You might want to . . . wash your hands . . . before you meet your guest."

She glanced down at her hands, still grimy from the flower bed.

"Max . . . this is about a job offer. This man has come all the way down here to offer you a job when you get out."

"A job?" His tone of voice seemed low, almost excited, and she lowered her voice to match. "I don't understand."

He shrugged. "You know you still show up in the media from time to time. Your case got a lot of publicity."

"Yeah . . . ?"

"Well, he's heard about you. He says he admires your courage and tenacity, and he's impressed with your background."

She blinked as her eyes adjusted to the fluorescent lights of the indoor hallway, where they stood. "What kind of business does he have?"

"I'll let him tell you about it. Here"—he gestured toward the ladies' room door—"I'll wait out here for a few minutes, and then I'll take you to him."

Because she didn't know what else to do, Max ducked into the ladies' room, washed her hands with soap, then examined herself in the mirror.

Pathetic.

She'd been allowed to keep her long hair, but she had to do it up every day in a tight French braid that was pinned to the back of her head. Of course, she was wearing no makeup, and though she had requested outdoor duty, it had been a cloudy, nasty winter, and the lack of sun showed on her pale face, which was fair-complected to start with. She could no longer remember a time when her eyes were not dark-circled, and the khaki work shirt bleached out the quixotic changeable color from her hazel eyes.

Splashing cool water on her face, she wet down the strands of blond hair that had sprung free of their pins. It was hopeless, really. No matter what she tried to do, she still looked like what she was: a prisoner.

Hell of a way to go in for a job interview.

A *job*. It sounded like a forgotten word from a language that she used to speak but no longer knew. As she followed Mike Jackson's broad shoulders down the corridor toward one of the meeting rooms, Max tried to quell all the questions that were bumbling around in her mind.

A job meant a future.

Max had survived all these years by forgetting about the future and allowing herself to exist on only one plane: the right here and right now. To even think about anything else was too powerful, the pain too swift and sure. There were no calendars in Max's locker with the days crossed off; the furthest she ever dared to look ahead was to the next visit with her mom.

And then Jackson reached a door, opened it, and stood back to allow Max to enter. Suddenly she didn't want to think about a job; all she wanted to do was plant bluebonnets.

Jackson gave her an encouraging smile, as if to say, "It's okay. Nothing to be afraid of."

But Max had thought that before, and look where it had gotten her.

The gentleman who was seated at the table got to his feet when Max entered the room. He was a handsome man in his sixties, with arresting blue eyes and thick, wavy silver hair beautifully styled and trimmed. The navy pinstriped suit was well tailored, the crimson silk tie precisely knotted, and the hand he extended was neatly manicured.

"You must be Rebekah Maxfield," he said in a cultured, sophisticated voice.

"Please, call me Max."

His handshake was firm and solid. "Garrett Sharp. Please, sit down." He pulled out a chair for her catercorner to his and, as she took her seat, she heard the door discreetly close behind her. She glanced back. Jackson had left them alone.

"It's a pleasure to finally meet you," said Sharp. Unlike most men his age, he did not wear glasses, and his keen eyes seemed to miss nothing as he appraised her.

She didn't know what to say. Six and a half years had left her a social imbecile when it came to small talk.

"You're much taller than I expected," he said.

"Five-ten," she said lamely, noticing that this man liked jewelry. He was wearing two diamond-encrusted rings.

"I understand your time here is almost up."

"Yes." She glanced down at her own hands, the nails unkempt and ragged. She curled her fingers into her palms, hoping he wouldn't notice.

From an inside jacket pocket he withdrew a gold engraved business cardholder, flipped it open, and withdrew a snazzy high-gloss black business card with embossed gold lettering and handed it to her.

COVERTCOM Electronic Eavesdropping Detection.
New York*Washington, D.C.*Beverly Hills*Miami*
Austin*London*Paris*Cairo*Moscow. Garrett Sharp.
1-800-SPYSHOP.

In spite of herself, her heart quickened. She glanced up.

"I know a great deal about you," Sharp said with an enigmatic smile.

"I'm sure you do, Mr. Sharp." She permitted herself a small grin.

"I've been following your case for some time now. I believe it was *Newsweek* that first broke the story about how you used your knowledge of electronic countersurveillance to elude your husband for over a year while you lived in hiding with your little girl."

She shrugged. "Either that or the *National Enquirer*."

Sitting back in his chair, he regarded her with the ghost of a smile. "I would think Judge Gabe Griswold would have had at his disposal any number of resources that could have been tapped in order to find his wife and child."

She said nothing.

"But in the end, you turned yourself in. Why was that?"

"Life on the run is no kind of life for a three-year-old child."

"You know your sentence could have been much

lighter if you had turned over the child to your husband."

"He's my ex-husband, Mr. Sharp, and I'd have gone to the electric chair before I put my baby in his hands again."

"Yes. I believe you would have." He leaned forward. "You are just the kind of person I like to have working for me, Max. You're courageous, stubborn, and careful. Not to mention highly intelligent."

Max's hands began to shake, and she clasped them together. "I've been out of the loop for a long time, Mr. Sharp. Electronic technological know-how doubles every eighteen months, as I'm sure you know. I'm hopelessly behind now."

He waved a dismissive hand in the air. "Sure, you're probably a bit behind in the most recent technological developments, but I have no doubt that you would catch up very quickly. Now, I'm prepared to offer you a job, starting just as soon as you are released from prison and have taken a little time to rest."

Her heart took on a slow, deep throbbing in her throat. She swallowed.

"You would start out in the Austin office, learning the ropes, meeting with prospective clients, brushing up on the latest bugs." He flashed a smile. His teeth were very white. "Your starting pay would be fairly modest, only fifty thousand, but you would receive a car and clothing allowance, plus benefits, of course. Eventually we would transfer you to our Washington office, where you would train with our elite Spy Squad—"

"Spy Squad?"

"Our countersurveillance sweep team."

"Oh."

"There would be a corresponding raise with that transfer of course, to seventy-five thousand, and when you're ready, we'll bring you on board in our New York offices, with your salary to start there at one hundred thousand with various stock options and, ultimately, the opportunity to make a great deal of money."

She stared at him. The man seemed to have forgotten that Max had been earning forty cents an hour for the past six years, with nowhere to spend it but the prison commissary. Even fifty thousand dollars seemed like a fortune to her . . . not to mention the car and clothing allowances . . . the transfers and raises . . .

"What's the catch?" she blurted.

He frowned. "Excuse me?"

Max's heart seemed to have moved up her throat and lodged at the base of her larynx. She could barely talk around the lump. "I'm sorry, Mr. Sharp. I don't mean to be rude or unappreciative—really. It's just that, well, when you live with cons . . . you learn to beware of anything that sounds too good to be true."

"Is that what you think this is?" His eyes were shrewd beneath the silver brows.

"Well, frankly . . . yes. I've been locked up here for almost seven years, and now you're offering me this job and all this money . . . It just doesn't seem real somehow."

He laughed. It was a smooth laugh, very polished. "I assure you that this is not the case. This is indeed a serious job offer. You have to understand, our clients are some of the richest and most visible people in the world. Corporate CEO's. Celebrities. Politicians. People with equally rich and powerful enemies. They depend on CovertCom to be completely discreet, highly professional, and the very best at what they do. Believe me, they expect the best because they *pay* the best, which is why I can't emphasize to you enough that the figures I quoted you are just the beginning."

With a wary glance, she said, "So why would you want to hire an ex-con? Wouldn't that upset the clientele?"

He shook his head emphatically. "Absolutely not. You were a mother, fiercely protecting her child. You hid successfully from a rich and powerful man—a federal judge—then you served your time without complaint, and to this day nobody knows where your little girl is, correct?"

She nodded.

"Then, you're *still* eluding him. More than anyone else, you could appreciate the needs of our clients, and they know it. Besides, your master's degree in electrical engineering doesn't hurt, either."

Max couldn't stop shaking. This was incredible. Unbelievable! It was the opportunity of a lifetime! A whole new start. And with that kind of money, who knows what she could do for Gaby?

So why, oh, why, couldn't she rid of herself of these nasty doubts that kept badgering her in the dark shadows of her mind? *There's no such thing as something for nothing.*

Call it instincts. Call it survival. Whatever. Max had learned long ago to heed those little warnings even when it made no rational sense to do so. Almost against her will, she found herself pushing the glossy business card across the table toward Garrett Sharp.

"Thank you for coming all the way down here to speak to me, Mr. Sharp. But I'm not ready to think about what I'm going to do when I get out. Not yet."

She had intended for Mr. Sharp to take the card and pocket it, but instead he pushed it back toward her with one manicured finger. "You need time to think," he said. "That's quite all right. I know you can't do anything right away anyway. But you keep my card. The job is still open for you when you're ready."

He got to his feet, and she did the same. It was hard to look into those sharp blue eyes. She felt foolish for even considering turning down this job. This was an opportunity beyond the wildest imaginings of anyone in this prison. So why wasn't she leaping for joy? She ought to be kissing this man's diamond ring instead of kissing him off.

That's when it dawned on her. Of course. Why hadn't she realized it sooner?

She didn't want to accept a job—or anything else— from Garrett Sharp because he reminded her too damn much of Gabe Griswold. Like Sharp, Gabe, too, had been smooth and polished and handsome and cultured and well dressed and successful. When he'd asked her to marry him, it had seemed like a dream come true.

Only she still hadn't woken up from the nightmare it turned out to be.

When Max walked out of the room, head held high, she left the card on the table.

She was still planting bluebonnets when the FBI came for her.

Chapter Two

Special Agent Jack Underwood could not believe his luck. He'd had Garrett Sharp under surveillance for more than six months, and this was the first big break they'd had.

Never had Underwood dealt with a more frustrating case. Two separate attempts to plant undercover agents into the CovertCom operation had failed. It seemed that a business which sold paranoia to its clients operated under more than a fair dose of its own. His first agent had been made as a fed right from the get-go; the second had been found out after less than a month of working for the company, through clandestine means Underwood had yet to figure out.

Planting bugs in any of their stores or offices or homes was a joke. No matter how crafty the fed soundmen tried to be, they were always found out in one way or another. Hell, half the people working for CovertCom were ex-spooks themselves; they knew all the tricks.

Even the Tough Shit Squad, as the Technical Support Squad in Washington was known, had failed.

He'd been reduced to assigning surveillance on Sharp, having people follow him around all day and all night in the vain hope that he would make some kind of false step that would hold up in court. Since Sharp had his own Gulfstream jet and bodyguards and bulletproof limo, even that chore was a bitch.

Headquarters was getting antsy, and Underwood knew that if he didn't come up with something soon, he'd find his ass transferred to some resident agency in fucking Del Rio, Texas, fighting over turf with the good ole boys and shuffling papers.

Or even worse, horror of horrors! Wind up at FBI

HQ, lost somewhere forever in the bureaucracy. People had been known to disappear in there and never be heard from again.

That this was the case of his career wasn't in doubt. It was the kind of case that if Underwood brought in a win, he could coast on it for the rest of his career; he could name his assignment, maybe even jump onto the management train and follow the track all the way to the best job in the Bureau: special agent in charge of a major field office, or SAC.

If he didn't, he could wind up like some of those poor sons of bitches who worked the Unabomber case. Some of them spent virtually an entire career chasing the phantom recluse, only to retire in bitterness, never able to get over their failure to stop him, then live to see him get caught by somebody else.

That was not going to happen to Jack Underwood.

Especially not now. Underwood had some good people in the field, and it took them less than an hour after Sharp had left the prison he'd visited in Texas to find out what he had been doing down there. In a stroke of almost unbelievable luck, Underwood happened to be in the San Antonio field office at the time, talking to some agents there who'd been keeping an eye on CovertCom's Austin office as part of the whole wide-ranging "Operation EAVESDROP."

Though there were still agents at the prison who could question Rebekah Maxfield, Underwood wanted to do it himself. This was too important to trust to some young field agent just out of the Academy. Before leaving for Bryan, Underwood had Maxfield's file faxed to him, and he read it on the way while another agent zipped in and out of trucker traffic at a speed Underwood preferred not to know. The file made for very interesting reading.

Though most parental abduction cases were turned over to the states for prosecution, and though most prosecutors chose probation rather than prison time for the offending parents, Maxfield had been slapped with a FRAID charge, a Federal Criminal Code and Rules acronym for a crime known as "Fraud and Related Activity in connection with ID Documents," since she had lived on the run with her daughter in various states for over a year by using false ID's, among other things.

When Maxfield refused to turn over her daughter or reveal the child's whereabouts to the court, the judge had added contempt of court charges and sentenced her to the fullest extent of the FRAID conviction: seven years.

Underwood wondered if the judge had been a friend of the child's father, federal judge Gabe Griswold. From the lack of mercy shown by the court, Underwood was willing to bet the answer was yes.

He was also willing to bet that they'd figured a few weeks in prison would wear the lady down and she would give up the child to win her freedom. Clearly, they'd figured wrong.

Rebekah Maxfield had shunned all media interviews of any kind, as had her family members and friends. She had respectfully requested through her lawyer that advocate groups leave her in peace. After the initial flurry of press following the conviction, she'd pretty much dropped from sight.

In her mug shot she looked wan, trapped, sad—not defiant as so many of them did. But in an old photograph that had been published in *People* magazine, she was revealed to be a real beauty, with blond hair past her waist and the height and figure of a model.

She was no model, though. From what little he could tell in the information he had in front of him, she was apparently some kind of electronics whiz, which would explain one of several reasons why Garrett Sharp might be interested in her.

And if Garrett Sharp was interested in Rebekah Maxfield, then the FBI was, too. It was important to Underwood to get to her quickly. He wanted to call Maxfield early in the game, before she had time to think about it.

The Federal Prison Camp warden, Janet Sinclair, was a no-nonsense black woman of singular grace and dignity, who gave Underwood a look that said she'd seen it all and yet still seemed surprised by the turn of events which filled up her office with FBI agents. It would seem that Garrett Sharp had worked his charm on her as he had many others who should have known better.

After a firm handshake and an offer of coffee, which Underwood declined, Warden Sinclair said, "I find it very hard to believe that Rebekah Maxfield could be in any trouble, Agent Underwood. She has been a model prisoner and an inspiration to the other inmates, and her time with us is almost up."

"She's not in trouble, Warden Sinclair. We simply want her help as a material witness in a case not associated with her own, and that's all I'm at liberty to say at the moment."

She frowned, her intense dark eyes never leaving his face. "Does this have anything to do with the visit she just received from the gentleman from New York? What was his name . . . Garrett Sharp. It was my understanding that Mr. Sharp wanted to offer a job pending her release date."

Underwood smiled at her. She did not smile back. When he said nothing more, she said, "I assume you wish to interview Max?"

"Max?"

"It's the name she prefers to go by. We've all gotten into the habit of calling her that."

"It just seems rather . . . familiar . . . for a warden to call a prisoner."

Leaning back in her chair, she crossed her arms over her chest, her body language communicating clearly that she did not like him and did not appreciate what he was doing.

It didn't bother Underwood. He was used to it.

"Max is not a typical prisoner, Agent Underwood, and when you meet her, you will see what I mean. She is educated and articulate, and—"

"And she committed a crime."

She pursed her lips. "Technically, yes. And she has paid her debt to society in full, and then some. I might add that her crime could actually be considered a heroic act, depending upon how you look at it."

"I'll keep that in mind."

She looked as though she wanted to say more, thought

better of it, and got to her feet instead. "I'll have Mike bring Max. You can use my office if you like."

"It's a generous offer, Warden Sinclair, and I appreciate it, but if you don't mind, I'd like to take her to a neutral location to question her."

"A neutral location? You mean . . . the police department?"

"I mean someplace where we can talk in complete privacy."

Her eyes flashed at the implied insult, but she merely said, "This is highly unusual, Agent Underwood. There are channels that must be taken before an inmate can be released into outside custody."

"I'll have FBI HQ fax you the proper authorization."

She hesitated. "All right. You do that."

Underwood nodded at one of the other agents, who left to make the necessary calls.

While he was waiting, he made a few calls of his own from the car, updating his supervisor and other necessary ass-covering, and then the big guy who was the warden's flunky brought Maxfield around to his car, parked next to a delivery van.

She was tall—taller than he was, he thought with no small chagrin, and so thin that the bones on her wrists stood out. Like most cons, she had an infinitely weary air about her, but her eyes were different.

If cops and cons had one thing in common, it was the expression in the eyes: a hardened, cynical, wary, suspicious, watch-your-back look that each could usually spot in the other, which was one reason some cops were so good at undercover work. But Maxfield didn't have that look about her, and it disarmed him somewhat.

She also had that kind of luminescent beauty that some blondes had, where the cool skin fit tightly over the shelfed cheekbones and the lashes and brows were delicate. Her eyes were an indeterminate color, but they were large and almond-shaped, her nose too big on any other face but just right on hers. At first Underwood thought she'd cut her long hair, but then he noticed that it was just braided and put up.

Maxfield was not cuffed, but her escort didn't seem to think it necessary, so Underwood didn't mention it. She stepped toward the car, but Underwood put a hand on her elbow and turned her toward the van, where a side door slid open. They got in, settling themselves in swiveling captain's chairs around various cameras with enormous lenses and other surveillance gear. The same agent who'd driven Underwood to the prison drove the van out past the gate and headed onto a highway that led out of town.

"Does this have something to do with my little girl?" she said first thing, before he could even introduce himself. The intensity of her face when she asked the question threw him momentarily off guard.

"No . . . this has nothing to do with your case at all."

"My ex-husband? Did he send you here?"

Interesting question. Shaking his head, Underwood said, "I told you, no. Now, my name is Jack Underwood, and I'm here to talk to you about Garrett Sharp."

At his first words, she had visibly slumped in her seat, her face a sketch of relief. Now she straightened and said, "What about him? I just met him. He offered me a job. That's all I know."

"What kind of job?"

She regarded him warily. "I'm not sure, really."

"But you'd be doing countersurveillance sweeps on clients, right?"

"Eventually. I think. That's the impression I got."

He nodded, keeping his face as blank of emotional reaction as possible. This was good. This was very good.

"I turned him down."

He glanced at her sharply. "Why?"

She sighed. It was a heavy, world-weary sigh. "I didn't trust him, that's why."

Underwood settled into the high-backed seat and studied her face. She was smarter than he'd realized.

"Why didn't you trust him? Did he say anything that would give you reason not to trust him?"

Shaking her head, she said, "No, no, nothing like that. He just . . . It seemed too good to be true, that's all." Her brow crinkled between her eyes, and she pinched it with a thumb and forefinger. Her nails were short and unkempt. "Do you have any aspirin? I've got a killer headache."

"Sure. Yeah. I think so." Underwood rummaged around for a bit until he turned up a bottle in the console between the front seats. He shook out two in the palm of his hand and handed them to her.

"I don't mean to be a bother, but I've been working in the gardens all day and I'm thirsty. Do you think I could have a drink of water?"

This time Underwood sighed audibly. Leaning forward, he directed the driver to stop at a roadside gas station, where he dispatched him to go inside and buy her a bottle of water.

"I'm sorry," she said, and then lowered her face into the palms of her hands. "I knew it," she murmured. "I knew better than to have any hope." Suddenly irritated with herself, she vigorously rubbed her eyes, pinkening her face. The driver returned with a bottle of Evian water, from which she took a long drink, washing down the aspirin.

They headed back out onto the highway, and she turned away, gazing at nothing while composing herself. Underwood watched all this without saying anything.

Finally, she said, "He's dirty, isn't he? He's under investigation for something."

"Let's just say we're keeping an eye on him," said Underwood. "And you can help us do it."

"What do you mean?" She swiveled back to fix him with a stern gaze.

"We want you to take the job that Mr. Sharp offered you. Do whatever they want you to do."

"You want me to be an informant?" she cried. "Are you crazy? Forget it!"

She began to gnaw at one of her fingernails, a gesture so unconscious she looked like a little kid.

"No," she said. "It's too dangerous."

"It's not dangerous at all," he lied.

She rolled her eyes.

After a moment he said, "I understand both your dad and your brother were Army Special Forces."

Glancing away, she murmured, "One of my other brothers still is a Green Beret."

"Your dad was killed while trying to rescue the Iranian hostages back in seventy-nine."

"A helicopter crash during a sandstorm in the desert," she said woodenly.

"And your older brother . . ."

"Brand. He was killed in Desert Storm. A rocket hit his helicopter."

"So you come from a proud heritage, then. A family of patriots and heroes."

For a long time she stared at her hands in her lap. It was a cheap shot, and he knew it, but he was willing to try anything.

Finally, she said, "What do you want me to do?"

"I understand Sharp made you a hell of a good offer. We want you to take the job, earn all the dough you can—you can keep any money you earn—do whatever he wants you to do. You help us make this case, it will be very beneficial to you."

"What case?"

"I'm not at liberty to say."

"Bullshit."

They locked stares.

With steely eyes she said, "You want me to put my ass on the line for you, you will damn sure tell me what the hell is going on so I don't get myself killed." Her face was flushed now, her eyes fully alive, and he saw for himself just how beautiful she could be.

After a long pause he said, "Okay. You'll find out soon enough, I'm sure. It can be the only possible reason he'd recruit an ex-con."

"Oh, I see. You mean, the only reason he could possibly have to offer me a job is so that he can get me to commit a crime," she said bitterly.

He shrugged.

She took a swig of water.

"We are investigating charges made by several of CovertCom's clients. Some say that after the CovertCom countersurveillance sweep, they think the 'Spy Squad' team, as they like to call themselves, are planting bugs of their own. Then they're taking the information they learn from those bugs and selling it to the client's enemies, or using it to extort money from the client in exchange for keeping the information secret."

"Charges. You mean you don't have a shred of proof that this is taking place."

Underwood said nothing.

"Oh, I get it! This is why you need me! Because otherwise you wouldn't have a case.

Shaking her head, she tapped the side of the water bottle with her long, blunt fingers. "You guys are a piece of work, you know that?" Rubbing her forehead with one hand, she added, "No way. Go make your case some other way. I'm no snitch."

He'd been afraid of this, going in. Well, he hadn't wanted to call her bluff just yet, but she was forcing his hand.

Without taking his gaze off her face, he said, "Your daughter is still at large, in hiding, is that correct?"

Her face blanched as if she'd been slapped.

"So, technically, you are still in violation of the law, Ms. Maxfield. You may have served all the time the laws allow in these cases, but your ex-husband still has parental rights outstanding."

She'd gone so white Underwood feared for a moment that she might pass out. He braced himself to catch her should she keel over.

"You wouldn't," she said, her lips barely moving.

"The FBI is the best and the richest law enforcement agency in the world, Ms. Maxfield. If we were to turn the full resources of the Bureau over to finding that child, we'd find her, I assure you."

She began to tremble so hard the little springs of hair around her face shook.

He didn't want to have to do this, but he needed this case, and he needed Rebekah Maxfield, and he was not going to fuck around with her all day. He pulled an extra ace out of his sleeve. "Now, you can accept Mr. Sharp's excellent job offer and start making a lot of money; or you can turn down the job, stay in prison, and know that the FBI is searching full-out to find your little girl, but that's not all."

She looked very ill. He hoped she wouldn't puke inside the van, or they'd never get rid of the smell.

"I'm afraid some new charges have come to light, Ms.

Maxfield, that could extend your stay at the Camp, oh, indefinitely." He arranged his face in a rueful expression.

"What? What new charges?" she shouted, half rising in her seat.

The agent driving the van glanced in the rearview mirror. His eyes met Underwood's as if to say, "Cool it before she wrecks the van."

Shaking, white-faced, she sat back down. "You bastard," she said. "You son of a bitch bastard."

Though he'd never admit it to anybody, Underwood felt a real twinge of guilt at what he was putting this poor woman through. Hell, he had kids of his own, and from what he could tell from reading her file, her ex was a real asshole.

But Garrett Sharp was blatantly breaking laws, blackmailing and extorting people, costing business losses in the millions, while all along arrogantly thumbing his nose at the Bureau. He had to be stopped, and this was the only way.

Besides, it wasn't such a raw deal, he told himself. Maxfield would get out of prison early, and she'd wind up making more dough than he did. All she had to do was cooperate a little. When the bust was made and the trial was over, she could take all that money and disappear someplace with her daughter.

He watched her as she glared at him with open hatred. It was his job, it had to be done, that's all there was to it. When he didn't blink, she drooped in her chair, closed her eyes, and rolled her head back on the headrest, her face anguished. A single tear crept from beneath her lashes and rolled slowly down the side of her face.

He almost lost it then. Almost said, To hell with it. He wasn't a fucking monster, but goddammit, he needed her to make this case! Without her leads and her testimony, they had nothing.

He waited.

Then, so quietly that he almost couldn't hear over the noise of the engine and the tires on the road, she said, "All right. Fine. My mom'll be happy anyway."

Alarmed, he said, "You can't tell her anything about what you're doing, you know. You cannot tell one living soul. Particulars of the CovertCom job, if you want, but as far as the investigation goes, I will be the only person you'll talk to about this operation."

Opening her eyes, she nailed him with one shrewd glance. In a voice laced with sarcasm she said, "Oh, don't worry, Agent Underwood. I wouldn't *think* of doing anything to mess up your little *operation*."

Motioning to the driver to head back to the prison, he said, "You will be briefed at a later date. For now, I want you to call Mr. Sharp and tell him you've reconsidered and you're going to take the job after all." Reaching into his inside jacket pocket, he withdrew the black business card Maxfield had left on the table after her meeting with Sharp and extended it toward her.

She stared at the card. Without moving, she said, "I remember the number, okay? Keep the damn card."

Underwood stifled a sigh. This was going to be one hell of a long case.

Chapter Three

Olivia "Liv" Maxfield was overjoyed to learn that her beautiful, brave, and long-suffering daughter, Rebekah (she never called her "Max"), would not only be coming home soon, but that the Lord had surely blessed her girl's patience and courage, for He had sent that wonderful man, Mr. Sharp, to offer her a job and *everything*. God did indeed move in strange ways, His miracles to perform.

There was so much to do and so little time to do it in! She had to fix up the guest room, and order a cake, and buy some more yellow ribbon . . .

Yellow ribbons. At first Liv had thought they'd take the yellow ribbons down when Rebekah got home, but gradually she had come to realize that they could never take them down, not as long as little Gaby was still out there, separated from her mother and her family by such a cruel twist of fate.

Things could change so fast in life, in the twinkling of an eye, and you could spend the whole rest of your life trying to get over it.

Though Liv was ashamed to admit it, the truth of the matter was that for months she had refused to believe Rebekah when her daughter had told her that Gabe had done such an unspeakable thing to that baby. How could anybody believe a man like that—so dashing, so suave and debonair and successful—to think he could ever do such a thing . . . well, she *still* couldn't even imagine it without feeling ill.

In fact, Liv might never have believed Rebekah at all if she hadn't been there one day when Gabe came to pick up Gabrielle for his regular visitation day. Up until then Liv had argued with Rebekah that a child deserved to be with its father and that it was unhealthy for Rebe-kah to keep them apart.

But little Gaby had started to cry and cling to Rebe-kah even when Gabe was just walking up the sidewalk to the front door. When he reached for her . . . well, Liv would never forget the look on that child's face. Absolute, stark terror. She had clung to her mother's neck and screamed this high-pitched wail of fear and despair that gave Liv chills just thinking about it.

And Gabe. Liv didn't know what she'd expected from her son-in-law. Perhaps soothing apologies or maybe even accusations that Rebekah had put the fear in Gaby's mind. But he hadn't done anything like that. He'd reached for the child and calmly pried her out of her mother's arms, and his face was just . . . *blank*.

They could still hear Gaby's screams even after she'd been buckled in her car seat and the car door closed—even when they were driving down the street. Rebekah had taken to her bed then and cried the whole rest of the day. It was a horror Liv would never forget as long as she drew breath.

It had been so hard, watching Rebekah suffer all these years, locked up like some kind of *criminal* when she hadn't done a dang thing wrong! And being separated from little Gaby, missing her growing-up years. It was just so unfair, especially after they'd lost Richard and Brand both. It just seemed like whenever the family got together at Christmas or whatever, there were so many empty chairs around the dining table.

Liv knew it wasn't right to judge other people, but she sincerely hoped the Lord had reserved a special place in hell for the Gabe Griswolds of the world.

Max had not allowed herself to mentally prepare for release day, so she found the entire experience to take on the aura of a dream, as if it weren't really happening to her but to someone else, and she was simply an observer.

Warden Sinclair personally shook Max's hand good-bye, enclosing one warm dark hand over Max's fair, cal-lused one. "I wish you everything good in life, Max," she said. "Just between you and me and the tree, I never thought you belonged in here in the first place, but you've always been a class act and we'll miss you around here."

"Well, I won't miss you," joked Max with a nervous laugh.

"No, I don't imagine so," said Sinclair, smiling.

While her mother signed the necessary security forms at the gate, Max gathered up her pitiful few belongings, which she'd hurriedly tossed into a cardboard box.

"I'll carry it out to the car," offered Mike Jackson gruffly, like a kid in junior high taking her books. Though the box was not heavy, Max relinquished it almost shyly. He was a nice man who had treated most all the inmates with respect, but he was still a *man*, and Max felt suddenly gawky and awkward—just the same way she used to feel in junior high when she had towered over every boy in her class and everybody called her Big Bird because of her yellow hair and asked her to do stuff like hold up her arm in the air so they could get better radio reception.

Apparently she was going to have to break in real life again just like a brand-new pair of stiff leather shoes.

Her mother drove out the gate and into the sprawling little city of Bryan. The prison was located in a middle-class, somewhat run-down neighborhood, but none of the houses looked real to Max. It still seemed like a dream.

"I can't believe I'm finally getting to take you home," said her mother.

"Me, neither."

"And I can't tell you how thrilled I am that you have already been offered a good job. It's just a whole new beginning for you."

Max stared out the car window.

"I have a surprise for you when you get home."

Glancing at her mom, Max suppressed a sigh. She didn't want any more surprises. All she wanted to do was crawl into a great big soft bed and sleep for the next nine years.

The drive to Austin took longer than Max expected. Clouds and mist had conspired with early March to lend a dreamy grayness to the normally lush Texas hill country landscape, which only made the trip more surreal. Her emotions seemed disconnected from her, almost inaccessible. Max found herself wondering if she had cut herself off from her own emotions for so long that she would never feel anything again.

Her mom tried to make small talk for a while, but Max couldn't keep up. She didn't know any of the people her mother wanted to talk about, and furthermore, she didn't care. Max knew that her mother was hurt and kept expecting her to be happy about getting out of prison. If she only knew!

Talk about jumping from the frying pan into the fire.

Still, Max made some effort to be sociable. After all, those endless weekend trips down from Austin during Max's incarceration year after year couldn't have been easy on her mom. But Max didn't really know what to say. Here she was, sprung out of jail, a member of the population of regular folks who went about their business every day . . . and yet, how could she really be a part of them? She was an ex-con, for one thing, and at the new job, which so excited her mother, she was a spy, spying on spies.

An outsider, it seemed, to the bitter end, walking the tightrope high above the crowd.

It was nearly dark when her mother headed up I-35 into the tangled snarl of streets and waterways and trees that made up the state capital. Recent years had seen a population explosion as Austin became known as an electronic center for many computer-age businesses and a sort of mellow mecca for New Age enlightenment seekers and burned-out yuppies. Max was overwhelmed by the high-speed traffic and the bewildering array of freeway exits, but there were some things about Austin that would remain forever Austin: rolling hills shrouded with shady trees intertwined with bike paths, spring-fed creeks arched over with walking bridges, wide boulevards, live oaks, stately old homes, and more bookstores, per capita, than any other city in the country. Even as Max's mom swished the wipers back and forth to clear the rainy sprinkles off the windshield and flipped on the headlights, Max gazed out through the mist and began to feel a small measure of peace steal over her soul.

Even so, she felt very old.

Her mother lived in a nondescript, three-bedroom brick tract house on a plain street corner in an unpretentious housing development that reminded Max of every military base house they had ever lived in. The house was not "home" to Max, especially. Her mother had moved in just about the time Max went on the run with Gaby, so there was little about it that provided a sense of familiarity. However, there was no missing which house was her mother's; every tree in the yard fluttered with yellow ribbons, and stretched across the front porch was a waterlogged sign on butcher paper which read: WELCOME HO.

For the first time in many months, Max threw back her head and guffawed. "Welcome *'ho*? You do know what that means, don't you, Mom?"

Her mother pursed her lips. "It *says* 'Welcome Home,' but the rain smeared the last few letters."

"Riiight," teased Max as they got out of the car. "Your neighbors sure have a lot of cars parked at the curb," she commented, maneuvering her box out of the backseat and following her mother across the wet grass to the front door. "The yellow ribbons . . . that's so sweet! It must have taken you all day to put them up."

"I had some help," her mom said, pushing open the front door.

Max stepped across the threshold, her mother snapped on the light, and a roomful of people yelled, *SURPRISE!!!*

The box fell to the floor as a gigantic mob surrounded her, and she was suffocated with hugs.

"Oh, my God, I can't believe you're all here!" she cried, bursting into tears of joy.

None of Max's brothers lived in Austin, and only one, Clark, an attorney and the oldest at forty, even lived in the state. He'd driven down from Dallas with his wife, Jennifer, and two kids, and with his silver-sprinkled chestnut hair he now looked so much like their dad had looked the last time they had seen him that Max felt as if she were hugging a ghost. Clark had represented Max at the hearing, and he had never forgiven himself for losing the case. She hadn't seen him for several years and clung to him a moment longer than necessary, a reassurance, a forgiving. When he pulled back finally, his eyes were wet.

Brett, at thirty-seven, three years older than Max, had flown down from Fort Bragg, North Carolina, with his new wife (number three), Janice. As usual, Max was never prepared for Brett. An identical twin to Brand, it was always like seeing Brand all over again, as if they'd never lost him at all. But then, it always felt stranger still that there was only one of him and not two. Brett had the tightly coiled, powerful build you would expect from an elite soldier, in spite of the fact that he was no longer so young anymore. When he hugged her, the vertebrae in her spine actually cracked from the force of his embrace, and taking a breath was out of the question. She didn't mind at all.

Zane, the youngest at thirty, still looked like a skinny adolescent. He was the only sibling who took after his petite mother and, like his mother, was shorter even than Max. Clark, Brett, and Brand were all over six feet tall, like their dad. Brett and Brand had shared Max's blond coloring, and Brett still looked like some kind of Viking prince, but Zane stood about five-eight (Brett liked to call him "the runt of the litter"), had thinning reddish hair he wore in a limp ponytail, and still bore the acne scars of his unfortunate youth. Zane had married young and divorced young. The classic computer hacker, he'd never remarried and worked out of an overstuffed computer-cluttered apartment out in California's Silicon Valley.

But Zane no longer had any reason to feel inferior to his accomplished older brothers, because he was the only person who communicated with Gaby's caretakers. He did it by computer, through electronic dead drops, and he made sure Gaby never forgot how much her mother loved her.

"Gaby sends her love," he whispered. Max, too overcome to speak, nodded and clung to him a moment longer than the others. As she stepped back, she couldn't help but notice how differently he was dressed than his older brothers. Where they were crew-cutted and conservative, Zane looked more like a junior high computer geek with his faded T-shirt bearing the logo of the fa-

mous underground hacker magazine, *2600,* a DEA windbreaker, a cap worn backward that said *Phreak,* and a
patchy three-day beard.

As if on cue, Brett reached over and snatched the cap,
held it over his head, and tossed it to Clark. "When you
gonna get a haircut, Zany?" he demanded, using the
nickname he knew his brother hated.

With a sardonic grin, Zane said, "Oh, whenever you
stop raping and pillaging and killing babies, I guess."

"You little shit—" began Brett, his face flushed.

"Now, boys. No fighting in the living room," interjected Liv absently as she headed for the kitchen.

For the second time that day, Max threw back her
head and laughed. It was so silly. It was so *family.* Clark
laughed, too, as did the wives in the room, and finally,
Zane and Brett.

Like always, everybody gravitated to the dining room.
While Liv bustled around in the kitchen, producing en-
ticing smells, Max sat surrounded by brothers and wives
both familiar and unfamiliar, while her overexcited little
niece and nephew—Clark's kids, born after she was incarcerated and sweet strangers to Max—scrambled
around underfoot, teasing her mother's geriatric old bulldog, Sarge, into mock growls and barks, and everybody
seemed to talk at the same time.

She felt a tap at her shoulder and turned to see Zane
standing beside her. "I brought you something," he said,
and handed her a folded-up piece of computer printout
paper.

Max unfolded the paper. On it was a grainy copy of
a photo that had been scanned onto a computer,
uploaded via a modem, and printed out at the other end
of the line. It was a smiling little girl about ten years of
age, her straw-blond hair tousled, her smile warm and
sweet. Her two front teeth were larger than the others,
and her face had the ungainly thinness of a beauty who
has yet to grow into her looks.

Max gasped.

The buzz of conversation around her faltered.

"Oh, Zane . . ." She fumbled for words and failed.
Tears blurred her vision.

"Well, it's too dangerous, you know, to send snapshots

back and forth through the mails," he said awkwardly. "The feds can catch you that way."

"What is it?" Liv elbowed her way through the throng of people peering and staring at the paper on the glossy dining table.

Max, her voice shaky and uneven, said, "It's a picture of my Gaby, Mom. And she's so beautiful!"

"What?" Liv covered her mouth with her hand, and Brett handed her the photograph. "How did you get this?" she asked Zane. "You didn't take any chances did you?"

Zane sighed. "Mom. I got it off the computer. Gaby scanned her picture, see, and uploaded it to me through the modem. Or her caretakers did. Anyway, I downloaded it and printed it up."

"You could still be traced," said Clark. "It's risky."

With a shrug Zane said, "No more risky than any of our other communications. And it's just one. It's not a whole damn photo album, for God's sake."

"Let me see it again," said Max, wiping tears from her cheeks impatiently. She cradled the piece of paper with shaking hands and studied the image of her little girl. "She's so big," she murmured. "Oh, my darlin' girl."

Someone squeezed her shoulder. Clark's wife, Jennifer, said, "That was a really sweet thing to do, Zane."

"Yes," agreed Max. "Thank you so very much." She put one arm around his skinny waist and squeezed, overcome with the moment. In all her years in prison, she'd clung to the mental picture she'd had of her baby, only three years old when she'd last seen her. And look at her now! Such a big girl. Almost grown.

The old familiar sadness crept into her heart, the bitterness at the years lost, the senseless, wasted years.

For a long moment everyone in the room grew silent as well, their collective memories crowding out the usual chatter and bustle.

Suddenly, Clark's four-year-old daughter, Hannah, stage-whispered, "Mama, I gotta pee-pee."

It was a perfect tension breaker, as everybody broke into slightly nervous laughter and began to move again. Jennifer took Hannah to the bathroom. Brett's wife, Jan, went into the kitchen with Liv. The brothers all pulled out dining chairs and sat around the table.

Somebody demanded a welcome-home poker game with Max—dealer's choice, any game she wanted—and somebody else went in search of her mother's huge jar of pennies for the pot. Clark cracked open a new deck of cards and began shuffling with show-off flourishes and fans, and Zane and Brett got into a shouting match over gun control (Zane for, Brett against). All of a sudden it dawned on Max that here she was . . . for the first time in more than seven years right where she belonged.

She was home.

And everything would have been all warm and fuzzy and happy ever after if her mother hadn't chosen that particular time to announce that she'd sold her house to the city to make way for another freeway loop which needed to cut through her corner . . . and she intended to move into Max's apartment with her.

Chapter Four

Dominic Antonio had no idea the toy business could be so cutthroat.

Glancing down the length of the long glass table, he caught Evan's eye and raised an eyebrow. Evan gave him a wink that was almost imperceptible beneath his bushy red brows. The military-severe flattop Evan wore almost tamed the fiery hair that was his Irish mother's legacy, but that same legacy still flashed forth from time to time from steel gray eyes. Though Dominic could never be sure, he strongly suspected that Evan sent money to a splinter faction of the Irish Republican Army to support acts of terrorism against the British.

Evan Ryder was the Spy Squad electrician. If there was a mike-and-wire setup lurking anywhere near the subsidiary wire lines, switches, or electrical outlets of a building or room, Evan could find it. He also kept them from getting their asses fried while snooping around behind walls and into lighting fixtures and other dicey places, looking for bugs. While doing a sweep, it was Evan who checked out any and all electronic equipment they might need, from a simple VOM (volt-ohm multimeter) to the more complicated spectrum analyzers, wideband receivers, oscilloscopes and field strength meters, to the highly complicated X-ray equipment and other toys.

Evan and Dominic were gathered with the other team members in the meeting room of the CovertCom main offices in New York, discussing an upcoming sweep with two nervous new clients, who worked in creative product development for Imagitoys, Inc., a small, newish company David in competition with established Goliaths like Mattel, Hasbro, Fisher-Price, and Kenner.

Both men were impossibly young and shaggy-headed, and wore denim shirts, wild Marvel Comics ties, and shorts. The Rollerblades they'd used for transportation to the meeting were piled in a corner of the room. Each had a habit of glancing at the other for reassurance when making a point. They would be very easy to manipulate.

"The big toy companies have spies everywhere," said the bearded one, a fidgety, wiry man by the name of Jason Crandall. "As soon as they get wind of a hot new product being developed anywhere else, they put teams on it right away to try and beat them onto the market-place. Smaller companies can't hope to compete with the kind of bucks the big boys have. They can back their stolen products with a blitzkrieg of advertising and marketing gimmicks." He glanced at his partner, a Japanese-American man with glossy black, shoulder-length hair and the incongruous name of Osamu Smith.

Osamu nodded. "Toyland—that's what we call the toy industry—is littered with the bones of upstart companies who had one good idea which made a fortune for somebody else while they went out of business."

"Can't they sue?" asked Dominic.

Both men nodded energetically. "All the time," said Osamu. "The business is rife with lawsuits for patent infringement, trademark violations, criminal counter-feiting, and so on. But if you lose the lawsuit, you can wind up bankrupt."

"It happened to Coleco," added Jason, "and in the mid-eighties they'd been making something like a billion bucks a year with their Cabbage Patch Kids."

"So how can we help you?" asked Dominic.

The two men glanced at one another. Jason, the more talkative of the two, said, "Me and Osamu have developed a new toy idea that we think will rock Toyland off its foundations." Osamu nodded. "Now, the annual Toy Fair is in February, here in New York. It's not the only one of its kind in the world, but it's the place to make a splash. We want to introduce our new toy there as a complete surprise, and we want to already be in production when that happens, so we'll have a natural advantage over the knockoffs."

"February . . . that's almost a year away," mused Dominic.

"Right," said Osamu with a quick nod. "We'll have to operate in almost complete secrecy until then in order to pull this off. And the first place we need to secure is our boardroom."

Jason shifted his weight in his chair and nodded at Osamu. "In a couple weeks we're going to make this big presentation of the idea to Imagitoys' CEO, the R and D people, the marketing people—all the department heads."

"And you would like CovertCom to do a sweep of the boardroom before then."

In a nervous rush of words, Jason said, "What we'd really like is to have the whole place swept, and have everybody screened, you know, but we can't afford that just now, so we'll have to start with the boardroom."

"What other security measures have you implemented?" asked Hakeem Abdul, the Spy Squad telephone specialist, with a slight Mideastern accent. Abdul was an exotically handsome man with brooding dark eyes who sported a cultivated goatee and liked to wear expensive, tailored suits. He never lacked for female companionship.

Jason and Osamu exchanged glances again. The habit was beginning to get on Dominic's nerves. Osamu said, "Well, we've got triple locked doors, and there's only three sets of keys to them. And nobody knows who has them."

"And there's paper over the windows in the work areas," added Jason, "and all the workers are sworn to secrecy."

Hakeem gave the men a pitying smirk. "I am sure the royal family of Great Britain would be the first to inform you that such measures are far from foolproof."

Jason flushed. Osamu stared at Hakeem with obvious distaste. "We don't own the company, Mr. Abdul," he said coldly. "There is only so much control we have."

"And as long as we are going to be presenting our new product idea to the rest of the guys, we'd like to be able to feel safe in that environment anyway," said Jason.

Sebastian Taylor, their expert on radio frequency devices, said, "And what about after the meeting?" Like all the men who worked for Garrett Sharp, Sebastian wore his surfer-blond hair close cropped, but his eyes were so blue that Dominic often wondered if the man wore contacts to enhance their color. He was just vain enough.

"What do you mean?" fretted Jason.

"Well, let's say your new toy is a hit with the brass, and everybody leaves the meeting for their respective departments, excited about the new product idea and eager to get to work developing it. They'll have to discuss it, won't they?"

"Well, yeah . . ."

"So if you're worried that the boardroom will be bugged, how can you be so sure the R and D or marketing rooms or whatever aren't bugged, too?"

This was the part of the sale that never ceased to amaze Dominic. It was called "increasing the paranoia of the clients." Basically, CovertCom advertised that they would gladly do single-room sweeps, but once they started working the clients, it was just a matter of time before the sweep had been expanded to include the whole damn building, which of course was far more time-consuming for the Spy Squad and far more expensive for the clients.

"I don't know," said Osamu doubtfully. "I mean, I know you're right and everything, but I don't think we can afford a building sweep."

"Yeah," added Jason, "our boss only gave us permission to pay for a room sweep."

Evan feigned an expression of horror. "You didn't discuss this at the office, did you?"

Jason and Osamu glanced uneasily at one another. Jason squirmed in his seat. "Well . . . sure."

The entire Spy Squad team shook their heads, almost in unison.

"Why?" asked Osamu worriedly.

"If the place is bugged, then you just announced to your competitor that you're getting ready to jump on something really hot. Naturally, they're going to step up their efforts to find out what it is," pointed out Evan.

"Did you know there are some transmitters no bigger than a grain of rice?" asked Sebastian.

"Not only that," said Hakeem, "but with hookswitch bypass infinity transmitters, your enemies can use the existing phone line to eavesdrop on the conversation of anybody who is speaking in the room from anywhere *in the world*—and you don't even have to be using the phone at the time."

The eyes of both men widened considerably.

Dominic added, "And anything from a paperweight to a briefcase to a pen can be a disguise for a bug."

"You're kidding!" cried Jason.

"Doing a sweep of the boardroom before an important meeting is an excellent idea," said Evan, "but if you don't focus on electronic countermeasures specifically, and information in general, company-wide, well, then you're just postponing the inevitable."

Osamu chewed on the inside of his cheek. Jason said, "It's going to cost a lot of money . . ."

"Which you will surely recoup when you sweep the market with this terrific new toy. Think about what the Power Rangers alone have earned for their creators."

The young men exchanged one long significant look, and Dominic knew they had them. "Okay," said Jason. "Let's go for it." Osamu made a little noise of agreement.

Dominic smiled. Greed. It worked every time. "Excellent. All right, the first thing we'll need is a set of blueprints for the building—"

"Blueprints? Why?" Osamu, ever the splinter under the skin.

"We may have to remove portions of walls, ceilings, or floors in order to do a complete search for bugging devices. Blueprints let us know where to find structural supports."

"And I'll need wiring diagrams from the building," said Evan. "Any wires that are not indicated on the diagrams would immediately arouse my suspicion."

"*Oooo*-kay," said Jason, scrawling notes.

"We will also want a set of building plans," added Sebastian, "in order to locate pipes, ducts, conduits, air spaces—anything that would allow sound to be transmitted from the target area."

"And I'll be expecting all the information pertinent to the telephone systems," interjected Hakeem. "Especially feeder lines from the Central Office, PBX lines, junction boxes, modular jacks, and so on. We'll also want to look at intercom systems or any other communications equipment you guys utilize in the building. I'll want to talk to the supervisor of communications. We'll obtain cable maps and pair information from telco, but your people should have the details concerning your Telephone Network Interfaces. I'll need the manufacturer and model of your PBX, along with the software version and setup information. We'll need wire maps for the PBX system and any intercoms you have, operational or not."

"And another thing," said Dominic. "*Never* speak of the upcoming sweep while in the office building, not to anyone. The mere mention of it could alert your eavesdroppers to disconnect their clandestine listening devices until after the sweep, which would make it much more difficult for us to locate them."

The only sound was Jason's furious scribbling. Osamu looked scared.

"We'll want to do a pre-sweep reconnaissance run beforehand, so that we can determine what equipment we'll be using and compare the blueprints to the actual layout of the place, including placement of furnishings," he droned on.

"You will be our guide for the recon run," said Evan, "but don't talk to us about it. Just let us handle everything, and if we need you to unlock a door or something, we'll get the message to you without compromising the sweep."

The young men nodded, their faces reflecting an expression of college freshmen just receiving their first term paper assignment.

Dominic felt a pang of sympathy for them. They were now thoroughly frightened and were about to commit their fledgling company to a great outlay of money. Still, he didn't go out in the street and drag people in here. Industrial espionage was very real and very costly—to the tune of an estimated two billion dollars a year for American businesses alone—and they all knew it.

There was a discreet knock at the door, and everyone

glanced up. Rose Peterson, the Boss's faithful assistant, motioned to Dominic.

"I'm sorry, sir," she whispered when he joined her at the door, "but Mr. Sharp would like to see you for a moment."

Dominic nodded, gestured to Evan to take over, and slipped out. Like the Boss's home, the offices were handsomely appointed, but with thick snow-white carpeting, glass-topped chrome tables, sleek modern furnishings, and stark, colorful Expressionist paintings. The effect was supposed to be airy and graceful, but Dominic called it "hospital waiting-room decor."

Garrett Sharp's office, like his penthouse, contained wall-to-wall windows, only these overlooked the East River and the Fifty-ninth Street Bridge. On the wall behind his desk hung a striking modern painting at least twelve feet long and six feet tall, which consisted of bold splashes of rainbow colors. It looked to Dominic like the artist had simply held buckets of paint in his hands and tossed them all over the canvas.

Sharp looked up from a pile of papers on his desk and waved Dominic into an S-shaped chair of chrome and black leather. It had no armrests, and Dominic hated it, but he took a seat anyway because that's what you did when you worked for Garrett Sharp: whatever he told you to do.

"Dom, I'm transferring you to our Texas office."

"Excuse me, sir?" Dominic tried to keep the edge of sudden panic out of his voice.

Sharp laughed. "Relax, Dom! It's not permanent! I only want you to go down there for a few weeks. After that I'm moving you to D.C. and then back up here."

This maddening habit the Boss had, of keeping things hidden from his employees until he could spring it on them and watch their reaction, drove Dominic crazy. It kept them all off balance all the time, which, of course, was the intended result. He suppressed a sigh.

"May I ask why, sir?" he asked.

"I've recruited a new employee, and I want you to personally oversee her training."

"Her?" he couldn't help but ask. CovertCom was notoriously sexist.

"Oh, she's a jewel," enthused Sharp. "She's going to bring in all kinds of new business. Sharp as a tack, too. Maybe you've heard of her. Rebekah Maxfield?"

Dominic scanned his memory banks. The Boss didn't like his people to be dense, but although the name did ring a bell, he could not place it.

"You know. She's the gal who snatched her own kid from her pervert husband—a federal judge, guy by the name of Griswold—and hid out for over a year. One of his running buddies slapped a seven-year sentence on her when she turned herself in, but she never did give up that kid."

"Oh! Right. That was a long time ago."

"She's out now, and I recruited her. She'd be great PR for the firm."

Dominic wasn't so sure about that, but far be it from him to argue with the Boss. "Does she know anything about electronics?" he asked delicately.

The Boss frowned. "Don't you read the papers? Keep up with things? That girl's one hell of a crackerjack with countersurveillance. How else do you think she was able to hide out from a federal judge for so long? One of the TV newsmagazines did a story on her." He chuckled to himself. "They offered to interview her for the story from prison. She told 'em to go to hell."

Dominic started to shrug, then thought better of it. "Seven years is a long time, sir."

"Damn right. That's why I want you to supervise her training."

Struggling to keep his frustration from showing, Dominic said, "How long do you think all this will take?

The Boss smiled at him as if he were reading his mind, and relishing every minute of it. "Well, now, Dom, that all depends on you. The better a teacher you are, the better a student this little girl will be. It's all up to you."

Nothing is up to me, thought Dominic as he got to his feet and extended a hand over the Boss's wide desk. "I'll do my best, sir," he said.

Sharp stood and shook Dominic's hand. "Just don't rush her," he warned. "It's going to take a little time for her to learn how we do things around here."

Dominic did not have to ask his boss what he meant

by that. He knew already, only too well. Bringing in somebody new was always tricky and risk-laden. There was always the chance that a newcomer could blow everything. Or turn out to be a fed and disappear. Though nobody knew for sure where Joe Dalton had gone, the rumor mill was pretty consistent with the story that he had been an FBI agent and the Boss had found him out.

Dominic didn't like to think about it.

Now the Boss was bringing somebody else into the sticky web of their clandestine little organization, and Dominic was already starting to dread it. No matter how sharp this woman was, she did not belong at CovertCom. Of that one fact Dominic was certain.

But there wasn't a damn thing he could do about it.

Max hit the brakes with all the force she could muster, and the little Saturn responded, fishtailing to a sudden stop. The shoulder harness of her seat belt yanked against her collarbone with painful finality as a backpacked, long-haired student zipped out in front of her on his bike, zig-zagged through the cars parked along the side of the street, and vanished into the labyrinth of side streets jam-packed with a hodgepodge of buildings and off-campus housing that made up the University of Texas campus.

"You always did drive too fast, Rebekah," admonished her mother from the passenger seat. "These kids out here are maniacs, and you just have to creep along and let them get past."

Max ground her teeth together.

"And I just don't see why you insisted on moving into this tacky duplex," she added as Max turned a corner, passed beneath an archway of live oak branches, and pulled into the single-car driveway. "We could have afforded to move to a nice, secure apartment complex."

"*You* could have afforded it, Mom. You." Max cut the ignition and sighed. "It's bad enough that I had to borrow the money from you to buy this car. And you don't have to live here, you know. You can still move into an apartment." *I don't know why you insist on living with me anyway,* she could have added, but didn't.

For seven years her mother had stood staunchly by

her side. How could she kick her out now? She couldn't tell her mom the truth about CovertCom, so what excuse could she possibly use? And anyway, was it fair to expect her mother to live alone at this stage in her life?

"Somebody has to keep you out of trouble," her mother teased, oblivious to Max's inner turmoil.

Max climbed out of the car and walked around to the back, where she popped the trunk lid and began removing bags of groceries. Her mother joined her, still talking. "And I just don't see why you are being so *proud*, Rebekah. I'm sure your boss would be more than happy to offer you an advance on your salary. I just don't know what you're going to wear when you start working."

"You know good and well that I had plenty of clothes packed away, Mom." Max followed her mother as they walked through the carport and into the side door of the house, where old Sarge, snoring in a corner, started up and headed for them, looking embarrassed that his hearing was no longer as sharp as it had once been.

Max's mom's back was ramrod straight, a sure sign of disapproval. It had been that way for several weeks now, as Max had argued with her mother over every stage of moving, packing and storing her mother's furniture and things, and renting this cheaply furnished duplex in a questionable neighborhood. Even as they moved around in the kitchen, they could hear through the thin walls the incessant thrumming of bass notes from their neighbor's CD player.

"Yes, and they all just *hang* on you, like you're some poor refugee or something. And the styles are all outdated, too," she complained. "Nobody wears those boxy blazers with the huge shoulder pads anymore. I *wish* you'd let me take you shopping!" With a *plunk* she smacked the grocery sack down on the chipped Formica bar, which separated the cramped, narrow kitchenette from the small, dimly lit den.

Max put down her bag and began placing Coke cans into the narrow refrigerator. "All right, Mom," she said wearily.

Her mother's face lit up like a little kid's. "You mean I can take you shopping?"

Max quirked a lopsided grin. It was the family secret

that her mom was the one who needed somebody to
look after her, and they all knew it. Deep in her heart,
Liv Maxfield had always been a child and she always
would be. "If it will make you happy," said Max, "you
can take me shopping and buy me some clothes to work
in—*if* you will let me repay you later."

"Oh, it will be so fun!" her mother cried, dancing a
little jig in the middle of the kitchen. "We haven't gotten
to do anything fun together in such a long time. And
I've *missed* it."

Gazing at her mother's pretty, flushed face, Max had
to smile. It was true. She had been such a *bitch* since
getting out of prison. She couldn't enjoy her new freedom because she knew that it had come at such a great
price, but she couldn't confide her heavy heart to a soul.
It made her so damn angry.

But she shouldn't take it out on her poor mom, who'd
put up with such an awful lot in recent years. Impulsively, she reached for her mother and gave her a hug.
The petite woman seemed to get shorter every year.

Hugging back, her mother said, "You were always so
independent, you know. When you were little, you used
to say, *My can do it, Mommy. My can do it.*"

Over her mother's head, Max rolled her eyes. How
many times had she heard that one? "I don't mean to
be difficult," she said awkwardly.

"I know."

"When I get a bigger place, we'll get some of your
stuff out of storage, I promise. You can furnish your
room with all your old bedroom stuff, and—"

Max's mother patted her arm and turned away. "I'm
not worried about it," she said. "I'm an old soldier's
wife, you know. It's just things. Just stuff. It doesn't
mean anything." Busying herself at the sink, she said,
"You're all that matters to me, honey. You and Gaby
and your brothers and their families. Furniture is
nothing."

Why does she always do this to me? mused Max. *One
minute I would gladly kill her, and in the next breath I
love her so fiercely I would die for her.*

As her mother picked up a bottle of dishwashing detergent and a sponge, Max protested. "I'll do that, Mom."

Bustling about the way moms do in kitchens, her mother shook her head. "You go rest, sweetie. You're looking tired again."

As badly as she hated to admit it, Max knew her mother was right. She had underestimated just how much those seven years of living on hold had exhausted her. Thought she'd been out now almost two months, she still could not seem to get enough sleep.

"I guess I could use a nap," she mumbled, and shuffled through the den, across the short hallway, and into her room, which was furnished like the rest of the place in spindly and nondescript garage sales furniture. Max flopped across the double bed, which consisted of a sagging mattress and box springs—no headboard. She really was a bitch to bring her little mama into a place like this, but it was only temporary. Mr. Sharp had told her that she would probably be moving to Washington, D.C., in three months.

"I'll make it up to you, Mom," she whispered as the tides of exhaustion drifted over her body.

As always, when she had trouble getting necessary rest, she lulled herself with memories. Mostly they came to her in brief flashes. During their time on the run, they'd lived for a few months in an isolated old farmhouse on the flat prairie of the Oklahoma panhandle. During one warm summer rain, Max had sat on the front porch swing and watched while Gaby danced out in the soft shower, clad only in her panties, her bare feet squishing through the fragrant grass, her sweet face upturned to catch the cool droplets on her tongue.

"Mommy! Come and play with me!" she'd coaxed, and Max had joined her at last. She'd swept the child up in her arms, and they had swayed to the music of the rain, their hair plastered to the backs of their necks, their laughter echoing in the completeness of their solitude. It was a moment of pure delight and utter joy.

But as always when things began to seem settled and safe at last, somebody had started to ask too many questions, and they'd had to leave again.

Toys and books were a luxury for a child on the run.

She could only possess as many as she could pack in a hurry. Gaby's favorite of her few books was Maurice Sendak's *Where the Wild Things Are*. At night, no matter where they were sleeping, Max and Gaby would cuddle together against the pillows and read *Where the Wild Things Are*. It had been a comfort to Max as well as her little girl, the idea that the demons which haunted them could possibly turn out to be harmless after all, and that they could go to sleep one night in safety and security.

They couldn't have friends really, either of them. There was seldom time, and it was always risky. So Max would play with Gaby, sitting cross-legged on the floor with raggedy old Pooh Bear, and they would have tea parties with pretend cups and pretend tea, and their world was, oh, so proper, and everybody was kind.

Other times Max would lie on the bed and let her long hair hang over the side, and Gaby would brush it and play with it, poking it full of colorful little barrettes. Afterward, Max would preen in front of the mirror and exclaim at how beautiful she looked. Once, to her daughter's endless glee, she even ran errands with the barrettes in place.

Then there came the time when the stress of the constant running and hiding became too much for Max, and she lay on the couch in yet another anonymous rented house, sobbing. Gaby was taking a nap—or so Max had thought—but she opened her tear-blurred eyes to find her little girl standing next to the couch, her little face worry-crinkled. She'd said, *"Mommy, are you so sad? Or does your head hurt?"*

And she'd pulled the child onto her body full-length, and wrapped her arms around her, and wept helplessly, and searched her weary heart for words of reassurance, but there weren't any, because she was so sad, and her head hurt.

More than seven years had passed since that day, and little Gaby had left her babyhood behind. She'd lost her two front teeth and grown new ones that were too big for her young face. She'd started school and learned to read *Where the Wild Things Are* all by herself. She'd gotten too big for tea parties.

And here was Max, seven years later . . . still so sad, and her head hurt.

The Austin CovertCom offices were surprisingly unpretentious, located in one of hundreds of similar office buildings spread out along the length of I-35. Max could not seem to get used to the throngs of traffic that now seemed to choke the city everywhere she drove, and by the time she'd missed her exit once, looped back around and underneath an overpass and down a one-way access road and into the wrong turn lane and across the paths of three oncoming cars to reach the parking lot, she was tense, overwound, and irritable.

She didn't even want to be there in the first place.

Postponing the inevitable, she escaped into the first rest room she could find and checked her appearance. Yanking it out, she dragged a brush through her silky hair and vowed to put it up next time. Though she was still pale and a little too thin, Max had to admit that her mother had been right about her clothes. The new suit she was wearing, to her mother's gleeful delight, was peacock green silk shantung and form-fitted to her long, trim waist. Her eyes, which changed color depending on what she was wearing, reflected the soft sheen of the suit like two emeralds.

Not that Max cared, really. After all, she was only going to be working around a bunch of criminals anyway.

After reluctantly exiting the rest room, she checked her new watch, found that she was already ten minutes late, wandered around looking for a building directory, then hit the elevator button with a shaking finger and headed for the fourth floor. Fifteen minutes late on the first day. Her military father would never have tolerated it.

The office was the last door at the end of the hall, and Max hurried down the corridor in her tight new pumps, clutching her new leather shoulder bag and feeling like an idiot. Her stomach was all jittery.

She did not want to be here, and yet felt a curious anxiety to do well, the curse of the overachiever.

A very pretty young receptionist with deep dimples in

the corners of her pink cheeks looked up as Max entered the office and gave her a dazzling cheerleader smile.

"I'm Rebekah Maxfield," she said nervously, trying to smile back but not quite making it.

"Oh, yes! We've been expecting you, Ms. Maxfield! Just one moment, and I'll tell Mr. Antonio you're here." She sprang to her feet and bounced out of the room.

The woman actually *twinkled*. Max would swear to it in a court of law.

She turned away, thinking, *I'd need a goddamned pair of shades to look at that kid again,* and wandered restlessly around, gazing at the expensive paintings, the muted dove-gray carpeting, the tasteful plants. Real ones that required care. She guessed that must be one of Twinkletoes's many important jobs.

Stop being a bitch, she scolded herself; and then, *I can't help it. It keeps me strong.*

She would have to stay very strong to survive.

Though her new boss's footsteps were muffled by the deep carpeting, his voice came to her like liquid butter. He said, "You must be Rebekah Maxfield. I'm Dominic Antonio."

Later Max would not remember turning around to face him. She would remember her mouth going dry so fast that she couldn't even say, "Please, call me Max."

She couldn't say anything, couldn't think anything, could only react.

He was, quite simply, the most beautiful man she had ever seen. Her attraction to him was visceral and powerful and instantaneous. When he shook her hand, a thrill like an electrical current charged up her arm all the way to her shoulder and spread warmly throughout her body.

He was tall, plenty taller than her, and when Max upturned her face to meet his eyes, she felt her face flush hotly, mainly because she was so afraid her thoughts were transparent.

All she could think was, *I haven't had sex in nearly ten years. Oh, God help me.*

As she struggled to bring her chaotic thoughts under some semblance of control, she cursed Agent Underwood. *He promised me that this job would not be dangerous.*

She wondered what else he had lied about.

Chapter Five

He was waiting for her in the frozen-foods department, and spotted her long before she noticed him. The difference in her appearance was astonishing. She was dressed in a ruby-red, small-waisted suit with black velvet lapels and black pumps. It was the kind of red that might wash out a wimpier blonde, but on her it was drop-dead gorgeous. When she reached around a shelf for a bottle of salad dressing, her impossibly long hair rippled down her back like a flowing stream.

Rapunzel in power clothes.

There was color in her cheeks now, a soft, natural flush. She crossed off an item on her list, then headed down the aisle. Her gaze brushed over him, where he stood leaning against the ice cream freezer, then back for a double-take of recognition.

Almost instantly, a scowl settled over her fine features, and he sighed.

"Underwood, are you following me?" she snapped. "What, you never heard of picking up a phone?"

He beckoned her to follow him through a door marked *Employees Only,* and as she trailed along behind him through the corridors of boxes containing toilet paper and canned goods, he could hear her heels clicking on the concrete floor like a little drumbeat of annoyance.

The last time he'd seen her, when she was still in prison, he had been "Agent Underwood." Now he was just "Underwood." He had to smile.

They emerged through an exit door. His car was parked in the alley behind the supermarket, and he unlocked and opened the passenger door for her. She got into the car without a word and did not bother to hit the button that would automatically unlock his door.

"You've been watching too many movies, Underwood," she said as he got in and started the ignition.

"Can't be too careful." He buckled his seat belt and eased the car out of the alley. He headed for a nearby park he'd seen, where they could sit behind a copse of trees and speak freely, in seclusion.

"Just your luck. I left my secret decoder ring at home." She drummed her fingers on the side of her smart black leather bag, just as she'd done with the water bottle in the van back at the prison. Only this time her nails were smooth and long and painted blood red.

Acrylic. A woman trick he'd never have known about if he hadn't been married.

The park entrance was only a few blocks from the supermarket, and he was safely hidden behind his chosen trees in less than five minutes. He left the engine running with the air conditioning on. It was already Texas hot, and he did not want to take a chance on leaving the car windows open while they talked.

"So. How're things going?" He swiveled in his seat and leaned against the car door, facing her.

"I've only been at my happy new job a week, Underwood. What do you expect me to know?"

"Who's in charge of training you?" He pulled a small spiral notebook and a pen out of his jacket pocket.

"D-Dominic Antonio."

The stutter was so rapid as to be almost undetectable, but Underwood noticed it and glanced up. "Big guy?" he asked. "Dark hair? Mustache?"

She nodded. "How did you know?"

He shrugged. "It's my job."

"Oh. That's right. I forgot. You're the Effin' B. I."

He said, "You know, this would go a hell of a lot easier if you'd get over this hostility toward me. I'm trying to help you."

Her laugh was sarcastic and unnatural, more of a snort. "No, you're not! You're trying to make your case and your career by using me as your personal snitch. Let's see now . . . Where is that pesky part about *you* helping *me?*"

He'd forgotten how smart she was. Always anticipating his next move. He wasn't used to that. Most informants were low-lifes who couldn't string together a coherent sentence. He'd have to stay sharp.

"For one thing," he said, "I'm offering you the protection of the Effin' B. I."

"Protection from what?"

"From the bad guys you work for and with."

"So if they're mean to me, you're . . . what . . . gonna come bustin' in with the S.W.A.T. team?"

"If I have to." He held her gaze while she pondered that. He could practically see her mind working.

"You can't make me like you, Underwood."

"I don't give a damn whether you like me or not."

"Well, then, you can't make me trust you."

He shrugged.

She broke the gaze first and stared out the car window. A couple of squealing young boys flashed past on bicycles, and she jumped, betraying her nervousness.

"Tell me about Antonio."

She turned her face to stare out the passenger window, so he was unable to read her expression. "What do you want to know?" she said. "I've only known him a couple days."

"I want to know everything you can find out about him. I want to know where he's from and how he came to be working for Garrett Sharp—anything about his background that you can tell me. I want to know what his job is, specifically. I want to know what he tells you about how the business operates, who's in charge of whom, and who does what. And as soon as you see him working a mark or setting up a scam, I want to know who, what, why, when, where, and how it happens. I want specifics. I want details."

Her mouth etched a grim line across her face. "Is that all?"

He shook his head. "Evidence," he said. "Paperwork. Documents. Order forms. Computer disks. Anything you can get your hands on."

"But it's too obvious!" she cried. "If I got caught sneaking stuff out of the office, they would know right away what I was doing."

Underwood smiled. "Now, now, Max. Aren't you just a little bit too smart for that?"

"What's that supposed to mean?"

"Well, you do work in the spy gadget business, don't you?"

"Yeah. So?"

"So . . . Do some spying. There must be all kinds of ways for you to find out information without arousing suspicion or leaving a trace of any kind that you were even there."

"What if I get caught?"

"I don't think that'll happen."

"What makes you so sure?"

"The stakes. There's too much at stake here."

"For you, maybe, but not for me," she said. "All that could happen to me is that I could get fired." Then she narrowed her eyes at him. "Wait a minute. Are you threatening me?"

He said nothing.

During the long moment that she stared at him, her face flushed ever hotter and her eyes blazed. "I'm not your fucking marionette," she said quietly. "You can't just pull the strings and make me jump."

"The more information you find out for us," he said, "the better it will go for you in the long run," and added, "the sooner you realize that, the better."

"Fine," she said, yanking on the car door handle. "Now, if you're done fucking me for today, I've got to finish buying groceries and get home, or my mom will worry. Unless, of course, you're wanting to fuck her, too."

With a weary sigh he reached for the gear shift. "I'll take you back."

"Kiss my ass." She climbed out, pulling her long legs after her like stilts, and slammed the car door so hard that it rocked the vehicle. As she stalked away, a sudden shot of wind caught her hair and flung it streaming behind her like a splendid silken guidon carried into battle.

Rolling his head around on his tense shoulders, Underwood headed back to the no-tell motel where he was staying to write out his 302, tally up his expenses for the day, make half a dozen phone calls, and take care of all the little requisite chores of being a federal agent on a case investigation.

But along the way, he stopped first at a liquor store and picked up a bottle of Chivas Regal. It was the only way he could think of to keep from thinking too much.

Not since high school had Max felt more idiotic or conflicted.

She wanted to kill her mother.

Not only had Liv surprised Max at work, but had invited her boss to dinner.

Somehow her mom had managed to make the cramped little house look cozy and inviting. Fresh flowers adorned the kitchen table where they would dine, the coffee table in the living room, and the mantel of the fake fireplace. Scented candles were everywhere, and their soothing fragrance mingled with mouthwatering cooking smells while soft jazz from the stereo wafted throughout. Somehow the place no longer looked sordid; it now looked comfortable.

It didn't help.

Max was a nervous wreck. *How* could her mom have invited this man into their home? At work it was hard enough being side by side with him in the office, brushing his arm at the coffee machine, standing near him in the elevator. (He smelled heavenly.)

She stared at herself in the mirror. "You will not fall into bed with this man, or—God forbid—in love with him. You can't. He's a crook. A criminal. A bad guy. You're supposed to be spying on him for the feds. Keep away."

The doorbell rang and she jumped, flinging her hairbrush to the floor.

"Rebekah! Dominic is here!"

Max was wearing a cowl-neck sweater in a deep turquoise color that made her eyes shine, and tight jeans, and as she headed for the door, she did have to admit . . . she looked hot.

"Stop it!" she whispered, turning the doorknob.

He was standing in the living room, his hands behind his back, studying a portrait of the twins where they were all decked out in their full dress uniforms and green berets, listening politely to their mother who stood next to him, talking softly. He was wearing a soft, stressed leather bomber jacket in chocolate brown over a crisp white sport shirt open at the neck, revealing dark curls beneath.

"I didn't know you were from a military family," he commented, turning as she entered the room. "Your mom's been filling me in."

Liv waved at Max and ducked into the kitchen, wooden spoon in hand. "I'm sure she has," said Max sardonically. "May I take your jacket?"

"Sure." He shrugged out of the jacket and as he handed it to her, and she enfolded the coat in her arms, she inhaled a warm leather scent that made her think of her dad.

"I was in the Marine Corps, myself," he said. "We did a little time in the desert, too."

"Yeah, the twins used to bitch about how the air force guys got concrete floors and air-conditioning, while the marines and army guys got sand fleas and scorpions." She smiled at the memory.

He laughed, his dark eyes crinkling at the corners. "They got that right!" Then he said, "I'm so sorry about your brother and your dad. I had a brother who was much older than me. He was killed in Vietnam, so I know how you must feel."

She nodded, and their gaze met. Quickly, she glanced away.

Her mother called Dominic to come and open the wine. While Max hung the jacket in the closet, she silently repeated the mantra, *He's a criminal*, to herself.

He's a criminal, and I'm a snitch.

She closed the closet door and joined Dominic and her mother in the kitchen, where the mood was much lighter. "Oh, Brand and Brett were the most protective big brothers you ever saw," her mom was saying. "Rebekah, remember when Brand snuck into the backseat and went along with you on your first car date?"

"Boy, do I." Max smiled. "That whole evening, we had no idea he was back there." She giggled at the memory. "Then, when the guy tried to take me parking—"

Her mother took over the story. "Brand sat straight up in the backseat and said," (and here, Max joined in), *"Take your hands off my sister!"*

They both doubled over laughing. Dominic roared, then, wiping tears from his eyes, said, "What did you do?"

Max said, "I got out of the car, dragged my brother out, and proceeded to beat the crap out of him."

As the laughter rang out over the kitchen, Max realized that it was the first time she'd heard laughter here since moving into the house. She *had* been a bitch, and it wasn't fair to her mother, who had no idea, of course, what was going on at CovertCom.

Max decided to relax and have a good time. She owed her mother that much. "Let's have a toast," she said.

"Great idea." Dominic, who had already popped the cork on the Chianti classico he had brought, poured them each a glass and lifted his own. Looking directly into Max's eyes, he said, "To the future."

Cold little goose bumps of hot desire crawled over Max's body. Trying in vain to ignore the sensation, she said, "To the future," and they all sipped.

Over a dinner of linguini and her mother's superb tomato sauce, Max's Caesar salad and hard crusty bread, they finished the wine, and her mother produced another bottle from the refrigerator. Max got to her feet and started to carry her plate to the sink. Her mother shook her head. "Leave them," she said firmly. "I'll get them in the morning." Then she yawned widely. "Oh, my goodness, pardon me. I'm just an old broad. Wine makes me sleepy."

Turning her back on Dominic, she winked at Max. "I'm going to turn in. You kids have a good visit."

Dominic got up, his face the picture of solicitousness. "I should be going. I wouldn't want to disturb you."

Her mother waved a carefree hand in the air, and Max glared daggers at her, which she pretended not to notice. "I wouldn't hear of it, and anyway, I sleep like the dead. An earthquake wouldn't bother me."

While Max stood, helpless, her mother left the room. And that was that. She was alone with Dominic. "Uh . . . why don't we take the wine into the living room?"

"Sure," he said, maddeningly dense to her mother's subterfuge, as only a man could be.

Max sat on the sofa, and he sat next to her like a slow

graceful cat, angling his big body slightly and resting his arm lightly over the back of the couch, his fingertips just barely brushing the nape of her neck. Candlelight flickered in his warm eyes and smoothed out his craggy features. The honeyed tones of Diane Schuur and the Count Basie orchestra doing, "We'll Be Together Again," drifted sensuously from the stereo speakers.

She did not dare look at him, but concentrated on her wineglass and cursed herself for drinking too much and getting light-headed.

"I'm glad your mother left us alone," he said, "because I've been wanting to say something all night."

She dared a glance up, felt herself melting, dove back into her wineglass.

"When I heard we were going to be working together, I looked up some stuff about you. I know about what you've been through, Max, with your little girl and all. And I've been wanting to tell you ever since we met that I think you are the bravest person I have ever known."

She didn't say anything. What could she say?

"You've been through hell and back, but you never cracked. You never let the bastards get you down. I've known soldiers in wartime made of weaker stuff."

She shrugged. Agent Underwood's face made a sly and frustrating visit into her mind, and suddenly, she felt very tired and she wanted to cry.

"You caught me by surprise," he said. "You weren't what I expected." Then, in a very quiet tone, he added, "You take my breath away."

She placed the wineglass carefully onto the coffee table in front of them, and let her breath out very slowly.

"And if I don't kiss you right now, I'm afraid I'll just disappear." His voice had gone husky and blurred.

She turned her face to his and dared to look deeply into his eyes.

He drew his fingers slowly through her hair, then cupped her face in his big hands, drawing her to him and kissing her as tenderly and softly as a butterfly's wings fluttering against her mouth. Without even meaning to, she arched her breasts against his chest, and he caught her to him so tightly she could barely breathe, with a kiss so hot and so liquid that her body seemed almost disconnected from her mind.

Then, suddenly, he pulled away from her, not in a brutal sort of way, but in a gesture full of unspoken reluctance and sweet regret.

"You're so beautiful it hurts," he whispered, leaning his forehead into hers. "My body wants to make love to you all night long."

She nodded. She was already past the point of no return. There was no going back for her. It had been too long since she'd been with a man.

"But we work together, Max," he continued, stroking her hair, tucking it back out of the way. "I'm your supervisor, basically your boss. I'm responsible for training you. I really like working with you every day, and I don't want to do anything to blow that." He glanced away, clearly struggling with himself. "It would really let Mr. Sharp down if he thought I was coming on to you or anything. I just don't think it's a good idea for us to see each other outside of work."

Max felt this great weight upon her chest, a lump in her throat. For a moment she dared not say anything. After all, he was absolutely right. It was certainly not a good idea for them to see each other, for a whole lot of reasons.

For a moment she had this hysterical desire to throw her arms around him and make love to him with all the pent-up desire she had. To say, *To hell with Underwood; to hell with Sharp. Goddammit, I deserve this!*

Instead she said, "You're right, Dominic. We really should not see each other except for work. That would be best."

There was nothing else to say.

He sighed and sat still a moment longer, as if he, too, were savoring it. Then he pulled away from her and got to his feet.

She got up, too, because she had to get his coat out of the closet, and the manly leather scent and buttery feel of it almost got to her, but she handed it to him very primly and said, "Thank you for coming, Dominic."

He said, "Tell your mother I really enjoyed dinner, and thank her for inviting me, will you?"

She nodded. "I will."

"She's a great lady. But then, I wouldn't expect anything different from this family."

She thought, *If you only knew*.

She walked him to the front door and stood awkwardly. It was a bad moment, and she didn't know what to do with it.

Apparently he didn't, either. "See you at work on Monday," he said, and ducked out the door as if he was afraid to touch her again.

The spring night was balmy and cool, and the air was sensual against her skin. The engine of his silver Mercedes roared to life, and he drove away in a flash of crimson taillights.

And she stood in the open doorway for a long, absent time, staring blindly into the darkness, still tasting his kiss, and wondering just how it was that her life had come to be so sad.

PART II

WILD CARD

kibitzer: *spectator who gives players*
           unsolicited advice

It should not be necessary to point out that
the addition of even one wild card . . .
considerably alters the picture . . .
                              ——Ted Thackery, Jr.
                                Dealer's Choice

Chapter Six

The CovertCom Washington, D.C., offices were located on Eleventh Avenue, just around the corner from the fortresslike, canitlevered FBI Headquarters building. It was a crowded, somewhat ugly neighborhood of bureaucratic offices that fed the voracious appetite of the United States government, but a few blocks' walk in most any direction led to green stately parks with their glorious monuments or the White House or the Smithsonian.

Dominic loved Washington even more than New York and especially now in early summer, before the humidity grew unbearable. For the most part it was a multicultural city of grace and beauty, surprisingly friendly and filled with a smorgasbord of things to do.

At the moment Dominic and Max were holed up in the windowless CovertCom boardroom with their most recent client, a short, intense, fiftyish man with thick salt-and-pepper hair, gold-rimmed glasses in outdated aviator frames, and braces on his teeth. Dominic tried not to stare at the obviously uncomfortable and surprising oral hardware. The client, Paul Zwibeck, tried not to stare at Max.

"Up until a couple of years ago," Zwibeck was saying, "Opco was one of the most successful fiber-optic firms in the country. We were in the process of closing a billion-dollar deal with the Chinese when a French company entered a late bid out of the goddamned blue, and undercut us by a huge amount. The French company got the contract, and as a result Opco lost over *half* its business, and we had to lay off *three-quarters* of our workforce." He sighed heavily. "I can't tell you how demoralizing this has been. Our firm regards its employees as family. The layoffs were just horrible. But if we hadn't done it, we'd have been bankrupted by the end of the year."

Max, who looked stunning in a trim black business suit, nodded. "You were hit by the DGSE."

Zwibeck blinked. "That wasn't the name of the company."

"No." She smiled. "I'm talking about the Direction Generale de la Securite Exterieure."

"I'm sorry. I don't speak French." The poor guy had a speech impediment, apparently caused by the braces, which sometimes made words like *French* provoke a spray of saliva onto his listeners.

Max did not seem to notice. "That's the Directory of Security for Foreign Affairs. The French government directly subsidizes and controls many of its high-tech companies. They routinely perform industrial espionage on American companies for the sole purpose of bringing economic advantage to French companies."

"Well, can't the CIA or somebody *do* something?" Zwibeck sputtered.

"In a free enterprise system like ours, it's not that easy," replied Max. "The United States government can't openly interfere, though they have passed laws that make cooperating in matters of economic espionage a crime, and they've protested to the French and expelled French citizens suspected of such activity and sent them home."

"Yeah, I think I read something about that," Zwibeck mumbled vaguely.

"But it's not just the French who are guilty of this, you know," went on Max smoothly. Dominic hid a smile. He loved to watch her work a client. "The Israelis, the Japanese, and dozens of other countries, including Russia, have plundered our high-tech industries for information that could save them a lot of time and billions of dollars in research and development, or help them undercut U.S. companies in bidding wars for high-tech contracts."

Zwibeck nodded. "Here's the thing. We've got some

new technology in development that would put Opco light-years ahead of the competition if we can be first to hit the marketplace with it."

Toys for big kids, mused Dominic.

"And I'm just scared shitless that somebody's going to steal it. If they did, we'd flat-out be out of business. That's why I've come to you guys." He hesitated. "I've told no one what I'm doing, not even my vice-presidents or board of directors." Miserably he added, "I just don't know who to trust anymore."

Max gave the man a sympathetic nod. "This must be heartbreaking for you. I know you started the company on a shoestring with your old college roommate and built it up. Now you have to wonder if even he could be leaking secrets."

One thing about Max—she always did her homework. Even Dominic had not known that tidbit about Zwibeck's company. Dominic watched the man's shoulders sag. There were a lot of technical geniuses working for CovertCom, but nobody had the human touch that Max did. As he watched her launch into an explanation of the difference between *overt* theft of information (data stolen by employees and sold to competitors), and *covert* (data stolen by competitors through bugging, wiretapping, and other devices), Dominic's mind began to drift.

After the awkward night at Max's Austin home, they had continued to work together smoothly—at least on the surface of things. Each pretended nothing had happened. Max had her hands full, anyway, getting caught up; seven years was an awfully long time to be away from the electronics business. But she had a mind like a whip. Sometimes Dominic felt as if *he* was trying to catch up to *her*.

No matter how much material he threw at her, it never seemed to be too much. On the edge of his attention, he could hear her talking technology with a techno-geek without even breaking stride:

". . . That's no problem. We use the CCS Portable X-ray system for that. It only weighs nine kilograms and will penetrate any nonmetallic surface to check for a microphone."

"What about developing the film?" asked Zwibeck.

"We use a Polaroid Radiographic film cassette and processor, and within minutes we get detailed X-rays. Most microphones use some metal or electronic components in their construction. If there's a mike hiding in, say, a desk, we'll find it."

"What about mikes that use semiconductor devices? Or plastic membrane mikes?"

"Well, since you know about plastic membrane mikes, and believe me, most people have never heard of them," she said with a grin that Zwibeck eagerly returned, "then you must surely know that they are extremely rare, very exotic. You almost never see them in the field unless it's some kind of government operation."

"True," Zwibeck conceded. He pondered that for a minute. "How do you detect RF emanations, then?"

"Boy, you are sharp, aren't you?" flattered Max. Zwibeck preened. "Okay," she continued. "There are several ways you can go with radio frequency transmissions. You can use a proximity detector, a feedback detector, wideband tuners, spectrum analyzers . . ."

Confident that she was handling herself with her typical aplomb, Dominic faded out again, marveling at Max's quick mind, as he so often did. She absorbed information on thermal imaging and infrared illuminators, pocket-size voice-stress analyzers, bomb-detection instruments that could practically see, hear, and smell; infrared intrusion detectors, and surveillance devices disguised to look like anything from sprinkler heads to briefcases.

Every night and every weekend she took home boxes of heavy texts and manufacturing instructions and computer program disks. He kept expecting her to complain or at least beg for mercy, but instead she was like a kid in a candy shop. Everything delighted her.

He watched her as she dragged out a large AM/FM radio/tape player—a typical "boom box," and set it on the boardroom table in front of Zwibeck. "Let me introduce you to the TRN-300," she said, punching a button. They listened to a few moments of the sound track to the *Beatles Anthology*. (Even the music was a good choice; this guy was obviously a baby boomer.)

"As you can see, it's a working boom box," she said.

"But it is also a tape recorder nullifier *and* an audio jammer. In audio jammer mode, the TRN-300 projects a protective audio zone up to six point five feet and within a sixty-degree angle of projection."

Zwibeck leaned forward, clearly fascinated. "Oh, man, this is cool," he said like a kid with a new toy. "So if I were to sit, say within range of the boom box with a colleague and we were discussing our new technology, and the colleague was trying to secretly tape-record the conversation—"

"The TRN-300 would defeat the device," said Max. "Any device in the human speech range of three hundred hertz to three kilohertz that uses a microphone."

"How does it work?" asked Zwibeck, fiddling with the boom box.

"It uses a phase-shift modulation technique. By sending out a constant pulse, it interferes with the mikes trying to capture your conversation on tape. And that ain't all," she added with a sexy, wicked grin.

Clearly dazzled, Zwibeck leaned closer.

"See back here? Just plug in your telephone line and phone set into this rear panel, and it will be virtually impossible for your phone to be tapped."

Zwibeck gazed at Max with lust in his eyes. Dominic had seen that look before. This woman was a true techno-head. And how many women fit that description? Dominic tried not to frown at their client. While he understood the man's attraction to Max, he resented it. There was so much more to her, even, than met the eyes, something this little creep would never take the time to find out.

Dominic never lacked for female companionship, especially in Washington, which was a virtual smorgasbord of intelligent, attractive professional women. Some were erudite, some preachy, some crazy, some airheads, some very nice and good company. He took a few of them to bed, but not very often and never twice.

And the reason, in spite of what Dominic had told Max, had nothing to do with what Garrett Sharp would or would not think. The low-down, nitty-gritty truth of the matter was that Dominic Antonio lived a dangerous lie each and every day of his life.

He could take a woman into his bed while living a lie, but he could not take one into his life.

Every day he looked at Max and couldn't help but wonder what it would be like to make love to her. But unlike the anonymous women he kept at arm's length, Max was already closer to him, simply because they worked together. He couldn't pull his little disappearing act with her. He wasn't sure he would even want to.

It was bad enough, living the lie in front of her. He dreaded the day when Max learned the truth about him. He didn't think he would ever be able to look her in the eye again after that. She would lose all respect for him, he was sure of it. And he hated to lose her respect because he respected her.

The Boss seemed to think that just because Max had done time that she would fit into the organization like a hand into a glove; but the Boss was an asshole who wouldn't know a quality woman of class if she came up and sat in his lap.

And *that* worried Dominic more than anything else. What if Max *didn't* "fit into the organization"? He kept thinking about the Boss's Faraday room in his New York penthouse, and about the missing Joe Dalton, who hadn't been loyal. What happened to him? And what would happen to Max if, once she realized the truth about CovertCom, she tried to get out?

He thought of this early time, especially since the transfer to Washington, as a sort of honeymoon period. Right now Max didn't know everything. So, around the office, they had developed a rhythm together, a delicate dance. They worked together with the clients as smoothly as Fred Astaire and Ginger Rogers. She never took the lead, but as someone had once said about Fred and Ginger: she did everything he did, only backward and in high heels.

Sometimes they would have lunch at one of Washington's assorted bistros or share a sandwich in one of the city's many parks, and sometimes he would walk her to her car if they had worked late. But except for guiding her by the elbow or the small of her back, or taking her hand to help her out of the car, he never touched her.

At work she was all professional cool; when they were

alone, she could be warm and funny. He sensed a strong mutual attraction, but she never acted on it. He was glad of that, because the situation was far more complicated than she could imagine, and his willpower only went so far.

Max had clinched the sale with Paul Zwibeck. Not only was he ordering a full Spy Squad sweep of the Opco offices and laboratories, but he was ordering a TRN-300 and several other little toys that cost a small fortune. When Zwibeck leaned over to sign his contract agreement and purchase orders, Max caught Dominic's eye and gave him a devilish wink. He gave her a big congratulatory smile and mouthed the words, *Good job*.

But when Zwibeck lingered, clearly reluctant to leave, Dominic left them and went to his own office. He tried to catch up on paperwork, but the late-afternoon June sunshine splashed warmly over his desk and he kept catching himself, chin in hand, mind lost.

Max left the office before Dominic did, and he wondered in an unreasonable spurt of annoyance if she had a date for a drink with Mr. Metalmouth Techno-Geek.

He indulged his melancholy as he usually did. He left the office just as the sun began to burn down toward the Potomac, torching the clouds and casting a bloody pall along the length of the reflecting pool. Walking straight down Eleventh, he crossed Pennsylvania Avenue until he reached the Mall, the great grassy stretch that sprawled east to the U.S. Capitol and west to the Lincoln Memorial.

Here he began to cut across the park, angling past the Washington Monument, which was not yet lit for night and thrust darkly up through the scarlet-edged sky. He headed beneath the line of trees that stood at parade rest along the shallow reflecting pool, guarding the shadows of some of the greatest historical events of the country. Here and there, young lovers lay sprawled in one another's arms beneath the drowsing trees. As he approached the Lincoln Memorial, spotlights suddenly appeared, bathing the brooding president with a somber amber glow that cast the angles and crags of his face in a great bas-relief of incredible sadness and the overpowering weight of responsibility. Dominic often found the big statue oddly comforting, but he was not here to see

Lincoln. Instead he cut across the sloping hillside that housed the memorial, past the souvenir vendors who were putting away their wares, and down the unadorned concrete walkway to his real destination.

Gathering twilight had, mercifully, sent the tourists scattering, and there were very few people around on this weeknight to distract or disturb him. As the walkway continued to slope down off the hilltop, the first jutting A-line of polished black granite was almost imperceptible in the grass, but the farther Dominic walked downward, the higher the wall seemed to reach, until he finally arrived at the apex and found himself surrounded by thousands and thousands of dead soldiers.

Technically, of course, it wasn't the actual soldiers, but just their names; only a vast wall of names, so many names you could never hope to count them all in a single visit, though Dominic already knew there were 58,132 of them, carved like stark memories into the black gulf of the nation's conscience, a gaping gash cut from the serene hillside of the capital city as a reminder to all who bought souvenirs and clicked snapshots and picked up postcards, that the freedom to do so had been paid for in blood.

Dominic already knew where his brother's name was. He'd been here many times before, had pressed paper to it and preserved the name on the paper with a pencil for his mother. As always, he reached up and touched the name, running his fingers over it like a caress.

The Vietnam Veterans Memorial had a tendency to engulf any daytime visitors who wanted to stand and think, pray, or caress a name. Insensitive foreign tourists crowded past with their Nikon cameras, backpacks, and baby strollers, posing for snapshots with idiotic grins on their faces while white-haired mothers stood unnoticed nearby and wept. Teenagers, too young to know better, horse-played and made loud jokes about post traumatic stress victims while graying veterans looked on with quiet resignation and fierce pride. It was too much. It was too hard. The first time he'd sobbed like a child.

But at night the black walls seemed more to embrace visitors, the spotlights to reflect their faces back to them like brothers gazing out from the grave. It was the closest Dominic could get to his fallen brother, who used to carry him around on his shoulders and toss a baseball to him in the backyard and threaten off all the bullies and chase away all the ghosts. Now his brother was a ghost. Yet somehow feeling close to him like this helped Dominic to clear his head and realign his priorities.

Dominic was trudging back up the hill and had just passed the seven-foot bronze statue of the three soldiers who walked together, weapons in hand, patrolling the memorial, when he heard Max's voice. It came to him clearly on the quiet evening air, and he caught the tone immediately: anger.

Glancing over in the direction of the voice, he spotted her, standing by the little building that was operated by park personnel during business hours to direct tourists and answer any questions about the memorial. Though the shadows of night were fast deepening, he could see her clearly enough to notice that she was talking to a federal agent.

For a fleeting moment Dominic froze. It seemed as if every blood vessel in his body turned to ice. He even forgot to breathe.

What the hell was she doing?

Dominic did not know the agent's name, but he knew the guy was a fed. He'd seen him around.

"Why don't you back off, Underwood?" she cried.

"Keep your voice down," the fed murmured, glancing around. Dominic dodged behind the statue of the three vets and used them for cover.

"I don't have anything to tell you," she said, making no attempt to lower her voice. Her tone was strident, stressed out, and scornful. "Why don't you go raid some survivalists or something?"

"It's been almost four months," the fed persisted, his voice even and deadly as only a fed could make it.

"Leave me alone." To Dominic's dismay, Max began striding straight toward the statue. It would not be long before she noticed him. He was completely out in the open, and the area was well lit by now; there was no place else to hide.

The fed dog-trotted after Max and roughly grabbed her arm. She tried to yank it away from him, and Dominic stepped from behind the statue, blocking their way. Pulling himself up to his full height of six-four, Dominic crossed his arms over his chest, glowered down at the smaller man (he pegged him at about five-eight or nine, maybe one hundred fifty pounds), and said, "Max? Is this man bothering you?"

A thunderbolt straight from the sky would not have shocked Max more. She felt the blood drain from her face as she stood there on the darkening path between Agent Underwood and her CovertCom boss.

In another life Max would have fumbled the ball completely at this stage of the game; she'd never been a very good liar. But living for a year on the run had taught her to think on her feet, and to do it without a flicker of expression.

One thing she'd learned during that life, and later, in prison, was that the best lies always had an element of truth in them. Almost without hesitation she said, "As a matter of fact, yes, Dominic, this man *is* bothering me, and I'm glad you're here."

She glanced back at Underwood, who was standing immobile behind her. It was impossible to read his expression. Gesturing toward him, she said, "This is Agent Jack Underwood of the FBI. And this is my boss, Dominic Antonio."

Underwood nodded at Dominic. Dominic did not take his eyes off him, nor did he offer his hand.

"Agent Underwood has been harassing me. It seems the FBI believes that even though I served my full prison sentence for keeping my daughter away from her dad, I should turn her over now so that he can exercise his perverted parental rights."

Dominic's gaze flickered from Underwood to Max and back to Underwood. "Is this true?"

Underwood shrugged. "Mr. Griswold still has rights outstanding, yes."

"So you're trying to get Max here to tell you where her daughter is?"

Without flinching, Underwood replied, "It would be easier on Ms. Maxfield in the long run."

Dominic's face set into a hard mask. His eyes glittered, and in that moment Max knew how dangerous he could be.

Dominic said, "The fact that her ex-husband is a federal judge wouldn't have anything to do with this little harassment you've got going here now, would it?"

"Absolutely not," said Underwood.

"Uh-huh. Well, Mr. FBI, I'm here to tell you that this woman would sooner slit her own wrists than let you get your grimy little paws on her child. She will *never* cooperate with you on this matter." He took a menacing step toward Underwood. "And since you have no legal recourse at this time, then I suggest you get the hell out of her life." He took another step toward Underwood, towering over the smaller man.

It was all Max could do not to leap for joy. Not only had Dominic believed her, but the story was not a total lie, and it was immensely satisfying to watch him scare the hell out of Underwood. She'd been wanting to do that for months.

Underwood swallowed. "Mr. Antonio, are you threatening me?"

Dominic smiled, but his eyes stayed hard. "Take it any way you like."

The two men locked gazes, but Underwood was the first to break it.

"Fine," he said. He glanced over at Max as if he wanted to say something, seemed to think better of it, and turned on his heel. Max and Dominic watched him go, gathering tattered vestiges of his pride about him as he went. They watched until the tree shadows gobbled him up.

Max looked at Dominic. "I guess he's gone to change his underwear," she said with a little smile.

He laughed. "I hope so."

They started strolling together across the grass promenade and from there, along the reflecting pool back toward the Washington Monument, lit up now against the night sky, the point of it seeming to shred the ghosty fabric of the clouds.

"Why didn't you tell me that guy was bugging you?" asked Dominic. "I'd have whupped his ass."

"I thought I could handle it myself," she said. "Mom always says I'm independent to a fault."

"She's right." They walked a bit longer in companionable silence, then he said, "Are you sure there's nothing else?"

Max glanced at him sharply. "What do you mean?" She tried to read his face, but in the muted lighting of the park after dark, she couldn't tell much.

"I mean, are you sure there's not something else this guy wants from you? Something you're not telling me?"

Her heart began a slow thud in her throat, and her mouth turned cottony. Maybe Dominic had heard more than she thought. Maybe she hadn't pulled off the lie as skillfully as he'd led her to believe. If Max had blown it now, this early in the game, then what would Agent Underwood do about Gaby? And would he uphold his threat to send Max back to prison?

It was hard to talk, but she did not want to betray her nervousness. "I'm not sure I understand," she managed finally.

He pursed his lips. "I just wonder if there is something else your judge ex-husband could want from you—some other reason why he would sic the feds on you now."

Max let out a long, slow breath, careful not to reveal the sigh of relief. So he didn't suspect her of spying on CovertCom. God, what a scare. She'd have to be more careful from now on. "You have to understand the mind-set of my ex-husband," she said. "He never loved Gaby. He *possessed* her. There's a difference."

He nodded. "And you stole his possession from him."

"Exactly."

"Still, this is as low as it gets, Max. I can't believe he'd let loose the dogs on you."

She sighed. "You don't know the half of it."

Dominic stopped walking and turned to her. "You're not in any danger are you? I mean, Griswold hasn't threatened you or anything?"

She gave him a sad smile. "No. I haven't seen my ex-husband since I was arrested. Believe me, putting his fed pals on me is threat enough."

They resumed walking. Dominic said, "Griswold's

rich, right? So why doesn't he hire some top gun to find your daughter?"

"Believe me, I worry about that every day. But she is very well hidden."

"Out of the country?"

She said nothing.

"Oh, forgive me," said Dominic. "I went too far; I didn't mean to pry."

"It's all right, really," she reassured him. "It's just natural curiosity. I don't mind." She hesitated. "I miss her every single day of my life."

He put an arm around her shoulders and gave her a squeeze. "You're doing the right thing, you know."

"I wonder sometimes. I had so many dreams for her . . ." Her voice broke, and she looked away, blinking, trying to get hold of her composure before she lost it completely.

He gave her a moment, and then gently said, "Why don't you go to her?"

She shook her head. "Can't risk it. Too much of a chance I'd lead Gabe or his hired guns to her. As much as I long to see her, it's just not worth the risk."

He glanced down at her. "So you have to . . . what? Wait till she's eighteen to see her?"

"Something like that."

"I'm sorry, Max." He shrugged out of his suit coat and folded it over one arm as he began rolling up the sleeves of his starched white shirt. "I just don't know what else to say."

"I know. It's okay. I learned to live with it a very long time ago. Whenever I get to feeling sorry for myself, I just imagine what it would have been like if I'd turned her over to him in the first place." She shuddered.

They had left the Washington Monument behind them, and in the distance the Capitol dome floated moonlike over the shadowy tree line. Night sounds drifted across the grass to them: nearby traffic, distant voices, a child's laughter.

The night air was heady, filed with the fragrance of fresh-cut grass and cultivated flowers, and out of the reach of park lights, the shadows sometimes sighed as lovers kissed. Dominic had loosened his tie. The jacket was slung over one shoulder, and his other arm swung at his side, where it occasionally brushed against Max.

The adrenaline that had surged through her body at the frightful situation of being caught with a fed by one of the CovertCom employees she was supposed to be spying on—and Dominic, at that—had left her skin tingling and all her senses aroused. They ambled onto the graciously landscaped park grounds leading to the Capitol. There was something reckless about walking with Dominic in the sensual summer night, her thoughts in a riot, her desire for him a sweet and terrible distraction.

"What were you doing at the Wall?" asked Dominic quietly.

She shrugged. "It'll sound silly."

"Try me."

"Well . . . it makes me feel close to Dad. He was a Vietnam vet, though he wasn't killed there. And it makes me feel closer to Brand, even though he'd served in Desert Storm and not Vietnam. I just . . . feel their presence. It's hard to explain."

He was silent for so long that she wondered if she had offended him. Suddenly, he reached for her and enfolded her in an embrace more tender than sexual. It felt like the most natural thing in the world to do, and she laid her head against his shoulder. He pressed his hand gently against the back of her head. She wondered if he could feel her heart beating, the way she could feel his.

It was so damn good to be held by a man again. She had dreamed of a moment like this with Dominic ever since he'd left her house that night, but it was a bittersweet moment and they both knew it, though for different reasons.

But even then . . . even as time held its breath . . . even as Dominic slowly released, her, but caught her hand in his as they continued walking . . . she couldn't help but wonder if Agent Underwood was out there somewhere . . . watching.

Thank God the Cold War's over, reflected Agent Jack Underwood as he edged around the perimeter of a tree trunk, keeping his body well hidden. *Now we've got all this cool spy stuff from the Russians.* Removing his glasses, he raised his NKVD "Glacier-Clear" Panther Scope to his right eye and squinted as he focused. Measuring a mere seven by three and a half inches, the scope was constructed of an ingenious configuration of prisms and lenses to provide a power of 10x, with a 96mm field of view at a thousand meters. With its big 46mm objective lens, the handy little scope had been specifically used by the Soviet Union's NKVD field operatives for spying on people, both foreign and domestic, in the dim light of dawn, dusk, or street lamps. It even boasted a carrying case that fit comfortably underneath Underwood's trench coat.

Trust the Russians for good spy stuff and great vodka.

Sheltered by the shadows of neighboring trees, easing only the side of his face and the Panther Scope around the tree, Underwood figured someone would have to have night-vision goggles and know where to look in order to see him.

It was a cinch Dominic Antonio and Rebekah Maxfield had no idea.

As he watched them walking along the reflecting pool, their heads bowed as they talked quietly, Underwood would have given anything for a parabolic microphone right now—or even better—a shotgun mike. There weren't a lot of people in the park, and with this relatively clear field of view, he could have pointed his little satellite dish or tube mike in the direction of the couple and picked up every murmur, every sigh.

Of course, he hadn't planned on this little surveillance gig, and he sure couldn't have hidden the bulky mikes and tripod stands underneath his coat.

Talk about your basic close call! Who knew Antonio would be hanging out at the Vietnam Veterans Memorial after work on a weeknight? Underwood was going to have to be more careful in the future, put more thought into arranging his meeting spots with Max. He'd about had a heart attack when Antonio showed up.

Still, he had to give the girl credit; she'd handled the situation like a real pro. He knew more than a few federal agents who weren't as sharp as she was.

The couple had walked the length of the reflecting

pool and the area of the park known as Constitution
Gardens and were heading in the direction of the Washington Monument. Underwood had to leave his tree and
leapfrog to a closer tree. Their image was getting blurry,
and he knew he would have to risk moving into open
territory for a while in order to keep them in view, but
their manner was completely relaxed and he noticed no
nervous glancing around for signs of a tail.

In fact, the more Underwood thought about it, as he
eased into the open and walked as casually as possible
thirty yards or so behind the couple, trusting in the darkness and in their own heedless lack of concern to cover
him, the more he realized that there was more here than
met the eye.

As the couple strolled between the Museum of Natural History and the Smithsonian Castle, Underwood
ducked behind a park police vehicle that was parked on
Madison Drive and lifted the Panther Scope to his right
eye, closing his left and focusing slightly.

Max and Antonio leapt into view—not exactly glacier-
clear at this time of night, but clear enough—and Underwood watched as Antonio took Max into his arms.
The scope dipped slightly as Underwood's jaw dropped.
She went willingly, and the embrace was long and
tender.

"Well, I'll be damned," whispered Underwood.

At that moment everything fell into place: the unconscious habit Max had of blushing and stammering whenever they discussed Antonio, her seeming reluctance to
turn over any information that could implicate him, the
eye-fucking, get-off-my-turf attitude Antonio had taken
with him . . . Of course, it all made sense now. They
were shacking up.

Shit, he thought. *This could blow the whole deal.*

He should have known this kind of thing could happen
when he used an informant instead of an undercover
agent. But what else could he do? He'd had no choice.

Underwood turned around, put his glasses back on,
and slumped against the bumper of the park police unit.
He had a blinding headache and was tired of playing
spy. He was tired, period. His supervisor was on his ass
about the man hours and expenses of the case, which

had, so far, produced nothing much but a pile of thin file folders that Underwood had tried with subtle language to make seem as if more was happening than it was. So far the transparent ploy wasn't working.

His wife, Abby, was harping day and night about how he was never home, never around their three little girls—even though when they got married, he'd thought she knew full well what she was getting into by marrying an FBI agent.

In eleven years of marriage, they'd moved four times, though it hardly mattered where they lived because he was on the road so much. He'd missed Bethany's birth altogether—Abby's sister had acted as labor coach, something Abby made sure he never forgot. When he was home, he was often buried in work, and when he wasn't, he was thinking about it. Lately, her complaints had grown increasingly bitter; nothing he ever did, it seemed, was right. She'd cut her hair as short as a man's and never even tried to look sexy for him anymore. Underwood was willing to concede that the strain of raising three children all born within the first six years of their marriage, with no more help than she got from him, was beginning to take its toll on Abby. His wife had also given up a successful career as a magazine editor in order to stay home with the girls, but that was her choice, wasn't it? It wasn't as if Underwood was forcing her to be chained to the playroom door.

With glum efficiency Underwood encased the Panther Scope inside his trench coat and started the long trek back to his car. It was getting very late. Abby would be pissed again.

And Max was shacking up with her boss.

Just perfect, he thought.

Chapter Seven

Liv loved their new life in Washington, D.C. Their spacious apartment in the Foggy Bottom neighborhood, near the George Washington University campus, was so much nicer than the Austin duplex. Rebekah could take the Metro into work every day, which meant that they needed only one car, and Liv used it to explore the city she had first discovered with her handsome young husband so many years ago.

Every now and then, when she was especially worried about Rebekah, she'd pay a visit to Arlington National Cemetery and have a talk with Richard about it. She tried to interest her daughter in a visit to her father's grave, but she declined. "It's too overwhelming," she'd said kindly. "I have my own places where I can find Dad." Liv had decided not to push the issue, because Rebekah seemed so troubled, so distracted all the time, but she refused to speak about whatever was bothering her, which worried Liv. She and Rebekah had always been so close, and now she felt shut out of her daughter's life just when they should be feeling excited about life again, after so many sad years. The best Liv could do was hover around in the background, keep an eye on Rebekah, and try to do what she thought Richard would want her to do.

On this soft June evening, as the dying sun gave a final fiery blast of crimson to the underside of the clouds and sank to its rest, streetlamps blinked on, casting a gentle glow on the animated faces of students set free for the day, tired professors shuffling home with worn bulky briefcases, and anonymous government workers, hurrying to pick up kids from day care or shop for supper groceries. Liv relaxed with a glass of wine on their small terrace, people-watching with Sarge until the mosquitoes drove them inside.

Her daughter, it seemed, had mysterious errands to attend to from time to time, and discouraged any questions in reference to them. Liv did not know a great deal about the nature of CovertCom's business, but by its very name, she guessed that at least some of it was clandestine. She knew better than to pry. After all, she'd once been married to a Green Beret.

Still, when several hours passed with no word from Rebekah, Liv began to fret. Every so often she paced to one window or another, as if it would hasten her daughter's return, but even though the street was well lit, there was no sign of Rebekah.

She's a big girl, Liv told herself. *She can take care of herself.*

Around ten p.m., Liv propped herself up in bed with a book, but by then, she was having to read each paragraph three or four times. She picked up the remote control and flicked on the TV in her bedroom and turned down the sound, allowing its background jabberwocky to soothe her. At ten-thirty, Liv caught the sound of a key in the front door lock, and every muscle in her body slumped with relief. *Thank you, Lord,* she whispered, though she wasn't sure why.

Rebekah appeared in Liv's bedroom doorway, and she smiled at her daughter. Rebekah's cheeks were pinkened with a high flush, and her eyes sparkled. She dazzled her mother with a smile. "Hi, Mom!"

Liv patted the bed beside her. "Come and tell me where you've been, you naughty girl. You had your old mom worried."

"Just walking," said Rebekah coyly, perching on the edge of the bed by her mom.

"Alone?" Liv studied her daughter's glowing face.

"Well, no, not exactly . . ." She glanced away.

Liv grinned. "You've been with Dominic!" She clapped her hands.

"Oh, Mom. It was just a walk, that's all." Rebekah bounced off the bed and headed for the door.

"Uh-huh."

"Dominic would like for you to come to lunch with us day after tomorrow."

"Me?" Liv's voice squeaked in surprise.

"Yeah. He'd like to see you again. He thinks you're cool. Go figure." She rolled her eyes.

"Well, I wouldn't want to intrude . . ."

Rebekah threw back her head and guffawed, her laughter provoking Liv's own laugh. "What?" Liv demanded.

Rebekah, still chuckling as she walked down the hall toward her room, called over her shoulder, "As if that's ever stopped you before, Mom."

"Wait!" Liv called. "Come back. I have something for you." She pulled open the drawer of the bedside table.

Rebekah appeared in the doorway.

Liv held out her gift.

Rebekah sat on the edge of the bed. "Silly thing. Buying me presents." She smiled at Liv as she tore off the gift wrap.

It was the computer printout photograph of Gaby, now handsomely framed.

"Oh, Mom!" cried Rebekah, tears welling in her eyes. "This is so beautiful! But do you think it's wise? If some-one sees it . . ."

Liv patted her daughter's arm. "It will be all right," she said. "You can't tell a thing about where she is. If it really worries you, keep it out of sight in a drawer or something."

"No." She shook her head. "I'll put it beside my bed."

"We have so few pictures of her," said Liv. "Certainly none past the age of three."

"Do you think she's happy?" asked Rebekah wistfully.

"She looks very relaxed, I think, very much at peace with herself. There is a twinkle in her eye that is genuine."

"Yes."

"She looks exactly like you did at that age. Just the spitting image."

"Do you think so?"

"Absolutely." Liv wanted to add, *There's not a hint of her father in her,* but didn't.

Rebekah sighed. "I have these . . . snapshots . . . in

my head. When I was in prison, I would take them out when I was alone or in bed, and look at them."

"I know what you mean," said Liv. "I do the same thing with you kids. Sometimes I miss you when you were little and your daddy was alive. The house was so boisterous then, so full of energy and life."

"It was fun," said Rebekah. "We didn't always have time to make good friends where Dad was posted, but we always had each other."

"You and Brett and Brand, the three musketeers. Always ganging up on poor little Zane."

"Well, poor little Zane had his ways of getting back, Mom, don't you worry." She grinned.

"And Clark . . ." Liv chuckled.

"Ordering us all around like a drill sergeant."

"Shoot, there had to be somebody around to help me keep you guys out of trouble."

Rebekah reached over and took her mother's hand. "It was a good life, Mom," she said quietly.

Liv nodded. "Yes," she said. "It was." *And sometimes,* she thought, *that's all I have to cling to, when the sadness gets almost too great to bear.*

The morning after Dominic had walked through the Mall hand-in-hand with Rebekah, he caught the shuttle flight to New York and joined Hakeem on a quick preliminary pre-sweep visit to Imagitoys, Inc.

They explained to Jason Crandall and Osamu Smith that Hakeem was going to plant countersurveillance, or antibugging devices into the telephone wall receptacles, and instructed Crandall and Smith to inform the rest of the people who worked at Imagitoys that they were NYNEX employees and they were there to update the phone system.

Such a ploy might not have worked for Opco, which, as a fiber-optics company, was top-heavy with engineers, computer nerds, and other technical experts who would have been suspicious and demanded further explanations. It seemed to Dominic that a toy company had a much more relaxed atmosphere, more a sense of fun. These people were expected to come up with products that would entertain children. If the phone company wanted to come and jack around with the phones, who were they to argue?

He and Hakeem arrived at Imagitoys dressed in legitimate NYNEX telephone repair coveralls and tool belts. Nobody paid any attention to them as they went about their business. Hakeem would remove each of the standard telephone wall receptacles, and Dominic would hand him what looked like an identical unit.

However, the new receptacle that Hakeem patiently screwed into place on the wall behind each telephone was actually a combination room and telephone transmitter. It received its power directly from the phone line, and therefore had unlimited operating time. A special control worked to suppress room audio during telephone conversations, which allowed both sides of the conversation to be transmitted clearly and distinctly.

Even better, when the phone was on-hook, a sensor recognized the change in line voltage, and immediately switched to transmitting room conversations.

In other words, not only could CovertCom monitor both sides of all telephone conversations going into and out of Imagitoys, but it could also clearly eavesdrop on conversations going on in the room even when nobody was on the phone.

On their way out, they planned to drop a bug into a flower vase that they could "find" during their Spy Squad sweep later on in the week.

At one point in their work, Jason Crandall walked by. He couldn't resist speaking to them. "How's it going?" he asked.

Hakeem scowled.

"Fine," said Dominic. "We'll be out of your way in a few minutes."

"No problem," said Crandall pleasantly. "Take all the time you need." He walked away whistling.

Like a lamb to the slaughter, thought Dominic. He rolled his head around on his neck, which was stiffening up in the cramped quarters behind people's desks. With these devices, CovertCom would probably have most of the specs for the top secret new toy within a month. What it did with those specs was Garrett Sharp's business.

And Garrett Sharp's business paid its employees very, very well.

"We're done," grunted Hakeem. They gathered the few tools that had been necessary for the job and left without speaking to anyone else in the building. As they were silently dumping their tool belts into the back of the van, a man approached them. He seemed clean-cut enough, if somewhat threadbare.

"Excuse me," he said. "Could you spare a quarter? My wallet was stolen, and I don't even have change to call my wife."

"Fuck off." Hakeem slammed the van door and turned away.

"I'm not a panhandler," said the man, clearly distressed. "I swear to God, all I want is a quarter to call my wife."

Dominic's pocket change was in his pants pocket, underneath the coveralls. The man seemed reasonable enough; he didn't look crazy or violent, and his demeanor was nonthreatening. Dominic didn't mind giving him a quarter. He started to unzip the coveralls.

The man touched Hakeem's elbow. "I know how this must look—"

With the sudden ferocity of a striking snake, Hakeem whipped around, his arm raised, and struck the man across the throat, sending him stumbling backward until he lost his balance completely and fell onto the street, clutching his throat and gagging.

"I said, fuck off," he snarled.

Before Dominic could say anything, the man sprang to his feet and took off running.

Hakeem laughed. "Let's go," he said.

Dominic still stood behind the van, his hand on the zipper of his coveralls.

"You coming?" Hakeem walked around to the driver's side of the van and got in.

Dominic watched as the man continued running to the end of the block and around the corner of the building. There wasn't anything to do then, but follow Hakeem.

Max was humming to herself, finishing up some paperwork at her desk just before her mother was due to arrive for lunch, when she heard a tap at her open door and glanced up to see Garrett Sharp standing there with Dominic. She jumped to her feet, upsetting an empty Coke can and fumbling to catch it before it could spill its last few drops.

Sharp smiled, showing all his teeth, and said, "It's good to see you again, Max. I thought I'd drop down from New York and see how you guys are doing. Dominic was telling me you're just about to leave for lunch. I hope you don't mind if I tag along. My treat."

"Uh, of course not, Mr. Sharp. Uh, but we may not be able to discuss business, though. My mother will be accompanying us."

"That won't be a problem at all. I'd love to meet your mother."

As if on cue, the receptionist buzzed Max's office to say that her mother was here. "Tell her we'll be right out," said Max with an awkward glance at the men.

She did not want to take her mother to lunch with Garrett Sharp. She did not want her mother anywhere near Garrett Sharp. But there was no prolonging the inevitable. She gathered up her shoulder bag, flashed a distracted smile to the two men, and preceded them into the reception area of the CovertCom office.

Max's mom was looking unusually attractive today. She had always been more youthful in her appearance than a lot of mothers of Max's friends: trim, perky, petite, with soft fluffy blond hair that framed her face, a flawless complexion, even white teeth, and intelligent blue eyes. In her day, she'd been a prom queen. When Max was a little girl, she'd loved to watch her mother and father dress up for the annual base military ball. Her dad would be resplendent in his full-dress whites, and her mother, who preferred chiffon gowns in frothy pastels, would look like an angel. They would pose together for a snapshot, taken by Max with her little Instamatic camera, and through the viewfinder she would see her father look at her mother with a light in his eyes that he held for no other.

They'd been married twenty-five years when he flew off in a veil of secrecy in the night for the Middle East in a valiant but ill-fated attempt to rescue the Iranian hostages who were being held captive at the American Embassy in Teheran.

Now Max's mom was a woman in her sixties, but she looked ten years younger. She exercised, ate right, and saw to it that well-paid hairdressers kept her blond hair only slightly silvered. Today she was wearing a sleeveless peach linen shift that hugged her slight figure and showed off her shapely legs. She kept her makeup and jewelry to a minimum, and wore contact lenses rather than the heavy plastic-framed glasses that unnecessarily aged so many women of her generation.

"Well, there is no doubt in my mind as to who this beautiful lady is," said Garrett Sharp before Max could make the introductions. Taking her mother's hand in his, he said, "You must be Olivia Maxfield. I'm Garrett Sharp, and it is indeed a pleasure to meet you." With that, he bowed low over Liv's hand and kissed it.

Before Max's eyes, her mother was transformed into the colonel's wife. Returning Sharp's smile with a gracious one of her own, she said smoothly, "It is indeed an honor to meet you, Mr. Sharp. I owe you a debt of gratitude for giving my daughter this wonderful opportunity to work for your company." She acted as though men kissed her hand every day.

Still holding onto her hand, he said, "You owe me nothing. Max has distinguished herself on the job many times over. She is a valued employee in her own right."

They continued to smile at one another as if no one else were in the room. Max thought, *Wait a minute, here. Wait just a damn minute.*

"I've made reservations at the Willard Room," said Sharp, turning to the others. He'd released her mom's hand but had taken her elbow in escort fashion. "I hope that meets with everyone's approval."

Liv's eyes sparkled as she said, "Why, that would be perfect, Mr. Sharp."

They took Sharp's limousine the relatively short distance to the Pennsylvania Avenue restaurant. The Willard was a historic landmark hotel located just two blocks from the White House. Luxurious and elegant, it was a favorite accommodation of visiting heads of state, former U.S. presidents, and other dignitaries. The Grand

Ballroom, with its crystal chandeliers and meticulously restored Beaux Arts architecture and decor, was the site of many society galas and glittering receptions.

The Willard Room itself had the intimate yet stately ambience of a private men's club, with its muted period rugs in shades of wine, dark-paneled walls, and heavy deep ruby velvet draperies. Max spotted the speaker of the House and the Senate majority leader tucked away in a secluded corner, nursing drinks and talking with quiet intensity.

While Max's mom chatted with Sharp about the wine list, Max caught Dominic's eye. She inclined her head slightly in the direction of her mother and Sharp, as if to say, *What the hell is going on?* But he only winked at her. She frowned at him and buried her head in her menu, but the words were blurred and she'd lost her appetite.

"Have you had a chance to catch the National Symphony Orchestra at the Kennedy Center?" Sharp was asking her mom when Max tuned back in.

"No, but I would love to," said Liv.

"They're doing a pops concert next Saturday evening—a full retrospective on the big bands."

"Oh!" cried Liv. "That sounds like such fun. You know, you just can't find anybody anymore who appreciates that wonderful music. It was great to dance to in its time, and great to fall in love to." As she dropped her glance, a demure smile upon her face, Max stared at her mother, agape. *She was flirting!* She was actually flirting with Garrett Sharp! Max could not believe her eyes.

"You are absolutely right," smiled Sharp in return. "And I happen to have a couple of third-row center tickets to the concert. Would you care to accompany me?"

Max's whole body jerked, and down went her wineglass. Grand Cru Bordeaux seeped all over the creamy-white tablecloth like a spreading stain of blood.

"Shit! I mean, I'm sorry," she cried, mopping miserably at the stain with her napkin.

"Don't worry about it," said Sharp kindly, signaling to the waiter. "It happens to everyone."

"What on earth is the matter with you today, Rebekah?" asked her mother.

"Nothing. I just—nothing." The waiter bustled about efficiently, soaking up the wine with a dish towel and bringing Max a fresh glass as if he took care of such clumsy blunders every single day, which Max doubted immensely. He even set a little crystal vase of roses over the stain so that it would not be a distraction during their meal.

Max was shaking, and she clasped her cold hands together under the table.

"Remember how everybody had a favorite band?" her mom was asking Sharp. "I loved Tommy Dorsey the best."

"He was all right," agreed Sharp, "but way too sentimental for an entire evening. Glenn Miller was more to my taste."

"To dance to, yeah, but for sheer listening, you couldn't beat Duke Ellington or Count Basie."

Dominic and Max might as well not have been in the room at all. The waiter brought Max's spinich salad with grilled chicken and honey-almond dressing. Dominic tackled his filet mignon. Max picked at the food.

She couldn't help staring at the flower vase. It was a beautiful piece of Waterford crystal. Pinpoints of amber light from the small shaded lamps clustered against the paneled wall hit the cut prisms in the glass and danced off like tiny rainbows. The roses were as vermilion velveteen, opening softly like a first kiss. The whole effect was a work of art.

But it couldn't hide that bloodred stain beneath.

When Max looked at the cut-crystal vase and the fragrant rose blossoms, she could not enjoy their beauty because they were meant to conceal something ugly.

And when she looked at Garrett Sharp, she knew that his insouciant charm, easy wealth, and handsome, graceful smile served only to hide something indescribably ugly underneath.

Something her sweet little mother would probably never see . . . until it was too late.

Chapter Eight

This time he met her at the San Antonio Bar and Grill in the underground mall at Crystal City. That way she could take the Metro straight to the underground shops area and make her way to the restaurant without ever having to go above ground. The underground mall was actually a small underground city-within-a-city; containing apartments, professional offices of all kinds, shops, restaurants, fast food and deli places, and access to aboveground parking. It was a considerable distance from either her office or her home, so he doubted they would have another surprise encounter with Dominic Antonio.

Still, he was unaccountably nervous. He was going to have to put the squeeze on her, and he was not looking forward to it. But if he didn't, he could kiss this investigation—and his career—good-bye.

He spotted her almost immediately, but then, she was hard to miss. For this Saturday afternoon meeting she was wearing some kind of white tank top that came to a low V in front, a pair of tight jeans, and a matching, loose-fitting short-sleeved embroidered denim jacket. Her hair was pulled back into a loose braid draped over the front of the jacket, and long blond tendrils framed her face. When she sat down in the booth across from him, she reached up to tuck a strand of hair behind her ear, causing her jacket to slip back onto her shoulder and reveal that she was not wearing a bra. He could clearly see the taut nipple beneath the white tank top.

He caught himself staring and, flustered, awkwardly averted his eyes. If she knew how long it had been since he'd been laid, she wouldn't wear shit like that to throw off his concentration. The thought made him suddenly irritable.

"What have you got for me?" he said brusquely.

She flushed. "I've been trying to tell you, Underwood, I need more time. I'm still a trainee. They don't leave me alone much. It's going to take several months—"

He leaned forward and grasped her wrist so tightly she gasped. In a voice that shook from the effort not to shout, he said, "You don't have several months. You don't even have several weeks. You'd better start using that pretty little head of yours for something other than flirting, or your daughter's cozy little hideout is *history*. Do I make myself clear?"

Her face had gone beet-red. "What the hell are you talking about?"

"Oh, don't take that sanctimonious tone with me. I know—" The waiter appeared with menus. Underwood jerked them out of the man's hand and gestured for him to leave.

"Wait!" cried Max. "I'd like a glass of ice water." Staring at Underwood, she added, *"If you don't mind."*

The waiter hurried away. After a moment Underwood said, "I know about your little fling with Antonio."

"What?" The waiter appeared with the ice water, then ducked away. "I'm not having a little fling with anybody," she said.

"Bullshit. I saw you with him."

"You saw . . . When? Wait a minute. You were *syping* on us, you little son of a bitch!"

He sat back and regarded her with a snotty little smile. "It's my job."

She was panting as if she'd been running a great distance, and her breasts were moving up and down, stretching the thin tank top with each breath. Underwood struggled not to stare.

"I'm not sleeping with him, Underwood. But then, I guess you already know that. You've probably got my bedroom bugged."

"Well, you would know if I did, wouldn't you?"

"I hate you."

He shrugged. The waiter timidly approached the table. "Would you care to place an order?"

She shook her head. Underwood said, "Yeah. Bring me the biggest burger you got, with onion rings and a beer." After the waiter had left, he said, "You know, I've been thinking about it. If you shacked up with Antonio, that might be just the break we've been needing. Who knows what you could find out with a little post-coital pillow talk?"

Her face paled. Between clenched teeth, she said, "I will not whore for you, you bastard."

"Oh, I expect you will," he said. "I expect you will do most anything to keep your little girl safe."

She stared at him, her eyes hard with loathing. Then she picked up her water glass and flung the entire contents into his face. While he was still sputtering, she leapt to her feet and ran from the restaurant.

Calmly, Underwood mopped at his face and shirt with his napkin. The whole encounter had left him shaken. Maybe he'd pushed her too far this time. Maybe he'd been thinking with his dick.

Careless. He would have to be more careful when dealing with her. She was volatile and unpredictable. If he pushed her too hard too fast, she might disappear on him, and if that happened, he didn't think FBI HQ would be impressed with any explanation he could come up with.

Max was so upset by the encounter with Underwood, she forgot that the Metro stop was located one level down and that she was supposed to take an escalator to get to it. Instead she got lost in the labyrinth of underground corridors, which seemed to have no beginning and no end. Some of the corridors were lined with shops and fast-food restaurants. Others contained only glassed-in advertising posters lining the long walls, but there were no shops or doors. For some reason Max grew spooked in one such corridor, nervous whenever a group of teens or a man approached or passed her, paranoid that she was being watched, hearing footsteps behind her when there was nobody there.

She entered another area of shops that included a Safeway grocery, a Roy Rogers restaurant, and offices. She was growing tired and flustered and near tears. Was her entire life to be a maze of invisible choices, dead ends, and blind alleys? Was she never to be free to choose her own path?

She headed back the way she had come, trudging wearily now, but when she found herself almost back at the San Antonio Bar and Grill, she frantically flagged down a security guard who took pity on her and walked her to the Metro stop.

The ride back to Foggy Bottom was long. Max leaned her head against the window, staring through her own sad, pale reflection to the tracks and tunnels hypnotically whizzing past. Here she was, in the nation's capital, taking the Metro back to her apartment . . . and she might as well be back in prison. Here, as in prison, there was nothing sacred or private about her life, nothing over which she had any control.

She raged inside at the injustice of it all, but what could she do? She could run, maybe. Disappear. But what would happen to Gaby then?

Gaby. That child was the one pure, uncorrupted thing in her life right now; the one overriding purpose for her existence. Her reason for living, for sacrificing, for doing anything. Gaby was happy and safe right now, and she was counting on her mother to keep her that way.

So that was it, then. She simply had no choice.

Dominic Antonio was watching Sebastian Taylor operate. Taylor, the Spy Squad specialist in radio frequency devices, had been dispatched from the New York office to D.C. by the Boss to contribute his expertise to Max's training. However, the buffed-blond surfer boy was contributing more than RF acumen at the moment, an observation that bugged the hell out of Dominic.

Taylor was working the VL5000P, which was a miniaturized version of the state-of-the-art VL5000 portable countersurveillance receiver, or proximity detector; what the guys in the Spy Squad called a "bugcatcher." Technically, he was doing a silent sweep of the boardroom of Opco, the fiber-optics business owned by Paul Zwibeck, whom Dominic preferred to call "Mr. Metalmouth Techno-Geek." They were the only people in the boardroom, and Taylor was sweeping the walls, doors, windows, floors, ceilings, furniture, phones, and office accessories with the small handheld radio frequency detector.

But mainly, he was showing off for Max.

They were doing this silent RF sweep during business hours. This was not Dominic's idea. He greatly preferred to work all night doing a sweep, and then set up a listening post with a monitoring spectrum analyzer in a room adjacent to the boardroom. This way they could check for any bugs that may have been planted on someone attending the board meeting. But, hey, Dominic wasn't the Boss, was he?

Consequently, since they were working during the day, they couldn't use the larger equipment, which often required more power than a battery could provide and would be difficult to smuggle in past curious employees. The VL5000P resembled a small transistor radio and fit easily in a suit coat pocket. Taylor wore headphones to prevent audible signals from revealing the search to any potential eavesdropper, and as Max looked on, he clowned for her, jauntily sticking a pen in the corner of his mouth like Groucho Marx's cigar, lifting his eyebrows comically, and otherwise making her laugh, which was a permissible noise for them to make while working.

Dominic ripped off a small Post-It note, angrily scribbled, "Let Max operate the bugcatcher. We need to rearrange the furniture," and smacked it to Taylor's forehead with more force than he intended.

Taylor mimed tying a noose around his neck and being hanged, which made Max laugh so hard she had to cover her mouth. Then he gently placed the earphones over her head and passed over the bugcatcher. Removing his coat and dropping it over the back of a chair, Taylor then proceeded to roll up his sleeves, revealing veined forearms and massive biceps. It was all Dominic could do not to roll his eyes. Together, he and Taylor lifted the heavy boardroom table and moved it a few feet over to the side. Then, with as little noise as possible, they pulled the sideboard away from the table and removed all the pictures from the walls, while Max checked every area that had been under, behind, beneath something, or otherwise hidden.

Moving the furniture had only buffed the guy's muscles more. Irritably, Dominic grabbed one end of the boardroom table by himself and hefted it. A sharp burn shot across his back, and he grunted before he could stop himself. Shit. Now he'd gone and fucked up one of his back muscles, no doubt. Grinning at him like a high school kid gunning the engine of his hot rod, Taylor lifted his end easily and put it back in place. While Dominic was arching his back, trying to stretch out the injured muscle, Taylor added insult to injury by moving back his end, too.

Little prick.

This part of the sweep was finished. A more detailed RF check would have to be made after-hours, along with checks of the phone lines, electric lines, the other offices, and so on. While Max rehung the pictures, Taylor rolled down the sleeves of his shirt and put on his jacket.

Back in the car, as they made their way back to the Eleventh Avenue offices, Dominic, trying to ignore his aching back, spoke very little as he maneuvered through D.C. summertime tourist traffic, while Max and Taylor traded repartee like a couple of stand-up comics.

"I mean, what's the point of Batman, anyway?" queried Taylor with a flash of his blue-blue eyes.

"Oh, you know," said Max, "to save Gotham City from the bad guys like the Riddler and the Joker."

"That's the part I don't get. Have you *seen* Gotham City? Could there *be* a more depressing place? I mean, geez, if you're gonna save a place from the bad guys, hell, make it Miami."

"Why Miami? Why not, oh, I don't know . . . Las Vegas?"

"Vegas? You kidding? Vegas is *way* too tacky. That place deserves the Riddler."

She laughed. "You have a point, there."

Dominic was getting pissed. Max had been in a bad mood for more than a week, for reasons that was a mystery to him, and now this little dickhead shows up and she's all smiles. He was surprised at her. He'd never have guessed her for the type to fall for such a shallow piece of work as Sebastian Taylor. A traffic light up ahead turned yellow, and Dominic gunned it. Nearly causing an accident, he barely made it through as it turned red.

"Dominic!" she cried. "Slow down."

He accelerated.

Taylor said, "He's probably trying to get to the emergency room to have his back treated."

Dominic whipped the wheel to the left, and they swept into the underground parking garage beneath their office building, making his way rapidly to the spaces reserved for CovertCom employees and snapping loose from his seat belt before the car even came to a halt. Taylor got out of the car and opened Max's door.

Dominic rode up in a later elevator. It took a while for the elevator to make its ponderous trip to the CovertCom floor and back down again, pick up Dominic and another man, and deliver them to their respective floors. By the time Dominic made it to his office door, Taylor was walking down the hall toward him. With a wicked grin he called over his shoulder, "That's great, Max. I'll pick you up at eight." Then he nodded at Dominic as he passed and headed for the reception area and out the door.

Dominic turned on his heel, stalked into his office, and shut the door. Then he sat down at his desk, picked up a heavy paperweight, and threw it so hard across the room that it left a dent in the wall paneling.

Chapter Nine

The Capitol building was far bigger, statelier, and more awe-inspiring than Max had ever imagined from seeing it on television or in photographs. On this Fourth of July holiday, it was closed to tourists, and their escort took them through an unassuming rear entrance, where a security guard nonetheless X-rayed Max's and her mother's handbags and passed a metal detector over the bodies of everyone in their party.

"Have you ever been in the Capitol before?" asked their escort, an attractive dark-haired young lady named Kathleen Anderson, who, in spite of the holiday, was dressed in a business suit.

"I have," spoke up Max's mom, "but my daughter never has."

"Oh, then we must take you to see the Rotunda," she said pleasantly. "I would take you to the floor of the House, as well, but Senator Kane is most anxious to meet you."

"He once met Richard during a training exercise at Fort Benning," said Garrett Sharp, "while his team was preparing for the Iranian hostage rescue."

Yeah, you told us that already, thought Max, irritated that Sharp would call her dad by his given name, as if they were old buddies. She trailed along at the rear of the gathering, following Ms. Anderson and the others through an incomprehensible labyrinth of small passageways, twisting and turning corridors, and up steep staircases, until they emerged at last into the vast, hushed Capitol Rotunda. Instinctively, Max craned her neck to see into its spectacular depths, and grew dizzy with the effort. Massive paintings in gilded frames which depicted pivotal moments in the country's history circled the floor

level of the Rotunda, interspersed with imposing statues
of notable historic individuals posed atop marble pedes-
tals. An unexpected spasm of sentimental patriotism,
perhaps brought on by thoughts of her father, gripped
Max's throat, and she swallowed hard.

"We'll have to come back and take a tour," whispered
Liv, as if speaking aloud would be an affront to the
statues. Max nodded, feeling an instant pang of guilt for
the inevitable tug-of-war she always experienced between the demands of her job and her mother's need
for her companionship.

Not that she lacks for company these days, she thought
resentfully, watching from behind as Sharp placed his
hand on the small of her mother's back in a way that
was both protective and intimate.

Kathleen Anderson, while genial enough, was no tour
guide and gently hurried the group through the Rotunda,
down another couple of corridors, and into an elevator
that whooshed them with brisk efficiency up a few short
floors to the old Senate offices. Most of the senators
preferred the ultramodern, if crowded, "new" offices,
housed across the street on Constitution Avenue. Senator Kane had earned his berth through the ancient practice of seniority; he was just finishing out his fifth term,
his second as Senate majority leader. In deference to
his contributions to that august body, he had even been
granted an exceedingly rare privilege—his own balcony.
It was to this balcony that Garrett Sharp had arranged
an invitation for Max and her mother, that they might
watch the evening's magnificent fireworks display in the
company of one of the most powerful men in the country, from the best seat in the house.

Who could *not* be impressed? wondered Max as they
exited the elevator and followed their escort along quiet
rugs, worn thin with use, and richly paneled walls that
seemed to stand mute guard over two centuries of secrets. Their entourage was led into an office overstuffed
with modern accoutrements of power never imagined
when the building was constructed: computers and print-
ers and copy machines and fax machines and telephones
tucked willy-nilly. Papers and books of every kind covered every nook and cranny, and extension cords and

wires ran amok along every floorboard. Max found the mess oddly comforting: It seemed the senator, who hailed from her home state of Texas, was obviously a worker and not a figurehead.

In one crowded corner the senator's Beaver 100 silver felt Stetson, with the ever popular cattleman's crease, hung from an ornate old hat rack. On another peg hung a stiff straw cowboy hat, preferred by most working cowboys in summer because it was cooler. The senator owned a sprawling ranch that took up much of the western half of the state. It was said that he got his first big break in politics when he bulldogged a full-grown steer to the ground once at one of President Lyndon Johnson's famous hill country barbecues.

The senator's drawling voice boomed from an adjoining room, "You can tell that sleazy little dickhead he can kiss my ass. I'm through fucking around with him. He can come around on this vote—what? I don't give a shit if we're in recess! It'll come up first thing in the fall. Hell, yes, I'm running for reelection. Where the fuck you live, a fucking cave? He votes against this candy-assed gun control shit, or I'll show him what a double aught buck is capable of. Whatd'ya mean, is that a threat? Tell him I said it, and you let the little weasel decide for himself!"

Max ducked her head and stifled a grin. She liked the senator already.

Kathleen Anderson fairly flew into the next room, and there was a muffled exchange, then she stepped into the doorway and said calmly, "The Senator will be with you in just a moment."

"Make yourselves at home, folks," yelled the senator from the other office. "Kathy, show 'em where the booze is at."

"Kathy" obeyed, scurrying across the room to a polished cherry wood armoire that must have stood seven feet tall, because even Garrett Sharp was dwarfed by it. The bottom cabinet hid a small ice-making machine, and the top doors, when unlocked and opened, revealed just about every type and brand of liquor Max could call to mind—and some she'd never heard of.

Alcohol, the oil that kept the machinery of government smoothly running.

Senator Truman Kane strode into the room with the crackling energy of a man half his age, his trademark snowy mane swept back from a leonine face. Thunderous ivory brows ruled his facial expressions and gunmetal-gray eyes that missed nothing, while a crisp white dress western shirt with pearl snap buttons accentuated powerful shoulders and wide leathered hands. As he crushed Max's hand in his grip, she noted to herself that he did not sport a bolo or string tie, another Hollywood touch which would have been a disappointment on a man she found she already liked in spite of his vocation as a politician. She did note that he was enough of a dandy that his dark blue Levi's were pressed and probably starched, and his cowboy boots had heels high enough to make him tower over most of his colleagues.

Though he let go of her hand, he took her elbow with his left hand as he took her mother's hand is his right. "It is a real honor to meet you, Mrs. Maxfield, and your lovely daughter, and especially on this day in which we celebrate our nation's freedom, which your great husband and your fine son died to preserve."

There were tears in his eyes as he said these things, and Max didn't know whether the whole thing was an act for the benefit of a couple of constituents in an election year or whether, like so many politicians, he was a veteran himself who idolized soldiers and hero-worshiped the war dead he himself may have sent into combat.

"Thank you, Senator Kane," said Max's mother with her typical aplomb. "I remember Richard phoning to tell me the day the contingent from Congress accompanied the president and came to give their blessing to the mission. You'll never know how much that vote of confidence meant to those men."

The senator had not let go of Liv's hand, and he was still touching Max's elbow. He shook his head. "Hindsight being what it is, Mrs. Maxfield . . . if we had it to do all over again . . ." He gave a helpless little shrug.

"I know," she said. "But those men believed in what they were doing. They believed in it with all their hearts, and I can tell you that they would have rather died doing what they could in service of their country than stand idly by and do nothing."

Max ducked her head and stared at her feet. She was feeling dangerously sentimental again and wished they would change the subject before she started to cry.

"Well, it's easy to see how those men can be all they can be, when they've got brave ladies like yourself cheering them on from the sidelines while the rest of us stand around with our thumbs up our butts."

Max laughed aloud. She couldn't help herself.

"Let's take a look at this view, whatd'ya say?" Kane asked jovially, letting go of Max. "Kathy, fix me a drink, will you?"

Without having to be told twice, the long-suffering assistant reached into the armoire, took down a bottle of Jack Daniel's bourbon, and poured a double shot straight into a glass. She handed it to the senator just as he was herding the group (which contained more people whom Max did not know) onto a portico overlooking the multitiered expanses of steps leading down to the Mall. Shaggy trees bordered the Mall area which lay outstretched behind the pool. In the hazy distance, the gray monolith of the Washington Monument spiked a sky now turned incandescent pearl in the muggy late afternoon sun. Thousands of people clustered throughout the park, having waited hours for the fireworks display.

Leaning against the balustrade, Max felt like royalty surveying her domain. It was almost incomprehensible to her that only one year before, she had gone to bed in her prison cell, with no fireworks. Her mother, sensing her thoughts, came up and put her arm around Max's waist. "My heart is so full it could burst," she whispered, giving her daughter a squeeze. "I wish your dad could be here."

Max shot a surprised glance in her mother's direction, but Liv had moved on and joined Sharp and Senator Kane farther down the balcony. Max stared at the senator thoughtfully. In some ways he reminded her of the old-style Texan politicians who had once ruled Congress with fists of iron: the LBJs and the Sam Rayburns and the Lloyd Bensons. Self-made men who might, say, speak in language peppered with racial epithets but who in the meantime rammed through civil rights legislation in a relentless juggernaut that had changed the complexion of the country forever.

But that kind of heavy-handed politicking was becoming a thing of the past, impaled on the cross of political correctness. Senator Kane was an anachronism, a favorite of satirists, late-night comedians, and political cartoonists. For the first time in his career, he was facing some serious challenges in the upcoming reelection campaign from young turks who were far too savvy to be caught saying anything that could be construed as controversial. Consequently, they were driven, not by strong ideals and powerful beliefs, but by raw ambition.

It took a moment for Max to recall that, due to her conviction for a federal crime, she would actually never be allowed to cast a vote again. The thought left her feeling hollow and sad.

Still uncomfortable in social gatherings of people she did not know, Max roamed restlessly around the senator's offices, suffering through small talk whenever she was trapped into it, avoiding it whenever possible, and impatiently awaiting the dark, when everyone would then turn their attention to the night sky and she would be left alone with her thoughts. Independence Day was a strictly American holiday, so her precious Gaby would not be enjoying fireworks tonight, and the thought made her indescribably sad.

Most all holidays were drudgeries for Max. Any day without Gaby was incomplete.

Finally, chairs were arranged in no particular order on the balcony, and Max took a seat near the rear. In the background, sounds from the symphony orchestra, ensconced on the pavilion of the Lincoln Memorial, drifted to the party in their privileged position above all the restless hubbub of the crowds. The liquor flowed freely, and the mood on the balcony was one of gaiety and anticipation.

It had been many years since Max had viewed a fireworks display. With the first starburst of dazzling silver and gold against the velvet backdrop of the night, Max cried, "Oh!" and sucked in her breath like a little kid on a carnival ride. The orchestra's bass drum pounded with each iridescent polychromatic explosion, which sizzled through the night and sparked the spear of the Washington Monument. The uplifted faces of the people watched a fire glow of phosphorescent crimson, amber, electric blue, and stardust silver.

The fireworks followed swiftly on the comet tails of one another with growing urgency, mounting in such an orgasm of blazing stellar competition that Max might have missed altogether the fact that Garrett Sharp had slipped from the knot of people congregated on the Capitol balcony and crept into the darkened offices behind. Something about his movements were too stealthy, too creepy to be those of a man finding his way to the bathroom, and Max decided to investigate.

While the sky erupted into a phantasmagoria of exploding color, and the crowd below shouted and cheered, Max slid down to the floor and crawled on her knees into the shadowy depths behind, holding her breath, though the noise without was enough to cover any noise within. It took a few moments for her dazzled eyes to grow acclimated to the black-on-black hulking shadows that became the armoire, the flags, the desks, and Garrett Sharp, huddled behind the copy machine.

Max moved around the perimeters of the room, which was not dark now at all, but illumined bloodred from a sudden burst of scarlet fireworks outside. Heart pounding, throat throbbing, Max dared to crane her neck for a closer look.

He was fiddling with electrical cords behind the copy machine. In the dim fluorescent glow of shadow and stained-glass light, it was impossible to tell what he was doing. Suddenly, he got to his feet, and Max shrank back against the wall, flattening herself behind a desk. He walked in front of the desk, not three feet away, stopped, turned his head, and looked right at her.

At least she *thought* he did—she could have sworn he did—but he did not acknowledge seeing her and continued on to the balcony to rejoin her mother and the others.

Letting out her breath in a relieved *whoosh*, Max

waited a moment. All hell was breaking loose outside in a cacophony of power and glory, shouts and cheers and cymbal crashes—this was the finale, and if Max did not hurry, she would be caught in the glare of the lights when everybody returned to the inner offices. In her hurry to see what Sharp had been doing, she stumped her toe so hard against a chair leg that it brought tears to her eyes. Hobbling, cursing beneath her breath, she dodged behind the copy machine and fumbled with the plugs.

Glittering gold exploded in rat-a-tat bursts of gunfire—or what sounded like gunfire—as the crowd roared like Romans watching the gladiators. There wasn't much time. She needed a flashlight, something, anything that would help her see what the hell she was doing. Bending down level to the electrical wall outlet, Max caught the sudden whiff of fresh plastic, like that of a brand-new toy released from its bubble pack.

Her mouth went dust-dry, because Max knew now what Garrett Sharp had been doing. He'd been substituting the regular adapter plug, which housed various plugs from the copy machine, lamps, and other electrical appliances, with a mains plug adapter transmitter.

In appearance, the transmitter looked and behaved exactly like a normal socket extension adapter. It was fully operational, and the copy machine and lamps and things would run just as they always had.

But in the meantime the transmitter would be relaying every word anybody said anywhere near it.

In other words, Garrett Sharp was now spying on Senator Truman Kane, and would soon be selling whatever juicy tidbits he consequently happened to learn to the highest bidder.

Chapter Ten

Olivia Maxfield was jubilant on the way home from the fireworks display. Arms clasped around the big basket of Texas wildflowers from Senator Kane, she snuggled a wee bit closer to Garrett and said, "Thank you so much for a lovely evening."

Garrett, too, was in a good mood. It was one of the things that made his company so enjoyable. "You're quite welcome," he said. "I enjoyed it, too. Didn't you, Max?"

Rebekah was sitting in the limo seat that faced Garrett and Liv. She'd been silent during the drive from the Capitol building, which took an inordinately long time due to the traffic. In fact, she was staring out the window when Garrett spoke to her, and seemed not to have heard him.

Liv almost squirmed in embarrassment. Rebekah could be so obstinate at times. "Rebekah!" she said, more sharply than she had intended.

Her daughter jumped and said, "Huh?"

"Didn't you enjoy the fireworks?"

"Oh, yes. They were wonderful," she said woodenly, turning her face once again to stare out of the window.

Liv decided not to let Rebekah's bad mood spoil her evening. Maybe she just missed little Gaby. To Garrett, she said, "I just adore Senator Kane. You know I've voted for him every time, I mean, if I was living in Texas. Even when Richard was alive and we were in the service and living on military bases all over the country, we always maintained Texas as our permanent residence." Liv stopped talking. She didn't mean to be prattling on like some women her age she knew, who insisted on including every single little boring detail in their stories, and never seemed to know when to shut up.

"He's a good man," agreed Sharp. "A doer. Knows how to get things done. A rare quality in a politician."

Liv nodded with no small amount of pride. Unlike some *men* her age she knew, Garrett really listened to her, as if her opinion mattered, and spoke to her as if she were intelligent. He never patronized her.

Glancing nervously at her mute daughter, she said, "Rebekah, didn't you like Senator Kane?"

"What? Oh, yeah. I liked him very much." Rebekah's answer, again, sounded as if her mind were a million miles away.

"He seemed quite smitten with you," persisted Liv. "I saw him talking to you."

"I'm not at all surprised that Senator Kane was so taken with Max," Garrett said. "She has this amazing . . . I don't know . . . ability or facility or what-have-you to draw the admiration of anybody who meets her."

"What a nice thing to say! Rebekah—wasn't that a nice thing to say?" she prompted.

"Thank you, sir," said her daughter, responding like a little kid who forgets to say thanks to Santa when he gives her a candy cane.

"I tell you, I have been so impressed with the job Max has done, that I've decided not to waste any more time. I want you two to start packing up. I'm transferring Max to New York on the first of August."

"What?" Liv was dismayed at the news. "It seems so soon to be moving. I thought we'd be heading for New York in, say, October or November. I thought Rebekah would still be in training that long."

"Well, so did I. But we both miscalculated. We forgot just how smart this girl is. No. I want her with me, Liv. I want to take her under my wing and mentor her in this business. She's got a future that is just . . . well, it's just limitless! What do you think about that?" He was asking Rebekah.

"Well . . . in New York, I'll be working directly under you, then."

"That's right. I think it's time we put you directly onto the Spy Squad team," added Garrett. Liv didn't know what the Spy Squad was, but judging from the tone in Garrett's voice, she could tell that this was a big deal. She felt a little thrill of excitement for her daughter. She wanted Rebekah to be pleased, to look forward to something in her life. She needed that so desperately. She needed to be able to anticipate good things in her future, because her past had been so dismal. Liv scrutinized her daughter's face, and though she was smiling at Garrett, the smile did not reach her eyes.

Nothing, it seemed, ever reached Rebekah's eyes anymore. Liv sighed.

"So I'll be doing sweeps, then?" asked Rebekah.

"You'll be doing sweeps, and you'll be working with me as well," said Garrett. "And I want you working only with our top clients, our A-list. The top of the pyramid."

"You mean . . . people like Senator Kane?"

Smiling, Garrett shook his head. "Senator Kane isn't a client, my dear. He's only a friend. An old friend."

"I see."

"But if Senator Kane had a job for us to do, you'd be the first one I'd put on the assignment."

"That's good."

It was all Liv could do not to kick her daughter. She glared at Rebekah as if to say, *Straighten up, missy*.

Rebekah ignored her.

"If you like," said Garrett, "I'll engage a service to begin apartment-hunting for you. Come to think of it, Liv, if you want, you can throw a few things in a bag and come back to New York with me. You can supervise the apartment hunt. Max can start wrapping things up out here in D.C."

Now it was Rebekah's turn to glare, and Liv felt herself blushing. She didn't know what to say. On the one hand, it would be a big thrill to fly to New York with Garrett. She'd never been on a private jet before. And she knew he would wine and dine her in real style. On the other hand . . . Well, there was the delicate little matter of where she would stay.

"We maintain a company suite at the Plaza," Garrett said, as if intuiting her discomfort. "You could stay there until an apartment is located and you are ready to move in." It was so typical of him, and so sweet.

"What do you think, Rebekah?" asked Liv. She didn't want Rebekah to be mad at her. She'd been so irritable since Liv had been seeing Garrett. Liv didn't like for there to be tension in her home. "You could come up next weekend and stay with me. It would be fun."

Rebekah shrugged. "Do what you like, Mom. You're a big girl."

Liv winced. She glanced surreptitiously at Garrett, but he seemed not to have noticed her daughter's lukewarm response to the entire plan.

Instead, he began discussing the fireworks display again, which was a big relief. They talked about it while Rebekah stared out the window. When they pulled up to the apartment, Rebekah said good night quickly, jumped out of the limo, and headed for the door without waiting for her mother.

She reached him in his car, through his car phone number. Very few people even had that number, and fewer still ever called it this late at night. The girls were still buoyant, elated by their exciting evening watching the fireworks in the park. Even Abby was in a surprisingly good mood, since Underwood had spent the entire evening with the family and had not even mentioned work. When he picked up the phone, Abby gave him a suspicious glance.

"Underwood."

"We have to meet."

"What?" He recognized her voice immediately, and his wife's sharp glare on his face seemed to pry into his soul. He lowered his voice. "Call me tomorrow. We'll set up a time."

"No. Not tomorrow. Now."

"It's late. Whatever you've got to tell me can wait."

"Union Station. At the kiosk where they sell wartime pins and memorabilia and stuff. I'm leaving for the Metro now. I'll be waiting." The phone clicked.

"Goddamn it!" He said, slamming the phone into its holder.

"Who was it?" He could see the tension already setting in on Abby's face, and in that moment, he knew the entire evening was ruined for her. The fact that he'd spent it in her company with the kids, enjoying their time together, would now be meaningless to her. With Abby, it had to be all or nothing.

"It's an informant. She wants to meet." Immediately, he regretted the reference to "she."

"Now?"

"I'm afraid so."

"Great. Just great."

"Abby—it's the Operation EAVESDROP case. This is the first break I've had in it."

"And it just happens to come from a female informant."

"Oh, for chrissake, Abby! If I was having an affair with her, do you think I'd be so fucking obvious?"

"Keep your voice down!" she hissed. "And watch your language in front of the girls." The three children to whom his wife referred had grown quiet in the backseat, well aware of the growing tension between their parents.

"Look, this is the first time she's ever requested a meeting. She may be in danger. I've got to check it out, Abby."

"Of course you do. You couldn't send another agent to take care of it. One who doesn't have kids."

"It's my case!" he shouted.

Her expression instantly turned to stone.

"I'm sorry," he said. "I didn't mean to yell at you. I'll take you and the girls home, and then I'll go see what's happening with this informant. It shouldn't take me more than an hour or two, I promise."

"Take all night," she said in a deadened tone. "I really don't give a shit." Then she turned away from him and did not speak to him again.

At the house he offered to help put the girls to bed before he left, but she said primly, "That's not necessary. I'm quite used to putting them down with no help from you."

This thoroughly pissed him off, and by the time he was back in the car, their good time at the national Mall watching fireworks with the kids was long forgotten, and he was glad to be getting away from the house.

Rebekah Maxfield could not have chosen a more inconvenient meeting place for him—not to mention a more inconvenient time—and he wondered if she'd done it deliberately. Union Station was all the way over at the other end of Washington, D.C., from Crystal City, and the traffic was still a bitch because of all the crowds who'd viewed the fireworks.

He fretted about her as he drove. What was going on? Had she been made? Had she been threatened in any way? Was she being followed?

Union Station was the behemoth antique train station that sprawled over several city blocks between Massachusetts Avenue and Second Street. Recently refurbished, it still housed stops for Amtrack as well as the Metro, but the modern plan included a three-tiered shopping mall that spanned the width and length of the huge facility.

Most of the shops and restaurants would be closed by now. The war veterans' memorabilia shop to which Max had referred was located on the bottom level of the station, outside the area that led to the trains. Max would be able to take the Metro straight to Union Station and wait outside of the booth for him, while he fought traffic and struggled to find a parking place.

If this was a joke on him, Underwood was not laughing.

By the time Underwood made it inside the cavernous station and headed in a brisk walk toward the shop, it was past one-thirty in the morning. At first he didn't see her, and felt a stab of fear in his heart, but she spotted him and got to her feet. She'd been sitting cross-legged on the floor, and he'd almost missed her.

She was dressed in a sharp navy pantsuit with a red silk blouse and a rhinestone and gold American flag pin on the lapel, as if she'd been celebrating the Fourth at a dressy occasion. Her face was wan and tired, and her hair needed brushing.

Without greeting him, she said, "You've got to let me tell my mother what's going on."

"Let's walk. And quiet down." He took her by the arm and steered her toward the middle of the massive facility. Glancing around, he said, "Were you followed?"

"No." Involuntarily, she glanced behind her. "I don't think so."

They walked in silence for a moment, until he felt reasonably certain that they were not being watched. It was fairly easy to do because the station was virtually deserted at this hour. Then he said, "No."

"You have to. She has to know—"

He shook his head vehemently. "Absolutely not."

She stopped and swung around to face him. Wearing low heels, she was even taller than usual, and he had to tilt his face slightly upward to maintain eye contact, something that irritated him immensely. "Mother's dating Garrett Sharp," she said.

He stared at her. "What?"

"My mom. Garrett Sharp's been taking her out. Putting the moves on her. I tried to warn her away from him, but she won't listen to me. You've got to let me tell her why!"

With a great sigh Underwood pinched the bridge of his nose between his thumb and forefinger, then replaced his glasses.

"This is why you called me out here in the middle of the damn night?"

"You can't let this happen!" She clutched his arm in near panic.

Underwood said, "The less she knows, the safer she'll be, Max. If you even breathe a word about what you're doing to your mother, she will betray you to him, and then you will both be in very serious danger."

"But she's in danger right now!" she cried.

"I don't think so."

"You don't *think* so? You son of a bitch, what if this was *your* mother?"

He grinned. "Nah. Mom's not Sharp's type."

She glared at him. The navy pantsuit made her eyes as deep blue and mysterious as sapphires.

"Relax," he said. "Sharp's a red-blooded American male. He's single. He probably likes your mom. I doubt she's in any kind of danger."

"He's seeing her just to get to me."

"Now, why would he do that? He has no idea you're

working for the feds." He cut a sharp glance over at her. "Does he?"

She stared away from him. "No. Not that I know of. No."

"Okay. Don't panic."

"He's moving us to New York."

This came as a huge surprise. Keeping his face impassive, Underwood said, "Already?"

"Already. He wants to mentor me."

Underwood smiled. This was excellent news indeed. "When?"

"Couple of weeks. August first."

Abby will be thrilled, thought Underwood with a wince. More time away from home. No more convenient meetings with Max at the Crystal City underground mall.

"There's more," said Max.

Underwood led her into a shadowy nook near the trains and waited. She stood very close to him. He could smell her perfume. The backlighting from the mall area made her blond hair stand out like a halo. "I saw Garrett Sharp plant a bug in Senator Truman Kane's office tonight."

Underwood frowned. "You were in Senator Kane's office tonight? Congress is in recess."

"Sharp finagled an invitation for Mom and me to join the senator and a few friends to watch the fireworks from his private balcony."

"The senator's private balcony," he repeated, flashing instantly to the heat and the crowds and the traffic he'd fought down below with his wife and girls.

"During the fireworks, Sharp sneaked into the senator's office and planted a mains plug adapter transmitter."

"Are you sure?"

"I followed him, and when he'd rejoined the others, I checked it out for myself."

"Did he see you?"

She hesitated. "No."

"Are you sure?"

"Yes!" she cried. "I'm sure."

"Okay, okay. Don't bite my damn head off."

"I want you to tell the senator what's going on."

Underwood shook his head. "Not yet. You need to get me a lot more evidence before I do that."

"What are you talking about, Underwood? I saw him do it! The senator is running a close reelection campaign. If you wait, he could be defeated because of Garrett Sharp!"

"That's not my problem," said Underwood carefully. "If we tell the senator, he could easily figure out that you are a government informant, and he could leak that information to the wrong people. You could get made, and we're nowhere near ready for that yet."

"He wouldn't do that. He—"

"No. Forget about the senator, do you hear me? You're moving to New York. New York is Garrett Sharp's base of operations. He maintains his central office there. If there is any evidence to be had, it will be in New York, and if there is anybody who would be able to get it, it's Garrett Sharp's own little protégée, and that, my dear, would be you."

In a voice that sounded alarmingly like his wife's of late, Max said, "Why don't you just hire my mother to get your sleazy information, Underwood? It seems to me that she would be in the best position to get it."

Ignoring the sarcastic tone, Underwood said, "She's an innocent. Keep her out of it, or you could be putting her in danger."

Between clenched teeth Max said, "You're damn right she's an innocent, and if anything happens to her, *Agent* Underwood, I swear to you, I'll kill you myself."

With that, she turned on her heel and stalked off.

For a long moment, Underwood stood alone in the shadows, her words ringing in his ears, wondering if . . . no, knowing that . . . she meant every word.

Chapter Eleven

"All's quiet along the Potomac tonight
Where the soldiers lie peacefully dreaming,
Their tents in the rays of the clear autumn moon,
In the lights of the watch fires are gleaming."

Max stood alone in a Washington twilight drizzle, the collar of her raincoat turned up to ward off the rain, her hair stuffed down into a scarf tied tightly around her face, reading the lines of poetry penned by Ethel Beers in 1879 and carved into the walkway of Freedom Plaza. To the northwest, poking grandly up over the clusters of trees, a corner of the White House was visible. To the west astride a valiant bronze steed from his frozen perch high upon a stone pedestal, General William Tecumseh Sherman surveyed the territory.

In spite of the late hour and the dreary rain, hardy tourists were not to be dissuaded from their busy itineraries, and they crowded the Plaza in their cheap ponchos, burdened like wandering packhorses with videocams and heavy camera bags, rushing along to the next photo op, trampling over the lovely words in their haste. None but Max stopped to read.

The openness of the location unnerved her; the tourists all looked like feds to Max. Still, she could walk and talk relatively unmolested, and should either Underwood or Sharp find out about the meeting and question her, she had her lies all worked out. Playing poker with her brothers had taught Max years before that the best bluffs are planned in advance.

He was easy to spot, striding down the street toward her with his head held high, his black trench coat sweeping behind him like the wings of a cape, his cowboy hat set at a rakish angle over one eye. Max was reminded of photos she'd seen in history books of the famous Texan Sam Houston, who'd worn buffalo robes given him by the Indians, who called him "The Raven." Houston had been a figure of grandeur and myth even while still alive, and Max thought she could detect a bit of the ghost of Houston in Senator Kane.

In spite of the greenery of the surroundings, the rain had washed out most color and given everything the smoky patina of ash. It was not a cold rain, yet Max felt chilled, as if the warm days of summer were ending and the long nights of winter, cold as death, loomed. The lowering clouds seemed to hold, not the promise of moisture and life, but stormy threats of fury and violence.

"You look like a drowned rat, little lady," said the senator with a big smile. "Why don't you let me flag down a cab, and we'll go someplace dry where we can drink something wet?"

She returned his smile. "No, thanks, Senator. If you don't mind, I'd like to talk out here."

"Suit yourself." While they crossed the street and entered the park that sheltered General Sherman, Kane pulled out a compact black umbrella. With an artful snap of his wrist, the umbrella billowed out and proved to be a bumbershoot big enough to carry Marry Poppins over the trees.

"There, now, that's better," he said, holding the umbrella over both their heads. The rain was coming down in angry torrents now, and it thundered against the cloth of the umbrella like distant gunfire. "What's this all about, darlin'?"

"I have something to tell you that must go no further," said Max.

He gave her a keen glance but said nothing.

"Senator Kane, I have reason to believe that your offices, and perhaps your car and maybe even your home, are bugged."

He stopped walking with an abruptness that almost caused Max to stumble. "Garrett Sharp tell you this?"

She looked him directly in the eye. "No, sir."

"Well, then, maybe I'd better hire him to check it out."

"No, sir. I don't believe that would be advisable at this time."

He narrowed his eyes into slits and regarded her for a long moment. "Why should I believe you, little lady?" Though the tone of his voice was genial enough, his eyes were guarded. "After all, I've known ole Garrett for years."

Without a blink she answered, "Because I am my father's daughter. I carry his name as well as my own, and I would never do anything to dishonor it."

When he made no reply, she added, "Don't take my word for it. Check out the plug behind the copy machine. It's really a mains plug adapter. It will pick up anything that is said in the general vicinity of the copier for an indefinite period of time."

With a thunderous scowl he said, "And just how would you know about this?"

"I discovered it during the fireworks display, and that's all I want to say just now."

Cars sloshed past on the streets outside the park, while tourists squawked and fled for shelter like seagulls diving for fish.

"Well, then. What would you advise? The FBI?"

"You could call the FBI, sir, you could. But I can't guarantee that they would do a . . . thorough . . . job for you. Some bugs might squeak past them."

He expelled a great gust of air from his nose. "Shit." After another long moment of staring into the rain, he resumed walking, still holding the umbrella over their heads, firmly steering Max along. Then he said, "How 'bout I hire you to do it?"

Max said, "I'd be pleased to, sir, but the truth is that . . ." She sighed. "The truth is that I'm being watched."

"By who?"

"I can't say, Senator."

"Well, great God in heaven." Thunder rumbled overhead as if in answer. "You didn't mention my campaign headquarters."

"That's just because I forgot. But I would suspect that your campaign headquarters would be especially vulnerable, sir."

"Who the hell's doin' it?" In his frustration and anxiety, the senator's Texan accent was growing more pronounced.

"I can't say for sure, but I can say that whatever they could learn from bugging your office or campaign headquarters might come in very handy to your political rivals in an election year."

"Well, why all this cloak-and-dagger stuff? Who are you, Deep Throat?" he asked in exasperation.

"Let's just say I'm a constituent who would like to see you reelected. If you get defeated in a fair race, then so be it. But this isn't fair. And I didn't want to be a part of it."

"A part of it? What are you talking about?"

Max was flustered with herself for revealing as much as she had. This time she stopped walking. They stood in a virtual curtain of rain that poured off the huge black umbrella around them. "Senator, I shouldn't be here right now. There are people who could bring great harm to me or to my loved ones if they knew I was telling you what I have told you. What we have discussed must go no further. I just wanted to warn you, so that you would not discuss sensitive issues where . . . eavesdroppers could hear."

Within the private gray damp of their small world, she held his gaze until he finally nodded. His craggy face breaking into a sudden grin, he said, "I always did like a broad with balls."

She returned his smile with a fleeting one of her own, and added, "I must also trust you not to talk about this matter with Mr. Sharp. It could have very serious repercussions for me."

"I understand," he said. "I think." After a moment he added, "I now owe you a favor." As she started to shake her head, he said, "Just don't you worry about it. It's the way business"—he pronounced it the Texan way: *bidness*—"is done in this town. You git in a jam, and I have a feelin' you will, you give me a call. I'll see what I can do."

"All right," she said. "I will."

The downpour continued with relentless determination, and most people had cleared the park area. Max

and the senator continued walking together, neither talking, their thoughts adrift in the mist that had begun to
collect in the shadows and corners. A cold dribble of
rain worked its way between her shoulder blades. She
shivered.

It was a bold step she'd taken, meeting with the senator and warning him about the surveillance. But the
truth was that she was still very much a prisoner, and
she didn't know, standing here in the chilly gloom of a
Washington rain surrounded by monuments to liberty,
whether she would ever again be truly free.

The rain continued in spirit-sinking monotony for
days. Normally, Max loved rain. Even in prison, there
was something comforting, something life-affirming,
about the sound of rain on the greenhouse roof as she
worked, and the riot of color that always followed was
a reward, a respite from her colorless world. But for
some reason, this time Max felt constrained by the rain,
isolated in the lonely apartment while she packed for
the move.

Mostly, she missed her mom. She even missed old
Sarge's snoring and the click of his claws on the floor in
the morning. She'd done what she could to lighten the
tension between them and she called her mother most
every day. But even though things seemed well enough
on the surface, there was an element no longer there,
an easy camaraderie, that she missed keenly.

On the night before Max was due to leave for New
York, as she tossed and turned amid her hot, tangled
sheets, she couldn't help but think, *I'm thirty-four years
old, and I haven't got a friend in the world except my
mother.*

Max kicked off the covers and turned on the light.
Crap on it. She might as well get some work done if she
was going to be awake anyway. She was getting sick of
her own company and could use the distraction.

Dominic had assured Max that it was not necessary
for her to master every area of electronics in which they
worked. Some members of the Spy Squad had their own
specialty, but as long as she had a general grasp of a
subject, then the rest should be left in the capable hands

of the expert. But Dominic didn't know that Max had to have a strong working knowledge of every area of electronic surveillance and countersurveillance in order to be able to recognize whenever a member of the team was doing the opposite of what he'd been hired to do. She not only had to be able to spot a crime when it was being committed, but be knowledgeable enough about what she'd seen to testify to it in a court of law.

Her weakness was telephone analysis. Before leaving the office, she'd gone through desk drawers here and there, pulling out any computer disks or manuals or anything else that looked as though it might be helpful. This would be as good a time as any to plow through them. Yawning, Max shuffled through the apartment, picking her way through packing boxes, and dug out a coffee mug and some instant decaf in the kitchen. Outside, thunder cannoned off glowering cloud shields. For a few minutes Max stood at the window, watching the tracer-volleys of lightning in furious combat, exploding over first one part of the sky and then another.

Gaby had always been so afraid of storms. Max would hold her and rock her and sing to her, saying, "Nothing's going to hurt you, sweet girl. Mama's here. Mama's here . . ."

She wondered, Was Gaby still afraid of storms? Was she too big now to be comforted by her mama?

Giving herself a mental shake, Max turned from the window and sat down at a desk nearby, flipping on her laptop and telling it what she wanted it to do. Sorting through the disks that she'd dropped in an unceremonious pile next to the computer, she picked one up that was labeled *Basic-Level Telephone Analysis Equipment,* inserted it in the slot, and called up its file listings, scanning through Portable Electronic Multimeter, Digital Capacitance Meter, Variable-Frequency Audio or Function Generator . . .

Yeah, this was just the thing to take her mind off her baby.

But after some browsing through the listings, Max decided she already had a basic grasp of telephone analysis equipment. Ejecting the disk, she sorted through more offerings, passing over *Medium-Level Telephone Analy-*

sis Equipment and going straight to *High-Level Tele-phone Analysis Equipment*. A power bolt of thunder pounded its fists against the windowpane, and Max jumped, almost upsetting her coffee mug.

She inserted the new disk, which contained a very brief file, offering only Time-Domain Reflectometer (TDR), and RF Detection Device (Spectrum Analyzer). Under the TDR listing were two headings: Capabilities and Limitations.

A raging thrust of lightning split the sky almost directly overhead the apartment building, tripping a loud *click* from every electrical appliance in the apartment, plunging the place into total darkness, and detonating a blast of thunder so loud and so close that it seemed the very earth had opened up and swallowed the building.

Everything stopped.

Ceiling fans no longer spun, digital clocks went blank, the hum of the air conditioner vanished, and the only lights that could be seen were outside. Max wondered if the apartment had been struck by the lightning bolt and worried about the possibility of fire. Groping her way to the front door, she opened it and listened, but there was no warning scream of smoke detectors.

They'd just lost their power.

The darkness wasn't so bad, but the stillness was creepy. It was so quiet that she could hear the actual sounds made by silence, could feel her own heart pumping blood throughout her body with each rhythmic beat. Outside, no traffic passed because it was so very late. The storm was moving past, taking its frightful battle elsewhere, but the rain stubbornly remained, flinging its wet fury against the walls of the building.

Suddenly, lights returned, clocks blinked, fans whirred, air conditioners hummed. Max felt the tension ease from the back of her neck, as if she'd been awaiting some brutal attack in the darkness and now it had been chased away.

The laptop, however, was not faring so well. Instead of the capabilities and limitations of Time-Domain Reflectometers appearing on-screen, a host of meaningless symbols and confusing instructions scrolled past, as if the machine were alive and, after surviving a bad shock, was talking to itself in confusion. Finally, it stopped scrolling and left only a simple notation: C:\>ANGEL FILE PRESS ANY KEY.

I'm game, thought Max, and pressed ENTER.

The screen went blank, then produced a file: *Angel Gabriel.*

A slow, deep strumming set in somewhere over Max's left temple, and it ran like an electrical current from her head down her spine; she could feel the throbbing in her fingertips. Max touched the ball on the side of the laptop that served as a mouse, trying to align the cursor arrow with the file *Angel Gabriel,* but she was shaking so hard that the arrow jerked and stabbed too close, too far, here and there, until finally she was able to hit the mark and double-click. A tiny hourglass bade her wait, but Max no longer had any concept of time; past, present, and future had melded into one pulsating bloody heartbeat.

The hourglass disappeared.

A CovertCom report appeared, one resembling many Max had written herself, but this one was flagged: *Extremely Sensitive. Eyes Only. Confidential. CC: Garrett Sharp, Gabriel Griswold. Not for general distribution.*

The report was dated early March of that year. Max began to read:

> After initial reluctance, subject agreed to come to work for CovertCom, beginning in the Austin office and progressing to the New York office. Subject will be monitored closely and her training will be supervised personally by myself. It is estimated that it will take from four to six months—possibly more—to build enough trust with subject that will enable me to ascertain location of child. Warning: it may take longer—as much as one year. Subject has demonstrated extreme intelligence and great skill in the past. Any attempt to rush the process could result in the flight of the subject. Weekly progress reports will keep the client apprised of the subject's progress in all areas. Any attempt made by the client to interfere in this process in any way will result in immediate consequences, RE: FRE R403.

The sound of whimpering came to Max first, and she realized that it was her own voice. Hands shaking so hard she couldn't hit the keys, Max fumbled around with the hidden secret file, looking for more, but there was nothing else. Apparently, Sharp had hidden the secret file beneath an innocuous-looking file on telephone analysis equipment, then either forgotten where he'd hidden it or started a new file altogether and forgotten to delete this one. Or maybe he *had* deleted the file, but the power surge had somehow caused it to reappear on the disk.

She found herself pacing the floor, only she had no memory of getting to her feet. Of all the nightmare scenarios Max had envisioned for the outcome of this job, this was the one thing that had never once occurred to her: that her ex-husband had hired Garrett Sharp in the first place to "hire" Max for the firm.

The idea popped into her head that she should maybe call Jack Underwood and tell him and get him to help her, but upon reflection she realized that Jack Underwood would not care why Max had been hired by CovertCom; all he cared about would be making his case.

Nobody would believe her. And even if they did, nobody would help her.

Rage bubbled and boiled to the surface like corrosive acid, and suddenly Max was screaming, *You poisonous, venomous snake!! How long are you going to curse my life?*

She hurled the coffee mug across the room. It smashed against the far wall. By then she was a wild thing, out of control, raving in a crazed frenzy of clenched fists, manic shrieks, and lunatic sobs, smashing lamps and tearing her hair like a madwoman on the edge of the abyss.

At first she didn't hear the pounding, but finally it got through to her and she stood, chest heaving, breath rasping, tears blurring her vision; she stood in the middle of the wrecked living room, lost.

"Excuse me. Is everything all right? Are you all right in there? Hello?"

The old lady who lived next door. She was knocking persistently on the door, checking on Max, trying to get her attention.

"I'm going to call the police!" the old woman cried.

"No! Don't do that," yelled Max at last. "I'm all right. Everything's all right."

"Are you sure?"

Max moved to open the door, then caught a glimpse of herself in the mirror, hanging on the wall nearby. She looked like a zombie, back from death. Instead, she lowered her voice and said, "It's all right, really. Thank you for checking on me."

"Okay. All right." The lady hesitated. Max didn't even know her name, and she was ashamed of herself for that. Her mom would know.

"Thank you. Really," said Max, and finally, she heard the woman move away from the door and return to her own apartment.

Pain scissored through Max's skull, and she sank to the floor, leaning her head back against the wall. Her emotional breakdown had left a deadness behind, a numbing exhaustion beyond anything Max had ever known. *I wish I could die,* she thought, *and then I wouldn't have to feel any more pain.*

She could do it easily enough. Just end it all.

But it wouldn't end. Without her, Gabe could close in on Gaby, could snatch her from her happy home and take her down to hell with him.

From somewhere down so deep she couldn't find its source, came a one-syllable sound, one word, one great glorious word that would, she could see now, set her free.

No.

She was not going to die. She was not going to quit. And she was not going to give Gabe Griswold—or anybody else—victory over her soul.

At first she was too weary to get up, so she clambered to her hands and knees and swayed there for a moment, her hair dragging the floor. Then, grasping the doorknob with one hand and pushing against the floor with another, she made it to her knees, where with one final grunt, she staggered to her feet.

She was drained. Empty. Her head was splitting, but there was a clarity of thought which burned with the sulfurous smoke of a lightning bolt that rends a tree clean down the middle and exposes the marrow.

Another single-syllable word branded itself into her brain.

Yes.

Yes. She would fight. Yes. She would find a way out of this. Yes. She would screw Gabe Griswold to the wall. Yes. She would bury Garrett Sharp. Yes. She would get Jack Underwood out of her life for good. And yes.

She would see her sweet Gaby again.

Max stumbled across the room to the laptop, where she printed up a copy of the report, then punched out the disk and began searching for a hiding place. She did not know what she was going to do, and she did not know how she was going to do it. The answer lay somewhere in New York, of that she was certain.

Right now she had very little to go on. She had FRE R403.

She had secret knowledge.

Something her dad had said to her once came to mind. The twins had beaten her at poker again, and she was pouting about it, and her dad had said, *"Max, never play to avoid a loss. Always play to win."*

Never play to avoid a loss.

Always play to win.

Moving calmly now through the leftover chaos of her own near-madness, Max threaded her way over dented lamp shades and crunched through broken pieces of coffee mug to the front window, where she parted the drapes and peered out at the wild night. The streets glimmered with the reflected shimmer of streetlamps in the rain-wet pavement, but overhead, ragged shreds of storm clouds, torn asunder as if by the fury of her own tempest, left a great tattered hole over the full moon. The light from the moon cast an otherworldly, ghostly glow that, in another time, might have struck fear in the hearts of onlookers.

But on this night Max stared the moon full in the face, and then she turned her back on it.

PART III

THE BLUFF

You may wind up nose-to-nose with some idiot who smirks at you and raises the limit every time.

——Ted Thackery, Jr.
Dealer's Choice

That is the great fallacy; the wisdom of old men. They do not grow wise. They grow careful.

——Ernest Hemingway
A Farewell to Arms

Courage is perhaps the most important single factor in the makeup of a poker player.

——Albert H. Morehead
The Complete Guide to Winning Poker

Chapter Twelve

August

It was good to be home, walking the busy streets of New York again. Though born in the Midwest, Dominic had discovered New York in his teens. He loved the energy of New York, the grimy intensity, the hodgepodge collection of other transplanted lost souls who had reinvented themselves.

New York in August was hot and edgy, with the threat of rain always looming but seldom delivering relief from the sticky tension. Every patch of grass was draped with supine bodies, dogs, kids, or all three. Cabbies and bus drivers were surly, doormen sleepy, waiters irritable. The crime rate always went up in August.

Dominic loved it all.

Dominic lived in a SoHo loft that occupied the top floor of an art gallery a few blocks south of Washington Square Park. The loft had once belonged to an artist who had committed suicide. On the day Dominic moved in, he found some words scratched into a broad windowsill: "It is my opinion that Van Gogh's paintings did not reflect his madness; rather, he was driven mad by people's indifference to his genius."

Dominic left the inscription as it was, to remind him of the arbitrariness of life.

The other Spy Squad members preferred apartments on the Upper West Side, but Dominic found its comparative sophistication boring. He preferred the nutty "unique fashions" shops of SoHo and Greenwich Village, the overstuffed bookstores, the messy corner basketball games, the art galleries, the students and gays and artists and other teeming life forms that gave New

York its multicultural spirit. There was a place, it seemed, for everybody. If you didn't fit in, all you had to do was walk a block or two and find your niche.

Dominic had restored the hardwood floors of his apartment and varnished them to a high gloss. The furniture was rugged and sturdy and spare, made solid with wood and leather, to withstand the rigors of the everyday life of a big man, and Dominic had filled the place with things that reflected his eclectic tastes and his travels: Navaho rugs and Native American pottery from the Southwest, folk art quilts from Appalachia, Japanese silk screens, piles of books, and carvings of polished driftwood from a West Coast artist Dominic favored. If he saw something he liked, he bought it and brought it home. Somehow it all fit together. The overall effect was interesting and pleasing to the eye.

Dominic was a man who favored order in a chaotic world. The place was usually neat and tidy, but he'd hired a cleaning crew to come in anyway to make sure everything would be in order for the Spy Squad Saturday night poker game. The poker game had been initiated by the Boss as some sort of bonding ritual, but everybody soon caught on that if the Boss didn't usually walk away with most of the winnings, work over the next few days could be pretty miserable. Consequently, it had become somewhat of a formality nobody particularly enjoyed anymore—except for the Boss, of course.

They usually rotated hosting the game, and since Dominic had been away for a while, it was his turn. The others usually liked to impress each other with various catered delicacies, but Dominic considered such pretentions bullshit and ordered plenty of pizza and beer instead. They didn't like it, they could kiss his ass.

He showered, shaved, groomed his mustache, and dressed in a pair of chinos and a denim shirt that had been laundered to just the right softness, and a pair of canvas boat shoes without socks. He was just rolling up the sleeves to the elbow when the intercom buzzer sounded. Frowning, Dominic glanced at the clock. Nobody ever came early to these things. The evening would be long enough.

Flicking the intercom switch, he said, "Yeah?"

"It's Max."

A little sizzle of shock bolted through Dominic. Max had not been invited to the poker game. "Come on up," he said, and released the security lock that would allow her to enter the freight elevator and come clanking up the four floors to Dominic's apartment. He waited for her, pulling back the metal grid as soon as the elevator came wheezing to a stop and taking her hand.

She had cut her hair.

Dominic gaped at her. She'd chopped off a full six inches. It was still long—past her shoulders—but freed of its previous weight, it tumbled about her face and over one eye in a flirtatious mass of blond waves. He had to suppress the urge to reach out and stroke it.

"You cut your hair," he said stupidly.

She cocked her head and gazed up at him. "Do you like it?" It was a question that coming from any other woman would be fraught with insecurity and begging for a compliment. From Max, it was more of a challenge. She didn't seem to have any doubts.

"Very much," he said, letting his gaze roam freely over her body. She was wearing a beaded form-fitting silk vest in shades of peach and cinnamon, bringing out the honey tones in her skin, no blouse, and flowing silk peachy trousers with matching sandals. "You look good enough to eat," he blurted

She gave him a lazy, seductive grin and sauntered away from him, looking around with curious eyes. "Pretty civilized for a guy pad," she said.

"We cavemen do have our moments," he said. "Uh . . . what can I do for you?" It was the least moronic thing he could think of to say.

"It is your turn to host the Saturday night poker game, isn't it?" She turned and nailed him with widely innocent eyes. Tonight, their color was a mystery.

"Uh . . . well . . ."

"Whassa matta?" she said, taking on a thick New Yawk accent, "No dames allowed, or wat?"

"Well . . ."

"Aw, c'mon," she said. "I won't get in the way, I promise." She smiled sweetly.

He capitulated with a roll of the eyes. What could it hurt?

"What would you like to drink?" he said. "I've got beer and beer." He led the way into the kitchen area of the loft.

"I'll take a beer." She followed him. He could smell her perfume, an exotic vanilla scent. It wasn't overpowering or too sweet, as so many women's perfumes were. It was just plain sexy.

Momentarily forgetting where he kept the mugs, he rummaged in the cupboard.

"I can drink it straight from the bottle," she said, laughing, so he popped the cap and handed it to her. Her warm fingers touched his for a moment. He turned away.

"Where is everybody?" she asked. "I thought the game started at eight."

"Nobody ever comes on time," he said, grabbing a beer for himself. Something had changed in her. He couldn't put his finger on it.

"I'll keep that in mind." She was standing very close. Dominic took a swig of beer and then another one. He couldn't remember when he had ever been so nervous. The new hairdo made a dramatic difference in her appearance—not that she had looked bad before—but the change in her was coming from within. A boldness, maybe. Something.

A vixenish little smile played across her soft lips, and it was all he could do not to grab her and start pawing at her like some hormonal high school kid. Though very classy and pretty, there was something a little naughty about wearing the vest without a blouse beneath it. It only had four buttons. He could have his hands inside it in about thirty seconds . . .

"Dominic."

The godlike intrusion of the intercom made them both jump.

Dominic stumbled over to the intercom and reluctantly buzzed up two of the guys. He suppressed a groan when the elevator grille pulled back to reveal Evan Ryder and Sebastian Taylor, whose lascivious glance at Max made Dominic want to drape one of his jackets over her shoulders. Evan stood stock-still for a moment, then solemnly said, "Thank God for women's lib."

Hakeem Abdul arrived soon after. The others had all met Max at the office during the previous week, and though surprised to find her here, did not seem to mind.

As always, the Boss arrived last. Dominic often wondered if he hid behind a corner in his limo, watching the building until everyone else had entered so that he could make his grand entrance.

"Why, Max! What a lovely surprise!" he cried, as though perfectly happy to see her, which Dominic doubted. After all, he hadn't told Max about the poker games, nor had he invited her. Dominic wondered how she'd learned of them. "Here, sit next to me," said the Boss, pulling out a chair for her in his usual courtly manner. They all took a seat around Dominic's dining table. He'd bought the handsome cherrywood furniture because he'd thought he might have need of it someday. So far he never had, apart from the ritual poker games and a handy place to dump junk mail.

Dominic picked up a remote control device, pointed it at his stereo sound system lining one wall, and pressed a button. Aaron Neville's lilting tones provided perfect counterpoint to Kenny G's incomparable sax.

Dominic watched Max laughing at something Evan was saying, her face softly bronzed from the evening light slanting through the windows. Since he was hosting the game, he placed a new deck of cards on the table, peeled off the cellophane, and shuffled them with sharp efficiency. "What's the game?" he asked. There was no such thing as dealer's choice when the Boss sat at the table unless, of course, he was the dealer.

"Let's start out with something simple," said the Boss, "so Max can keep up."

"Thank you, Mr. Sharp," she said graciously, as though he had not just insulted her.

"Don't worry, honey," he said, patting her hand. "You'll be playing like a pro in no time."

"You never played poker in the dorm or nothin'?" asked Evan.

"Oh, I played some with my brothers, a long time ago."

"Nah, they play those little ladylike games like spades in the girl's dorms," commented Sebastian smugly.

Dominic wondered about Max's time in prison, but said nothing.

"How about seven-card stud?" said the Boss. "With a pot limit."

Of course everybody agreed. Dominic had noticed that the Boss always positioned himself to the right of the dealer so that he would be the next to last to bet in games like this, which gave him an inherent advantage. Dominic hadn't decided if that made the Boss smart or just a cheat.

Dominic dealt the first two hole cards and then the first round of up cards. He had a seven up and a jack and a ten in the hole. Evan showed a two, Sebastian a queen, Hakeem a seven, Max a ten, and the Boss a four. Everyone placed a modest bet to start; "modest" in this game meant that the white chips stood for one dollar, the red chips five dollars, and the blue chips ten dollars.

In the second round of hole cards, Dominic drew a two. Unwittingly, he glanced over at Max. She had a perplexed expression on her face. Sebastian was putting on his version of the poker face, but as usual, was betraying himself by jiggling one knee. Evan's face was unreadable, Hakeem's surly, and the Boss had a gleam of satisfaction in his eye.

Dominic figured he was still in the game for a straight if he got lucky. Evan bet a couple of white chips, Sebastian saw that and raised the stakes to a red. Hakeem matched it, as did Max. The Boss raised Hakeem's red with one of his own and a couple of whites. Dominic bet a red chip.

He dealt the second round of up cards and pulled another two for himself. Evan showed a six, Sebastian a nine, Max an eight, Hakeem a king, and the Boss another four. Dominic didn't see any way to stay in the game with a ten, a jack, a seven, and a pair of twos; not as long as the Boss was showing a pair of fours and Sebastian was showing high cards, so he folded but continued to deal the next round of hole cards. After that round Hakeem also dropped out, leaving Sebastian, Evan, Max, and the Boss. Sebastian recklessly bet a blue chip. Evan bet a red. Max matched Evan's bet, and the Boss matched Sebastian's. The chips piled up in the center of the table.

Dominic dealt the next round of up cards. Sebastian drew an ace, Evan a five, Max a six, and the Boss another four. Sebastian and Evan folded.

"I've got three of a kind, dear," said the Boss kindly to Max. "What do you want to do?"

"Um . . . I think I want to call," she said. "I mean raise. I want to raise you a couple of chips." She tossed in a blue plus two white chips to the pot.

He blinked. "Are you sure? You do know that three of a kind beats most other hands in this game, don't you? And as far as you know, I'm holding a flush in the hole." He glanced around at the others. Sebastian, the pet sycophant, chuckled appreciatively.

Max studied her cards, a little frowny wrinkle between her brows. "I'd really like to keep playing, I think," she said.

The Boss smiled and shook his head. "Okay," he said, spreading his arms expansively. "Don't say I didn't warn you. Dealer? Hit me."

Dominic placed a card in front of each of them. The Boss got a king, and Max a queen.

"I raise you a red chip," said the Boss with a wicked little smile. "Are you in or out?"

"Um . . . gosh . . . I don't know." Max hesitated, looking flustered. "That's five dollars, isn't it?"

"Yep. Too rich for your blood?"

She drummed lacquered fingernails against the polished surface of Dominic's dining table. The room was growing dark; shadows collected in the high, murky corners of the punched-tin loft ceiling. Dominic flipped on the crystal chandelier hanging over the table, and adjusted the setting until the light was muted and easy on the eyes.

"You've got . . . what . . ." said the Boss helpfully, "a ten, an eight, a six, and a queen showing? Even with an ace, you wouldn't have much, unless, of course, you're hiding two of them in the hole." He grinned, and most of the men grinned politely along with him. Max chewed the side of her lip. Finally, she said, "No, I'll raise you."

"What?"

"Isn't that what you call it?" She tossed two red chips onto the table.

A flicker of anger gleamed in the Boss's eye. "All right," he said in a deadly quiet voice, adding his chips to the pot. Without taking his eyes from hers, he said, "Dealer?"

Dominic placed the final cards facedown in front of each player. First the Boss and then Max lifted a corner of their cards and peeked.

"I bet the pot limit," she said, counting and then shoving stacks of chips to the center of the table.

Dominic felt his eyes widen. Why was she being so reckless? What did she have to prove? And what kind of hand could justify that kind of wild bet?

"Are you crazy?" blurted Sebastian.

A dangerous glint appeared in the Boss's ice-blue eyes. "If that's the way you want to play, little girl," he said, pushing several of his stacks over to join hers in the middle of the table, "Then I call. Show us your stuff, sweetie." He smirked at the other men.

In seven-card stud, the player had to display only his five top cards, and sometimes choosing which cards could make or break the hand. Dominic felt the muscles in his stomach tighten as though to prepare for a blow.

Without fanfare, Max slowly turned over a nine, a ten, a jack, a queen, and a king and gazed at her boss with level, unreadable eyes.

Garrett Sharp showed a five and the leftover king to go with his three lowly fours.

Dominic cringed. He'd have to explain to Max the unwritten rule about letting the Boss win most of the time, and *never* beating him on the first hand. Three of a kind was usually a winning hand in seven-card stud, but only if the three of a kind were high cards. Only an idiot would sit on three fours when his opponent was showing a possible straight or flush.

In other words, Max had made a fool out of the Boss. Furthermore, she seemed unrepentant.

"My, my," he said slowly. "What a little bluffer you are."

She gave him a sweet smile and said, "Must be beginner's luck."

"Must be," he said.

But it wasn't. She beat them all under the table all night long. Dominic had never seen such a ruthless poker player. She played fearlessly, nasty and low-down—the way high-stakes poker was played. She took appalling risks—but only when she was winning. Her strength, he noticed, was that she tended to play the players and not the cards.

And she could read the players very well, which made her behavior all the more baffling.

She seemed to know most forms of the game, from straight draw to stud, and was patient and gracious when any of the others (usually Sebastian) made ignorant blunders.

And if the Boss was increasingly regarding her like a snake about to strike, she seemed not to notice, which made no sense whatsoever to Dominic, since clearly, she noticed everything else.

Then, toward the end of the evening, she started playing a little looser, a little less close to the chest—enough so that each player could recoup some of his losses and regain a modicum of dignity.

Everyone, that is, except for the Boss. With him she never dropped her guard, never gave in, never blinked.

Dominic tried to give her various subtle and some not-so-subtle warning signals, but she ignored him. At some point it ceased to be a card game and turned into a power struggle. Though the Spy Squad members managed not to lose their shirts in the end, the Boss forfeited every chip in his stash and had to resort to cash.

She cleaned out his wallet.

Dominic's chest constricted with fear for her recklessness. He prayed Sharp would forgive her for being a novice to their group. He prayed Sharp would forgive her, period.

Finally, the Boss pushed back his chair. "Well, I'm not about to take off my clothes for you, girl," he said. Empty pizza boxes and beer bottles littered the table.

Lights gleamed from the buildings and reflected off the clouds in a sulfurous yellow glow peculiar to New York. Down below, a road crew worked in the streets of the city that never sleeps. He got to his feet, and everyone else stood up as well. "I guess this is the first time I've ever been hustled by somebody on my own staff."

Max smiled. Beneath the soft focus of the chandelier, it seemed to Dominic that the smile did not reach her eyes, and something about that chilled him. "It's been so long since I've been able to play the game against a worthy opponent that I guess I just got carried away," she said in a small voice.

For a long moment nobody spoke. Then the Boss reached over and chucked her chin, as if she were a rebellious teenager. "I knew you were good when I hired you," he said. "I just didn't know how good."

The tension seemed to drain out of the room with that, and everybody moved to take their leave. Dominic walked each of them to the elevator. Sebastian said, "I'll share a cab with you, Max," and Dominic said, without even thinking about it, "I need to talk to Max for a minute if you don't mind, Sebastian. I'll see her safely home."

Sebastian's white-blond eyebrows quirked in surprise. "Max . . . ?"

"It's okay, Sebastian. I'll see you Monday."

Sebastian shot a keen glance Dominic's way, but Dominic did not register any expression on his face in response to the other man's challenge. After loitering and making maddening small talk, he finally left, and Dominic was alone, at last, with Max.

When the final clanks of the elevator had echoed to the bottom of the building, and Dominic could see the last of the guests on the streets below, he turned to her and said, "What was that little performance all about?"

"What do you mean?"

"C'mon, Max. Don't try to play little miss innocent with me—you're way too smart for that."

"Honestly, Dominic, I have no idea what you're talking about," she said unconvincingly, turning away from him so that he couldn't read her face. They were standing near the windows of the dining area. Soft yellow light from the chandelier lit up the pizza and beer carcasses, the scattered cards, and backlit her hair with a golden aura.

"I'm talking about your little card mechanic act with the Boss."

She whirled to face him, her eyes crackling with anger. "I never cheated him. Never. A card mechanic is a cheat, and that's not my game."

"Then, what is your game, Max? Making an idiot out of a man in front of his staff? You'll be damn lucky if you've still got a job left on Monday."

Her answering laugh was bitter. "Oh, I'll have a job. You needn't worry your pretty little head about that." She almost spat out the words.

Dominic stared at her. "What's going on with you?"

"Nothing." She crossed her arms over her chest defiantly. "Not a damn thing."

"What are you so angry about?" He stepped closer to her. "Is it your mother?"

"Huh? Oh, that. No. I mean, I'd rather that my boss wasn't seeing my mother, but I'm not angry about it."

"Then, what?" He took another step closer. City lights gleamed through the tall windows and glistened in her eyes. "Let me help you."

She sighed. "You can't help me, Dominic. No one can." A stark, simple loneliness in her tone and in her words sounded a note so deep and so profound that it resonated with full measure into the depths of Dominic's own sad aloneness and found an answering throb. For a beat or two she reached into his soul with her gaze, and the connection was a tangible thing, almost physical. Then, with a slight shake of her head, she suddenly turned away from him.

"I just wanted the son of a bitch to know that he can't walk all over me," she said.

"Oh, yeah, that makes perfect sense," said Dominic. "The guy gives you a crackerjack job after you've been locked up for seven years, pays you a fistful of money, shows your mother the time of her life, and behaves like a gentleman in every sense of the word around you—yeah, Max, I'd say it was time you taught him a lesson."

"How *dare* you!" she cried, whipping around so fast

some of her hair caught in her eyelashes. Furiously she brushed it away. "I can't believe you're *defending* him!"

Dominic blinked under the sheer force of her rage. Actually, he couldn't believe it, either. "I'm not defending him," he said, "I'm just trying to get you to back off a little. Garrett Sharp is . . . I mean, he can be . . ." Dominic hesitated, uncertain how much he should tell her. "Dangerous," he said finally. "He can be dangerous."

"I'm a big girl. I can take care of myself."

Dominic felt his temper and his patience give way in the face of her stubbornness. "You have no idea what you're talking about!" he shouted. "And until you do, you damn well better back off!"

"*You're* the one who's clueless!" she yelled. "*You* back off!"

She moved to brush past him and leave. He grabbed her wrist and yanked her close to him. "Goddammit Max!" he cried. "Are you *blind? I can't back off!*"

"Let me go!" Her chest was heaving, her face flushed. She tugged and pulled her wrist. "Let me go." Her voice had dropped to a breathless whisper.

"I can't," he said helplessly. "Goddammit all to hell. I can't let you go."

She stared at him, her mouth opening into a little O. Her eyes shimmered with unspilled tears.

Dominic crushed her to him, smothering her mouth with his. She slipped her wrist from his grasp and entwined her arms tightly around his neck. He lifted her off her feet. Their passion had a crazed frenzy to it, like lovers in a war zone, grabbing a moment that might be their last.

In two strides he'd reached the dining table. Still holding her close to him with his strong right arm, he reached out with his left and swept pizza boxes, beer bottles, and cards to the floor with a heedless crash. She went down on the table, her hair spreading out on its dark mirrored wood like yellow silk, working his belt buckle while he groped at the vest. Two buttons popped completely off and ricocheted off the table like bullets; the other two came loose effortlessly. Her breasts strained against the lace of her bra in two satiny swells. The hook was in front, between the breasts, and he dispatched of it with two fingers just as she released his urgent erection from its painful hold and cupped it with an assurance that made him gasp.

"Oh, God." His breath quickened, and he nuzzled her throat.

"Take me now," she whispered. He pulled back and studied her face. She let go of him, unbuttoned the waistband of her trousers, and lifted her hips, tugging loose.

She was not wearing any panties.

He pulled the trousers off of her and bent to kiss the soft furry down between her legs. "No," she said, pulling him up, over, and into her. "Take me now."

His need for her, and her response to him, was almost overwhelming. After a maddening, almost comic, dash for a condom, Dominic clambered on top of the table and guided himself into her, ramming in deep. She was wet and ready and cried out. She wrapped her long legs around his waist.

It was wild and hot and uncomfortable and crazy. The table groaned beneath them. Dominic tangled his fingers in her hair and glued his mouth to hers. He wanted to make love to her all night long. He wanted to show her so much.

But it was not to be. To his intense surprise and utter humiliation, he was only able to last half a dozen thrusts before he climaxed. Turning his hot face away, he apologized.

She took his face in her hands and turned it slowly back to hers. In the sultry light from the windows and the chandelier, she looked exquisitely beautiful. Smiling, she said, "It's all right. Don't worry about it. It's been a hell of a long time for me, and anyway, we're just getting started. Now, take me to bed, my sweet lover, and let's go back to the beginning."

Chapter Thirteen

Olivia Maxfield sat straight up in bed, heart pounding so hard it felt as if it were going to jump right out of her chest. Somewhere far below, a siren was screaming past.

Another interminable siren.

There was no particular reason for the siren to have awakened her; there had certainly been sirens outside her window in Washington. Her and Max's apartment building was located in a nice neighborhood on East Fifty-fourth Street off Park Avenue; the doorman knew their names; and the streets were very well lit at night.

It was just all wrong, is all.

The easy camaraderie she'd enjoyed with her daughter in Washington had been replaced with a sort of watchful tension. Though they still talked and exchanged warm hugs, Liv sensed that her daughter had withdrawn from her into some private place she was not allowed. It had happened before, after Rebekah had discovered that Gaby was being molested by Gabe but before Liv had completely accepted it as fact.

It hurt. It had hurt then and it hurt now.

Liv threw back the covers and padded over to the window, where she parted the drapes and looked out. In a building across the street, she could see a woman sitting silently in her window, watching Liv watch her. Liv glanced at the clock. Two a.m. She quickly closed the drapes.

Liv found life in New York to be bewildering at best and overwhelming at worst. The bus routes baffled her, and the subway frightened her. She hated to spend the money on cabs and so spent most of her time shopping for groceries in the overpriced corner market and exploring the streets within a few blocks of her own apart-

ment. The crowds and the long lines everywhere gave
her a headache. Gone was the independence and high
spirits she'd possessed during their brief months in
Washington.

They had been replaced by a sort of dark dread. Of
what, Liv could only imagine. She'd carried this feeling
around within her chest like a stone on only two other
occasions: when Richard left to rescue the hostages in
Iran and when Brand shipped out to Desert Storm.

Perhaps it was merely the free-floating anxiety one
often experienced when living in a large city, fueled by
watching sordid and bloody news broadcasts that made
it appear as if horrific crimes lurked around every street
corner, looking for victims.

Or maybe it was the tension she picked up from her
daughter. When Rebekah had joined her mother in New
York the weekend before, the haircut was only one surprising development that Liv noticed. The very air, it
seemed, crackled and sizzled around her daughter. From
her quick outbursts of temper over small things, to her
bitter laugh, to her morose silences, Rebekah's rage
clung to her like a seething black cloud. At first Liv had
feared that Rebekah was angry at *her* for continuing to
see Garrett Sharp. But eventually she had come to realize that whatever was bothering her daughter was much
deeper and far more serious. She tried to talk to Rebekah, but she only evaded her mother's questions and
generally refused to talk about it.

*This is the exact same way she acted right before she
disappeared with Gaby,* fretted Liv as she attempted to
court sleep. Sometimes Liv worried that Rebekah was
plotting to vanish again and join Gaby, but deep down,
Liv doubted it. She couldn't imagine that her daughter
would take such a potentially costly risk.

Perhaps she was just miserable in love, and maybe
now that they were in New York and she no longer had
to work under Dominic's direct supervision, she would
feel more free to act on it. This very night she was supposed to be playing poker over at Dominic's, and the
fact that she was so late returning home *had* to be a
good sign, didn't it?

Unless she got mugged on the way home.

Stop it.

Liv had to admit that her continuing to see Garrett was not helping the situation with Rebekah much, but this was one time in her life that Liv was going to be stubborn. Garrett was good for her, and if her daughter couldn't live with that, well, then, she was just going to have to grow up and get used to it.

So why, *why* did Liv have this awful feeling deep inside, this terrible dread? Rebekah had a great job, they had a good home, Liv was seeing a wonderful man, the boys were doing well, Gaby was safe . . . what?

What?

Staring into the darkness, Liv strained her eyes, as if the answer lurked somewhere up there in the shadows. Another siren wailed down below. Liv squeezed shut her eyes and bit her lip. The answer would not come to her, not when she needed it most.

Experience had taught her that.

Max snuggled up close to Dominic and rested her head on his shoulder.

"Tell me about your mother," she said. "You've never talked much about your family."

"There's not much to tell. It was a typical suburban, midwestern upbringing. I grew up in a town outside Chicago. Dad drove in to the office every day. Mom taught school, so we weren't latchkey kids or anything. Dad died in a car wreck when I was in college."

"I'm sorry, Dominic. That must have been hard on you, so young and all."

"It's something we have in common, I think. Losing our dads at a young age. You know how it changes the entire family dynamics."

She hugged him. After a moment she said, "How many brothers and sisters did you have?"

"Just the one. My older brother."

"So with all those years' difference in your ages and all, you were kind of an only child."

"Kind of."

She played with the curly hairs on his chest. "I can't imagine life without my brothers. I mean, I've been forced to now, but when we were kids growing up. I can't imagine not having had them."

"What's it like, being the only girl in a family of big brothers?"

"Noisy." She laughed. "I guess I learned how to think like a man. And I've got a lot of traits that might be considered masculine—I'm very competitive, for one thing. Very outspoken. And I like guy things, like electronics."

"They didn't try to take over and run your life?"

"Oh, yeah! Of course! I learned to be tough and fight for my space." She laughed again. "But it's always been this kind of warm and fuzzy, *protected* feeling, you know? That I've got these brothers out there who love me and who would be there for me in a heartbeat if I needed them."

"So if I break your heart, they'll come and kick my ass?" he said lazily.

"Something like that." She hesitated. "So . . . how did you come to be working for Garrett Sharp?"

"I applied for the job."

"Very funny. C'mon, you know the story of my life. Time for a fair exchange of information." She tugged at the hairs between her fingers.

"But it's boring! You won't like me anymore when you find out how dull my life really is."

"Try me."

"I was working for another electronics firm here in New York, and Sharp sent a headhunter over and stole me."

"What were you doing when this alleged theft occurred?"

"Working on the assembly line."

She sighed. "Dominic."

"Oh, okay, okay! I was doing sweeps."

"Where?"

"Does it matter?"

A sharpness to his tone caught Max by surprise. "Well, no. I was just curious, is all."

He was silent for so long that Max began to wonder what she'd stumbled onto. Finally he said, "I worked for a firm that was employed almost exclusively by the Giancani family."

"You mean . . . You don't mean . . . I mean . . . *organized crime*?"

"I'm not a wise guy, if that's what you're wondering."

"No, you just worked for them."

He sat up and pulled away from her. "Somebody has to. Their money's as good as anybody else's. They hired our firm to sweep their residences and their businesses and we did it. Period."

Max wasn't so sure about the money part. Mob money was not "as good as anybody else's," not as far as she was concerned. Not when it came from racketeering, illegal gambling, prostitution, and drugs.

C'mon, old girl, she thought. *You're a big girl. You went into this with your eyes wide open. You knew he was a crook from the beginning. Why play all sweet and innocent now?*

"Dominic—" She reached for him.

"I'm going to take a shower," he said without turning toward her. As he got up, his naked body was in silhouette to the city lights from outside. It was a beautiful male body. The buttocks were small and firm, the legs long and lean, the shoulders broad. She had explored every inch of it, and it was still not enough for her.

He walked like a dancer, full of sinewy grace, into the bathroom, and she lay on the bed and watched him. Desire for him was already beginning to build within her, burning between her legs and throughout her body. It was shameless and made her forget who and what he was.

She could hear water running in the bathroom, and then the pulsating thud of the shower. She would surprise him in the shower. Then he would forget his irritation at her, and nothing else would matter. Untangling his sheets from her legs, she got out of bed. She seemed to remember his rummaging through one of these drawers for a condom before they made love in the bedroom. Max pulled open a drawer in the black, high-gloss, ebony dresser. Underwear, neatly folded. She closed the drawer and pulled out another one. Plastic credit cards rattled around in the drawer.

Wait. Not credit cards.

Turning toward the window's city-light nightglow, Max withdrew one of the cards from the drawer, and peered closely at it. It was a driver's license, but it was not a driver's license for Dominic Antonio. The photo on the laminated plastic appeared to be Dominic, but the name was not his.

The name on the California driver's license was "David Shumaker."

With a trembling hand, Max dropped the driver's license back into the drawer, and that's when she could see what had been rattling around. More driver's licenses under different names. Social Security cards. Credit cards. Other forms of identification.

Not one of them said "Dominic Antonio."

Chapter Fourteen

"What are you doing?" said Dominic.

Max jumped and turned from the dresser. Smiling, she said, "You caught me," and held out her hand. A condom nestled in the palm.

The shower was still pulsating full-strength; Dominic was standing dripping wet in the doorway of the bathroom, and she couldn't see his face because it was backlit and turned toward the darkened bedroom. "I was going to surprise you in the shower," she added.

After a pause he said, "Maybe we won't need it." Though she strained to detect a difference in his tone, she found none.

"Why not?"

"Come here and I'll show you."

Once Max was standing naked beneath the warm water, and Dominic's arms were around her, she forgot why she'd ever been nervous in the first place.

She remembered on the way home. They'd both wanted her to stay, but Max didn't feel right about leaving her mom home alone. She knew her mother was uncomfortable living in New York, and it worried Max. Everything had changed since Washington, and Max felt responsible. Her mom had always understood that a transfer to New York was inevitable, but Garrett Sharp had given her little time to prepare for it.

So Dominic called her a cab. Before walking her down to the street, he reached into a drawer on the nightstand, and pulled out a compact, shining semiautomatic pistol.

Max stood motionless and stared as he ejected the magazine. With smooth, efficient movements, he checked the clip, snapped it back into the custom grip, jacked back the slide for a quick glance, pressed the safety, and tucked the gun into the waistband of his trousers. "My Smith and Wesson M6906," he said with a cocky little know-it-all grin. "Nine millimeter."

Pointing toward his crotch, he added, "By the way, they always do this in the movies, and it's the dumbest thing any human being could ever do. But I'm working on the assumption that we won't run into too many bad guys on the way downstairs and that I don't need to bother with my holster for this quick little trip."

She swallowed. This was the real world. It was not a movie. This was her lover, who had once worked for the Giancanis. Now he was working for a man who was making a fortune by defrauding his own innocent, trusting clients. (And friends, if one were to count Senator Kane.)

This was her lover, a man of many names. And she did not know the real one.

Within the rabbit warren of offices that made up the WMFO (Washington Metropolitan Field Office) was the office of the SAC, which overlooked the sluggish Anacostia River. Agent Jack Underwood had been summoned to the office by the special agent in charge himself, Wade Barrows, a tall, well-spoken black who had once been an All-American wide receiver for Northwestern. Barrows, unlike many SAC's, was well-liked among the rank and file. He was known to be fair, but the word was that if you got on his bad side, he could be ruthless.

He didn't keep Underwood waiting long and didn't waste much time on preliminaries.

"Jack," he said, regarding the nervous agent over the steeple of his long fingers, "you're in charge of EAVESDROP, aren't you?"

"Yes, sir." Underwood shifted his weight in his chair. The SAC knew full well who was in charge of every investigation in the WMFO.

"I just received a phone call from the director that I thought might interest you."

Underwood swallowed.

"Seems he got a phone call himself, from Senator Truman Kane. You know him?"

"Kane?" Underwood stalled. "Only from the media. I don't know him personally."

"Well, he's got an idea that Garrett Sharp is bugging his offices and selling the information to Kane's political rivals. Do you know anything about that?"

Underwood's mouth went too dry to swallow. *Maxfield!* She must have told the senator. Well, if there was one thing Underwood had learned in all his years in the Bureau, it was how to lie.

"No, sir. I wasn't aware of that."

"Don't you have Sharp under surveillance?"

"Yes, sir, but these bugs can be extremely easy to plant. He could have done it during a social occasion with the senator."

"A social occasion at the Capitol?" Barrows pressed.

"Well, those offices are open, you know."

Barrows scowled at him. He tried not to squirm.

"What about your informant? What's her name . . ." Barrows glanced down at a file on his desk. "Rebekah Maxfield. She know anything about it?"

"No, sir," Underwood lied without a blink.

"You've been on this case, how long, Underwood?" Barrows consulted the file and answered his own question. "Six months."

"Yes, sir."

Barrows leaned back in his chair and fixed keen black eyes on the uncomfortable agent. "What can you tell me to update this?" He tapped the file with one long finger.

"Quite a bit, actually. Um, Maxfield has been promoted to the New York office and will now be working directly under the supervision of Garrett Sharp. Up until now she's been a trainee, so she's had little chance to observe the illegal planting of devices or the theft of information or extortion of clients. That should all change now that she's in New York."

"I see."

Underwood could feel the slow, hard throb of his heartbeat in his throat. He made a Herculean effort not to appear nervous or insecure, not to jiggle a knee or clear his throat or talk too much or too fast.

"All right, then, Underwood. I want you to move to New York."

Underwood sat bolt upright. "You mean . . . be transferred to the New York FO?"

"No. You'll still be working this case from the WMFO, but I want you to get up there and stay up there until we can close this goddamned case, do you understand that?" His tone had changed dramatically.

Abby would shit bricks.

"Um, sir, um . . . That could take two or three months, at least, and—"

Barrows got to his feet and towered over Underwood. "I don't give a shit if it takes two or three more *years,* Underwood! I want this case *closed,* do you understand?"

Underwood tried not to cower. It was hard. "Yes, sir. I understand."

"I'm sick of this fucking around, you hear? The senator's on the director's ass, the director's on my ass, and do you know who's going to be on *your* ass, Underwood?"

Underwood nodded.

"You fuck around with me on this, and I guarantee you'll find yourself off the case doing background checks in Tyson's Corner. *Do I make myself clear?*"

The SAC was referring to the mind-numbing boredom of running background investigations on various political appointees—a chore that fell to the Tyson's Corner, Virginia, resident agency and used up three of its eight squads for no other purpose. Nobody *ever* volunteered for such an assignment.

Underwood said, "Perfectly clear, sir."

Barrows sat back down. Still frowning, he said, "I've spoken to the New York SAC. He's going to loan you a couple agents to help out. I'll expect daily reports from you, Underwood, and I want them sent straight to me."

"Yes, sir."

"All right. Good luck."

He was dismissed. Underwood rose onto wobbly legs and headed gratefully for the door.

"Underwood?"

He stopped and turned, trying not to telegraph his reluctance through his stiff back.

"You do good on this thing—please the senator and

all—it'll be a feather in your cap, know what I'm saying?"

Underwood nodded. He knew very well what the SAC was saying. Not that he had to be told. This was a career-making case, no doubt about it. It was also a career-breaking case. It could land him in an office like this or it could deposit him in Tyson's Corner.

He returned to his small, overstuffed, windowless office, and stared at the wall for a very long time. No matter how he looked at the situation, there was absolutely no positive spin that he could put on it that would even placate, much less please, his wife. She hated the Bureau, and he was beginning to wonder sometimes if she hated him.

Finally, he decided that there was nothing he could do but get it over with. He crammed some reports and other things into his briefcase and left the office, telling the secretary who handled him and three other agents that he had to go home to tend to a personal matter and that he could be reached there.

In spite of the fact that he'd left a little early, traffic was tourist-congested and maddeningly slow. Still, he managed to make it home before dark, which was early for him. Along the way, he stopped and picked up some flowers and a bottle of Beaujolais to soften the blow.

The girls were eating supper, and bounced from their chairs in happy surprise to see him, falling over themselves like eager puppies to get in the first hug. He looked over their shining heads to meet Abby's eye, holding out the flowers as he did so.

She was smiling but suspicious. "What's going on?"

"I just thought I'd come home a little early," he hedged as the girls settled back into their chairs around the kitchen table, their eyes glued to the tiny portable TV perched on one corner.

Abby eyed the flowers. "Are we being transferred?"

"No! No, of course not. We're not being transferred." He handed her the flowers, kissed her, and began rummaging in the drawers for a corkscrew.

"Bottom drawer," she said absently, sniffing the flowers.

He found the corkscrew there and started working on the cork.

"Jack."

He glanced up.

"I know you're trying to butter me up. It's the only time you ever get me flowers. Either that, or when you want to apologize." She made no move to find a vase or even to unwrap them.

He concentrated on the wine bottle. "I've just been working a lot lately." He began to withdraw the cork.

"Jack."

The cork came out, dripping red like blood.

"Quit screwing around and tell me what's going on."

"Nothing's going on. It's just—"

"Ahh." She turned away. "I knew there was a *just*. Within the Bureau, there's always a just."

He stood slump-shouldered in front of her, gazing at her stiff back. "It's just this case—"

"Yeah, I know. It's always just a case." She turned back and gazed at him with hardened eyes.

"They want me to go to New York. Just until we close this case—"

"And how long will that be, Jack?" Her arms were crossed rigidly over her small-breasted chest, the flowers dangling limply from one hand.

He shrugged. "A few months."

"A few months? A few months!" Her voice had risen to a shrill stridency. Three little faces instantly turned toward them.

With a significant glance toward the children, he placed his hand on her elbow. "Calm down."

"I will *not* calm down! You have *no right* to ask me to calm down!" she shrieked, her eyes wild.

"Kids, go on into the den to watch your program," said Jack, directing them toward the small room at the rear of the house, where he liked to escape to watch ball games.

"But, Daddy, we're not finished eating," said Bethany, the youngest.

"Take your plates with you," he said, not taking his eyes off his wife's.

Without argument, the three girls gathered up their plates and cups and filed quietly out of the room.

Poor kids. Poor all of them.

When the girls were gone, Jack said, "Abby, it's New York. It's not the Mideast. I can commute on my days off. You can even come up once in a while, bring the girls if you like—"

"When you pack your bags," she interrupted, "take more than just enough clothes for a few months."

"Wh-what?" A cold fist closed over his heart. He was having trouble breathing.

"If you insist on upsetting this household *yet again* because of your job, Jack, then you can do one of two things. You can quit the Bureau, or you can get out."

"I can't quit the Bureau," he blurted.

"Fine. Then, you can damn well quit this marriage."

Underwood could not believe what he was hearing. He stared stupidly at the wine bottle, still in his tight grip. "Abby, I don't want to get a divorce."

"Well, I do." She spoke firmly, with no quaver, no tears, in her voice.

"You can't do this to the kids."

"Do what? They hardly know you anyway."

A knife to the gut wouldn't have hurt him more. "That's not true."

"It is true. You work all the time. By the time you get home, they're in bed. They won't even miss you."

Underwood blinked at his wife. The lights in the room had gone suddenly dim, and he was afraid he was going to pass out. He clung to the wine bottle and tried to take a deep breath. He'd never dreamed, when he first married her, that she would ever be capable of such cruelty.

"I love the girls, Abby. And I love you."

Her face softened. "Then, quit that godforsaken job, Jack! It is not your life! We are."

But they both knew that wasn't true.

"Don't do this," he pleaded. "I swear, when this investigation is over, I'll—"

"Move on to *another* investigation." She lifted her chin and narrowed her eyes. "And then another one. Hell, Jack, I could compete with another woman better than I can compete with this damned job. Have you ever spent time at a Bureau function, talking to other Bureau wives?"

Of course he hadn't.

"If their husbands are ambitious and on the management track, they will move twenty times over the course of a career. They will move no matter how happy their kids are in school or how well they're doing. They'll move more than an army family. And when they get into a new house, which they have to start all over again, fixing up—they can be sure they'll hardly ever see their husbands, because the guys are gone all the time on Bureau business. I can't do it, Jack. I just can't. You've got to make a choice here: me and the girls, or the Bureau."

His eyes filled with tears of frustration and pain. A long, pregnant moment passed between him and his wife, a wordless moment in which everything that had to be said was said. The infinitesimal thread that had bonded them together for better or for worse was severed during that moment. He saw the break. He saw it in her eyes.

And he was helpless to do anything about it. Because deep, deep inside, the miserable truth yawned dark and wide in his soul: his wife was right. He did love his job more than he loved her. He couldn't give it up, not for her, not for anybody.

He couldn't.

Then she gave a small nod and said, "Fine."

With a last angry gesture, she flung the flowers at him. In reaction he grabbed for them—and knocked the wine bottle to the floor. It hit the side of the cabinet with a tiny explosion, splattering bloodred wine and dark shards of bottle glass all over the floor, followed almost instantly by the flowers, which scattered apart as they fell, and finally, lay dying and bruised amid the wreckage of Jack Underwood's marriage.

"I miss the boys," Liv said morosely. It was Sunday afternoon, and though she'd been prowling restlessly around the apartment all day, she'd refused an offer for Max to take her to the Metropolitan Museum of Art.

"Why don't you go to Dallas for a visit, Mom? I'm sure Clark and Jennifer and the kids would love to see you."

Her mother shook her head. "They're all so scattered out now. Zane is all the way out in California, Clark in Texas, Brett down in North Carolina. I just don't have a family anymore." Her voice broke.

Max put an arm around her mother's shoulders. "I miss them, too," she said with a sigh. "Come on, Mom. Let's get out of the house."

"I don't want to go anywhere."

"Nonsense. It's a glorious Sunday afternoon in New York City. What could be better than that? Did you realize that Trump Towers is just around the corner, Radio City Music Hall and Rockefeller Center are just a few blocks away, and we're within a quick walk to Central Park?"

"Okay," her mother said reluctantly. "But I'm not going to take my good camera. It might get stolen."

They left the building and walked into windy, sun-splashed streets. Uptown New York on a Sunday had a different feel to it from the rest of the week. The office buildings were closed and all the obsessed, nerve-thin young turks who worked in them and dwelled in the suburbs gone. Most of the people left were urban natives, and they cruised the streets casually in T-shirts, sweats, and jeans, pushing baby strollers, walking dogs, window-browsing, and nodding at each other like insiders to a really good joke.

It took only a few minutes to reach the park, and they entered through a lovely plaza, where they passed a lady selling balloons from a colorful clutch that danced in the breeze over her head. A horse drawing a hansom cab clippity-clopped past them. Max nudged her mother and pointed. "That's John Kennedy, Jr., on Rollerblades."

"No! Where? Are you sure?"

"Mom, who could mistake that face?"

"Oh, my. Just right out here with everybody?"

Max laughed. "Why not? He lives here, too." She took her mother's hand affectionately.

"I'm glad you brought me," said her mom.

"We can explore for the rest of our lives and never

discover everything New York has to offer," enthused
Max. "You'll learn to love it, I know you will."

Her mother grinned up at her. "I didn't know you
liked it so much here."

"Gabe brought me a couple of times when we were
first married. I always thought it would be a great place
to live if you could afford it."

"And now you can."

"And now I can." Max smiled.

After a while Max's mom began to grow tired, so Max
deposited her on a bench and went in search of an ice-
cream stand. She found one at one of the park entrances
and had just ordered two Fudgsicles when a familiar
voice said, "Max."

She started like a guilty felon and whirled about. Jack
Underwood was standing behind her in jeans and a Penn
State T-shirt.

"For God's sake, Underwood!" she cried. "I'm off
work today; why can't you be?"

He looked terrible. Dark circles ringed his eyes, and
his whole face seemed to droop. She noticed he'd missed
a small patch while shaving.

"What the hell's wrong with you?" she said, not without sympathy. "Are you sick?"

"My wife left me," he blurted.

Max blinked. She paid for the Fudgsicles and handed
one to him wordlessly. He took it, tore off the paper,
threw the wrapper in a nearby trash can, and started
eating the cold treat as if he'd missed three meals.

"I'm sorry," Max said. "I really am." She felt badly
for the guy. Not that she didn't still despise him, but
she'd never wish this on him. For a moment Max considered telling Underwood about the disk she'd discovered
right before leaving Washington, the one implicating her
ex-husband with Garrett Sharp and the arcane reference
to FRE R403.

Maybe Underwood could actually help her bring down
Gabe. At the very least, he could help her figure out
what FRE R403 meant.

Underwood shrugged. "Technically, she kicked me
out." He bit off a huge chunk of the Fudgsicle and said
around it, "In any event, I'm here now in New York,

for no other reason than to fry Garrett Sharp. That means you've got to get off your pretty little ass and get me some usable information or I will make your life a living hell." He swallowed, licked the stick, and tossed it into the trash.

Max could feel the sticky chocolate melting off her Fudgsicle and onto her hand.

She felt a sudden chill. Fumbling for a tissue, she wet it with a little of the water, and wiped off her hands.

"By the way," continued Underwood. "I ran a check on your boyfriend. Thought you might want to know that Dominic Antonio does not exist. Not in any computer anyplace that I could find. Not in the Department of Motor Vehicles of any state, not in the Internal Revenue Service, not in the Social Security Administration, and not in the NCIC," he said, referring to the National Crime Information Center. He was studying her face as impassively as an entymologist might regard a cockroach. "You might want to think about that the next time you're giving him head."

Max turned her back on Underwood, paid for a fresh Fudgsicle for her mother, and walked away without another word. One thing was for damn sure. She would never feel sorry for Jack Underwood again.

And she would never, ever trust him.

Liv could tell the minute her daughter handed her the ice cream that something was wrong. Her whole manner was jerky and angry.

"What's wrong?" she said.

"Nothing." Rebekah stared straight ahead, turned her stony profile to her mother.

"You were gone an awfully long time. Did anything happen?"

With a long-suffering sigh, Rebekah said, "No, Mom. Nothing happened, okay?"

"Okay." Liv took a dainty lick of her Fudgsicle. Cutting a sideways glance at her daughter, she said, "Didn't you want one?"

"Huh? No. I mean, yes, I did. I had one already."

"Before you came back?"

"I didn't want to drop yours," snapped Rebekah. "Okay?"

"Okay," Liv repeated. After a moment she said, "Do you want to walk some more?"

"Sure."

They got up and strolled along. "Thank you for the ice cream," said Liv demurely. "It really hits the spot."

Rebekah looked at her as though her thoughts were a thousand miles away. "I'm glad," she said.

They departed from the main path. Liv discarded her stick into a trash can, and they wandered onto a winding, rocky, tree-crowded trail. Presently they arrived at a burbling brook, and Liv posed for a snapshot on the little wooden bridge arched over the brook. Then she made Rebekah pose. Through the viewfinder of the small camera, her daughter seemed so infinitely sad. Liv didn't know what to do or what to say. Clearly, something had happened in her daughter's absence, but she'd gone straight back to that private place of hers and stuck up the "no trespassing" sign. Liv was shut out again.

"When you're so sad like this and I don't know why, it breaks my heart," said Liv.

Rebekah stared at her. "I'm not sad, Mom."

"You are. Something is worrying you terribly, but you won't let me help you."

"Oh, Mom." Rebekah stared over her mother's head and then said, "It's just some work-related problems. Honestly. And there's really nothing you can do to help me."

"Are you sure?" fretted Liv.

"I'm sure. And I'm sorry if I upset you. I didn't mean to, believe me."

They walked in silence for a while, then Rebekah said, "Let's catch a cab at the park entrance. There's a great restaurant overlooking the plaza at Rockefeller Center."

"You mean where the ice-skating rink is?"

Rebekah laughed. "It's only an ice-skating rink in winter, Mom. In summer, it's an outdoor restaurant. We'll shop for souvenirs to send Clark's kids."

"That sounds like fun." Liv was beginning to perk up. "I used to love to buy little surprises for you kids when we would travel to exotic places."

"I remember." Rebekah seemed to be relaxing somewhat, getting over whatever had angered her, and Liv was glad of that.

"It got harder, of course, as you got older. And that Zane. I just never know what to get him anymore. I stopped being able to buy good gifts for Zane when he became such a computer nerd. I just don't know anything about computers. But that Zane, he's just a genius. You give that boy a floppy disk and a keyboard, and he's just in seventh heaven . . ." Liv stumbled to a halt. Rebekah was standing in the middle of the sidewalk, staring at her as if she'd just sprouted horns and a tail.

"Rebekah? What is it?"

Her daughter's mind was whirring like a top—Liv could practically see the gears shifting.

"Oh, my God, Mom. You are a living, breathing genius, and I am the world's largest dumbass!" She laughed aloud and picked Liv up right off her feet and swirled her around like a rag doll.

"Stop it! Put me down! Have you lost your mind?" People were staring. But Rebekah was hooting and hollering and wiping tears off her cheeks.

"What in the world? What is it? What?"

Her daughter said, "The answer was right there in front of me all along, and I was deaf, dumb, and blind to it."

Liv laughed a little, uncertainly.

Rebekah shook her head. "Just last night, I was telling Dominic that my brothers would be there for me in a heartbeat if I ever needed anything." She beamed at Liv.

"Of course they would, honey. You know that."

Rebekah threw her arms around her mother, which prevented Liv from reading her face or even understanding all of what she was saying. All she could hear was something like, "And, boy, do I ever need them now."

Which, of course, made absolutely no sense whatsoever to Olivia Maxfield.

Chapter Fifteen

As soon as Dominic had seen Max safely into the cab and on her way, he'd headed straight back into the building, up to his apartment, and into the bedroom as quickly as he could. Snapping on the light over the dresser, he yanked open the drawer with all the false ID's in it and stood for a moment, concentrating. At no time had Max given him any indication that she'd seen the ID's. At least not that he could tell.

Cursing his stupidity and carelessness, Dominic took the pistol out of the waistband of his pants and tossed it onto the bed. Then he pulled the drawer from the dresser and dumped the cards onto the bed next to it. The scent of her perfume lingered on the tangled sheets and distracted him with memories of her body writhing beneath him.

Dominic never brought women to his apartment. Never. Nothing that had happened between them that evening had been planned. From the desk by the window, Dominic took a large brown envelope. Scooping the cards into it, he taped it shut, drew an X through the tape, and stuck the envelope into the hidden drawer where he kept the key for his safety deposit box. He'd put the envelope into the drawer at the bank first thing Monday morning—something he should have done long ago, when he first assumed the Dominic Antonio identity. Then he picked up the pistol, double-checked the safety, and put it back into the nightstand drawer. Only then did he flop back onto the bed and allow himself to think about her.

He could kick himself six times over. What had he been thinking? He couldn't get entangled in a relationship now—not with her, not with *anybody*. It was a luxury he could not afford. In his business love was dangerous. Love could get you killed.

"Oh what a tangled web we weave," he muttered, "when first we practice to deceive."

What the hell was he going to do about it? Now that Max and his work had somehow gotten all balled up together; he couldn't stick her into some convenient little compartment in his mind, the way he could stash his various identities in a bank box, and walk away.

He couldn't walk away, period. That was the problem.

Every day the problem became bigger and bigger. Soon it would be unmanageable.

And that's what scared him.

At Monday's board meeting, Dominic had trouble concentrating. He wondered how much Max knew about the real dealings of CovertCom. There was no indication on her face that she was aware of anything untoward, but then, he'd seen her play poker.

"Now, moving on to the next item on today's agenda," droned Sharp. "I'm making one little change in staffing assignments. I'd like Max to work with Hakeem Abdul for a while."

Max's chin jerked toward the Boss.

"Well, you've been working in close proximity with Dominic for some time now," purred Sharp, "and Hakeem's specialty is phone systems." He smiled. "I thought it would provide you with an excellent opportunity to pick up some pointers from Hakeem on telephone surveillance and countersurveillance measures." He turned to Abdul. "Hakeem, does that meet with your approval?"

"Certainly, sir. It would be a pleasure to work with Max." He nodded toward Max.

Sharp glanced toward Dominic. It was an involuntary gesture, a betrayal by body language of his hidden agenda: he was punishing Max for his humiliation at her hands during the Saturday night poker game.

As the Boss guided the meeting to other matters, Dominic risked a glance Max's way. Her expression was again impenetrable, but when she caught him staring, she quirked one eyebrow delicately, and he knew then that she did indeed understand what had just taken place. Fortunately, she was smart enough to say nothing about it.

Dominic hid his own disappointment—and his worry. Evan Ryder was an occasionally volatile presence, no doubt about it. Sebastian Taylor was a shameless hound dog when it came to women. But Hakeem Abdul was a loose cannon. There was something murky about him, a secretiveness, a look in his eye of a man who could be deadly when crossed. When Dominic looked into Abdul's eyes, he saw something coiled, something best left unprodded. Around Dominic, at the office and on the job, he was highly skilled and unfailingly polite, even ingratiating. But whereas Taylor and Ryder would clown around or relax somewhat, especially after a few beers, Abdul never let down his guard.

Then there was the little matter of the poor guy who needed a quarter to call his wife. Hakeem's reaction proved that he could be violent with the least provocation. Even worse, Dominic suspected, Hakeem hated women.

If Dominic had worried about Max before, he had been able to mitigate that worry by the knowledge that he was always around to keep an eye on her. He still did not have any idea how she would react once she fully understood how CovertCom operated. Would she take some sort of moral high ground, threaten to bring the law down on them, show *disloyalty*?

Max still didn't know about Joe Dalton, who had disappeared after working for them for a month or two. She didn't know about the Boss's Faraday cage, tucked back in a secret room in his penthouse. There was so much Max did not know. And it could get her killed.

Dominic was still pondering these depressing thoughts when the door slammed back against the wall. Instinctively, Dominic shoved back his chair and sprang up on the balls of his feet, his hand automatically poised inside his jacket.

Jason Crandall and Osamu Smith, the two wiry young men Dominic remembered from Imagitoys, Inc., shoved their way into the room almost abreast of one another, with Rose Peterson fluttering impotently in the background, disapproval etched all over her face. Crandall, his face thunderous with barely contained fury, hurled an object onto the table, provoking the rest of the people sitting around it to scramble to their feet.

But it was not a grenade, after all; it was a toy. Dominic peered at the toy. It was an action figure, some sort of plastic heroic character about six inches tall, clad in desert camouflage fatigues with a black beret cocked over one eye, arms and legs crouched in a pugilistic pose, face twisted in a grimace not unlike Crandall's.

Before anyone could speak, Smith tossed another object after the toy. It appeared to be a remote-control device.

"Check it out," snarled Crandall, gesturing toward the toy. "The brand-new remote control action figure, Recon Viper, guaranteed to turn this year's toy season on its ear." He glanced at his partner for backup.

"It'll revolutionize toy sales and sweep the market in time for Christmas," added Smith, his eyes stone-cold black slits in his angry Japanese face.

"Nobody's seen anything like this since Barbie dolls," said Crandall, his voice curdled with bitterness. "It'll sell more than the Cabbage Patch Kids."

Smith and Crandall exchanged glances. Smith said, "Maybe we should have brought two of them, Jason."

"Yeah," said Crandall. "We should have thought to bring Viper's enemy, Abdul the Desert Rat."

Dominic looked over at Hakeem Abdul. There was a dark glint to his eye, but he said nothing.

"This lady and these gentlemen could see for themselves the brilliance of both toys," continued Smith, "how the action figures can be manipulated by the remote-control devices to fight with one another, shoot at one another, whatever the kids want them to do."

"Oh, don't worry, Osamu," added Crandall. "They can see for themselves when Stratego Toys blitzes TV with their commercials and saturates the market with their promos in a few months."

Dominic gave an uneasy glance toward Sharp. His face was impassive as the two younger men vented their rage and frustration.

"You sons of bitches," said Crandall. "We trusted you, and you screwed us over."

"Gentlemen," said Sharp, gesturing toward the chairs around the table. "Please, why don't you take a seat and tell us what this is all about."

Placing the palms of his hands squarely on the polished glass table, Crandall leaned forward and said, "Oh, I think you know perfectly well what this is all about."

"We paid you a fortune," interjected Smith. "A *fortune*. We had to beg our bosses to do it, but they did it because they believed us when we told them that you guys would make sure there were no bugs, no way any of the rival toy companies could have even a whisper of what Imagitoys was developing."

"But I guess we were too trusting," said Crandall. "Either you missed a few in your so-called sweep—"

"Or you've been screwing us to the wall all along," broke in the more suspicious Osamu Smith. "It has occurred to us that the company we hired to protect us from industrial spies could very well be spying on us itself and selling our precious virgin product to one of the biggest toy manufacturers in the goddamned world, who could of course rush production and get the thing out before we could even introduce it to the Toy Fair in February."

Crandall balled up a fist and smashed it onto the hard table. "You *ruined* us! Do you understand that?" he shouted. *"We're ruined in Toyland!"*

Garrett Sharp, his voice soothing and calm next to the wild and furious accusations of the two young toy men, said, "Do you have any proof of this?"

Smith and Crandall exchanged uncomfortable glances.

"Not exactly," muttered Crandall.

Without a blink Sharp glanced around at the Spy Squad assembled at the board table. Some had taken their seats. Some, like Dominic, still stood. "Do you see what I was talking about earlier? Why it is important to sweep not just the offices of a company that suspects industrial spying, but the homes of certain key employees as well?"

Smith's jet-black eyebrows came together between his eyes. "What are you saying?"

"I'm saying that not everyone in a given company is entirely trustworthy. They could be displaying admirable loyalty on the job, and then going home and spilling company secrets to the highest bidder."

Crandall's jaw dropped. He reached up a nervous hand to tuck a loose strand of hair behind one ear. "Are you saying Imagitoys was betrayed by one of its own?"

Sharp said, "It's possible."

"That's preposterous!" cried Osamu Smith.

"Is it?" asked the Boss. "People have been known to sell out intelligence personnel within our own government—actually have them killed—for money."

Crandall's face flushed darkly.

"The first place the government looks for moles," added Sharp, "is at employees who have shown signs of financial distress over previous months, which would make them vulnerable to the machinations of a foreign government. Or, conversely, they look at employees who suddenly seem to be displaying conspicuous signs of wealth not commensurate with their salary."

Osamu Smith stared straight at his colleague. "You moved into that nice new apartment," he said ominously, "and took that vacation to Disney World."

"I told you! I sublet that place from my uncle! It's rent-controlled!"

Smith crossed his arms over his chest. "I suppose Disneyworld is rent-controlled, too?"

"No, but my credit cards are all maxed out now, because I took my girlfriend and her kid there this summer, so what?" Crandall's expression telegraphed all sorts of righteous indignation. "What? You're going to turn on *me* now? What's the matter with you?"

"What's the matter with *you*? You're moving into new apartments and taking nice vacations when we've got our whole *futures* on the line here?" Smith's tone grew nasty.

Crandall rolled his eyes. "*Our* futures? I thought we were talking about the future of Recon Viper, maybe, or even the future of Imagitoys." He shook his head. "Get a life, man." Gathering up the toys from the boardroom table, he headed for the door.

"Imagitoys *is* my life," murmured Osamu Smith. As

he leaned over the table, his shoulder-length hair fell forward in a silky black curtain. Without looking at anyone, he said, "I suppose I owe you an apology. We are both very upset. This has been an extremely stressful situation." As he straightened, he stared sadly at the Boss and said, "Mr. Sharp, I pray you are wrong. But if you are right . . . well, I just don't know what to think anymore."

With that, he walked out of the room, closing the door softly behind him.

That night Max met her brother Zane where she always met him: in a private chat room of a fanclub newsgroup on the Internet. For this meeting they'd chosen a *Star Trek* forum.

She opened the conversation the same way she always did: "How's Gaby?"

"She's doing terrific," he answered. *"She's excited about starting school. She's already met her fifth-grade teacher at the American school and loves her. She's been saving up all her report cards to show you whenever you are finally able to meet."*

Tears blurred Max's eyes as she typed, "Fifth grade. I can't believe it."

"I know. Me, neither. Her caretakers want you to know she's taller than anybody else in her class. Hey, sis sounds like somebody else I know."

Nodding through her smile, Max ignored the tears that plopped onto the computer keyboard. Same thing that always happened. It was a wonder the thing didn't short out on her. She typed, "Does she know I'm out of prison now?"

"You kidding? I made sure she knew that first thing. She's so proud of you, Max. We all are. She knows you're in New York now, and she asked if you would get her a replica of the Statue of Liberty."

"Consider it done." Max sobbed as she typed, a common reaction to every conversation with Zane. "I'll save it for the time she can show me her report cards."

"Max—I've been asking around as per your request."

"What have you found out?" Max grabbed a tissue and blew her nose.

"Hacker friend of mine who got busted by the feds and served a little time in jail says that FRE is a legal term. It stands for Federal Rules of Evidence."

Max frowned. She couldn't believe she hadn't made that connection. But then, why would she? "So R403 must mean Rule 403."

"Sounds logical."

"I wonder what rule that is, and what it has to do with Gabe."

"You're asking the wrong computer nerd, sis, but I know somebody who could help you find out."

"Who?"

"Dummy. Think about it."

"I'm too tired to think!" She plunked out a little emoticon to show her displeasure: :-(

"LOL," said Zane, referring to the on-line abbreviation for "laugh out loud." He was laughing at her, and she was not getting the joke. *"Boy, you MUST be tired,"* he added. *"It's not like you to be this stupid."*

"Been a long day," she typed in irritation. This was so like Zane, to toy with her and make her guess rather than just coming right out and saying it. They'd never gotten along when they were kids.

"I'll give you a hint: Brotherly love."

"WELL, YOU'RE MY BROTHER, AND I'M NOT THINKING VERY LOVING THOUGHTS RIGHT NOW!" she typed, jabbing the keys and using all caps to indicate shouting.

"Hahahahaha."

This was the problem with on-line communications, seethed Max. You could not do bodily harm to the person with whom you were conversing.

Then she stared at Zane's "hint."

Oh, man . . . She really was tired . . . or maybe she really was stupid. "I get it now!" she said, her fingers flying over the keyboard. "I get it!"

"About time. Now, go call him and ask what he thinks."

"I don't dare," she said wryly. "Phones are probably tapped."

"Okay. I'll ask him, then. My big brother Super-Clark,

Attorney at Law, can leap tall torts with a single bound. Besides, he owes me a favor anyway."

"What kind of a favor?"

"Don't ask."

Max rolled her eyes. The magic her brother could coax out of a computer often left the other members of the family thunderstruck. It was a wonder Zane hadn't served a little time himself for some of his hacking antics. They chatted awhile longer, discussing Zane's work and their mom, and set up their next cybermeeting, at an *X-Files* site for groupies and fans of that cult science fiction television show. Like most hackers, Zane loved sci-fi and fantasy. As for Max, she felt it pretty much suited her life.

By the time Max disconnected she was beginning to feel something she hadn't felt in a very long time: hope.

The feeling carried her along on a certain buoyancy for several days, a good mood that was probably fueled as much by her affair with Dominic as anything. Knowing she would be able to see him every single day almost made her forget what she was supposed to be doing. Almost.

But then she came home from work one evening a few days after the Imagitoys blowup to find her mother skipping about like a child. "Come look what Garrett gave me! Come look!"

Max followed Liv over to the living room windowsill, upon which set an exquisite little dish, shaped like a leaf with a butterfly perched on top. The glass was as delicate as spun sugar, and multicolored, reflecting sunlight like a rainbow.

"It's pate de verre glass," said her mother. "Isn't it just scrumptious? I admired it in an antique store, and of course Garrett insisted on buying it for me."

"It's pretty, Mom," said Max. "That was nice of Garrett."

Her mother's eyes sparkled impishly. "But that's not all," she said. "Look what was nestled inside the dish." She held out the palm of her hand.

Max stared at a gold butterfly pin encrusted with dazzling rubies, sapphires, emeralds, and yellow diamonds in a filigreed wing design so dainty it appeared ready to take flight.

"Isn't it just the most gorgeous thing you've ever seen?" said her mom, tilting the pin to make it sparkle in the sunlight. "And it's real. The jewels I mean."

"Mom. Have you lost your mind?"

"What are you talking about?" Her mother was still smiling at the pin.

"This is way too expensive! Mr. Sharp must have spent thousands of dollars. You can't accept a gift like this from him."

The corners of Liv's mouth turned downward. "It's not too expensive for Garrett. Pocket change. And I'm keeping it." Then she turned on her heel and walked away.

Yet another miserable confrontation with her beloved mother over this man's manipulation of their lives. Max was sick of it. She was sick to death of all of it.

She would get Jack Underwood his evidence. And she would do it soon.

Saturday night, while the men gathered at Sebastian Taylor's for the requisite poker game, Max, wearing a hooded windbreaker over her trademark blond hair, jeans, and sneakers, showed her office ID to the night watchman, and took the silent, solitary elevator to the CovertCom offices.

She'd explained to Sebastian that she had cramps and would have to beg out of the game. Predictably, he had winced at such an intimate female revelation, and predictably, he had remembered his inglorious defeat at Max's hands the previous Saturday night, so predictably, he gladly promised to make excuses for her.

She would deal with Dominic later.

Letting herself into the office with her own key, Max stood for a moment in the shadowed foyer, thinking. Zane had explained to her that no matter how paranoid a business might be, they had to depend on the *people* who ran it to maintain security, and most people were notoriously lax. Hackers ("social engineers," as he called them), for example, would masquerade as, say, telephone company or maintenance workers. This would

allow them to invade an office and find top-secret pass-
words on Post-It notes, stuck to the back of the main-
frame computer; keys to locked drawers Scotch-taped to
the bottom of open drawers next to them; security codes
penciled on a scrap of paper and actually stuck to office
bulletin boards in full view.

The CovertCom computers and fax machines ran all
night long, depending upon what was going on at offices
around the world and in different time zones. Its workaholic personnel frequently worked into the night, or returned to the office after a brief stop at home or dinner
at a nearby restaurant. Consequently, the inner offices
were seldom locked. In fact, Max had specifically chosen
Saturday night as the only time she could be reasonably
certain that she would not be interrupted by a rambling
Spy Squad member.

She went straight to Garrett Sharp's office. It was
locked.

Frustrated but undaunted, she headed for Rose Peterson's desk. Rose, she was certain, would have a key
to the Boss's office. Taking a seat at Rose's swivel chair,
Max rummaged through the drawers until she found a
small key chain full of keys.

It took six tries, but one finally worked.

Max's sneakers made no sound on the plush carpet as
she slipped through the door, locked it behind her, and
crossed to Garrett Sharp's crowded desk. The office,
high over the muffled streets below, was so quiet Max
could hear the ticking of a clock and the thumping of
her heart.

The nighttime view out the wall of windows was
breathtaking. The black water from the East River far
down below reflected the city lights off its glossy surface,
while the lights from the Fifty-ninth Street Bridge hung
suspended over the river like the spangled diamonds of
some giant, gaudy bracelet.

Max turned from the view and clicked on a small
study lamp on the desk. Sharp's black leather chair
scrunched as she sat down.

She had absolutely no idea what she was looking for.

Pulling out one drawer, she poked through some papers, then tried another drawer. The desk didn't seem

to have anything very interersting, so she tried the file cabinets. They were locked. When none of Rose's keys worked, Max searched around for a hidden key and found it in a potted plant.

The first drawer she pulled out was stuffed with files. One of them read, *Imagitoys*.

Max began to breathe faster. Plopping down onto the carpet, she spread the file folder out before her and sorted through various computer printouts.

No.

Transcripts.

These were tape-recorded conversations that had been transcribed. Fumbling through the pages, Max followed along until she came across what must have been the records of a meeting in the research and development department of Imagitoys, Inc., concerning the specifics involving a proposed remote-control action figure.

It appeared to Max that those specifications had been replicated almost exactly by Stratego Toys in Mr. Recon Viper and his archenemy, Abdul the Desert Rat.

Heart throbbing in her throat, Max reached inside her windbreaker and withdrew the portable document scanner she'd carried with her.

Underwood was right. She had a few spy gadgets of her own.

So intense was the ferocity of her concentration as Max worked the document scanner, with its eerie green light, over the pages in the file on the floor, that she was not aware that someone had entered the CovertCom offices until she heard the sound of a key jingling in Garrett Sharp's office door.

Chapter Sixteen

In one electrifying, heart-stopping moment, Max leapt to her feet, doused the light, and grabbed up the file, papers and scanner, crushing them to her chest, which left her a breathless half second to plaster her body against the wall just behind the door as it swung open.

In the spare, minimalist office, which relied on the view for decoration, there was absolutely no place to hide.

Her body had gone into full-fledged adrenaline-rush flight-or-flight response. Heart clanging away in full alarm, blood pumping to the roots of her hair, Max stood deer-still as the door yawned open and thumped gently against her breasts. Out of the corner of her eyes, she could see that the file cabinet drawer was still agape, and she clenched her teeth while a thousand lame excuses raced through her mind.

If she was caught on a Saturday night in the Boss's locked office with an armful of files and a document scanner in hand . . . there was, quite simply, nothing she could say.

What would they do? Would they kill her?

Squeezing shut her eyes, Max concentrated on breathing with painful, slow silence.

And then she smelled it, and the scent was a shock to the senses.

Dominic.

She would know that fragrance anywhere. She didn't know the name of the brand, or even whether it was aftershave or men's cologne, but whatever it was, it was distinctively Dominic.

What was he doing here?

He wasn't looking for her, was he?

She waited.

If he closed the door, she was caught.

The small desk light snapped back on. Max stood perfectly still behind the open door. She could see nothing from where she was.

The leather chair scrunched as he sat down.

She waited.

The sounds of computer keys clickety-clacking came to her, along with more chair movements, followed by a gentle whirring, which lasted only a few moments.

Max's helter-skelter grip on the files in her hands was slipping. A sheet of paper worked its way loose and drifted down to the floor at her feet. A corner of it jutted beneath the door.

If Dominic looked down when he closed the door . . .

The chair scrunched again, and the light went out. The subtle scent of her lover came to her again as he passed through the doorway. Now she could see a slice of him through the door crack by the hinges. If he turned his head, he would see her, too.

The door swung away from her with a slight draft of air, connected, and then she heard the key in the lock again.

Trembling violently, Max sank to the floor and relaxed her grip on the files and the document scanner. She had no way of knowing if Dominic was still in the CovertCom offices or if he'd left. She dared not turn the light back on again; it might show beneath the door.

Leaning her head back against the wall with the exhaustion left in the wake of panic, Max stared blindly out the wall of windows at the city nightscape. What had Dominic been doing, and why? Could Sharp have sent him to the offices on an errand?

Not likely.

Was he double-crossing Garrett Sharp?

Nausea gripped Max's stomach; she tried in vain to calm herself. If Dominic was undercutting the Boss in any way, he was a dead man, Max was sure of it.

But he had used a key.

So had she.

But she'd taken hers from Rose Peterson. Where had Dominic gotten his?

Maybe he was some sort of trusted lieutenant of the Boss, and had been given his own key by Garrett Sharp himself.

Max's nerves were stretched as taut as frayed rubber bands. She felt dangerously close to snapping. Nothing made any sense, and she was scared.

She was very scared.

Jason Crandall was hot, sweaty, and pissed off. Weaving his bike between two yellow cabs, he bumped up over the curb, dismounted, and picked up the bicycle in his arms along with his baseball bat and mitt. His softball team had just gotten the shit kicked out of them, partly because their star pitcher, Osamu Smith, had finked out so he could stay home and pout.

Crandall clanked and banged his way into the front door of his apartment building. The damn helmet didn't fit properly, and sweat drooled beneath it, down his temple, and along the side of his face. He pressed the elevator button. It was a muggy and hazy Sunday afternoon in New York, but it was still a welcome change from work, which had grown decidedly chilly and stormy.

He had not yet been fired, but Crandall had a feeling that it was just a matter of time. He wondered how many of their coworkers had heard the shouting between him and Osamu Friday afternoon. Crandall could not believe that his old friend had actually accused him of being on the Stratego payroll! The man had lost his mind. The whole situation with CovertCom, the Recon Viper, and Stratego Toys had just made Osamu crazy.

Stumbling from the elevator, Crandall rolled his bike down the corridor to his apartment and let himself in. He was thirty-two years old, and he felt like sixty-five. He and Osamu had worked their asses off on the Viper, weekends and nights—but it hadn't felt like work. They'd been that excited about it. They'd known from the beginning that this was going to be the toy that would set them up in Toyland for life.

Instead, it had damn near destroyed them.

Leaning his bike against the living room wall by the front door, Crandall tossed his bat and mitt onto the nearest chair. Then he went over to the sputtering wall unit air conditioner, turned it up, and banged on it. Flinging his helmet onto the couch, he held his face in front of the air-conditioning vents for a few moments, then headed for the shower, stripping off his clothes as he went and throwing them onto the floor. Hell with it. It was one of the joys of living alone.

A long, cool shower and change of clothes restored his spirits somewhat. While heating up a can of chili, he drank a whole quart of Gatorade, and ate the chili straight from the pan in front of the TV.

The apartment grew dark, and Crandall turned on a light or two so it wouldn't get too depressing. When the buzzer sounded from downstairs, he wondered immediately if it might be Osamu, come over to make amends. He hoped very much that that was the case.

"Yeah?"

"Mr. Crandall, this is Hakeem Abdul. From CovertCom."

Crandall hesitated.

"May I come up? I'd like to talk to you about something concerning Stratego."

Crandall's stomach turned cold. Maybe this guy was here to rat on CovertCom. Maybe he'd be able to salvage this thing after all. Visions of high-dollar lawsuits, of vindication, danced in his head.

"All right." He pressed the release button.

When the quiet knock sounded at the door, he was waiting. Through the peephole, he could see Abdul standing there in a suit, tie, and trench coat.

Crandall wondered how the man could stand the trench coat in the heat. He unlocked the door and let him in.

Abdul stepped inside quickly, almost furtively, and he did not immediately make eye contact with Crandall or offer his hand. Instead, his eyes darted around the room as though he was looking for something. Crandall felt uncomfortable, but he wasn't sure why. He told himself he was being ridiculous.

"What's this all about?" he asked. His voice sounded nervous, and he cleared his throat.

Abdul took a couple of steps and stopped in front of the chair, but he did not sit down. "I have some information that might interest you," he said. "It concerns your business with CovertCom."

Crandall nodded. The man's eyes were so dark that they were unreadable. Crandall's discomfort grew. He had an unreasonable urge to flee, to get out, to run.

He started to offer Abdul a seat, but thought better of it. He wanted this man out of his home, and the sooner the better. With increasing nervousness, Crandall regretted letting him in in the first place. There was something creepy about the way Abdul was looking at him.

"I have proof that CovertCom cheated you and your partner, that they planted bugs at Imagitoys when they were supposed to have been sweeping for them, and that they sold the information to Stratego."

Crandall's heart leapt in his chest. *He knew it!* This was just the kind of information he needed to get himself out of this mess, even if the Viper was lost to them forever. He and Osamu were a team. Without this black cloud hanging over their heads, they could start over, they could think of another incredible toy!

Struggling to hide his elation from his face, he said, "Why are you telling me this, Mr. Abdul?"

Abdul said, "Because it is the last thing you are ever going to hear."

"What?"

The word left Crandall's lips even as he caught the blurry sight, just out of the corner of his eye, of the baseball bat—his own bat—whizzing through the air and connecting, *Crack!* with the side of his head.

Abdul was wrong, after all. That crack of his own skull splitting open was the last thing Jason Crandall ever heard.

A highly public place would be an unexpected meeting venue, Jack Underwood decided, so the next time he met with Max, it was at the top of the Empire State Building on a windy Sunday afternoon. Dwarfed skyscrapers bristled all around them and stretched out into the distant haze to the Hudson River. On the horizon across the river a molten ball of sun shone weakly through the mauve smudge of smog and clouds. Late August, and you could look right at it.

Underwood didn't have much use for New York.

Max had stuffed her hair under a cap, and was wearing an *X-Files* T-shirt with the program's trademark slogan emblazoned on it: *Trust no one.* On the back of the shirt was the phrase: *The truth is out there.*

A throng of tourists speaking German and snapping pictures crowded around them, and they moved wordlessly to an unoccupied corner of the observation deck. She placed a Bloomingdale's sack at her feet between them and turned away for a moment, busying herself with one of the telescopes that ringed the deck. Underwood picked up the sack and glanced inside. It was stuffed with documents.

A thrill of excitement jetted through him, and he smiled. *Finally,* they were getting somewhere.

While peering through the sight of the telescope, Max said, "Transcripts."

He could barely hear her and leaned close to her, as if they were looking through the scope together. He could smell her perfume and tried not to think about it.

"Intercepted conversations carried on in meetings of clients who hired us to do sweeps. I got what I could from files in Sharp's office, but the only one I could testify to is the Imagitoys file."

"Were you in on the sweep?"

"No, but I was at the meeting when two of the employees, Jason Crandall and Osamu Smith, burst in and accused CovertCom of stealing info on a new toy and selling it to Stratego Toys."

Underwood turned his face toward hers. *"Toys?"* he muttered.

He felt a momentary crush of disappointment. This was just plain silly. Toys. Christ.

"Imagitoys hired CovertCom to do a sweep of their offices while a hot new toy was in R and D. Supposed to be the most dramatic breakthrough in toys since Barbie."

He sighed. "Okay."

She narrowed her eyes at him. "I thought you had kids."

"I do."

"You never fought off a delirious crowd two days before Christmas, trying to get your hands on the last hot whatever-it-is that your kid absolutely has to have?"

"Well . . ."

"What do you think your kids would do to get hold of a remote-control action figure?"

"I have girls."

"Underwood—"

"All right, all right!" He laughed, holding his hands out in surrender. "You're right. I'm wrong. There, now. Happy?"

She frowned.

He said, "Look, you're right, okay? I realize we're talking millions of dollars here—maybe even billions, in the long run."

"You have no idea. These toy companies are *killers*."

"I don't suppose you have the tapes."

"What tapes?"

"The tapes from which these transcripts were taken?"

"Oh, yeah, right! I almost forgot!" Sarcasm dripping from every word, she stalked away from him in supreme frustration. He waited. After a moment she came back.

"Look, Max. This is great—it really is. I'm not trying to be an asshole—"

"You don't have to try. It comes naturally."

He stopped and studied her face. She was trying not to laugh.

"Okay. So I am an asshole. However, I need more."

"How much more?"

"As much as you can get."

"It's too late for Imagitoys. I mean, I wasn't there when they did the sweep—"

"I understand. But the next time you run a sweep with Dominic—"

"I'm not with Dominic now. Mr. Sharp put me with Hakeem Abdul."

Underwood hesitated. "Why?"

"Who knows why?" She blushed and turned away. In the distance the pewter river reflected the lavender sky.

After a moment he said, "Abdul's the phone man, right?"

"Right."

He pursed his lips. "That'll be tougher. He won't be planting mikes in phones."

"Not necessary with hookswitch bypasses."

"Right. Hmmm. Can you tell when a phone's been altered in that way?"

"Yes, but I'd have to come along after him and check—I'd have to take the phone apart and look for myself to see if he bypassed the hookswitch."

That could be dangerous. If Abdul caught her jimmying around with a phone after he'd finished with it . . .

"Tell you what," said Underwood, "if you suspect that Abdul has set up surveillance through a phone line, call me and I will send out one of our guys to check it out. They'll be able to tell. All you need to do is let me know."

"That won't work, Underwood."

"Why not?"

"Because when a hookswitch has been manipulated for that purpose, using a Zener diode bypass, it does more than just wiretap the phone. The transmitter then acts as an open mike, picking up conversations from anywhere in the room, whether someone is using the telephone or not. All you need to do to listen in is be near a phone line anywhere in the world." She sighed. "If that's even how he did it. There are devices, transmitters, that are designed to look like regular telephone wall jacks, you know, mounted receptacles. There are a number of different ways he could have done it, but they would all have the same end result."

"So?"

"So if your guy comes in—even if he's just acting like a telephone repairman or something—eavesdroppers can hear, be alerted, and get the hell out of Dodge."

"Shit."

"Look, you don't have any choice. I got these papers for you didn't I?"

"Well—"

"From Garrett Sharp's *locked* file cabinet in his *locked* office."

"I'm impressed," he said truthfully.

"So I can check out Abdul's work, too."

Underwood knew that he should insist that she not take such a dangerous risk. But he also knew that if she didn't, they might never make their case. What she had retrieved for him from Sharp's office probably looked terribly important to her, but the sad truth of the matter was that a skilled defense attorney could shred every document with motions to suppress and all sorts of sleights of hand before a jury ever saw them.

He sighed. "Just be careful, will you?"

"Admit it. You'd be sad if I got killed, huh?" she teased.

He grinned. "Well, yeah; the paperwork would be a bitch."

She laughed.

Somehow, somewhere along the line, they had become allies against a common foe.

Underwood turned and gazed out toward the setting sun. For a few moments, while the moist ocean wind whipped and tugged at their clothes and the brassy sun dipped down behind the champagne Hudson, they stood together.

It was nice for a change. Not that it would last.

It took Underwood until almost eleven p.m., working in his little cubicle at the NYFO, to identify, document, catalog, and report on the papers Max had retrieved for him from Sharp's office, or rather, the *copies* of papers. To get the originals would take a search warrant, and Underwood was nowhere near ready to go that route yet.

Wearily, he pushed his glasses up onto his head, rubbed his eyes, and went wandering in search of a good cup of coffee. The NYFO was down to a skeleton crew for weekend duty, and Underwood nodded at some of them as he dragged himself into the break room. A small television set jabbered from a corner. While Underwood rinsed his cup and refilled it, the late-night news came thundering on with its urgent jingle and its if-it-bleeds-it-leads take on the world, or at least the world of New York City. He listened with half an ear while he rummaged in the small refrigerator for some cream. There was a nearly empty carton of half-and-half, clotted.

"The body of twenty-nine-year-old Jason Crandall was found bludgeoned to death in his apartment early this morning—"

Underwood whirled from the refrigerator, coffee mug in hand, and stared at the TV.

"Neighbors have reported hearing a quarrel between Crandall and his friend and business associate, Osamu Smith, earlier that evening. Officers who questioned Smith about the murder then received permission from Smith to search his apartment, where they reportedly discovered a bloody baseball bat in his bedroom closet. The bat—and Mr. Smith—are now in police custody . . ."

Forgetting all about the cream, Underwood channel-surfed for a while, looking for more information on other affiliates, but they had all moved on to other stories. Mug in hand, he hurried down to his cubicle, picked up the phone, and asked the operator for the voice-mail extension of an agent he knew, name of David Young, over in the violent crimes squad of the NYFO.

After waiting impatiently through the multiple rings and the computerized drone informing him that Young was away from the office and to please leave a message at the tone, Underwood said, "Dave? Jack Underwood here. Listen, I need you to find out anything you can about the murder of a guy named Jason Crandall. Manhattan borough, I think. His death could have a direct bearing on a case I'm working on out of the WMFO. The sooner you can get back to me, buddy, the better. Thanks. Oh—there's a case of beer in it for you if you're a good boy." With a chuckle he left his extension number and hung up.

Underwood took a sip of coffee, scowled at the bitterness, and sorted through the papers on his desk that Max had given him, as if there were some clue there which would answer all the questions clamoring around in his mind.

Underwood realized that he was trembling; caffeine-overdose jitters, probably. Adrenaline rush.

Or could it be . . . *fear?*

Not for himself, certainly, at least not at this point in the investigation. Right now he was basically invisible to the bad boys.

But not Rebekah Maxfield.
She was right out there in the open.
A moving target.

Dominic was dozing through an old *Magnum, P.I.*
rerun on late-night TV when the intercom squawked.
Frowning at the clock, he shuffled over to the intercom
in his bare feet and a pair of running pants. "Yeah?"

"Dominic, it's me."

"Max! What are you doing here this late! Get your
ass up here before you get mugged." He buzzed her up
and hurried through the apartment, turning on lights as
he went. Even before he pulled back the grille, he could
see that she was crying.

"What the—" She flung herself into his arms before
he could say anything else, and he held her for a moment, stroking her hair, while she trembled and wept
against him.

"What's wrong, honey? Is it your mom? Are you all
right? What is it?"

"Those two toy guys . . ." she mumbled through her
tears.

"Toy guys? Oh, you mean the guys from Imagitoys?
What about them?"

"Jason Crandall's dead. Osamu Smith beat the crap
out of him with a baseball bat, and now he's dead."

"What? Where'd you hear that?"

"On the news. Don't you watch the news?" She pulled
away from him and walked off a little bit, dabbing her
face with a damp and raggedy tissue.

"Well, usually, but . . ."

"Dominic." She turned and stared him full in the face
as if she were about to say something, then hesitated.

"What?"

She seemed to make some inner decision. "It's our
fault, isn't it?"

"Who's fault?"

"CovertCom."

It was all Dominic could do not to flinch. "What are
you talking about, Max?" He kept his voice carefully
controlled, betraying nothing.

"Osamu Smith was right, wasn't he? We bugged their

offices and sold the plans for Recon Viper to Stratego, didn't we?"

This was it. The big showdown. On the one hand, Dominic was relieved that she'd brought her doubts to him and not to somebody like Hakeem Abdul. On the other hand . . . there would be no turning back now.

"We did." She turned away from him. "I can see it in your eyes."

Dominic wanted to say something but didn't know what would be the safest approach, not until he had some sense of how she felt about it. "Max?"

She turned back, and her eyes were veiled. The poker player, back in the game.

It saddened him. He said, "What if we did? What if I told you that's what CovertCom does with most of its clients?" He swallowed. "What if I told you we were all crooks?"

With a sigh and a shrug, she said, "Dominic, where do you think I've been the last seven years?"

"I know where you've been."

"All right, then. Surely you must know that I didn't just come in from some small town in Middle America, all gaga over the big bad city."

"What's your point?"

"My point is that I'm not naive—"

"Nobody said you were."

"I mean, I've known something . . . wasn't right . . . from the beginning."

Dominic frowned. "From the beginning? What do you mean? I never broke any laws or asked you to during training in Texas or in Washington." He didn't mean for his voice to come across so sharp and suspicious, but there it was. She could not have possibly known, could she?

"It wasn't you," she said. "It was Garrett Sharp. That first day, in prison, when he offered me a job." She stared at her hands and said dreamily, "I was planting bluebonnets in one of the prison flower beds. And they said he'd flown in all the way from New York to offer me a job."

"Why is that so hard to believe, Max? Surely you must realize how good you are at what you do."

She shook her head. "No, it wasn't that. It was him. I just knew it was . . ." She looked up, straight into his eyes, and said, "I just knew it was too good to be true."

He read absolute truth in her voice, her face, and her body language. He didn't think it was a bluff. He said, "What did you tell him?"

Smiling a little at the memory, she said, "I told him it was too good to be true."

For a moment Dominic stared at her, then he laughed. Nobody else would dare say such a thing to a man like Garrett Sharp. "What changed your mind?"

She turned away and walked over to the window. "My mother. She was so excited about the offer, and she had been through so much on my behalf all those years . . . I just couldn't bear to disappoint her."

He nodded. Sounded reasonable. "She's never suspected . . . anything?"

She gave a short, bitter little laugh and said, "You kidding? The woman's bedazzled by Garrett Sharp. I mean, who wouldn't be? He gave her a butterfly."

"Huh?" Somehow they'd shifted subjects; it was the one trait of women he could never seem to adjust to.

"A butterfly pin. Covered in precious jewels."

"Oh."

"He does stuff like that all the time. In Washington, he took her on a helicopter tour over the city at night."

"What's wrong with that?"

"Nothing. Everything." Her voice had dwindled down to a very small, soft, sad trickle.

Dominic went to her and put his arms around her. She swayed into his body, and they stood together by the window for a long moment. He wanted to protect her, shelter her, take her away from all this.

But he couldn't. Not anymore.

Chapter Seventeen

"Goddammit," mumbled Hakeem.

Since it was unusual for the man to say much of anything around Max, she found the expletive to be quite dramatic and moved a bit closer in order to see what ailed him. "What is it?"

"No remote service port."

"Oh," she said. "That's bad, isn't it?"

Frowning as he worked, Hakeem grudgingly educated the ignorant woman. "It means I will be unable to call the remote service port, log in as a service technician, and have them activate the spare pair for service observing," he said. He was referring to the spare pair of telephone lines available in many telephone connections, which are often never used, thereby providing a perfect circuit for a wiretap.

"And bypass the hookswitch that way," she guessed aloud.

He made no response to her comment, which she took as a yes. Hakeem, she had observed, squired many beautiful women around town on his arm and was himself possessed of great charm—but Hakeem, she was certain, had nothing but contempt for them. She assumed he was of the Muslim faith, but she had never seen him practice the five-a-day prayers the devout never missed, kneeling on their prayer rugs facing east, nor had she ever heard him make a remark such as, "It is the will of Allah."

She strongly suspected that the only will in Hakeem's life was his own.

Of the Spy Squad members and other CovertCom employees Max had met, Hakeem was the only one who, at some primal level, frightened her.

They were examining the phone systems for X-Tech,

Inc., a company that manufactured sophisticated X-rays and other devices for security purposes. X-Tech had hired CovertCom because new Federal Aviation Administration regulations had dictated that the nation's largest international airports use the new and costly mass spectrometer machines. These machines were capable of "sniffing" nitrogen compounds present in all explosive devices, from TNT to PETN, thereby detecting plastic and other explosives that did not show up on standard X-ray machines, as a deterrent to terrorism. Consequently, the few companies capable of manufacturing the expensive machines were involved in a bidding war for the coveted airport contracts.

X-Tech wanted to guarantee that its bid would not be undercut by foreign or other manufacturers.

Max and Hakeem were standing in the unair-conditioned basement of a high-rise office complex that was home to the X-Tech offices, and she was holding a flashlight for him while he rummaged around in the wiring closet, where all the telephone trunk lines from the building were routed. They were both wearing coveralls over their dress clothes, their jackets removed and left behind in the van. To her, the many-colored plastic-sheathed lines were as bewildering as a multilaned L.A. freeway—and the destination just as mysterious—but Hakeem seemed to see them the way a weaver might see threads of yarn in different hues: the pattern was in his head.

"Okay," he muttered. "Tie-line trunk."

Sweat drooled off Max's face and tickled her armpits. She gathered from Hakeem's mumblings that the phone system relied on a trunk connecting two PBX's, or Private Branch Exchanges. Tapping such phones was not impossible, but it was more complicated than a phone system connected to a central exchange, and required more equipment. Hakeem was going to have to pick and choose specific telephone instruments to wiretap. Considering the nature of this business and the bidding war, Max guessed that he would pick several key fax machines.

Though the home offices for X-Tech were located in New York, the factory itself was in Plano, a suburb of

Dallas. The engineers down in Texas would be faxing bid suggestions and updates daily to the brass in New York and vice versa before the final decision was arrived at.

This was a lucky break for Max.

A facsimile machine, or fax, worked by scanning a document and converting it into a series of electrical signals. These then transmitted over a telephone line to a receiving machine, where the signals were converted back into an identical copy of the original document.

"Ahhhh," muttered Hakeem. "The faces are on dedicated analog lines."

"Which means we can set up a high-impedance bridging connection in another office somewhere in this building," Max volunteered. She gathered from Hakeem's answering grunt that she was correct.

He said, "Why don't you go now and see about leasing office space?"

In other words, "Go away, little girl, ya bother me."

But Max was nothing if not agreeable. She was used to being underestimated and, if anything, encouraged it. It was her strong suit, especially with an Armani-clothed pig like Hakeem.

A couple of days later, they'd set up an "office" in the same skyscraper that housed X-Tech—replete with a couple of folding card tables, some chairs, a computer, a telephone, a fax machine, a coffeemaker, some Styrofoam cups, and the sophisticated STG Facsimile Intercept System, which fit in a standard briefcase.

Max called X-Tech and told the official with whom they were working that CovertCom was sending along a fax to them to test the integrity of their machine and to please be watching for it. They were more than happy to comply.

After the fax went through, Hakeem called CovertCom. "We're sending you the X-Tech test fax," he said. As the normal-looking slip of paper vanished, he said, "Did it go through? Okay? Good," and hung up without saying thanks.

Max watched the entire process very closely. She thought she caught Hakeem making a tiny but significant mistake, but she said nothing. Not only would he scorn any advice from the dumb-blond female, but she never wanted to give away her advantage with a man like Hakeem Abdul.

"The handshake was negotiated," he mumbled, telling her something so obvious as to be insulting, but of course she made no response. "I'm setting up this monitor to capture all the faxes they send and receive on a hard drive. We can check it whenever we want and print up what we like."

"Good idea," she said with fake admiration, smiling through her teeth.

"Would you get me some coffee?" he asked. "Black, no sugar. I'm, uh, busy."

"Why, sure, Hakeem," she smiled. "No problem."

For Max, this would be the first hard evidence she would have to provide to Agent Jack Underwood of illegal acts performed by CovertCom. Once the wiretaps were in place and the STG Facsimile Intercept System running, it would then be up to Max to get her hands on hard proof that would hold up in court—proof such as secret in-house X-Tech bidding information faxes which would be covertly obtained by CovertCom and sold to a rival company. The rival company would then use the information to undercut the bid and win the coveted airport contract.

In some ways, Max hated what she was taking part in, the duplicity with and deception of the X-Tech people, who trusted CovertCom and, by extension, Hakeem and Max herself. She was taking part in a fundamental betrayal of that trust, which could have very serious repercussions for the business and for the people who worked there. The only way her conscience could justify that betrayal was by Max assuring herself that if she helped bring down CovertCom, they wouldn't be able to double-cross any other businesses. Max understood now that without her help in making the FBI's case, CovertCom and Garrett Sharp might go on unimpeded for years.

She found that she could no longer live with that knowledge, not anymore. It wasn't just about her, or even Gaby. It was about so much more, and in the next few months, every hand she played would be crucial.

*   *   *

"Jack?"

"Yeah."

"David Young, here. You wanted info on the Jason Crandall murder."

"Yeah, David. How ya doin'?"

"Oh, I can't complain. Hey, uh, I heard about your divorce. Sorry."

Jack frowned into the phone. The FBI was the worst small town in the world; it thrived on gossip, rumor, and innuendo. Button-down agents hog-tied by rules and regulations nevertheless entertained themselves endlessly by gossiping about one another, cases under investigation, and pronouncements from on high.

"Thanks, David, but don't worry about it. I'm doing fine." He wasn't, of course, doing fine, but it behooved any prudent agent to make other agents believe that he was. To do otherwise was to draw attention from management, which was the last thing any field case agent wanted to do. "What can you tell me?"

"The Jap swears on a stack of Mama's Bibles that he didn't off his good buddy Jason Crandall. His defense attorney says he'll even hire his own lie detector test. He admits that they quarreled over some new toy their company was developing, but he denies that he killed the guy. Says he doesn't know how that bat got into his closet. Cops say he had the motive, the method, and the means to kill Crandall, but the defense claims it's all circumstantial."

"Oh, yeah? I'm sure he has no idea how that bloody bat got into his closet."

"Just between you and me?"

"Yeah?"

"Cops think the guy's legit. This one homicide detective I know, he says his gut tells him that this guy's telling the truth, but the D.A. wants to go ahead with it anyway."

"Huh. Well, that's really all I needed to know, David. What's your brand of poison?"

"Well, since you're buying the beer, Underwood, make it something imported. I want it to be expensive."

"Gee, thanks," laughed Underwood as he hung up the

phone. It had been a long day. Underwood knew he
needed to go back to his hotel room and get some sleep,
but he found himself filling time the way he did at the
end of every day. He had literally given up his family
for this job, but in all his years of working long hours
for the Bureau, Underwood had never really realized
how much that family had meant to him. On the one
hand, it was a relief not to have to deal with Abby anymore and her angry silences and her furious outbursts.

But he missed the girls. God, how he missed them.

With a sigh, he picked up the phone again and called
an agent he knew who worked at FBI HQ in the white-
collar crime section, Sarah Sandstone. Though it was
early evening, he knew Sarah would still be at work; she
was an ambitious workaholic just like him. They'd been
in the same class at the Academy. The last Underwood
had heard, she was going through her second divorce.

After the requisite small talk, Underwood made his
request: could Sarah get him a list of the most recent
purchasers of Stratego Toys stock? It was a long shot,
but Underwood was hoping to make some connection
between Garrett Sharp and Stratego beyond what little
had been provided him by Rebekah Maxfield. If he
could show a direct correlation between the information
she had copied from Sharp's office and some sort of
personal enrichment of Sharp because of that information, then it was possible that he could make a case for
racketeering. Some of the country's biggest mobsters had
finally been brought down not by murder or other hei-
nous crimes, but by simple racketeering.

It was worth a try, he thought, and Sarah agreed. Because all stock purchases were registered with the Secu-
rities and Exchange Commission, she said it would be
no problem getting him the information he needed.

When Underwood hung up the phone, he was surprised to find they'd been talking a whole hour. Maybe,
when he returned to Washington, he would take her
to dinner.

It was the least he could do.

Max was late for her meeting with her brother Zane
in the *X-Files* fanclub newsgroup on-line chat room.

"Where ya been? I was about to give up on you."

"Working for a living," Max typed, too weary to offer excuses. "What did you find out?"

"Super-Clark sez Rule 403 stands for 'Exclusion of Relevant Evidence on Grounds of Prejudice, Confusion, or Waste of Time'."

Max's heart sank. "What's that supposed to mean?"

"How do I know? He checked it out in the Federal Criminal Code and Rules book. It gives the judge in a federal case wide discretion in excluding certain forms of evidence from trials if he thinks they're a waste of the court's time. He said it might have something to do with Gabe's cases. Told me to check them out on-line in the Federal Supplement or the Federal Rules Decisions. Something about Westlaw and Lexis offering opinions or something."

Max leaned forward, as if she could crawl right through the computer screen. This was something. It was actually something. She typed, "Well, did you check it out?"

"Hey, sis, I'd like to. Really. But I got a life, you know? I didn't have any names of any defendants to do a word search, so I tried one with Gabe's name. You have no idea how many cases that guy has adjudicated. Or whatever the hell it's called. Jesus, Max, it would take days and days to go through them all, and I don't even know what I'm looking for, you know?"

Max grit her teeth in frustration. This was so typical of Zane. She wanted to strangle him. She let out a long sigh and leaned her chin on her hand, contemplating the little blinking cursor, wanting to curse, herself.

On the other hand, how could she expect her computer-hacker brother to plow through hundreds of cases when he really didn't even know what he was looking for?

She thought about asking Clark to do it, then thought better of it. Clark was an extremely busy attorney, himself a family man; unlike Zane, he did indeed "have a life."

Max could call up the cases on-line, herself, but again, it would be a tedious, time-consuming search. What she needed was some direction, some specificity. How, specifically, could "exclusion of relevant evidence" connect federal judge Gabriel Griswold and CovertCom, Inc.?

"Never mind, Zane," Max typed. "Thanks for the trouble you went to. I'll figure something out." They visited awhile longer, then left the chat room and Max got out of the *X-Files* forum. For a while she roamed around cyberspace, exploring different options, coming up empty-handed and frustrated. Finally, she disconnected the modem and turned off the computer.

Her head was aching, and she was exhausted. It was late. Max went through the apartment, turning off lamps and checking locks, then followed the flickering light peeping out from under her mother's bedroom door. She found her mom sitting up in bed, watching late-night television. Max went in and stretched out on her stomach on the bed next to her mom.

"I miss your long hair," said Liv. "I miss brushing it."

"You can still brush it," mumbled Max, her cheek resting against the jumbled covers.

Her mom ran her fingers through Max's hair, and she shut her eyes.

"It's not the same," said her mom. "Nothing's the same."

Max said, "I thought you were getting used to New York, Mom. It's September already. It'll start getting cooler, and the leaves will start to change on the trees. I know you like that."

"I do. It's my favorite time of year."

"Then, what's wrong?"

"I don't know." Her mom sighed. "I've been thinking . . ."

Max waited.

"Maybe I should go to Texas for a while. Visit Clark and everybody. I miss the grandkids."

Suddenly, Max's eyes popped open.

A trip to Dallas might be just the thing.

Why didn't she think of it in the first place? Gabe's federal district court was located in Dallas. She could go straight to the courthouse and find out what she needed to know.

It would not be easy, though. Nothing she did anymore was. For one thing, she had to be extremely careful of drawing Garrett Sharp's attention.

Just as swiftly came the thought, *What if Gabe finds out I'm nosing around?*

If Gabe found out, it could be bad. It could be very bad.

No question about it: Gabe held all the cards. Gabe and Garrett Sharp had Max sandbagged between them. She was a cold player on a losing streak.

And the stakes were very, very high.

Chapter Eighteen

Agent Jack Underwood stared in dismay at the FedEx package that had arrived for him from FBI HQ. Though it had a return address from Sarah Sandstone's office, the damn thing weighed five pounds. Warily he opened the box. It contained computer printouts of every stock exchange that had occurred in the past year, and not just for Imagitoys, but for every business which sold stock.

Angrily, he picked up the phone and jabbed Sarah's number. "What the hell is all this?" he demanded.

"What is all what, Jack?"

"I asked you to send me stock info on one business, Sarah, not the whole friggin' country."

"Well, Jesus, Jack. You ARE an investigator, aren't you? So investigate. You'll get it all sorted out soon enough."

"Soon enough? What, are you nuts? It'll take me five years to go through all this shit."

"Well, golly gee, Special Agent Underwood, it IS your case, isn't it?" She was laughing when she hung up.

Underwood was not amused.

"We're not getting any fucking intercepts!" Hakeem was angry, and Max noticed that when he was angry, his face darkened noticeably. "Why aren't we getting any intercepts?"

They were sitting on folding chairs in their leased "office," checking the fax intercept machine, which they'd set up to trap faxes being sent back and forth from X-Tech's New York office and their Plano, Texas, factory. It had been ten days since the fax intercept had been set up, and Hakeem was pounding on the computer keys as though the harder he smacked them, the more information would appear on the monitor screen.

"This does not make any sense!" he fumed. "We *tested* the fucking machine!"

"What kind of machine does X-Tech use?"

He ignored her.

"Hakeem?"

"Xerox," he muttered, jiggling wires at the back of the fax machine.

"Doesn't CovertCom use Sharp fax machines rather than Xeroxes?"

"Yeah, so what?" He was checking the plugs in the electrical outlets.

"So two different types of fax machines have to go through standard G-3 protocol at the handshake to negotiate before the digital information is exchanged, right?"

He didn't say anything. Probably ignoring her.

"Don't we intercept the data during those little electronic negotiations?"

Busy doing important stuff, he seemed not to be paying attention to the stupid woman.

"Well, I was just wondering . . . I mean, I don't know a whole lot about phone systems, but I was thinking . . . What if X-Tech uses Xerox fax machines at both the factory and the offices?"

He was not looking at her, but he had stopped doing whatever he was doing.

"If a Xerox fax handshakes with another Xerox fax, then they both know right away that they're not going to have to go through the protocol. They both speak the same language, so to speak. So they can zip through a little shortcut instead and bypass the code."

He turned and stared at her.

Widening her eyes, she gave him her best *Duh* expression. "Hakeem . . . If that happens, our fax intercept system would miss the fax, wouldn't it?"

He pursed his lips. After a very long moment, he gave a slight, almost imperceptible nod.

"I don't know anything about it." She shrugged. "But I was just wondering what would happen if we had the same kind of fax machine here in this office that they use company wide over at X-Tech."

With a scornful glance, he turned back to his work and said, "We'd need the make and model numbers off the fax machines at the factory in Plano."

"Well? Why don't we go find out?"

He frowned at her. "You mean break in, Max. I know of no other way we could legitimately obtain this information from the company."

Well, then you don't know very much about social engineering, thought Max, picturing her computer hacker brother. Zane could find out whatever they needed to know in five minutes. Ten, maybe, if he was busy.

But that would miss the whole point, wouldn't it?

She reached over and touched his arm. He recoiled from her as if she meant him harm, and she let her hand drop. *Asshole.* "I'm up for a little black bag job, Hakeem. How about you?"

"I don't know—"

"Aw, c'mon! We could fly down to Dallas, be in and out of the Plano X-Tech factory, and get the fax intercepts going in no time at all. It would be fun."

"It's never fun to get arrested."

"Who said anything about getting arrested? We're the *Spy Squad,* aren't we?" She giggled.

"This isn't a movie!" he cried brusquely, gathering up his briefcase. "You are advocating that we break the law. If we were caught—"

"We won't get caught, though, will we? C'mon, Hakeem. I know you guys have done this sort of thing before."

Snapping shut the briefcase, he said, "Fine, then. I can go to Plano and get the information myself. I don't need the help of a woman."

"Of course not," said Max. "But if you left me behind, Mr. Sharp might wonder if you were trying to hide something from him."

"What?"

She examined a polished fingernail. "This is a paranoid business, you know. And Mr. Sharp likes loyal team players, not lone rangers. I mean, *you* know and *I* know that I wouldn't really know what I was doing, but at

least if I went along on the trip, Mr. Sharp would have
no reason to doubt your loyalty, Hakeem." She smiled.

He stared at her for a long moment. His eyes were
unreadable; cold and dark and shiny as a snake's. Then
he said, "Fine. I will speak to Mr. Sharp about a trip
to Texas."

He walked out and Max followed him, trailing along
behind at a respectful distance, keeping her face a careful blank and her thoughts to herself.

Chapter Nineteen

Dominic encountered Hakeem, overnight bag in hand, in the hallway between their offices. "Where you headed?" he asked, riffling through some mail.

Hakeem smiled. "Just a little black-bag job down in Texas."

Dominic stopped and looked up from his mail. "What are you talking about?"

"We're going down there to complete work on the fax intercept job for X-Tech."

"By 'we,' you mean . . ."

"Myself and Max."

Dominic frowned. "Does the Boss know about this?"

"Approved it personally." Hakeem smiled.

"And I assume Max has been thoroughly briefed and apprised—"

"It was her idea, Dominic," Hakeem said, fixing his dark-eyed stare on Dominic's face.

Glancing around, Dominic stepped into his office and gestured for Hakeem to follow him. Closing the door behind them, he said, "Are you sure this is a good idea?"

"The X-Tech job has presented certain . . . obstacles. This is the only way to surmount those obstacles."

"It's extremely risky, Hakeem. You know we don't do these jobs unless it's absolutely necessary."

"Mr. Sharp seemed to think it was," said Hakeem without breaking his stare. "What is the matter, my friend? Are you afraid I'll make a move on your girlfriend? I find her quite attractive, you know." His eyes were taunting Dominic.

Dominic hardened the muscles of his face, clenched his fists, and stepped to within inches of Hakeem. He was taller than the other man, and used his height to full advantage. He did not touch Hakeem, but every sinew in his body was coiled into a threat. He said, "Let me tell you something, *my friend*. If anything happens to Max; if one hair on her head is mussed, if she is comes to harm in any way, you will have me to deal with, is that clear?"

Hakeem did not flinch or even blink. Without breaking eye contact, he said simply, "Perfectly."

The man had icicles for balls.

Without a word, Dominic turned and sat down behind his desk, busying himself with paperwork. He heard the door open and close.

Why hadn't Max told him she was going to Dallas with Hakeem? On a black-bag job, no less.

Swiveling around in his desk chair, Dominic steepled his fingers and stared out the window at the dying day. The wind was beginning to bluff and bluster, and he could see people down below bending into it like tough little walking trees. A cold front was due in; scurrying clouds were already snagging the highest buildings and draping themselves over the city.

Dominic felt off center and uneasy.

It wasn't as if Max weren't thoroughly capable of looking after herself, not just on the job, but where Hakeem was concerned.

So why did he feel so queasy?

Perhaps the queasiness was due in part to Dominic's growing conviction that the fabric of their little team was beginning to fray around the edges. He had a feeling that it was all going to unravel very soon, but he didn't know why.

Not yet, anyway.

Propelling himself from his chair, he paced the floor restlessly. Yellow lights were blinking on in the street down below. Raindrops scattered across his window like bones rattling.

There was nothing more he could do here tonight. Shrugging into his trench coat and snapping off the desk light, Dominic stood for a moment, watching darkness descend and trying in vain to quell the little fears that gnawed at his gut like vultures, poking and prodding the dead.

As soon as the plane touched down at teeming DFW and Max and Hakeem began negotiating through the crowds to a car-rental booth, the butterflies that had been fluttering in Max's stomach during the flight now swarmed all over her body and broke out across her skin as cold goose bumps. The last time she'd been in Dallas, it was courtesy of the county jail.

Hakeem rented a Buick Regal—big enough that he could ride in comfort but not so ostentatious as to annoy the Boss. The freeway traffic seemed insane to Max, and she was more than happy to let Hakeem drive. He seemed to know where he was going, which was a relief, because Max was hopelessly lost. The freeways tied back into themselves like congested knots, and since it was after dark, the only landmark Max recognized was Texas Stadium. No doubt Gabe still maintained his luxuriously appointed private box and still attended all the Cowboys's home football games. In another century, on another planet, a young and foolishly happy Max had sat beside her husband and cheered on the team, feeling so privileged, so *lucky*.

Hakeem drove aggressively, weaving in and out of traffic like a stock car racer, and the smooth riding Buick was making Max carsick. She was a nervous wreck, and all she wanted to do was get away from him, sink into a hot bath, and think.

No. All she *really* wanted to do was just get away, period. Catch the first plane out of that big, noisy airport, and fly anywhere that was as far away from Judge Gabriel Griswold as she could get. She'd underestimated how frightened she was just being in the same city as her ex-husband.

Stop it, thought Max, staring blindly out the window as Hakeem shot off an expressway ramp, boomeranged around a circle, and rocketed past the famous Hyatt-Regency, with its tower, outdoor glass elevator, and big lit-up ball of a restaurant dominating the Dallas skyline. *Keep your head. This isn't about what-ifs. This is about getting the job done.*

Nausea gripped her stomach; her mouth was dry and gummy; her thoughts racing about like scattered little rabbits. She had to get a grip, or she would never find a way out of this labyrinth; she'd spend the rest of her life bumping into dead ends.

She was beginning to get her bearings again, and could see that Hakeem had skirted downtown Dallas and was heading northeast.

"Where are we going?" she blurted. They were the first words she'd spoken since deplaning.

"Plano," he said.

"But . . . can't we at least check into our rooms first?" Max did not want to tell him how ill she was feeling; she could never display weakness of any kind to Hakeem that wasn't feigned. Like an animal in the wild, she knew that much.

"I need to recon the X-Tech factory by night," he said. "Check out their perimeters and security, make plans."

And I'll baby-sit the car, Max thought dryly. Not that she cared. Hakeem's scorn for her help would be instrumental in getting her to the courthouse without alerting him. She had a few plans of her own to make. She just wished she could make them someplace that wasn't moving at the time.

The drive was interminable. It took them a full two hours to get there from the airport.

The X-Tech factory was not a factory in the traditional sense of the word. It was a slick, sterile building three stories high and tucked back on well-groomed lawns like many other businesses of the area. The streets were spotless, the parking lots large, and the buildings faceless and bereft of personality. The whole effect was one of control and efficiency. Things were constructed here, not on an assembly line, but under a microscope.

Hakeem eased the car slowly past the building, muttering under his breath. "Idiots don't even have a fence. No visible perimeter of security. 'Course, they could have buried seismic sensors or electronic field sensors. Or they could have a microwave system." Pulling into a shadowy section of the parking lot, which was also unfenced and unguarded, he said, "Wait here. I'm going to go check it out." He left before she could speak, one way or the other.

Max did not care. Finally, the car was at rest and she could sit very still and try to settle her tumbling stomach. She wasn't sick enough to throw up, just sick enough to be miserable. Thinking sluggish, weary thoughts, she rested her head back on the headrest of the car.

If this were a poker game, she thought grimly, *I'd fucking fold.*

Gabe was the dealer, and he always stacked the deck.

She drifted awhile and dozed, and when Hakeem opened the car door, she jumped.

"It's so easy my fucking *grandmother* could break into this place," he chortled. "There's glass shock sensors on the windows. Big deal. Who needs to break windows when you can just walk right in the goddamned door?" He backed out of the parking space and headed for the street, his lights off. "There's only one security guard. Do you believe that? *One!* A rent-a-cop who wanders around once in a while when he's not watching TV in the break room. The doors use Sentex Pro-Keys. No sweat."

"How will you break the code?" asked Max, who'd lapsed once again into her duh-which-way-did-they-go voice that she usually used around Hakeem.

A couple of blocks down the road, he switched on his lights and laughed at her. "Why should I have to break the code? It's a standard ten-digit keypad. Pair of binoculars'll tell me what I need to know."

"What if you can't read the keys people are punching?"

He shrugged. "I'll just tailgate."

"What's that mean?"

With an impatient sigh, he said, "You just walk in right behind somebody who's just gone through the door. You step in before the door closes."

"Oh. Won't you need some kind of ID?"

"Not necessarily. There's ways around that."

"Wow," said Max. "This is exciting."

He smirked at her and maneuvered the Regal onto an expressway ramp, jetting in just in front of an eighteen-wheeler. The truck driver blasted his horn, and Hakeem held up his middle finger in the glare from the trucker's headlights as he sizzled past two other slower-moving vehicles.

Max silently prayed he'd get a speeding ticket. She'd love to see the son of a bitch get an ass-chewing from the Boss. She was beginning to despise Hakeem Abdul and strongly suspected that the feeling was mutual.

By the time they checked into a north Dallas Hilton, Max was so exhausted that she took her room key-card from the reception clerk and headed straight for the elevators while Hakeem was still filling out forms and checking them in. Their rooms were on the tenth floor, side by side, but not adjoining, she noticed gratefully as she let herself in, locked the door and bolted it.

Max dumped her things onto the king-sized bed and fell flat onto it, burying her face into a pillow. The car-sickness had passed, but she was so weary she ached, and so frightened she could barely think. They would spend most of the day tomorrow, she knew, staking out the X-Tech factory, and would slip in to retrieve the information they needed after dark. Hakeem would probably want to catch the red-eye for New York immediately afterward.

She had one shot, one little window of office-hours daybreak to somehow get herself all the way back across Dallas, into the bowels of the downtown area, to the courthouse, get the information she needed, and get the hell out of there before either Hakeem or Gabe caught wind of what she was doing.

One misstep and she could lose everything. *Everything.*

Never play to avoid a loss, her dad had said so many years before. *Always play to win.*

Losing, she had been taught, was merely an excuse for giving up.

Chapter Twenty

Max decided to open this round of the game by taking the initiative. Guessing that Hakeem would want to spend the afternoon surveilling the X-Tech factory and the evening break-in, Max knew he would want to sleep in and indulge in a big lunch before leaving for Plano. Trying to sidestep any orders he might give her for the day, she left the hotel before eight o'clock the next morning and dropped off a message for Hakeem downstairs that she'd decided to spend the morning shopping. Since Hakeem had the keys for the rental car and she wanted to avoid enraging him any further, Max called a cab.

She made a mental note to stop and buy something—anything—somewhere before returning to the hotel.

The traffic was heavy; the trip long and nerve-racking. The sky was overcast and dull, with enough chill in the air to put an edge to the day. It was Max's intention to get in and out as quickly as possible to avoid arousing Hakeem's suspicion.

The closer the taxi drew to the downtown Dallas area, the more Max felt a slow, sticky terror creeping up on her. Her hands were shaking from too much coffee and nerves, and it was all she could do not to jump out at a traffic light and take off running. The cab took a turn on Commerce, and before Max knew it, they were pulling up to the big ugly white Earl Cabbell building that housed the United States District Court for the Northern District of Texas.

Max suffered a momentary crisis of confidence. Every man who walked past looked like Gabe at first glance, and she found herself suddenly feeling exposed, even with the short black wig and dark shades she'd hastily donned during the drive from the hotel, much to the cabdriver's bemusement.

Fumbling with the twenties, she shoved two toward the driver and ducked out of the cab as if dodging a bullet.

The courtrooms, she knew, were located on the third floor. Her destination was the office of the clerk of court. As long as she stayed away from the third floor, she should be all right. Max had to look up the clerk's office on a building directory, then submit to a search of her bag from the security guard posted between the two elevator banks. When he was satisfied that she did not carry a cell phone, a camera, a laptop computer, a tape recorder, or a gun, she was allowed to take the elevator. She did not carry a briefcase, just in case Hakeem should waylay her someplace before she made it back to her room and demand to know what she was doing, going shopping with a briefcase. However, her tote bag was enormous and roomy enough for any amount of papers she might wish to stuff into it.

Crowding into an elevator with a bunch of well-dressed and attractive lawyers and other court officials talking shop and wisecracking, Max kept her head bowed and her eyes glued to the floor until she could make her hasty exit. Max's heart racketed against her rib cage every time she saw a tall, trim, graying man round a corner or step out of a doorway. Although she was aware that Gabe would have changed somewhat since she had last seen him almost eight years before, there was no question that she would know him the instant she saw him.

And he, her. In spite of the quickie disguise, she was sure of it. *Nothing wrong with a healthy dose of paranoia when somebody IS out to get you,* Max thought grimly.

By the time she had passed through a metal detector frame outside the clerk of court's office and finally attracted the attention of someone behind a desk who could help her, she was almost stuttering. "Uh, I w-would like to be able to, um, check the case transcripts of one of the federal judges," she stammered to a hawk-eyed woman "of a certain age" with an iron-gray helmet of hair and an ample bosom, who wielded authority and clearly enjoyed it.

"You're going to have to be a little more specific than that, dear," said the lady, looking at her in much the same way Hakeem did. "There are hundreds of cases that are filed in this court each year. I would have to have the name of the judge and the case number." She wore half glasses perched on her nose and peered over the top of them at Max.

"I don't have a case number. I mean, it's not a specific case. It's a judge."

"You want transcripts from every single case a certain judge has tried?"

"Well . . ."

"You know, transcripts are not filed on a case unless it's being appealed or a formal request has been made."

Dismayed, Max stared at the woman. "They don't file court transcripts?"

"Not on every single case, no. You can study motions that the judge hands down on a particular trial, but it won't have transcripts unless it's being appealed or a formal request has been made." She glanced around Max as if she was a simpleton, holding up important business.

"Well, I just wanted to study the cases of one judge."

"Which judge?" the woman asked sharply, as if Max had proposed breaking the law.

"Gabriel G-Griswold," Max said, lowering her voice and glancing around furtively, as if her ex-husband had appointed spies to lurk around, watching for her.

"You want to study all the cases that were presided over in federal court by Judge Griswold."

"Yes."

The woman heaved a long-suffering sigh. "Since when?"

"Since . . . I don't know," Max faltered.

The woman squinted at Max over the top of her glasses as if she emitted a faint but foul odor. "Do you realize how long Judge Griswold has been on the bench?"

"Yes. Uh, ma'am." She tried not to tremble visibly.

The woman shook her head. "Look. I don't have time

for this. You can find this stuff out yourself by using PACER."

Max looked around again, making sure she was unobserved and that Gabe was nowhere nearby. "What's a pacer?"

The woman turned to a computer terminal and began clickety-clacking away at the keys. "It's a software program. Actually, it's an on-line service. Public Access to Court Electronic Records—PACER. You can download docket sheets, party and attorney information, Local Rules, select local forms, and other miscellaneous information. You can sign up for it and find out anything you want to know about any of the judge's cases. It's free to subscribe but costs sixty cents a minute to use."

Max felt time slow down at that moment, like the stop-action slowing of a film. "Can I sign up for it here?" she heard herself asking.

"Yes, but it's not necessary. You can do the whole thing on-line, just like you would sign up for Compu-Serve or America Online or Prodigy or any of the commercial on-line services.

"I can?" Now she was sounding stupid, but her mind was roaring ahead like Andretti at the finish line, and through the cloud of smoke, one fact stood clear: *She could have done the whole thing from her home computer up in New York.*

In other words, she'd taken this terrible risk of being caught by Gabe . . . *for nothing.*

"Ma'am?" asked the woman, her voice cutting into Max's thoughts like a knife through butter.

"Yes . . . I'm sorry."

"Here. Fill out this form. You'll need a major credit card number. You'll get a PIN number, and your account will be immediately activated. After that, you can log on at your leisure, using any PC and modem."

"Um . . . how do I . . ."

"Instructions will be given on-line," said the woman, then leaned forward conspiratorially. Max leaned closer to her.

"Just between you and me and the tree," she said, "the information you're wanting would most likely be in the Federal Supplement or the Federal Rules Decisions, which you can obtain through any of the on-line services at any library, or through the Internet. It would be cheaper than using PACER, but PACER would be much faster. If you used both, you could save a little time *and* a little money."

"Why . . . thank you!" said Max, flashing a genuine and grateful smile. Assessing the woman for the first time since talking to her, Max said, "I'm in law school at SMU, and one of my professors is just *impossible*. But if I don't pass his course, I can't get my degree." She shrugged helplessly.

The woman nodded. "I understand. Both my sons are lawyers."

"Really?" said Max. "You must be very proud."

"Oh, I am." The woman finally broke into a smile.

Max filled out the form as quickly as possible, and handed it to the woman, who gave her an information sheet about PACER.

Stuffing the PACER information sheet into her bag, Max bolted from the office . . . just as Gabe Griswold rounded the corner at the end of the corridor.

It had taken him two days, but Jack Underwood was finally able to compile a list of stock investors for Imagitoys and Stratego Toys. Imagitoys had gone public only a couple of years before and was still a small, tightly controlled company. Stratego Toys was more established. Though it wasn't as huge as Kenner or Fisher-Price or some of the other toy giants, its track record at hitting a market niche and running with it was impressive.

Starting with the Stratego list, Underwood began the tedious process of weeding out; it was one of the most boring—but also the most proven—methods of investigation.

It was unthinkable that a man as shrewd and savvy as Garrett Sharp would purchase stock in his own name. That he might be registered with one of the larger firms was a possibility, but at this point, Underwood wanted to weed out the chance that he may have invested under the name of a DBA—a Doing Business As—or dummy company. Should he find no evidence of that, Underwood would make the rounds of the larger firms, flashing his creds and checking out their client list—such a time-consuming prospect that he actually preferred tackling that dragon later. So this time he started by eliminating the larger, more well-known investment outfits.

He wasn't exactly sure what he was looking for, but he knew that when he found it, he'd know it.

When he had compiled a separate list of company and charitable foundation names that were unfamiliar to him, Underwood began checking them out by looking them up in *Standard & Poor's Register of Corporations, Directors, and Executives* and *Dun & Bradstreet Principal International Business.* Underwood was able to do all of this at his desk, working on-line. He also looked up unfamiliar names in the *Foundation Directory,* which listed all legitimate charitable foundations.

At the end of another long day, when his eyes were getting bleary, his neck stiff, and his hands cramped, Underwood had found only one company invested in Stratego Toys that was not listed in any of his usual sources: Arcanum Trust.

Before bone-weariness finally drove him home, Underwood checked, just for the hell of it, the databases for *The New York Times,* and *Wall Street Journal,* and *Business Week* for any references to Arcanum Trust.

There were none.

And if Underwood's Latin wasn't too wobbly, he seemed to remember that *arcanum* was the Latin root for the word, *arcane,* which meant *mysterious.*

Kicking his chair underneath his cubbyhole desk and yanking his coat off the back of the chair, Underwood had to grin.

A mysterious trust, eh?

He was starting to smell blood.

It took Max thirty miserable minutes to finally emerge from the rest room where she'd hidden and work up the courage to leave the building. She was so afraid of being seen by Gabe that she forgot to call a cab. Rather than return to the hellhole that was the federal courts building, she hurried across the street and used a pay phone inside another building. While fumbling for a quarter, it suddenly dawned on Max that she had filled out a form in which she had put down her full name. Would the suspicious woman remember her as Rebekah Maxfield, or as Max Griswold? The thought turned her stomach to cold jelly.

But she couldn't think about it just then, and there was nothing she could do about it anyway. Right now, she had to get back to Hakeem as soon as possible.

By the time she got back to the Hilton, it was almost lunchtime. She'd forgotten to buy anything and had been forced to make the driver turn around and take her to a mall so that she could grab a few things off the shelves and race back to the waiting cab. Even then, she barely remembered to remove the wig and shake out her hair. Her fare wound up costing almost a hundred dollars.

Shopping bags flying, hair in her teeth, Max fled the cab into the Hilton—to find Hakeem sitting in an upholstered chair facing the entrance, his powerful arms crossed over his chest, his face set in a thunderous scowl.

"Where the hell have you been?" he seethed, jumping to his feet and planting himself directly in the path of the elevators.

"I told you," she said with a dim-witted smile, "I wanted to do some shopping."

She tried to step around him, but he grabbed her wrist and twisted it until she yelped in pain. Yanking the shopping bags from her hand, he dumped the contents right out. Filmy lingerie fluttered to the floor.

"Ach!" With a spiteful kick at the frothy pile and a murderous glare at Max, he said, "Don't you *ever* do anything like that again, do you hear me?"

It was not much of a stretch to feign anxiety. "I'm sorry, Hakeem! I didn't think you would mind." Having read once that a gorilla in the jungle is threatened by direct eye contact, she dropped her glance to the floor.

"You stupid little bitch! This isn't a vacation! We're here to get a job done! Now, take that crap to your room, pack your stuff, and get your ass back down here in five minutes," he snarled. "We're going to Plano, and I want to be ready to get the fuck out of there and head straight for the airport when the time comes, you got that?''

She nodded. "Okay, but um, Hakeem? It might take me ten minutes."

"Just fuck off," he growled. *"Now!"*

Hurrying toward the elevator, Max could hear Hakeem cursing in a foreign tongue. As she stood in front of the bank of buttons, head still bowed submissively, she ground her teeth together, Everything in her world was starting to career wildly out of control, and there was absolutely nothing she could do to stop it.

She felt something break loose inside of her, something she'd kept tightly tethered deep in her soul for so very long; something so savage, so feral, so bloodthirsty and dark she dare not look it fully in the face.

She could feel it now rising up inside, like a ferocious grizzly shaking loose from a long, cold hibernation, maddened with hunger.

As the elevator doors opened, and Max stepped inside and turned to stare poker-faced at Hakeem waiting impatiently for her, she knew then that she would not be able to control it much longer.

She would not even want to.

Chapter Twenty-one

It took Jack Underwood another day or so to track down the fact that Arcanum Trust was a fictitious name created as a repository for assets transferred from another company: Recondite, Inc.

"*Recondite, Inc.?*" he mumbled to himself, dragging his fingers through his short hair. "What the hell is that supposed to mean?" He again checked every business reference he could find, but none listed "Recondite, Inc.," or attempted to explain what kind of business it actually was.

Finally, driven by desperation and frustration, he dug through the trash and takeout bags and stale Styrofoam coffee cups on his desk until he managed to produce a dictionary. Sure enough, there was a definition for "recondite." Basically, it meant something that was obscure and difficult to understand.

Underwood laughed aloud. It was a weird sound, listening to his own laugh. He glanced around at the other cubicles and desks around him. Darkness had crept up and crowded against the windows. Many of the day-shift agents had left. The Bureau had strict rules about overtime; a certain amount was expected and factored into the agents' pay, but excessive overtime was forbidden because it was so expensive. Underwood, however, had long since ceased worrying about it. This wasn't even his field office. He didn't give a shit.

He guessed it must be quite late by now because most field offices severely scaled down their nighttime staff unless there was some emergency investigation taking place. At the moment all was quiet. He spotted one agent, playing solitaire on his computer over at a shadowy corner desk; no doubt the game had been smuggled in from home to relieve late-shift boredom. Underwood stared at the guy. What was his name? Pierce? Dirk? Sharp Object?

Shit, all these young agents had names he wouldn't give a dog.

Still, they weren't without their uses. For one thing, unlike creaky old-timers like Underwood, these kids had grown up on computers and used them the way an old newspaper man would use a manual Underwood typewriter.

Underwood staggered to his feet, stretched, yawned, and wandered over to Dagger or whoever the hell he was. "You look busy," he opined.

The kid jumped, glanced up at Underwood, and began stammering an explanation.

"Relax," said Underwood. "Do I look like a suit?"

"Well . . ."

"I need some help," said Underwood. "Up for a little chase?"

"Yeah!" the youngster yelled. Underwood placed a restraining hand on his shoulder before he could strain a groin muscle leaping to his feet.

"Hold on there, Lance," he said, marveling at the fact that the guy's name had finally come to him, just in the nick of time. "I just need you to do a little hacking for me, son."

"Oh. Okay." The kid punched out the game, still so eager to help that Underwood halfway expected him to start panting.

"I need to know the names of the investors for a company called Recondite, Inc." He jotted down the name on a Post-It notepad. "It's a repository for a DBA called Arcanum Trust. It's not legit. It's a cover for bad guys who are getting rich doing bad things."

"Got it," nodded the earnest boy, his fingers already flying over the keys.

Underwood felt his jaw come loose at the hinges. The kid was a virtual wizard.

"Why aren't you over at NCCS?" he asked, referring to the FBI's National Computer Crime Squad.

"Oh, I *wish*!" cried the wonder boy. "I've been *begging* to be transferred over there, but this is my first assignment out of the Academy, and the ASAC says I've gotta do three years here first."

"Uh-huh." Underwood was staring at the computer screen. The kid had not stopped striking keys while he was continuing to talk to Underwood; it was almost as if he had a split brain.

"So I'm stuck over here tracking down stolen cars and shit. I hate it."

"Well, you know, I work out of the WMFO," mentioned Underwood offhandedly.

"You *do*?" yelped the kid, so dazzled he actually spun around in his chair to look up at Underwood. "That's where the NCCS is; they work out of the WMFO."

"That they do," agreed Underwood. "And I'm pretty tight with the SAC over there."

"Wade Barrows."

"Right. You do a good job for me here, kid, then I'll put in a word for you with the SAC at the WMFO."

Behind his glasses, the kid's eyes widened. "He could get me transferred into the NCCS?"

"Oh, yeah." Underwood smiled. It was so easy to get what you wanted out of rookies. Besides, he wasn't kidding. He needed an ally over at NCCS.

"Okay. You bet." The young man whirled around in his chair and started making his computer do things Underwood had never imagined. For a few moments he stood transfixed. Then he shook himself, jotted down his home phone number on the back of his business card, and laid it at Lance's elbow.

"Call me when you get the info," he said.

The kid appeared not to have heard him.

Underwood walked back to his desk, shoved all the trash into the overflowing wastebasket, made a note or two to himself, tore up some phone messages from Abby, which he did not intend to return, and shrugged into his coat.

When he turned around, Lance was standing there, a shit-eating grin on his face.

"Here're your names," he said smugly, handing over a printout to a dumbfounded Underwood.

"Let me know if you need anything else," he added,

and headed back to his desk, where Underwood watched as he started up the solitaire game.

Underwood couldn't believe that the kid had actually gotten those names. That was crazy. That was stupid. He couldn't possibly have gotten the names of the investors of a fictitious company that easy. Still blinking, Underwood glanced down at the printout in his hand.

The first name on the list was Garrett Sharp.

The second name was Gabriel Griswold.

Time stopped.

Everything else in the room blurred at the edge of his peripheral vision, then blackened out altogether. All Jack Underwood could see, at that moment, was the list and the name.

He held in his hand proof of a connection between a federal judge and a felonious businessman under investigation by the Federal Bureau of Investigation.

Ho-ly *shit*.

This went way beyond Operation EAVESDROP or even just CovertCom.

Thanks to Dirk or Pierce or Lance or whoever the hell he was, Underwood's case had taken a crooked turn and wound up in a labyrinth of public corruption.

Shit.

This meant everything would change now. Underwood would have to collect and present enough evidence to the Public Integrity Section of the United States Department of Justice, and from there to the United States Attorney's office. Now they'd be not just slamming one spy shop operator for fraud and theft and whatever else they could conjure up, but they'd be going after a federal judge, most likely invoking the RICO statute.

It was your basic high-profile, once-in-a-lifetime fed wet dream.

Underwood broke out into a little soft-shoe. Shit, it practically gave him a hard-on, just thinking about it. When he was done with this, his career would be *made*; he could practically name his assignment. Visions of sugarplums danced in his head.

Before tap-dancing his way to the elevator to head for home, it occurred to Underwood that there was a good possibility that Max was unaware of the connection between her ex-husband and CovertCom. He wondered, briefly, if he should warn her.

She'd freak out, he thought. *She'd shit bricks.*

And that was that, he decided. No way was he going to jeopardize this investigation by taking Max into his confidence. She could blow the whole thing.

He'd come too far, sacrificed too much. This was way, way too big.

No. The less she knew, the better.

By the time the elevator doors had opened, Underwood was practically skipping.

Liv had never visited Garrett Sharp's penthouse suite before, and she was nervous. He'd sent a car and driver around to get her at eight sharp, and as she pressed the button on the elevator panel for the top floor, she looked at herself in the mirror-shining steel elevator doors. She hoped her dress wasn't too revealing. It was a floaty saffron chiffon street-length dress with a daring plunging neckline partially concealed by a little yellow jacket. Liv had noticed that the older sixtysomething Academy-award winning actress Elizabeth Taylor had gotten, the lower her necklines had gone. She figured if Liz could do it, then so could she.

But as the elevator shot upward, sending her stomach toward the floor, Liv wasn't so sure.

Garrett's penthouse elevator did not stop to take on passengers, and it was a quick ride. When Liv stepped out into the opulent corridor, she gawked at the angelic ceilings like a tourist visiting the Sistine Chapel. Although army colonels and their families had access to some of the best housing on base, Liv had never lived anyplace so sumptuous. It looked like a European palace.

Actually, Liv reflected with a sniff as she pressed the door chimes button, *it's just a wee bit show-offy.* She didn't think she'd be very comfortable, living in such splendor.

Almost immediately, Garrett answered the door himself, wearing a periwinkle-blue cashmere turtleneck sweater, which exactly matched his eyes, and a double-breasted navy sport coat. "Liv, darling, you look abso-

lutely spectacular!" he cried, kissing her. "You remind
me of Doris Day in her prime."

"Oh, don't be silly," she murmured modestly, blushing
with pleasure. Doris Day had always been one of her
favorite movie stars.

He led her into a fabulous room with a wall of windows looking out over Central Park. The muted Persian
rugs had the look of old money, as did the delicate
French and English antique furnishings. One solid-
looking and rather worn rocker struck a somewhat dis-
cordant note with the rest of the furniture, until Liv realized what it was.

"Oh, my Lord! Did you buy one of President John
Kennedy's rocking chairs?" She covered her mouth with
one hand in awe.

"I sure did," said Garrett, beaming at her. "Would
you like to sit in it?"

"Oh, I couldn't!"

"Sure you could. It won't break." He chuckled
indulgently.

"Are you sure?" She stepped hesitantly toward the
rocker.

"Go ahead! Everybody wants to."

Gingerly, she took a seat, her back ramrod straight,
running her hands along the arms of the rocker. Her
eyes filled with unexpected tears. This, too, had once
belonged to a man young and splendid and in his prime,
cut down too soon. Thinking of the president's beautiful
widow and brave young children, Liv wanted to lay her
head down and cry.

"Cost me an arm and a leg," said Garrett, crossing
the room to a wet bar. "But it's one of the best investments I ever made. No telling how much it'll be worth
some day."

Blinking away the tears, Liv got to her feet and stood
awkwardly. Money. What a rotten thing it could be
sometimes.

Garrett opened a bottle of Dom Perignon champagne
and filled two crystal flutes with the sparkling white
wine. Liv loved champagne, but it made her tipsy. Garrett held up his glass, and she held up hers.

"To us," he said.

They clinked glasses, and the sound was a deep resonant bell tone. Liv's mother had once taught her that good crystal had a deep bell tone, not a clink, and that good champagne did not blow the cork across the room but poured smooth and dry and bubbled in the glass, as hers was doing now. Everything Garrett touched was first-class. Liv's mother would be pleased.

Unfortunately, the more time Liv spent with Garrett, the more she began having these little niggling doubts. Nothing she could put her finger on. Just doubts.

"Would you like to see the rest of the house?" Garrett asked genially.

"Oh, yes," she said, taking another sip. She'd never been in a rich man's New York penthouse before. She didn't want to miss any of it.

She followed him through a formal dining room. The muted glow from an overhead chandelier caused the deeply polished cherry wood pedestal table to mirror a Waterford crystal vase filled with sprays of baby's breath and fresh white roses delicate and dainty as snowflakes. But before she could comment on that, or on an enormous mural painted on the end wall that depicted a lush Italian vineyard, Garrett had whisked her through a swinging door into a kitchen so dazzling as to almost hurt the eyes.

Everything from the commercial-size oven and refrigerator to the front of the built-in dishwasher was sparkling stainless steel. Hanging from a round ceiling rack over an island stove was a full set of stainless-steel cookware that looked as though it had never seen a stove top, although a cook stood at the sink, dressed in an authentic chef's jacket—only it was denim, not white, and matched his jeans perfectly. Mouthwatering aromas filled the kitchen.

"This is my pride and joy," boasted Garrett. "Those pots and pans? Genuine Calphalon professional cookware. Most chefs prefer the Calphalon hard anodized," he added, "but I prefer the stainless steel because it looks better, don't you think?"

Liv, who'd never heard of Calphalon—hard anodized or any other kind—nodded mutely.

Behind the sink was a backsplash of hand-painted,

crackle-glaze tiles depicting stylized bunches of grapes in shades of plum and verdant green against a white background. Even as Liv exclaimed over the tiles, she noticed a table in the nearby breakfast nook which was covered with matching tiles that repeated the grape motif in the corners and center of the tabletop. White floor tiles also contained matching grape patterns.

"Garrett, this is the most beautiful kitchen I have ever seen," she said truthfully.

Beaming, he said, "Wait till you see it first thing in the morning."

She felt her cheeks grow hot and refrained from comment.

He poured them both another glass of champagne. Liv was surprised she'd already finished the first. It must be her nerves.

"C'mon, I'll show you the rest," he said, and she trailed along behind him out of the brilliant, spotless kitchen. She knew without asking that Garrett was no cook; he didn't collect gourmet cookware to use for himself, he just loved having the best of everything.

He led her past several closed doors, and she didn't pry as to what was behind the doors because she didn't want to appear nosy. Ornately framed paintings, each with its own individual shaded light, hung on the hallway walls; she thought she recognized a Renoir. Garrett vanished through a doorway at the end of the hall, and she followed to find herself in his bedroom.

The sheer masculinity and power of the room almost overwhelmed her. The wallpaper was solid bloodred. A fireplace, complete with stone hearth, warmed the room with firelight. A king-size, dark mahogany Nob Hill sleigh bed with burnished leather and brass accents dominated the room. A matching Bar Harbour trunk occupied the foot of the bed. A world globe in shades of amber and lit from within glowed from atop the trunk. A plush comforter in English flannel tartan plaid in shades of ruby red, hunter green, and navy covered the bed invitingly. Pillows were piled sensuously on top, some deep red, some the matching tartan plaid.

Garrett sat on the edge of the bed and bounced a little. "This is the most comfortable bed on the planet," he said. "On top of the mattress here is a handmade goose-down featherbed mattress pad. The sheets?" He flipped back the comforter to reveal navy sheets. "Egyptian cotton sateen, three hundred fifty thread count. I tell you, it's like sleeping on a cloud."

Liv didn't know what to say to that. She had just noticed the small round table in front of the fireplace. It was covered with a crisp, wine-red linen tablecloth. Gleaming beneath the soft sheen of candles in golden candelabra were gold-edged plates, cut-crystal gold-rimmed stemware, and heavy golden flatware. Resting demurely across one of the plates was a single white rose, soft as velvet.

"Garrett," she began, but he got quickly to his feet and laid a gentle finger against her lips.

"Shshshsh," he whispered. "Don't worry about anything." Taking her champagne glass from her hand, he placed it on the trunk behind him and kissed her. It was a long, melting kiss that made her knees weak.

"I've waited for this a long time, my sweet," he said.

"I know, but I'm not sure—"

"Don't talk, darling," he said, taking her by the hand and leading her toward the table in front of the fire. She was beginning to feel a bit woozy from the champagne, and she giggled. He poured her another glass and one for himself as well.

"Vinnie's making us prime rib," he said, "and spinach ambrosia, and chocolate bavarian cream for dessert," he said.

"How decadent," she said, giggling again.

"Yes, that's it exactly," he said with a wicked little grin. "I want this entire night to be decadent."

"I've never been decadent before," she said with a lighthearted laugh, sipping her champagne.

"I know! And it's high time you were, don't you think?"

Tossing back the last of her wine, Liv said, "Why not? I'm an up-grown lady. I mean a grown-up lady." What a funny thing to say! She laughed some more.

He took her hand and kissed it. "I'll tell Vinnie we're ready for our salads. Stay right here, okay? We've got so much to talk about, you and I."

He sprang to his feet with the vigor of a man half his age and strode from the room.

Liv stared blankly at the fire for a moment, then reached for the Dom Perignon and poured the last drops of it into her glass to finish. She was trying to remember something she'd been thinking about before, but couldn't, so gave up. When she'd drunk the last of her champagne, she reached over, picked up Garrett's glass, and drank the rest of his as well.

She was being *sooooo* naughty!

But Garrett was right. She'd been a good girl all her life, and it was high time she had a little fun.

What had he said? That they had so much to talk about.

But Liv didn't really think they were going to do much talking in this room. The thought brought a blush to her cheeks. Emboldened by the champagne, she took off her little jacket and hung it over the back of her chair.

Well, if you got it, fling it, she thought. *I mean, flaunt it!* How funny! She was even slurring her thoughts! She giggled some more and upended the champagne bottle onto the tip of her tongue.

She was a bad girl. Yes indeedy.

Garrett returned to the room. He was such an attractive man, and his eyes were just electric tonight. From behind his back, he produced another bottle of champagne. "Look what I've got, Livvy!" he said with a big grin on his face.

"If I didn't know better, I'd think you were trying to have your way with me, sir," she said.

"Well, maybe you don't know better," he laughed, pouring more champagne in her glass. "Now, the salad will be here any moment. Let's have a drink and talk a while."

"Okeedokee," she said.

"Tell me about your granddaughter," said Garrett Sharp with a toothy smile.

The first thing Max and Hakeem argued about was the type of body transmitter he would wear when he entered the X-Tech factory, while she waited out in the car. Hakeem's area of expertise was telephone systems, but because Max was a woman, he refused to consider her input about the body transmitter.

Max tried to point out to Hakeem that the single biggest source of interference with a body-worn transmitter *was* the body. The human body, she said, was the biggest absorber of radio frequency transmissions because it was *conductive,* which made it an efficient power absorber. Consequently, she wanted him to use a transmitter with an antenna at least one-quarter wavelength long.

Hakeem insisted that because Max would be relatively close—sitting in the parking lot adjacent to the building—that he could work with a shorter antenna.

If there was any steel in the structure of the damn building, she pointed out, it could interfere with the radio transmissions. Not only did he refuse to listen to her warnings—but he also refused to field-test the transmitter; a crucial omission, since every human body was electrically different, and transmissions could be affected by where the transmitter was worn, dryness of skin, clothing, and so on.

Max wanted Hakeem to carry a higher-power UHF AID (audio intelligence device) body wire, which had better signal frequency characteristics for getting out of buildings, but Hakeem wouldn't listen. Instead he took a cheap, lower-powered VHF transmitter kit, which only had a 143 megahertz frequency and featured a built-in electret microphone. (Max hated built-in microphones.)

He also left her with what she considered a piece of shit receiving system, since it was not designed to filter out stray radio interference, static, or distortion. She'd have felt a hell of a lot better with an I-Com R 7000 communications receiver.

She'd have felt a lot better if she wasn't even here. Or if she had to be here, she'd have felt a hell of a lot better with *any* of the other Spy Squad members. Damn Garrett Sharp and his fucking chickenshit little hand-slap punishment power plays!

Damn them all to bloody hell.

Hakeem made it into the building easily enough, and after an anxious wait, Max heard him murmur the make and model number of the requisite fax machine, which

she recorded on the built-in tape recorder included with
the receiver system housed in a briefcase.

Then a loud wave of static fucked up the reception,
and Max had no idea what was happening inside that
building.

Asshole! she thought, peering anxiously toward the
quiet building. *Stupid fucking sexist pig asshole.*

She tended to curse in times of extreme stress—a leftover, perhaps, from prison.

The static wave passed, but the words that came
through were garbled. Straining to hear and adjusting
the volume control—which didn't help; it served merely
to make the distortion louder—Max thought she could
detect that Hakeem was involved in a conversation
with someone.

This was not good.

He was supposed to get in, get the info they needed,
and get out. He was not supposed to have to stop and
explain himself to anybody.

Shit.

Starting the ignition of the rented Buick, Max crept
the car forward, headlights doused, until it was parked
catercorner to the exit door. After first unscrewing the
dome lightbulb, Max leapt out of the car, with the engine
still running, and raced around the opposite corner of
the building.

Hakeem had said that the windows contained shock
sensors. So what they needed was a shock—something
to divert the attention of whoever was waylaying Hakeem and give him time to make his getaway.

Max cast about frantically for a stone, but there was
none. The grounds were meticulously landscaped; the
shrubs and flowers planted in the rich black soil that,
Max remembered, turned to gummy mud and could pull
off a man's shoes when wet. She was about to despair
when she discovered a large chunk of concrete that had
broken off a sidewalk, probably during a heavy rain, and
had not been repaired. Grasping the ragged chunk and
breaking off three nails in the process, Max heaved the
concrete over her head and smashed it into the nearest
window, which immediately activated a loud alarm.

She made it to the car just as Hakeem came sprinting

out the door, and burned rubber getting them out of the parking lot and down the street before the overweight security guard had time to read their license plate or even get a good make on the car.

Since nothing had been stolen or otherwise disturbed, Max doubted that the police would be called. The guard would chalk it up to vandalism and probably not connect it to the strange telephone repairman someone remembered talking to in a separate room.

"What the fuck do you think you're doing?" yelled Hakeem when they'd rounded a couple of corners, turned on the headlights, and continued down the street toward the freeway on-ramp at the normal speed limit. "I told you to keep the car parked where I put it!"

"I was saving your ass, you son of a bitch," said Max quietly.

Quick as a bolt of lightning, his hand shot out and slapped her across her face in a resounding blow that would have staggered her if she'd been standing.

"Don't you *ever* disobey my orders again!" he cried.

Right in the middle of the street, without warning and with no word, Max slammed on the brakes so hard that the car fishtailed, and threw the gearshift into *park*. While Hakeem stared at her openmouthed, she picked up her tote bag, reached into the backseat for her carry-on bag, released her seat belt, got out of the car, and walked away.

They were parked smack-dab in the middle of the street in the center of an industrial area of the city dissected by an expressway full of speeding nighttime traffic. There were no homes or convenience stores or other signs of life. Most of the buildings were locked up for the night.

As she continued walking away from the car, Max heard Hakeem slam his car door, shout at her in Arabic, shut the car door on the driver's side, and roar off in a screech of tires.

She did not even look back.

Since Max and Hakeem returned from Dallas late at night, Dominic was unable to see Max until the staff meeting the next morning. She arrived late, looking haggard and exhausted, and took her seat without a glance in Hakeem's direction. Dominic looked at Hakeem. He seemed unruffled.

Dominic didn't pay much attention to the ebb and flow of the meeting, except to note that Hakeem seemed to regard the Dallas trip as having been a success, judging from his brief, self-congratulatory report. Max stared at the tabletop and said nothing.

When the meeting broke up, Dominic loitered, pretending to examine something in his briefcase, until the others had left. To his great surprise, Max laid her head down on the table, resting it on the crook of her arm as though she planned to take a little nap before returning to her office. Dominic had been all poised to go on the offensive, demanding to know why she'd left for Dallas without telling him about the trip, but something about the vulnerable line of the back of her neck stopped him short.

He went around the table and laid a gentle hand on the back of her head.

"Are you all right?" he asked.

"Just tired," she said without lifting her head. "I didn't get in until very late."

Something about the use of the pronoun "I" instead of "we" gave Dominic pause. Surely they had returned from Dallas on the same plane. Wouldn't it be more natural for her to have said, "*We* didn't get in until very late?"

Pulling out a chair next to her, he sat down and softly brushed the hair back from her eyes, which were dark-shadowed and wary. For the first time he noticed a small round bruise right on the corner of her mouth; lipstick had hidden the little split just beneath it.

Dominic felt the hairs on the back of his neck stand straight out. Speaking in a carefully modulated tone, he said, "What happened to your lip?"

"Nothing." The word was final. He knew he would get no more from her about it.

Intending to pull her into his arms for an embrace, Dominic grasped her wrist, but even as he tugged it out from under her, she winced in pain and pulled back.

His scalp crawling, the way it always did when he was

alerted to danger, Dominic loosened his hold on her wrist but did not let go. Instead he turned the small white wrist over in the palm of his hand, examining it. The skin was so translucent he could see the blue veins beneath.

Four bruises, the size of a man's fingers, striped the narrow part of Max's arm like obscene tattoos.

Slowly, he raised his gaze and met her eyes, but she glanced away. Like a man coaxing a frightened animal out of a corner, Dominic said quietly, "Come here. I've missed you." When he said nothing about the bruises, she huddled against his chest and he wrapped his arms around her, cradling her head.

"Next time, don't run off without telling me, okay?" he said softly.

She nodded. "Okay."

Stroking her hair, Dominic gazed across the room over her head. Everything he saw had turned red, as if filtered through blood.

"Why don't you go on home and get some rest?" he said. "You won't be any good to anybody, tired as you are. I'll come see you this evening, after work."

She did not object. With a slow nod she pulled away from him, gathered up her briefcase, and left the boardroom. Her shoulders were slumped. It was all he could do to contain himself.

He waited.

When Dominic was reasonably certain that Max had left, he walked slowly down the hall like a panther on the prowl and entered Hakeem's office without knocking, closing the door quietly behind him. Hakeem was standing at the window, his hands clasped behind his back, gazing out over the buildings like the crown prince surveying his kingdom.

"Hakeem," said Dominic.

Hakeem turned from the window.

Dominic approached Hakeem with his hand outstretched as if he wanted to shake Hakeem's hand, and Hakeem reached out in response.

What happened next took place swiftly. As the hands of the two men touched, Dominic took hold of Hakeem's hand with both of his, grasping the meat of Hakeem's palm and separating the four fingers down the middle as he did so. Shoving the palm of Hakeem's hand backward toward his elbow joint, Dominic stepped to a forty-five degree angle of Hakeem and allowed the natural momentum of Hakeem's body to fall to the floor even as it was recoiling from the pain.

With a loud bellow, Hakeem hit the floor on his back, but even as he tried to spring to his feet in a countermeasure to Dominic's move, Dominic immediately planted himself on his knees to either side of Hakeem's forearm, pressing it solidly to the floor between his knees and bending the palm backward as if he wanted to break the hand right off the arm, which indeed, he did.

His face twisted in pain and surprise, Hakeem stopped struggling. It pleased Dominic to see that even though the man was a psychopath who seemed to have no conscience and to therefore feel no shame or guilt . . . he did definitely feel fear.

"That's right," he said through clenched teeth. "You *should* fear me, because I swear to *Allah,* if you ever touch Max again, I'll kill you."

Giving a last unnecessary, but very satisfying, twist to Hakeem's trapped wrist, Dominic sprang to his feet and walked out of the office.

Heading straight down the corridor, he barged right into the Boss's office without knocking, striding rapidly into the room, and planted both of his big hands on opposite corners of Sharp's desk. Pushing his face to within inches of Sharp's, Dominic said, "If you don't get Max away from that sadistic bastard and team her up with somebody else, I will do something we will *both* regret, do you understand?"

Sharp maintained eye contact fearlessly with Dominic for a long beat, but when Dominic did not blink, he slowly nodded.

Dominic stood up.

Sharp said, "Would you mind telling me what provoked this outburst?"

"No," said Dominic. "I wouldn't mind telling you at all. He put bruises on her, and I guarantee that's the last time he's ever getting near her again."

"All right, all right." Sharp held up his hands, palms

out, then said, "I'll assign her to work with Sebastian Taylor. Does that meet with your approval?" He smiled at Dominic with a wicked glint to his ice-blue eyes.

In his present mood, it took a great deal of self-control for Dominic not to put his fist right in the middle of that smug face. But he didn't. Instead he nodded, turned, and walked out without closing the door.

He was getting really, *really* sick of CovertCom.

Chapter Twenty-two

Liv expected Garrett to phone her up after their evening together, but instead he didn't call at all for the rest of the day. She couldn't help but wonder if maybe now that he had what he wanted from her, he would dump her.

It seemed so ridiculous to be worrying about it, like a high school girl waiting for her boyfriend to call. Liv had never been very big on dating, and this was the reason why. She hated all the little game playing that had to go on. Playing hard to get. That sort of thing. At her age she should be tooling around the country with her husband in a Winnebago, visiting the grandkids and seeing the sights. Instead, here she was sitting all moony-eyed by the phone, willing it to ring.

One uncomfortable thought intruded even more into Liv's mind than did her worries about her physical intimacy with Garrett, and it was so uncomfortable that she tired not to think about it at all: *How much had she told him about Gaby?* Liv honestly could not remember. It was too worrisome even for her to deal with, so she just pretended to herself that everything was all right.

Garrett finally did call later that evening, and Liv could detect no different in his tone. Still, Liv was flustered by the situation and didn't know what to think. Was he going to ask her to marry him? Was he going to dump her? Was he going to expect her to sleep with him now after every date?

What were the rules? Liv didn't know what the rules were anymore.

Under any other circumstance, Liv might have talked it over with Rebekah, but she dare not. Rebekah was still not happy that Liv was seeing her boss, and when Liv saw her that morning after her trip to Dallas, she looked tired enough to fall down. Still, though Liv begged, she went to work anyway.

Later, Rebekah surprised her mother by returning home early and going straight to bed.

Everything was off-kilter, out of balance, and Liv was darned if she knew why.

Later, she came across Rebekah, sitting at the dining table, clacking away at her laptop as if it were life and death. Liv noticed a sheet of paper on the table next to the laptop that had the word PACER across it, but when she leaned forward for a closer look, Rebekah suddenly laid a book over the page as if it were some sort of top-secret document or something.

Frustrated, embarrassed, and more than a little lonesome, Liv wandered into the kitchen for a snack. It was a small, cramped kitchen so typical of a New York apartment, and yet so different from her big sunny kitchen at her home in Austin. Liv could still remember how wonderful it had been, the day Rebekah came home from prison, to have the house crammed full of kids and grandkids and food and laughter. Lord, how she missed them all.

Walking back into the dining room, Liv said, "Rebekah?"

Her daughter, concentrating intently, did not look up. "Rebekah?"

When there was still not response, Liv cried, "Max!"

Her daughter jumped, blushed sheepishly, and said, "Oh, Mom . . . I'm sorry. I didn't hear you." She was pale, her hair disheveled, and she still looked tired.

Liv said, "Let's go see Clark this weekend. It's the end of October, and the temperatures are only in the eighties down in Texas."

Rebekah smiled. "The trees won't be changing yet like they are up here. Not till the weather gets a little cooler, anyway."

Liv shrugged. "I don't care about that. I want to visit family. Do come with me, won't you? You've been working so hard, dear."

Rebekah sighed. "I just got back from Dallas, Mom."

"Did you call Clark?"

Glancing down at the computer screen, Rebekah said, "No, Mom. I was very busy and I didn't have time."

Walking around the dining table, Liv put her hands on her daughter's tense shoulders. "I never get to see you anymore. You're either with Dominic or you're at work or—"

"Or you're with Mr. Sharp."

"Well . . . yes, I suppose that's true. I just thought that maybe we need to get away from it all so that we can spend some time together. Honestly, darling, I don't think you will ever relax as long as you're so wrapped up in CovertCom."

"Boy, you got that right," said Rebekah with a slight giggle.

Liv didn't get the joke, but she didn't press. "Then, come with me. Please? Just for a few days."

Rebekah took hold of the mouse and clicked around until the screen went blank. She snapped shut the laptop and said, "You're right, Mom. I need to get away from here. Besides, I need to talk to Clark about some things."

Liv clapped her hands together. "Oh, I'm so glad!" She laughed. "I'd like to see them follow me around down there."

Rebekah swiveled in her seat and looked up at Liv. "What are you talking about?"

Embarrassed that she'd blurted out such a foolish thing, Liv waved her hands in the air as if it were no concern and said, "Oh, it's nothing, really. It's just that sometimes I get the feeling that someone is following me. I think this city is making me paranoid."

Rebekah got to her feet and studied Liv's face so closely it made her blush.

"Mom. What makes you think someone is following you?"

Uncomfortable under the scrutiny of her daughter's gaze, Liv turned away and fussed with knickknacks on the sideboard. "I noticed a man in the library one day. I saw him again at St. Patrick's, and I just got this, I don't know, creepy feeling. I could have sworn he was following me."

"Did you see him again?" At the sharpness in her

daughter's tone, Liv fumbled with a ceramic figurine of an angel.

"Mom?"

"Well, all right. Yes. I thought I saw the same man yesterday morning in front of . . . in a cab right behind mine."

Folding her arms over her chest in that defiant, determined way her mother knew so well, Rebekah began to pace, her brow furrowed in thought. Finally, she reached down to the floor beside her dining room chair and took hold of the briefcase nearby. She heaved the briefcase onto the dining table and opened it.

From inside the briefcase, Liv watched as she withdrew a small black device the size of a cigarette package with an antenna protruding from the top. Liv thought it might be a transistor radio. She started to ask about it, but Rebekah put a finger to her lips to shush her and whispered, "I'm just testing something." Then she connected a set of headphones to the device and put them over her ears.

And before Liv could even say how do you do, her daughter had begun holding the device a few inches from the surface of the dining room table, first on top, and then down underneath it. From there she moved on to the sideboard, then along the walls and electrical outlets, and on into the living room, as if she were engaged in some sort of weird voodoo ritual.

Totally befuddled and bewildered, Liv thought, *This kid just beats anything I ever saw.*

Max's brother Clark lived with his wife, Jennifer, and their two children in a beautiful, sprawling upscale home located on the banks of Lake Ray Hubbard near the Dallas suburb of Rockwall. In late October the young trees surrounding the house were just changing color, and bright yellow sunshine sparkled off the blue lake and drenched the faux-country kitchen with happy warmth. Max's mom smiled in languid contentment as Clark's two small children rolled around on the floor with their Sheltie dog, Skye.

To Max and her mom's delighted surprise, Brett and his wife, Jan, had joined them for a brief visit. For Max, it was especially gratifying. She knew this was Brett's way of checking up on her and seeing for himself how she was doing since her release from prison. He and Brand had always been protective of her in that way. In high school, she had resented it, but now she appreciated it.

Max sat at the table, watching Clark goose his pretty wife as she frosted a cake at the counter. Jan was sharing military gossip with Max's mom while Brett read the newspaper.

She felt set apart from it all, old and immeasurably sad.

Seven long years of her life had passed her by in prison. Wasted, squandered years of Gaby's precious little life; years Max could never retrieve; years gone forever. She loved a man she could never have, and was trapped in a situation she did not want. Somehow, somewhere, her life had spun out of her control. What had started out as a glorious dream had run amok and turned into an ongoing horrifying nightmare with no ending.

If it weren't for Gaby, she thought for the hundredth time, *I'd throw myself in that lake and never come up.*

"Clark! You're worse than the kids!" cried Jennifer, laughing as he scooped up a rut of icing off the top of the cake with his finger and loudly sucked it off. "Go away!"

Max got to her feet and said, "C'mon, brother. Let's take a walk."

"Good idea," he said cheerfully, whistling at Skye and holding open the sliding glass panel door that led to the backyard.

Brett poked his head above the paper. "Exercise? Outdoors? Can I go?"

Before Max could object, Clark said, "The more the merrier."

Max bit her lip. She wasn't prepared just yet to take Brett into her confidence. It wasn't that he couldn't be trusted, it was just that he tended to tell her what to do all the time.

A glistening green lawn stretched down to a path by the lake, which led to a boat dock where Clark kept his sailboat, *Jenny Too*.

"We'll take you guys for a sail while you're here," said Clark as Skye bounded ahead, his fluffy white tail wagging with each step.

"That'll be nice," said Max woodenly.

"Cool," said Brett. "Good thing Zany's not here. He'd get seasick."

Clark and Brett laughed.

Clark glanced sharply at Max. "Sis, you act like you've come down here for a funeral."

"I'm sorry," she said, linking her arm through his as they walked. He pressed her arm close to his side, and it made her want to cry. Everything these days, it seemed, made Max want to cry.

"What gives?" he asked.

Max swallowed and glanced over at Brett. It was a positively perfect day, seventy-two degrees, high puffy white clouds pushed across the clean sky by light breezes, sunlight warming her hair . . . but all Max could see, everywhere she looked, was darkness.

"I'm in trouble, guys," she said simply, the words standing bald between them.

They stopped, and Clark gave her a shrewd, assessing stare. "What kind of trouble?"

"Mom doesn't know any of this . . ." she faltered.

"Understood. Talk to us," said Brett. They began walking again, and Max hurried to keep up.

"The job I got out of prison? CovertCom?"

"Yeah. What about it?"

"It's all a sham. I've been working as an informant for the FBI on a case they're trying to make against my boss and . . . others . . . for fraud and theft and God knows what all else."

"I knew it!" cried Brett. "I had a funny feeling about that job from the very beginning."

"Jesus," said Clark.

Max explained about Agent Underwood's offer, and how she'd been coerced to take the offer against her better judgment, for Gaby's sake. Brow furrowed, Clark stared at the ground as they walked, saying nothing. From the side, with the gray just starting to brush his temples and his thick hair shining chestnut in the sun, he looked so much like their dad that it was almost creepy.

"Wait a minute," Brett interrupted. "This guy you work for. Is he the same guy Mom's been seeing?"

"Yes."

"For God's sake, Max! Why don't you stop her? The guy's a crook!"

"I know he's a crook, Brett, but you tell me how to get Mom to stop doing anything she's set her mind to do and we'll both be miracle workers!"

For a long moment he stopped and put his hands on his hips, gazing out at the dazzling lake through squinted eyes.

Clark stared at the ground. "What does your fed friend think about it?"

She snorted. "Underwood? He couldn't care less. But he won't let me warn Mom. He's afraid it could jeopardize the case."

Clark sighed. "Dammit, he's right. But it's not his mom we're talking about."

"Tell me about it," she said gloomily.

Brett's expression was grim. "Have you tried talking to her?"

"No, Brett, I've just let her innocently screw up her life! I find it amusing."

"Okay," said Clark. "Calm down." He took her arm again, and they continued walking.

"There's more," she said miserably.

Both brothers stopped walking and confronted her. She felt like a little kid, about to get into trouble with her daddy. "I discovered that Gabe's behind this whole thing—my being offered the job and all, I mean. He's trying to use my boss to find out where Gaby is."

"Oh, God!" Clark took both her arms in his. "Max. Are you absolutely sure about this?"

She told him about the computer disk containing the secret report.

"Shit!" cried Brett. He started to pace in a little half circle around them.

"What does what's-his-name . . . Underwood . . . What does he think about it?" asked Clark.

"I haven't told him."

"Why *not*?" yelled Brett.

"Because I don't trust him, Brett, that's why! All he

cares about is his stupid fucking case! He doesn't care about my daughter or my mother or me. Even if I did tell him, it wouldn't make any damn difference, I can guarantee you that!" Tears of frustration burned her eyes.

"Okay, okay. Calm down," said Clark, giving Brett a threatening glare. "You're probably right. I've had some dealings with the feds before, and they can drive you nuts, that's for sure." Brow furrowed, he dug his toe into the ground.

"God, I wish I still smoked cigarettes," fumed Brett.

"It's just that I don't know who to trust anymore," she said gloomily. "Aw, hell, I've told you this much, I might as well tell you the rest of it."

She glanced from brother to brother. "Mom thinks someone is following her."

"What?" they cried in unison.

Heaving a world-weary sigh, Max said, "That's what I thought. I mean, why would anybody think *Mom* would know anything? But she just told me this a couple days ago, so I swept the apartment, just for the hell of it, you know? And I found some bugs."

"Whose apartment?"

"Mine and Mom's."

This news brought Brett up short. "Gotta be her new boyfriend. Your boss."

Max shook her head. "I don't think so, Brett. There's an . . . amateur . . . quality to it that Garrett Sharp would never display. I mean, if he had somebody following Mom, it would be somebody good enough that she would *never* suspect it. I might, you see, but never Mom."

Clark nodded thoughtfully.

"And the first bug I found? It wasn't even cleverly hidden or disguised or one of a million high-tech doo-dads we've got access to. It was just haphazardly stuck on the bottom of the butterfly dish Garrett gave Mom. I mean, it was one of those not much bigger than a grain of rice, but I still felt like an idiot that I hadn't checked it before. But then, I was so damn mad about the butter-fly pin—"

"Butterfly pin? What butterfly pin?" said Clark.

Max rolled her eyes. "Don't ask."

"So who do you think is doing it?" asked Brett.

"I think Gabe has hired someone to follow Mom when Garrett's not working on her. It would be like Gabe not to trust Garrett."

"Why would he have someone follow Mom and not you?" interrupted Clark.

"Possibly because he might think there would be more of a chance that Mom might make a careless mistake that could lead him to Gaby."

"Oh, my God," said Brett, turning pale.

For a few moments they walked together in silence, and then Clark said, "What I want to know, is how the hell Gabe came to know your boss in the first place. He must know CovertCom is engaged in illegal activity."

"We don't know that for sure," she said. For the first time Max had used the word "we" to describe her situation, and it felt so good. Some of the tension began to drain out of her stiffened neck muscles.

"There *must* be a connection!" he cried.

"No kidding," added Brett.

"I thought so, too," she said. "I went to the federal courthouse in Dallas during a business trip, and I signed up for PACER. I thought maybe I could find some kind of connection there."

"Why? It'll just have a record of Gabe's court cases," mused Clark. "Oh! I get it! You're thinking *that* might be the connection!"

"I don't know, Clark. I just thought it might be a good idea to look into it, you know?"

"Do you know how to use PACER?"

"Not really. I haven't had much time to try."

"C'mon." Doing an abrupt about-face and whistling toward Skye's direction, which brought the little dog running like a miniature Lassie, Clark started back toward the house, striding so rapidly that Max had to take two steps for his every one. Brett matched his pace evenly.

It was almost like being with Brett and Brand again, like the old days, and even though it was Clark and not Brand, it still felt good. After so many long months of being alone with her fear, Max felt almost giddy with relief. Her brothers were going to help her.

Maybe there was some hope, after all.

Back at the house, firmly ensconced in his spacious office, the French doors closed against both kids and dogs, blinds darkened to prevent glare on the computer screen, ceiling fan lazily whirling overhead, Clark whizzed through the preliminary setup motions on his state-of-the-art computer. Max was seated at a second chair just behind and to the right of Clark, so that she could look over his shoulder while he worked, and watch for anything that might provide the connection between Judge Gabe Griswold, and CovertCom.

Brett was straddled backwards on a kitchen chair to Clark's left.

Her brothers' shoulders were so wide and strong and comforting. Max silently scolded herself for waiting so long to ask for their help. Her mother was right. She was independent to a fault.

"You know what it will mean if we make a connection, don't you?" asked Clark as he waited a few moments for the modem to transfer information.

"I think so," she said.

"It will mean that we can bring down the grand and glorious federal judge once and for all, and you can see Gaby again."

"I'd dearly love to be there to see it," said Brett. "The takedown, I mean."

"I'd sell tickets," said Clark. They smiled at each other.

A burst of excitement exploded throughout Max's body at the mere thought, but she quickly snuffed it out. One thing prison had taught her was to take life one day at a time. She didn't dare get her hopes up. Besides, she couldn't afford to get sloppy and make a crucial mistake that could tip her hand before she was ready to play it.

The eminent judge's cases appeared on-screen, and Clark scrolled slowly through every one, so that Max could read the names of the defendants and see if anything sounded familiar. They were listed in chronological order, and she didn't know how far back they should go.

Outside, dusk crept over the lake and shadowed the room. Clark turned on a gooseneck desk lamp with a green shade. Max developed a headache, and they took a little break for cake and coffee. Her mom seemed bewildered and somewhat hurt that Max and Clark and Brett were spending so much of their brief visit holed up together in Clark's office, but Jennifer, who intuitively understood that her husband must be providing Max with legal help of some kind, took Liv and Jan and the kids shopping and to a movie, leaving the house quiet and still while they worked. Max didn't know what Jan thought of it all, although she did seem more tolerant and good-natured than Brett's previous wife had been.

Skye scratched on the door, and Clark relented and let him in to curl up under the desk at Clark's feet. Nightfall cloaked the house. Max went around turning on lamps so that the family wouldn't return to a dark house, and returned to continue working.

Brett ordered them a pizza. Max took another dose of Excedrin. For a little while, Brett stood behind her and rubbed her shoulders. His hands were so strong that it hurt, but she didn't complain because she was so touched at the gesture.

In the end, she almost missed it.

Her fatigue was blurring the screen and her patience—what little of it she possessed—was fraying at the edges. She had already begged Clark once to give it up and turn the damn thing off, but he refused and she knew there would be no budging him. Once he set his mind to solving a problem, he'd keep at it like a pit bull with lockjaw.

"Dudly Do-Right," whispered Brett in her ear, and she laughed out loud at the old family nickname.

"What?" mumbled Clark. He glanced over his shoulder. "Am I being mocked?"

"I couldn't help it," said Brett. "Zany's not here."

They all chuckled, and Max wondered how other families dealt with stress. Hers joked their way out of it. She was yawning loudly, not even bothering to cover her mouth, when the next case scrolled slowly past on the screen.

The United States vs. Hakeem Abdul.

Her gasp was so loud in the quiet room that Clark jumped and Skye awoke, thumping his tail uncertainly.

"What is it?" said Brett.

"I know that guy! I mean, I work with him," she stuttered. "I mean, he's on the Spy Squad. I mean, he's at CovertCom!"

"This Abdul guy?"

Heart jarring against her rib cage with every beat, Max nodded.

Her brother laid a calming hand on her forearm. "Settle down, sis. Don't hyperventilate, here. Take a deep breath while I check this out."

"Okay." She took a deep, shaky breath. "Okay."

Giving her one more brotherly pat, he turned back to the computer and attacked the keyboard with a vengeance, mumbling to himself. "All right. It says the Docket Report is 210 pages long. How do you want to view it?"

"What do you mean?"

"Well, that's a long report. We can choose from several options. We can scroll through it one screen at a time, or view only the first screen, or only the last screen, or . . ."

"One at a time." Max tried to suppress her growing impatience. Her brother could be so meticulous at times that it bordered on plodding.

"C'mon, Clark," said Brett. "Let's just get on with it."

Clark began to scroll through the docket report. Max read over his shoulder as he summarized the report, translating the legalese into plain English for her benefit.

"It was a conspiracy case," he said. "Hakeem was part of a group who was planning a terrorist act. Feds busted them up before they could carry it out. Hmmm. Okay, all right. Abdul's attorney pushed for—and got—a separate trial for his client. Smooth move, Ex-Lax."

At the corny comment, Max exchanged a grin with Brett. It was the kind of thing Clark was always saying when he was a kid. Not that he ever was one. As the oldest of the Maxfield kids, Clark was the classic firstborn: serious, driven, achieving, marshaling the younger siblings around like little troops.

She'd always adored him.

"Okay. He was acquitted, Max."

"By Gabe?"

"No. He had a jury trial." Fingers flying over the keys, Clark spent a few minutes looking up some other factoid. Max, still in a state of shock, stared blindly at the screen. Brett began to jiggle a foot.

"Hmmm. This stinks. This stinks to high heaven."

"What do you mean?"

"Well, the other members of the conspiracy were all convicted. They're doing time right now. Your friend Abdul was the only one who got off."

"Please. Do not refer to the man as my friend."

He wasn't paying any attention. He checked into several other sources, then reluctantly pulled out of PACER. "There won't be any transcripts of the trial, sis."

"I know. Because he was acquitted."

"Right." Pounding away on a few more keys, Clark got off-line, disconnected the modem, and turned off the computer. He swiveled around in his desk chair to face her and Brett.

"If Gabe was the sitting judge who heard the trial, then he had a hell of a lot to do with guiding the direction that the trial went, by choosing which objections to sustain and which to overrule, and by handing down various decisions concerning evidence and other rules, and even by the instructions that he gave the jury."

"Right," said Brett.

Exhaustion, the nagging headache, and emotional overload were numbing Max's mind. She couldn't think.

"I mean, Jesus, Max," said Clark, "federal judges sit at the right hand of God in the judicial system. At least they get to thinking that they do."

"No kidding," she said. "You don't have to remind *me*. I did seven years because of that son of a bitch."

Clark ducked his head and stared at his hands. Instantly Max regretted her words. He still thought she blamed him for his failure to shorten her time on appeal. She touched his hand. "It wasn't your fault," she said gently.

"Yes, it was."

"Well, I never blamed you. *Never*."

He took her hand in his. "I know, sis. But I never
stopped blaming myself." After a moment he glanced
back at her. "This is a golden opportunity for me to
redeem myself, you know."

"What are you talking about? You don't have anything to redeem."

He squeezed her hand, and she squeezed back. "Let
me do this for you, okay? If you won't let me do it for
you, then let me do it for myself. And for Gaby."

"Do what?"

"Let me help you nail that bastard once and for all."

"Hey, I wanna play, too," said Brett.

Relief washed over her body in waves, and Max had
to wait a moment to speak so that she wouldn't embar-
rass herself by bawling. "I knew you guys'd help me,"
she said finally.

They shrugged, the gesture identical. Once again, Max
was reminded of Brand. Brett said, "We're family. What
are families for if you can't depend on them to bail you
out when you're in trouble?"

After that, there was nothing more to be said.

Chapter Twenty-three

Brett and Jan left the next day. Liv turned in early, the kids were settled down with a Disney video, and Jennifer went to fetch a bucket of chicken. Clark and Max huddled together in his office and began tracking down people who might know something about the case of *The United States vs. Hakeem Abdul.*

Though it was a Sunday night and many of the principals involved had unlisted telephone numbers, Clark had enough connections in the legal community, and an impeccable enough reputation, that he was eventually able to acquire the numbers he needed from friends and associates. Using the speaker phone for Max's benefit, Clark first called Linda Garcia, who had been the prosecutor on the case.

"Clark!" she cried. "I haven't seen you since that boring cocktail party at the Hyatt last summer for Judge Seacord's retirement."

"Well, some of us had enough pull to be invited to the boring dinner afterward," he teased.

"Hey, I got invited! It's just that I had a life to go live, unlike some butt-kissers I could name."

Clark responded with a loud kissing noise.

"Oh, I see! Now you're kissing mine! I've often fantasized about this moment."

Laughing, Clark asked Garcia if she remembered the case.

"Geez, Clark. How long ago was that?"

"Three years."

"Oh, yeah. I was pregnant with Sophia then. I'd puke my guts up in the rest room before trial every morning, then go kick Frank Hoffman's ass. At least, I thought I was kicking his ass, and in fact I would have kicked his ass if Judge Griswold hadn't been so fucking biased, excuse my French."

"Well, that's what I'm asking about, Linda. I want to know what you mean by biased."

"It's nothing I could put my finger on. I mean, technically, he did nothing illegal, really. Do you know very much about the case?"

"Just that it involved a conspiracy to commit an act of terrorism."

"No kidding. Abdul and a few of his other buddies from Iraq had gotten visas to stay in the country because they said they had helped some American soldiers in Desert Storm and that if they were returned home, they'd be beheaded. At the time, there was all this patriotic fever burning all over the country for the returning GI's, you know, and so they got sympathy visas pretty quick.

"A couple of years later, undercover feds busted up this plot they had going to bomb the Pentagon."

"Are you kidding? That doesn't sound too bright to me," said Clark, rolling his eyes in Max's direction.

"It was more sophisticated than you could ever believe. They were going to plant the explosives in the Metro system that stops at the Pentagon mall, and during emergency rescue they were going to set off some more, which would cause massive chaos and confusion, since EMS and police would be killed in that one, and then they were going to take advantage of that to move in on the Pentagon. Who knows if it would have worked or not? It's just scary as shit to think about it."

"Linda, why didn't they try the case in D.C.?

"Because the plotters lived and worked in Dallas, and all the plans and the undercover feds were here in Dallas."

"Okay. So where did Ga—Judge Griswold come in?"

"Let's just say he leaned pretty heavily on FRE 403. Time and time again he excluded or suppressed important evidence on the grounds that it wasn't relevant. He maintained that the probative value of the evidence was substantially outweighed by the danger of unfair prejudice and misleading the jury. The defense was claiming all along that Abdul was never involved in the conspiracy itself, but that he just happened to live in the same apartment as the coconspirators."

"Yeah, right."

"He also excluded the testimony of one of our witnesses, a neighbor who'd heard the men discussing the plot while they were cooking outside next door to his apartment on a little hibachi. He says Abdul was right in the middle of it. Griswold excluded him because he ruled the testimony to be hearsay."

"Unbelievable."

"You're telling me? I had more than one reason to throw up every day, believe me."

"So what about the undercover fed? Couldn't he put the make on Abdul?"

"Clever defense questioning shed doubt on that. Whenever the fed visited the apartment, Abdul was not around. And since the fed was doing most of his business with the leader of the group, who was not Abdul, then technically, he couldn't make him, and we couldn't turn the other members of the conspiracy, although God knows we tried."

"Linda, sweetheart, I've got one more question."

"Anything for a butt-kisser."

"Why wasn't Abdul deported after the trial? Shipped back to mother Iraq?"

"Well, for one thing, he was acquitted of all charges by a jury of his so-called peers. And for another, soon after the trial he landed this really great job working for a spy shop outfit up in New York. So now he was a fine upstanding young taxpayer, and they had no good reason to kick him out."

"Linda, you are a doll, and I now owe you one," said Clark.

"You'll be *sooooor-ry,*" she sang with a laugh, and they hung up.

For a long moment Max and Clark both sat staring at the speaker phone as if it had something more to say, something definitive.

Finally, Clark said, "This still doesn't prove anything, Max."

"I know." She sighed.

"Gabe always was slicker than butter. No way is he

going to do anything which would alert attorneys or anybody else involved in the criminal justice system to the fact that he's throwing trials. Lawyers gossip. News leaks. Reporters swim around the courthouse like sharks, hitting up their best sources for anything that smells like blood."

"Somebody would have said something by now."

"Oh, without question! You wouldn't believe how many ambitious U.S. attorneys there are, looking for judgeships. Not to mention state court judges looking to move up in the world. Oh, people like Linda might complain, but like she said, there's nothing you can put your finger on."

"We have to find a connection between Gabe and CovertCom."

"Exactly."

"What if he owns stock in it?"

Clark considered this. "Well, that would be iffy, no doubt about it. It might draw charges of impropriety, but I don't think it would be a conflict of interest in this case, since Abdul was not involved with CovertCom at the time of the trial in Gabe's court."

Max nodded, feeling that old weight pressing against her chest, the one she'd felt in prison every morning when she woke up, looked around her, and knew she was caged.

There was a discreet rap at the door, and they both looked up to see Jennifer standing there, juggling paper plates, sodas, and a chicken bucket. Jennifer Maxfield was a petite, beautiful woman with a frosted blond pageboy held back now in a sky-blue band matching her eyes, a quick smile, and a figure—even after two babies—that made most women drool and most men stare. According to Liv, once Clark had laid eyes on his future wife, he never looked at another woman.

Max jumped up to help her, and Jennifer elbowed her way in, bringing smiles, kisses for Clark, and a breezy "How's it going?"

Clark said, "I talked to Linda Garcia. She was the U.S. attorney in the case against Abdul, but although she could corroborate that Gabe's rulings tended to favor the defendant, she couldn't make a solid connection between Abdul, CovertCom, and/or Gabe."

Appalled, Max shot a glance over at her brother. With an apologetic shrug, he said, "Sorry, sis, but Jenny and I tell each other everything."

Max didn't know what to say to that, and so busied herself with a Southern-fried chicken breast and a paper napkin. She was so used to living in a state of tight secrecy that she was alarmed to think that Clark could jeopardize her situation by talking to *anyone* about it—even his wife.

Jennifer pulled up a chair to sit close to the desk and said, "Who was the defense attorney?"

"Frank Hoffman," said Clark.

Tossing her husband a napkin, she nodded. "He just came through a nasty divorce last year."

"He did?"

"Oh, yeah, Clark, where have you been? His wife Rachel was raising all sorts of allegations of mental cruelty, adultery, whatever she could think of that might destroy his reputation." She took a dainty bite of cole slaw with a white plastic fork.

"Remind me of that next time I want to fool around on you." He winked at her, and she gave him a sexy little grin from beneath her lashes.

Max felt completely excluded. She knew that it was not Clark's, or even Jennifer's, intention to make her feel that way, but it was a natural consequence of being in the same room with the couple for very long. They were devoted to one another. For a long time Max had envied them.

What must it be like, she wondered, to have such complete and total trust in someone else?

"I think you guys should talk to Rachel," said Jennifer, turning to include Max in the remark.

"What's she got to do with it?" mumbled Clark around a huge bite of buttery biscuit.

"Oh, it's obvious, lover!" Leaning forward, Jennifer dabbed the corner of Clark's mouth with her napkin. "Men lawyers often talk to their wives about their cases, some more than others. If Frank said anything to Rachel at the time about any kind of impropriety on Gabe's part, then she'll have it hoarded up along with all the other bitter little facts she may dwell on in a given day of hating her ex-husband."

Max sat straight up. "So she'd tell us, then, wouldn't she? If she thought it might come back to give her ex-husband any grief, she'd talk!"

"That's what I'm saying, yes," said Jennifer. "At least, she'd talk to you, I think. It takes a woman to know a woman, right?"

Max smiled at her sister-in-law with great fondness. She genuinely hoped that some day she'd have a chance to know her better. Clark and Jennifer had gotten married while Max was on the run with Gaby. Although she had known Jennifer before the wedding, she'd never really had a chance to know her well. Hopefully that all would change one day.

Hopefully everything would change one day.

"Mom and I are going back to New York tomorrow," she said, more to herself than to anyone in the room.

"Why don't you take my car now," offered Jennifer, "and go see Rachel? She lives in Plano. Do you know where that is?"

With a sardonic grin Max said, "Oh yeah, I know where Plano is." She frowned. "But I don't know this woman. I don't even know if she's home. How can I just barge in on her?"

"Don't you worry. I'll take care of that," said Jennifer with a perky grin. A woman of boundless energy, she sprang to her feet and went in search of her address book.

"I can see why you love her so much," said Max quietly to Clark.

"There's nobody like her in the whole world," he said. "She's my soul mate. God, Max, I hope you can find that someday. Nobody deserves it more than you."

Max stared at her plate. *But I already found him,* she thought miserably. *That's the whole problem.*

Rachel Hoffman lived in a grand, sprawling brick home with a spiral staircase in the all-white living room, and two-story-high windows overlooking the pool in the huge den with beamed ceilings and parquet floors. She led Max to a sunken "conversation pit" near the wet bar, made herself a stiff martini, and brought Max a wine spritzer in a delicate crystal glass. There was no sign of children or pets anywhere.

Hoffman was a handsome, imposing woman with fierce black hair pulled straight back in a severe chignon and haughty dark eyes that missed nothing. She chain-smoked.

"So. My friend Jennifer tells me you've been fucked to the wall by your ex-husband." She lit one cigarette with the butt of another and squashed the other out in an ashtray full of lipsticky butts.

"I'm not sure what she's told you . . ." began Max.

"Relax. I don't know your life history. But I do know that your pervert ex-husband wants to get his hands on your little girl. I read that much in *Newsweek*."

"That was a long time ago," said Max awkwardly.

Hoffman waved her cigarette in the air. "That's neither here nor there. The fact remains that I remember when Frank defended that rag-head camel-jockey creep. Frank would defend Adolf Hitler if he thought there was enough money and or publicity in it for him." She took a deep drag on her cigarette.

"I know my ex-husband suppressed evidence—"

"No shit, Sherlock. Frank was so elated at the end of the every day during that trial that he couldn't hardly stand himself. God knows I couldn't stand him."

"Do you think Fra—your ex-husband . . . Do you think he had some sort of . . . arrangement going with my ex-husband concerning the outcome of the case?"

Hoffman exhaled a stream of smoke and gazed at Max through narrowed eyes. "Wouldn't put it past the bastard." She polished off her martini and went to fetch another one.

Max's eyes were beginning to burn from the cigarette smoke that layered the room like nightclub fog. She sneezed.

"Want another one?" called Hoffman from the bar, holding up a wine bottle.

"No, thanks, I'm still working on this one," said Max, digging through her tote bag for a tissue. She sneezed again and blew her nose.

"Allergies," said Hoffman. "It's that time of year." Through all the smoke, she seemed to Max to be in soft focus.

"Um, after the trial. Your husband's client got a job at a spy shop outfit up in New York called CovertCom?"

Taking a healthy sip of her martini, Hoffman nodded. "Not the first time, either."

A jolt of electric nerves shot through Max's body. "What do you mean, *not the first time*?"

While Max fidgeted impatiently, Hoffman took a deep drag on her cigarette. Nodding, she said, "He had another client one time who was tried in Judge Griswold's court. I can't remember his name. Anyway, he got a job up there, too. Or I should say, he got a job up there before the rag-head did."

"So he was acquitted?"

"Shit, yeah. He hired Frank, didn't he? Man's a cocksucker, no doubt about it, but if my ass was in trouble—*especially* if I was *guilty*, shit, I'd hire him myself! He wouldn't give a shit who I was as long as the case was either high profile or involved a lot of money, or preferably, both."

"And the other guy? The one who went to work for the spy shop?"

"What about him?" Hoffman drained her martini glass.

"Was it a high-profile case?"

"Nah. If it was, I'd remember the case. But there was a shit-pot lot of dough from it, though, I can tell you that. Practically paid for this house." She grinned wickedly.

"Where did the money come from? Was the client rich?"

Hoffman giggled. "Well, let's just say he was *connected*." Placing the martini glass carefully on the coffee table, she laid her hand against the side of her nose, crooking it over to the side of her face as if it was broken.

Max shook her head. "I don't understand."

Lighting a cigarette with the butt of the one she'd just shortened, Hoffman savagely stubbed it out in the ashtray. Two butts fell over the side of the ashtray in a fine powder spray of ashes. Glancing up at Max, who was watching with a sort of fascination, she said, "Honey, you *do* understand the words *organized crime,* don't you?"

Chapter Twenty-four

The day Jack Underwood lost contact with Rebekah Maxfield, he broke out into a cold sweat. For three days he searched for her with the help of a couple of surveillance teams who kept an eye on the CovertCom offices and the Maxfield apartment for him.

By the third night he was fighting panic. She seemed to have dropped off the face of the earth.

The fact that Max had eluded authorities for over a year in just this way made Underwood even more uncomfortable. If he lost a key government witness in a high-profile case, his career would be over before he could say *Tyson's Corner*.

When one of the agents on surveillance reported on the fourth day that Max and her mom had shown up at the apartment, hauling luggage as if returning from a trip, Underwood practically leapt out of his chair, grabbing his coat on the run and dodging out the door to relieve the surveillance agents and catch her before she could disappear again.

The movies made surveillance look so easy, reflected Underwood as he sat in the window of a restaurant across the street from Max's building and watched for her. In truth, the only way to keep from losing a subject was to have forty or fifty agents involved in the surveillance, dressed in different types of clothes and driving a wide variety of vehicles both behind, in front of, and approaching the subject, so as not to draw attention; to have a bumper beeper attached to the car that was under surveillance, and maybe a chopper or a plane overhead.

Underwood was painfully aware that he had few agents to help him. In some ways that was good—there was less margin for a mistake that could be overlooked in the confusion—but in another way it put even more pressure on Underwood not to screw up.

When it grew dark out, Underwood huddled in a doorway of a shop that was closed for the night, his hands jammed down deep in the pockets of his coat, his collar upturned against the wind. November was howling down out of Canada, and he could feel every cold breath.

He had just about convinced himself that it would be all right to go home and get some sleep, when he spotted her leaving the building and heading down the sidewalk at a brisk pace. Underwood followed along on his side of the street until he saw her enter a small corner grocery. Crossing against the light, Underwood dodged a taxi and stationed himself in the shadows just to the side of the store, which he knew she would have to pass on her way back to the apartment.

Cursing himself for not thinking to bring gloves, Underwood cupped his numbed hands and blew on them, then rubbed them together to generate warmth. *Right now,* he thought, *I'd shoot somebody for a hot cup of coffee.*

It seemed to Underwood that Max was in the store inordinately long, and by the time she emerged carrying two plastic shopping bags full of groceries, he was in an ill temper.

"Decided to come in from the cold, did you?" he asked as she walked past.

Startling violently, Max dropped one of the bags, its contents spilling over the pavement. "Jesus Christ, Underwood!" she cried as she stopped to retrieve the groceries. "You scared the hell out of me! What's the matter with you?"

Folding his arms across his chest, he peered down at her as she gathered the bags and, without offering to help, said, "I might ask you the same question. Where the hell have you been?"

When she stood up, Underwood could see that she was wearing high-heeled designer boots, which made her even taller than him than she normally was. He did not like that.

With long, angry strides she headed down the sidewalk toward her apartment building. "I took my mother to Texas to visit my brother, Underwood," she snapped, "as if it's any of your business."

Underwood grabbed her arm and yanked her to a halt. "But that's just it, you see. It is my business. Every single move you make is my business, Maxfield, because I *own you*. Do you understand that? Until this case is closed and you have testified in a court of law, you don't step foot outside that apartment without my knowledge. Don't you *ever* even *think* about leaving the city again without talking it over with me first, you got that?"

In the gauzy, pollen-yellow streetlights of the upscale Manhattan neighborhood at night, she turned her face slowly toward him. Hatred glinted from her eyes like the cold slice of a scimitar.

"I got it," she said. *"Warden Underwood."*

He watched her as she turned on her heel and stalked the rest of the way to her building, and he watched her as she disappeared inside. Something about the look she'd given him had left him, deep down inside, cold and alone as death.

And somehow, he knew, that even as he had struggled manfully to hold on to her, she had slipped right out of his grasp.

The trip to Texas had been just what the doctor ordered for Liv, and she was feeling quite rejuvenated. She still didn't know what the future held for her and Garrett, but she knew that, whatever it was, she would be able to handle it.

Liv wandered to the window and looked in the direction of the little market down the street, but she could not see her daughter. She didn't like Rebekah to go out alone at night—this was New York, for heaven's sake! But Rebekah, it seemed, was one thing Liv herself was not.

She was fearless.

Liv admired that quality about her daughter, but she worried sometimes that it might lead her to be reckless. *I brought four magnificent sons into this world,* thought Liv absently, *and you might know it would be my daughter who came the closest to being just like her father.*

And that's what worried Liv.

The phone rang and Liv grabbed for it, halfway believing it might be Rebekah, but to her pleasant surprise, it was Garrett.

"How was your trip?" he asked.

"Oh, it was wonderful!" she cried. "We had so much fun with the boys and their families. Clark took us sailing."

"I'm glad," said Garrett, his butter-smooth voice so warm and sexy; it reminded her of the crooner Bing Crosby. "Liv, I've been thinking about our last evening together."

"Me, too," she said, her cheeks burning in embarrassed remembering.

"We just don't have many opportunities for private moments, do we?"

Liv felt a little thrill in her stomach. She'd been afraid that Garrett might not want to see her again, but this sounded as if he wanted to be with her again after all!

"That's true," she said carefully.

It was important that a lady not seem too eager to a gentleman. She had to retain a little mystery to herself. It made her more desirable. This was something all these modern young girls never seemed to learn.

"Darling, have I ever told you about my cabin in the Adirondacks?"

A little sizzle of excitement took hold of Liv. *Calm down, old girl,* she told herself. To Garrett, she said, "No, I don't believe you have."

"Well, you understand, of course, that I use the term 'cabin' somewhat loosely." He chuckled. "It's a magnificent log home in Franklin County, in the upper Saranac Lake area. It was once a lodge. I bought it some years ago and had it renovated for my private use. It has a spectacular view of the lake and is surrounded by woods."

"Oh, it sounds wonderful!"

"It is, it is. Now, unfortunately, the best of the fall foliage colors have already climaxed, but it's still very beautiful there this time of year. It's my getaway. Very few people even know I have it. I want to take you there, Liv, just the two of us. No security people. No one at all. Just you and me. Would you like that?"

"I would love that!" she cried.

"We could spend a long weekend together, darling, just you and me, and see what kind of future we might have together."

This was a surprise indeed. And it was so sudden!

"Let's plan on it, then," Garrett continued in his usual take-charge way. "Next weekend. Don't tell anyone—not even Max."

Liv hesitated. Not tell her daughter where she was going? How could she not tell her? "I don't know, Garrett," she said. "I don't want Rebekah to worry about me."

"Nonsense. She's a big girl. And so are you. You have a right to do what you please without asking your little girl's permission."

"Well, I wasn't going to ask, exactly," she said, "but she needs to know how to get in touch with me in case of an emergency."

"Oh, for God's sake!" he cried, his voice suddenly sharp and tight with annoyance. "You can think of something, can't you? I'll give you a voice-mail phone number you can leave for her. We'll check in every day, all right? If anything happens, we'll come straight home."

"Well . . ."

"Liv. Do you want to be with me or not?"

There was a frightening note of finality to the question, almost as if Garrett were asking Liv to choose between himself and her daughter.

How silly. He wouldn't be doing that. Would he?

Liv, who was intimidated by confrontations and hated for anyone to be angry at her, felt confused by the sudden pressure-turn of the conversation with Garrett. She didn't understand why simply telling her daughter where she was going would be such a big deal, but Garrett was right. It was time Liv learned to live her own life and quit worrying about what her kids thought. Like Garrett said, Liv could leave a telephone number where she could be reached, and her daughter would just have to live with it.

"Of course I want to be with you," she said. "I'll think of something to tell Rebekah."

For Liv, it was a brazen stand of independence. Her daughter would not be pleased, and the knowledge made Liv feel a little giddy, as if she were a kid sneaking out on her parents, instead of the other way around.

It would be an adventure.

She couldn't wait.

Max's mom opened the door to Dominic that evening, and not only was her smile warm and genuine, she put her arms around his waist and hugged him like a son. Dominic responded with fondness. In his crazier moments, the ones where he allowed himself to fantasize that everything would somehow all be straightened out someday and Max would be his wife . . . he would find himself thinking that Liv would not make a bad mother-in-law at all.

"It's so good to see you, Dominic," she said. "I never get to see my sons anymore, so I hope you don't mind if I adopt you as a substitute."

"It's a pleasure, Liv," he said. "I don't get to see my mom much, either."

"Well, I know you didn't come to see an old broad like me. I'll go get Rebekah."

She left the room, and Dominic, ever-restless, got up and wandered over to the window and stared at the infamous butterfly dish the Boss had given to Liv. (He'd noticed she was wearing the pin.) Dominic couldn't blame Max for being concerned. Liv was an innocent, if there ever was one, and Dominic seriously doubted that Garrett Sharp had ever known one innocent day in his entire life.

Just for the hell of it, he picked it up.

"What are you doing?"

The tone of Max's voice, edged with suspicion and coming from right behind him, caused Dominic to jump and almost drop the dish. Feeling suddenly guilty, and not entirely sure why, Dominic set the dish on the windowsill and turned to face her.

The angles of her face were sharp, her eyes inexplicably stony.

"Jesus, Max, you scared the shit out of me." He gestured behind him. "I was just checking out the butterfly dish."

"What about it?"

Dominic stared at her. "Are you mad at me?" It was a simple-minded thing to say, but it was the first thing that occurred to him. Her body seemed to bristle with anger, and he was damned if he could figure out why.

She crossed her arms over her chest. "No."

"Well, according to Body Language 101, I'd say you're pretty severely pissed. I'm just trying to figure out what I did wrong."

Her posture slumped and she turned from him. "I'm not mad at you, okay? I've just got a lot on my mind right now." Widening the gap between them, she crossed the room and sat on the sofa.

Following behind, he sat next to her, but gave her the benefit of a foot or so of space between them. She looked haggard. "What's wrong?" he asked, caressing the side of her face with the back of his hand.

"Nothing. I'm just tired."

Okaaaay. If that's how she wanted to play it. . . He let his hand drop to his lap. "By the way, in case you're wondering about your recent change in assignment, you can thank me. I took care of it for you."

"Took care of what?" She seemed as if she weren't really paying much attention to him.

"When you got back from your trip to Dallas with Hakeem, I had a little talk with him, and then I spoke to the Boss, and he assigned you to work with Sebastian." He smiled.

Her face crinkled into a frown. "What do you mean you *had a little talk* with Hakeem?"

He shrugged. "Let's just say he won't be strong-arming you any longer."

With an elaborate roll of her eyes heavenward, she sprang to her feet and began to pace. "Who do you think you are," she cried, "one of my big brothers? Look, I can handle a pig like Hakeem Abdul. If I need your *big strong help,* I'll ask for it!"

"What's the matter with you?" he said, starting to

grow angry. "Did you forget how you looked that morning? You were a wreck!"

"Well, thank you very much, Calvin Klein."

"Oh, for God's sake, Max! Be reasonable! Hakeem is a violent man who hates women. A man like that will only respect a superior show of strength. Believe me, I've known guys like that my whole life."

"So have I. So what? Did you think I was going to follow along behind him and ask him to slap me around some more?"

"Of course not!"

"Then, why didn't you let me handle it?" she shouted.

"Because goddammit, I love you!" he yelled.

The words hung in the air between them. Dominic didn't know who was more horrified, him or Max.

He tried, and failed, to think of something to say. After a beat or so, it occurred to him that, in situations such as this, it was usually the girl's turn to say I love you back to the boy.

Instead Max said, "You don't know me, Dominic. You don't know me at all."

What a mysterious, vexing thing to say. He heard himself say, "I know enough."

To his amazement, her eyes filled with tears.

Tears were definitely not part of the script.

"We're strangers to each other, Dominic," she said, the words falling soft and sure in the room like a smooth round pebble into a pond, sending shock ripples in ever-widening circles. "I don't even know who you are."

Icy needles of fear pricked Dominic's body from head to toe. For so many years he'd been able to fall back on what he called "the empty-eyed stare," that look that he always used whenever anyone got uncomfortably close to the truth.

But then, in all that time, he'd never loved anybody.

Max had this way of peeling back the layers to expose the quivering core deep within. His instinct was to try and cover himself. Faking a laugh (which sounded fake), he said, "Nonsense. You know me better than anybody."

"Okay," she said, targeting him with her eyes. The

words flew swift as an arrow. She said, "Tell me your name."

As those simple words hit the bull's-eye, Dominic could feel the blood drain from his face. Struggling to assume the empty-eyed stare, he took a deep breath and said evenly, "It's Dominic, you silly girl, Dominic Antonio."

For a long, unbearable moment, she stared at him, those eyes nailing him to the wall. Then, slowly, she nodded. Finally, she said, "I think you'd better leave now."

What was happening? What the hell was happening?

Clambering awkwardly out of the overstuffed couch, he got to his feet and stood right in front of her. Her face was upturned to his, and he cupped her chin with the palm of his hand. A single tear broke loose from her lashes and tracked its slow, heartbreaking way down the side of her face. He caught it with his thumb. "Max?"

Her voice breaking, she said, "We can't do this anymore."

"What are you talking about? Why not?" There was no hiding the hint of desperation in his voice, and he despised himself for it, but there it was. He couldn't help it.

"Too many secrets."

"What? What secrets?"

"Too many secrets between us. Between you and me. You won't—or can't—even tell me who you are. And I can't tell you . . ." Shaking her head, she pulled away from him.

"What can't you tell me?" Dominic was so fucking confused he didn't know which way was up and which way was down. He had no idea what she was talking about.

Turning her back to him, she said, "I can't tell you . . . I can't tell you that I love you. Not as long as there are . . . lies . . . between us."

He wanted to deny it. More than anything in the whole damn world, Dominic wanted to deny it. He wanted to shout at her that there were no lies between them, that there were no secrets.

But he couldn't. Because if he did . . . it would be just one more lie.

He saw himself out. As he closed the door, he looked over at her, but her back was still turned to him, and he knew it was over.

A rush of wild craziness overtook him, made him want to fling the door back against the wall and shout out the truth to her, throw it in her face, see what she thought of him *then*.

But what would be the point? It would be agonizing enough, not having her in his life.

For her to hate him would be absolutely unbearable.

I should have trusted my first instinct, he thought bitterly as he let himself out the door. *I never should have gotten involved with her.*

The next few days were miserable. The less he was able to see her, the more he found himself obsessing about her. Though he tried with all his might and dignity not to mope around after her at the office, the effort took such fierce concentration that other areas of his work began to slide.

At home, he had a miserable time sleeping or even taking care of simple things like eating. Emotional and physical exhaustion crept up on him almost behind his back, and since he'd never really been in love before, he didn't notice the warning signs of stress, didn't realize, in fact, that he was literally grieving.

Had he not been so preoccupied by the shambles of his personal life, he would have been aware of the danger signals at work.

He would have realized that Max's life was in terrible danger before it was too late.

Chapter Twenty-five

Mid-Game, early November, 1997

In all her life, Max had never felt more alone, not even in prison.

There are many more kinds of prisons, thought Max gloomily as she sat with her chin propped in the palm of her hand, doodling at her desk Friday afternoon, *than those with bars on the windows.*

When the phone at her desk rang, she was tempted not to answer it. She didn't want to talk to anyone about anything. On the third ring she picked it up.

"Max? I'm glad I caught you. This is Clark."

Serrated little blades of panic sawed through Max at the sound of her brother's voice. He had never called her at CovertCom before. She knew without having to be told that it was an emergency.

"What is it? What's wrong?" She gripped the telephone receiver as if it were a lifeline and she a drowning victim.

"Maybe nothing, sis. Maybe everything. But I thought I should warn you—"

"What? About what?" She couldn't even think. Only react.

"I got to thinking that there had to be some reason why Gabe got a job for Hakeem and whoever else it was at CovertCom. There had to be some connection between Gabe and CovertCom that went beyond finding jobs for accused felons. So I was thinking about what you said, about Gabe buying stock in CovertCom, and how that wouldn't be any big deal, really. But you told me that CovertCom was defrauding its clients and stealing valuable information from them, so—"

"Clark!" cried Max. "I can't guarantee the security of this line."

He paused. "What line?"

"The phone line! I'll call you back. Are you at your home office or work office?"

"Work."

"Okay. Give me a few minutes to change phones."

Panic-driven, Max threw on her trench coat, grabbed her tote bag, and ran straight out of the office without a word to the astonished Rose Peterson.

Although Max had never checked the phones for a tap, she would not have put it past Sharp to tap his own office phones and spy on his employees. She mentally kicked herself for letting Clark say as much as he had.

Since the day she got out of prison, this was the most scared Max had ever been.

There was a cluster of pay phones on the corner. Two were occupied, and one was out of order. Max had to wait, screaming inside, until one came free, then she frantically dialed Clark's office phone. "It's Max," she said.

"Geez, Max, I'm such an idiot! It never occurred to me that the guy might tap his own phones! I'm so sorry!"

"Don't worry about it," she said with more assurance than she felt. "Just finish what you were telling me."

"Okay. Where was I? Oh, yeah. So I called up Zane, and I asked him to see if he could hack into Gabe's personal financial records, maybe find some connection there."

"You mean, from his bank?"

"No, no. His home PC. Like most of us, he's on-line at home, see, and he does a lot of business and all from his home computer. I figured Zane could sneak in through a back door that way, see what he could sniff out."

Max, still out of breath from her mad dash to the phones, began to become aware of her environment. Like most city dwellers, she paid little attention to the weather unless it inconvenienced her, and at this moment it was inconveniencing her a great deal. Storm warnings, in the form of powerful wet winds, had come crying in off the Atlantic while Max was buttoned down in her office, thundering through the canyons of the high buildings and battering Max now where she stood, hunkered in the flimsy shelter of the phone booth.

"So what did he find out?" she shouted, plugging one ear with a freezing finger.

"Well, that's just it. He got caught."

"What?" A cold hand closed over Max's heart. "What do you mean?"

"Apparently, Gabe had a security device on his home computer that detects an unauthorized intruder, and immediately traces the call."

"Oh, my God." The razor wind sliced at her legs, but that was not the cause of Max's sudden violent trembling. "Are you telling me that Gabe knows it was Zane who was hacking into his financial records?"

"Yes. He knows, Max. And that's not all."

Panic tugged at Max's arms and legs. It told her, *Run, run.*

"Wh-what else, Clark?"

"Somebody told him that you were snooping around the courthouse."

The woman at the courthouse. "Oh, *nooo!*" The last word came out sounding like a keen, or a howl, something primal, something stark.

Run, run, run.

Tears of cold and fright blurred Max's eyes, and she tried to blink them away. People bustled past, hunched into themselves against the cold, hurrying home.

Home.

"Clark—make sure that Zane gets word to Gaby's caretakers to be very careful, okay? I don't think Gabe knows where she is, but we can't take any chances."

"Will do. I'll call him as soon as we hang up."

"I'm going straight home. I'm putting Mom on a plane for Dallas, okay? Is that okay?"

"That's fine. We'll take care of her. Max—what are you going to do?"

"I don't know yet. I just don't know. I'll take care of Mom first, and then . . . and then I guess I'll go on the run again, Clark. Like before." Desperation caught in her throat, and she struggled not to break down.

"Sweet girl . . . be careful, okay?"

Thunder growled from on high, and a cold drop of rain splatted against Max's face like God's tear.

"I will. I love you guys."

"We love you. Let us know when . . . when you're safe."

"I will."

Rain-lashed wind ripped at Max as she hung up the phone, but she plunked an icy quarter into the slot and immediately dialed home with cold-stiffened fingers.

Ring, ring, damn you!

On the fourth ring, Max hung up. She wasn't about to leave a message on the machine. Where the hell was her mother?

Standing alone on the street corner, torn by indecision and the elements, Max knew that it was dangerous for her to return home. If Gabe knew that Max was on to him . . . if he knew that she'd made the connection between himself and CovertCom, then he would take whatever means necessary to stop her.

He had to know now that there was far more at stake than finding Gaby. His career—everything that made him who he was—was at risk.

When had her brother said that Zane had hacked into Gabe's PC? Last night? The night before? Two days ago? When?

He hadn't said.

She started to call him back and ask, but decided against it. She had to go home. She had to find out where her mother was. She had to get her mother to safety.

Underwood.

Again, Max hesitated. Should she call him? Should she ask for his help? Wasn't it his job to help her?

Not really. It was his job to make a case against CovertCom. If she told him her ex-husband, the great federal judge, was dangerous, he probably wouldn't believe her anyway.

Fuck it. From the very beginning, Underwood had been more trouble than he was worth. She didn't trust him.

She didn't trust anybody.

She *couldn't* trust anybody, not as long as Gaby was depending on her mother to keep her safe.

Time was of the essence. The quicker she could put miles between herself and CovertCom, the better.

Running straight out into the street, Max beat on the window of a cab that was slowing for a light and leapt into the backseat before the driver could object. "Fifty-fourth and Park," she said. "And there's an extra twenty in it for you if you can get me there fast."

Although the cabbie made the trip in record time, Max was tormented by demons at her heels. The apartment was ominously cold and quiet. A note on the kitchen counter in her mother's breezy hand brought a chill to Max's soul:

> Darling. Garrett and I have gone away for a roman-
> tic weekend. I know you may not approve, but I as-
> sure you everything is all right. If you need me, I've
> put a voice-mail phone number at the bottom of this
> page. Otherwise, I'll see you Sunday or maybe Mon-
> day. I love you. Mom.

Something was wrong. Even though the tone of the letter was cheerful enough, her mother had not said *where* she had gone with Garrett. That was completely uncharacteristic of her. In fact, Max could not think of any reason why her mother would keep her destination secret other than that she had been told to do so by Garrett.

Hollow, bone-cracking fear buckled Max's knees, and she sank onto a kitchen chair, holding her mother's note in a trembling hand.

Her mother didn't know it, but she'd just been taken hostage.

How could I have let this happen? Max thought.

She shook her head. No time for regrets. What to do. She had to think what to do. Call Underwood? And tell him what? That her mother had gone off for a romantic weekend with the man she'd been seeing for several months—call out the SWAT team?

Yeah, right.

After a few fearful moments, calm came to Max. The

game wasn't over yet. Oh, no, it was not over by a long shot.

Hurrying into her room, Max changed clothes, putting on jeans, a thick sweatshirt, and a sturdy waterproof coat, along with cushy socks and a good pair of hiking boots. Into her tote she threw a few things, then reached up and rummaged around in the top of her closet, where she retrieved a thousand dollars in cash, a specially equipped briefcase, and a few other items she knew she was going to need.

It was night. Outside, the wind shrieked and the rain pummeled the windows, as if nature were throwing a temper tantrum. Stuffing her hair up under a leather cap with a good visor, Max took a moment to collect herself, then hurried out the door. She didn't know if her building was being watched or not, so she took the stairs and headed for a corridor that led to the basement laundry room and a back exit.

Rounding the corner, she blundered almost smack into Hakeem Abdul and her ex-husband, Gabe.

Hakeem already had a gun drawn. The moment he saw her, he assumed the stance and pointed the gun straight at Max.

She froze.

Gabe smiled at her. It was unreal, standing face-to-face with her ex-husband once more. His hair was much grayer, almost silver, and the lines around his mouth and eyes were somewhat deeper, but other than that, he was the same man she had once loved.

Max's thoughts began to dash about like trapped little animals. Hakeem's gun looked like a cannon to her untrained eye, and she knew that they intended not just to frighten her or get information from her, but to kill her.

I don't want to die, she thought. *I promised Gaby I'd come back.*

Gabe spoke. "I know that Gabrielle is in Switzerland," he said in that compelling courtroom voice she had once found intoxicating. "Tell us who are her caretakers and where we can find her, and I will let you live."

Living nightmares, Max found in that instant, were not so very different from the dream-state ones. Images grew jumbled; time stopped, then speeded up in fast-forward, then stopped again; and nothing, nothing seemed real.

This was a living nightmare.

Max could not be standing here, staring at her ex-husband while a cold-blooded killer held a gun on her; she could not be standing here, hearing her husband say that Gaby was in Switzerland.

It was not happening.

How could he know? How could he possibly know?

Nobody knew that Gaby was in Switzerland. Nobody but Max . . . and . . . her mother.

But Liv would never, *ever* dare reveal Gaby's whereabouts to a living soul—too, too much was at stake! She would never take such a terrible risk!

Max tried to speak. Her mouth was so dry that her tongue stuck to the roof of her mouth. "What have you done to my mother?" she asked in a voice trembling with terror she could not hide. "You've done something to her, haven't you?"

Gabe smiled again; actually, it was more of a smirk. How could she not have known, from the very beginning, that his smile was never, ever real?

"I haven't done anything to your mother. You'd have to ask my friend Garrett what has become of her. But I don't care about your mother, my dear. All I care about is finding my daughter. You have defied me for the last time. You have kept my daughter from me, and now you will tell me who she is with and where I can find her or you will die."

And if I die, she thought, *what hope will my mother have?*

Hakeem Abdul, Max knew, would be able to obtain any information Gabe wanted from her scared and very vulnerable little mother . . . right before he killed her, too.

Something about the wind and rain outside, or maybe it was the horror of the moment, but in the lickety-split way of her scattered thought processes, Max felt a sudden calm, and in that petrifying moment of quiet, she thought of a strategy she might use, a weapon, as it were.

She said, "Gabe, it might interest you to know that for the entire time I've been working for CovertCom,

I've been an informant for the FBI. I've told them everything. Should anything happen to me, anything at all—
they'll know it was you. They'll come after you, and your
precious career will be over."

As soon as Max said "FBI," she saw the barrel of the
gun take a sudden dip, and she glanced up from the ugly
black weapon to Hakeem. His face had turned a sickening
shade of yellow. Then she looked at her ex-husband.

She could see her words working on him, could see
him assessing her, searching for the lie in her eyes.

"You're bluffing," he said.

For a long, excruciating moment, their eyes met.

The lights went out.

That split second of hesitation was all Max needed.
Plunging straight ahead, briefcase held aloft like a shield,
she hit Hakeem with all her strength. Caught off guard
and surprised by the ferocity of her attack, he lost his
footing and went down. A muzzle flash and a muffled
thud sent Max scrambling for the door.

The lights flickered back on.

When everything started to unravel, it happened
quickly, until the entire tapestry of her life was soon
reduced to a worthless tangle of unrelated, brightly hued
threads that dangled beneath her and tripped her up as
she ran, clutching the briefcase in her sweaty hand as if
it could shield her from the bullets which whizzed past
her head and thudded into the wooden door as she
passed through. Splinters stung her cheek.

There should have been an answering echo of gunfire—enough noise to raise an army—but he was too
smart for that. A silencer shrouded everything but muffled little thuds as each bullet was fired and found their
mark, breathlessly close to her ear.

The rainbow embroidery of her mother's strength, her
daughter's sweet trust, her brothers' courage, her lover's
tenderness—even the black snarls of her time in prison,
the deaths of her father and brother Brand, and her ex-
husband's cruelty—which had once woven together,
good braided into bad, to provide the brilliant texture
of her existence, now threatened to serve only as a tattered burial shroud instead.

Someone yanked the sleeve of her blouse and lay a

hot branding iron against her left arm; however when she glanced down, she saw that a bullet, not a hand, had left the rip. Blood oozed from the wound, but even as she hitched up the arm for a closer look, she felt a tug at her hair and knew his aim was getting better.

Heart pumping at her throat, hot needles of panic pricking her skin, she ran flat out, through the back door of the apartment building and out into the cold, wild, wet night. Her breath coming in little clouds of mist, she made an attempt at a giant leap down the concrete stoop and failed.

She hit the alley hard as she skidded face forward onto the extended briefcase, as if it could somehow break her fall. Almost instantly, she stumbled clumsily to her feet, sprinkling crimson droplets of blood. In the gleam of a fluorescent light, the blood glimmered back.

The fall had sucked the breath out of her, and she staggered, gulping for air, as more shots cracked against the shining wet alley, sending little shards of concrete shrapnel stinging into her body. The stark realization burned into her brain that she was going to die right here, right now, shot down before she could see Gaby again.

That thought alone almost brought her to her knees.

She didn't even hear the car until it was almost upon her. It bore crazily down on her like a dark demon from hell, careening around the corner and down the alley with a sickening howl and filling the air with the screaming screech of brakes.

The passenger door flopped open and was immediately hit by gunfire, leaving a small neat hole right in the center of the car door, a bull's-eye on a target.

"GET IN!"

Wind-tossed trees in the nearby adjacent street jostled patches of luminescence into freakish patterns, but there was enough light from the dome bulb inside the car to enable her to see the driver clearly. Still, this was no time for hesitation. Gripping the briefcase, she dove in headfirst, grappling for the door handle as the tires spun backward in a wild flail of arms, legs, blood, and the smoke of burned rubber.

PART IV

COLD PLAY

cold play: *when a player on a losing streak makes a desperation bet against a superior hand.*

There is a land of the living and a land of the dead and the only bridge is love, the only survival, the only meaning.

Thornton Wilder
The Bridge of San Luis Rey

Chapter Twenty-six

Liv was surprised when Garrett picked her up in an imposing, dark blue four-wheel-drive Range Rover. It was the first time they had ever gone anywhere without a driver, or for that matter, without the limousine. The weather had gone all raw and nasty. Garrett looked so rugged and handsome wearing jeans, a plaid flannel shirt in navy and tan, a navy cable-knit crew neck sweater, and a buttery tan leather jacket.

"We're driving?" she said as he stowed her bags in the rear.

"Sure," he answered. "I thought it would be nice for a change. Upstate New York has some of the most beautiful scenery in the Northeast. You can't possibly get the full flavor of it by flying over."

"Is it terribly far?"

"Nah. Only about five or six hours, driving. New York isn't as big a state as Texas, my dear." He winked at her as he opened her door. "Besides, I thought you wanted to spend some time alone together."

"Oh, I do," she said, getting in. "I'm just surprised at you, that's all." She clambered into the truck-like vehicle and reached for her seat belt.

"I'm a man of many surprises," said Garrett as he closed her door and walked around to his side to get in.

For a man who was spoiled by being driven everywhere, Garrett nonetheless handled the Range Rover with great assurance. Traffic didn't seem to bother him, and he knew his way, so Liv relaxed, sorting through his CD collection until she found a selection of Andrew Lloyd Webber's greatest show tunes.

While Betty Buckley's incomparable soprano soared through "Memory," Liv wondered at how quickly they

seemed to leave the city behind. Though insulated somewhat from the gigantic storm buffeting New York City
that afternoon, the Hudson River Valley was draped
with gauzy layers of mist that seemed to lift like curtains
from time to time, revealing picturesque villages, patches
of green pastures, steamy ponds, magnificent riverside
estates, and hillside woodlands aflame with the fiery colors of autumn.

For the first time, Liv allowed herself to fantasize
about what it would be like to be married to Garrett
Sharp. Would they visit his lakeside log cabin often, and
would they have favorite haunts along the way?

As night approached, gathering mists soon changed to
drizzle. By the time they entered Essex County, it had
grown quite cold and Garrett was running the car heater
continually. Conversation had slowed to a standstill, and
Liv had noticed that Garrett was becoming somewhat
preoccupied. She was also growing hungry and wondered if they would stop to eat or pick up groceries on
the way to the cabin. Truthfully, she was tired and in no
mood to cook. When the car phone rang, she jumped.

Garrett picked it up. "Yeah."

Liv glanced at his profile. She could see the muscles
in his jaw clenching. "I can't believe it," he said. Then,
"Hell, yes, we're driving. Would you rather I file a flight
plan for all the world to see?"

The one-sided conversation bewildered Liv, but something about the remark concerning a flight plan injected
a cold little chill into her stomach, though she couldn't
say why. Perhaps it was the rapidly changing mood she
saw taking place on Garrett's face.

Perhaps it was the lie he'd told her, about driving so
that they might enjoy the view.

Just then he turned to look at her, and his eyes were
as deep and cold as the waters of the Saranac Lakes.
Into the phone he said, "Look, I can take care of my
end easily enough. You're the one who fucked up, and
you're the one who's going to have to fix it."

With that, he slammed down the telephone receiver so
hard that the bell gave a confused little ring, and cursed
under his breath. Liv did not ask about the call. She was
used to Garrett's volatile work-related temper tantrums,

but this was different. Maybe the fact that the phone call, with its disturbing news intruding into their private, cozy little car world, shattering the misty peace, could explain why, this time, Liv felt strangely frightened.

Rain and darkness eventually blotted out their surroundings, until it was just Liv and Garrett, alone in a Range Rover, driving deep into the mountains to a place Liv had never seen, and toward a destination she'd told no one about. It was supposed to have been romantic, but Garrett's stony face, etched in anger, was anything but.

They left the Northway and picked up a country road north toward Lake Placid, where Garrett stopped for gas. To Liv's complete mystification, he placed a couple of phone calls from a pay phone outside the gas station, rather than using the car phone. Still, she chose not to ask about it because she'd long since learned that CovertCom was a secretive business.

By the time they'd reached Mirror Lake, the rain had frozen into icy sleet. Although Liv was disappointed when Garrett picked up a couple of Big Macs, coffee, and fries at a drive-through highway McDonald's rather than stopping at a restaurant, she could understand his eagerness to get to the cabin before the weather worsened.

"Is everything all right?" she asked timidly as the Range Rover sat idling by the drive-through window.

"Everything's fine," he said without looking at her.

"It's just . . . we were having such a good time, and then . . . you seemed to get some kind of bad news," she hazarded.

Still staring straight ahead, he said, "That's none of your business, Liv."

His words stung, and she turned her face toward the passenger window to hide her hurt. He was an enigmatic, difficult man to understand. Although Richard had had his faults, he'd always been straightforward and upfront with her. If he was angry, he told her so, in no uncertain terms. When she pleased him, he told her that, too.

With Garrett Sharp, she never knew where she stood. It was perplexing, and it kept her constantly off balance.

They left the highway and took a couple of turns down narrow roads closely lined with trees, passing rural houses exuding warm light from their windows. For some reason, this made Liv feel suddenly very melancholy.

The weekend no longer looked as appealing as it had when they first set out. The Range Rover was designed for rugged country use, not for comfort, and Liv's back was beginning to ache when Garrett turned the vehicle down an unmarked, rutted, single-lane road that tunneled darkly through the trees, their wet boughs slashing against the windshield and shrieking across the roof of the vehicle like the curling fingernails of skeletons.

The vehicle eventually emerged into a gravel clearing layered with soggy leaves. Garrett's log "cabin" loomed like a natural two-story extension of the towering pines and other trees. Heavenly amber light spilled from the windows, which were set back behind an immense wraparound porch, and a white stream of smoke curled lazily from the huge stone chimney.

"I had someone open up the place for us," explained Garrett when Liv exclaimed in delight.

Being with Garrett was like riding a roller coaster, she reflected as she got out of the car. Up, down, up down—you never knew what to expect. The cold wind whipped away her breath, and she hurried up the stone steps to the front porch, where Garrett pushed open the door.

"Welcome to Hearthside," he said with a smile.

"Oh!" cried Liv. They entered a magnificent great room sprawled beneath a peaked ceiling at least thirty feet high and trussed by mighty timbers. A massive mountain stone fireplace extended the full length of the opposite wall, flanked on either side by floor-to-ceiling windows that overlooked a deck and beyond that, the lake. Handsome rugs were scattered around on the hardwood floors, which were polished to a high gloss. Wrought-iron chandeliers hung low and cast soft warm light on the handmade Adirondack birch-wood tables, a moose head and crossed snowshoes hung over the hearth, and cozy mohair throws were tossed casually over the overstuffed chintz-covered chairs and couches. A cheerful fire danced in the fireplace, and books and magazines were in plentiful supply.

Huge logs supported second-story lofts, which opened

up on three sides of the room, with smaller logs making up the balconies and stairway balustrades. In the shadowy alcove beneath one of the lofts, Liv could see a kitchen with a long, heavy, thick pine trestle table and the matching handcrafted cabinets.

Everywhere was the soothing scent of wood.

Liv turned to Garrett to tell him everything that was in her heart, how she felt instantly at home in this place, how much she loved it, how glad she was that he had brought her here, how she couldn't wait to explore the surrounding woods . . . but she stopped, and all the words crowded into her throat and died.

Leaning on his elbows over one of the loft balconies on the opposite side of the great room, his hands clasped and his ankles crossed as if he were the homeowner welcoming the guests, stood Sebastian Taylor, his blond hair glowing flaxen in the flickering firelight.

"So you finally arrived!" he called jovially to Garrett.

Liv whirled back toward Garrett, questions clamoring for answers, but he ignored her.

"Go get the bags," he commanded Taylor, tossing the car keys onto a nearby table. "Where's Evan?"

Loping down the half-log staircase, Taylor said, "He went out to get some more firewood."

In that masterful way of his, Garrett strode across the room toward a handsome wall unit tucked beneath a loft that contained a television set and CD player and some cabinets. "I need a drink," he muttered.

Liv, still standing dumbstruck in the middle of the floor, said, "Garrett?" Her voice was tentative, questioning.

Garrett reached the wall unit and began rummaging in one of the cabinets. He did not answer her. A back door opened from inside the kitchen, and Evan Ryder came in, bringing a whorl of outdoor air with him. His arms were filled with firewood, and he carried them over to the hearth and deposited them into a large basket on the floor nearby. When he was done, he unzipped his goose-down parka and shrugged out of it.

He was wearing a flannel shirt and, over that, a shoulder holster with a gun in it. The front door swung open then, and Sebastian Taylor came banging in, bearing luggage.

"Garrett!" cried Liv, anger and confusion making her bold.

"What?" He poured himself a tumbler of whiskey.

"I demand to know what's going on!" Lifting her chin a bit to cover the quaver in her voice, Liv swallowed.

"Where do you want these?" asked Taylor.

"Put mine in my room," said Garrett, "and put hers in the room next to it."

"Right." He went bounding up the stairs, as if the bags were filled with air.

Evan Ryder said, "Judge Griswold called, and the shit hit the fan."

Cutting a glance over at Liv, Garrett said, "Shut up."

But it was too late, of course.

It was too late because *now* Liv understood what was going on. She understood everything. It came to her with a flash of insight that was a culmination of every nagging doubt she'd ever had about Garrett, and every little secret her daughter had kept from her through the months.

Her first thought was, *God help me . . . I've been such a fool.*

Her second thought was of Rebekah.

Her third thought was eclipsed by a sudden rushing flood of fear so powerful it covered everything else in Liv's life, leaving her paralyzed as the cold waters swept up over her ankles, crept past her crotch, lapped at her face, and finally threatened to drown her, before she could make a single solitary cry for help.

Jack Underwood was diving in the depths of sleep when the jangling phone split the night and brought him swimming reluctantly toward the surface. Still half submerged, he fumbled for the receiver and said, "Hello?" without opening his eyes.

"Jack?"

"Yuh-huh."

"This is David Young."

"Huh?" Groping through a scotch-induced fog, Underwood stumbled around in the mental mists, searching for the name.

"From Violent Crimes."

"Oh! Yeah." Propping himself on one elbow, he grappled through the items on the bedside stand, found his glasses, and put them on, though his eyes were still closed.

"The SAC said I should call you about a shooting over on Fifty-fourth and Park. He said it might have something to do with Operation EAVESDROP?"

Underwood's body went stone-cold. Sitting bolt-upright, eyes wide open, he said, "What shooting?"

"There was a shooting incident on the bottom floor of an apartment building at that address. A tenant who was doing her laundry said she saw a couple guys chasing a woman she ID'd as . . . Rebekah Maxfield. They shot at her several times, but apparently she got away. I checked at her apartment, but there was nobody home. I wouldn't have bothered, you know, because it's an NYPD matter, but the SAC said . . ."

"You did the right thing, David. Listen . . . meet me there in half an hour, okay?"

"Okay."

Underwood pulled on some clothes with shaking hands. He cursed himself for drinking so much before falling asleep. Washing down two aspirin with some Alka-Seltzer, he called a cab, checked the clip and safety of his FBI-issue Model 1076 Smith & Wesson 10mm, holstered it, put on his trench coat, and hurried downstairs.

On the drive to Max's apartment, Underwood's heart raced at twice the normal rate, and he broke out into a sick sweat. Though he tried to blame the booze, the truth was that he feared his whole investigation had just turned into a giant clusterfuck; Max's life was now in terrible danger and it was all his fault.

He just wasn't sure how.

Young was waiting for Underwood in the lobby with the building super and the doorman. The NYPD detectives had already left. Young explained to Underwood as they walked toward the rear of the building that since there was no known crime victim, and since there was no complaint or even so much as a missing person filed, then there was little they could do.

"Did you see Max at all today?" Underwood asked Ralph, the doorman.

Ralph nodded. "This morning she left for work normal, just like always. Then she came home a little early—"

"What time?"

He shrugged. "Five-ish."

"Did you see her leave again?"

He shook his head.

"What about her mother?"

"Mrs. Maxfield? Oh, she left for a romantic weekend with that nice gentleman she's been seeing. I'm taking care of her old bulldog, Sarge, for her, just like I did when she went— "

Underwood interrupted. "What do you mean, a romantic weekend?"

Ralph said, "She told me. And she was dressed for the country. I thought it was interesting because they didn't leave in his limo, like they usually do. No, this time, he was driving, and they loaded her bags into a blue Range Rover."

"He was driving? Are you sure?"

"Sure I'm sure."

They'd reached a rear corridor leading toward a laundry room and an exit door. There was no yellow crime-scene tape strung up, but the police had circled the bullet holes with black markers, a fact that annoyed the super, a man named Schneider, no end.

"A hole is bad enough," he complained. "You can get by with a hole, maybe, but these black circles? Now we've got to repaint the whole thing."

Ignoring him, Underwood turned to Young. "Shell casings?"

"None. If they were using an auto, they either picked them up later or they were using a brass-catcher."

"What do you think?" Underwood examined a sizable chunk of splintered wood in a door facing.

"Pretty big plugs. I'd say a .45, but it's hard to tell for sure. The witness says the gun didn't make very much noise, and nobody on the second floor even heard it, so I'm assuming they used a noise suppressor."

"What's this?" Pointing at some dark sprinkles on the

linoleum, Underwood crouched down. He wiped his finger across them. The droplets were, for the most part, dry, but he was able to smear some of the substance. "It looks like blood!" he cried.

Young knelt down beside him. "How come the cops didn't notice this?" he said angrily. "Morons."

"She was hit," said Underwood. Snapping on a light switch that cast faint illumination on the concrete stoop, he followed the blood splatters. "Look at this." He glanced over at Young. "If she was hurt bad, there'd be a lot more blood, wouldn't there?"

"Probably." Young shrugged. "Depends on the wound." He was carrying a bright flashlight and cast its halo of light around on the alleyway. "It looks as though she fell and slid a bit, then scrambled to her feet." Pointing the light farther, he indicated two skid marks. "I'd say a car took the corner practically on two wheels over there, hit the brakes, then backed up in a real hurry to get the hell away from whoever was shooting at them. The witness couldn't say for sure who it was, since she was cowering in the laundry room at the time, but it would appear the lady caught a ride."

"What happened to the bad guys?"

"Nobody knows."

"Gimme the flashlight." Underwood got on his knees beside the skid marks. "I don't see any blood here," he said hopefully.

Young said, "It was raining, Jack."

Underwood felt light-headed. He eased himself onto the bottom step of the stoop and sat there, staring out at the rain-slick streets of New York. Steam belched out through a street grate from the bowels of the city.

For the first time since beginning Operation EAVESDROP, the investigation didn't seem to matter anymore to Underwood. Somewhere out there, Max was bleeding, and probably scared to death. She was running for her life from somebody who wanted her dead.

"I promised her I'd protect her," he murmured.

"Protect who?" Young lowered himself to the step just above Underwood and lit a cigarette.

"My informant. I promised I'd look after her, and I blew it." A damp chill took hold in his gut, and he wanted to throw up. If anything happened to Max, he knew he'd never forgive himself.

"We can't be everywhere, man," said Young as he exhaled a stream of cigarette smoke. "It'll be all right," he added. Under the circumstances there wasn't much else he could say.

It wasn't going to be all right, though. Underwood knew that. Something had gone crazily, terribly wrong. Somewhere, he'd dropped the ball.

He'd let Max down. No wonder she hated him.

"You guys need anything else?" asked Schneider from the doorway with poorly disguised irritation.

"Jack?" prompted Young.

"Yeah. Tell him we'll want to look around Max's apartment."

Flicking the cigarette butt into the alley, Young got to his feet and went to deal with the super.

Underwood's glasses were fogging up. He watched as the glowing ember burned bright, then faded and died.

Dominic's main goal was to put as many miles between Max and her would-be killers as he could. To that end, he drove with fierce concentration, breaking nearly every traffic law on the books as he maneuvered the Mercedes out of the city. He even used a few evasive techniques to ensure that they were not being followed. The German-made car responded like a lover, and they made good time. For her own part, Max said nothing. It was a full half hour before Dominic glanced down and noticed that her arm was bleeding.

"Jesus, Max! You're hit! Why didn't you say something?" Instinctively, he grabbed the arm, which provoked a yelp of pain from Max.

"It's all right," she said, yanking her arm out of his hand. "Just a graze. I'll live."

"Let me look for a drugstore, anyway," he insisted. "I can get some gauze and bandage it."

"No."

"It could get infected—"

"I said no!"

Dominic looked over at her. She was white-faced, and

her eyes were wide with fear. *She doesn't trust me,* he thought, and his heart sank.

"How did you know I was in trouble?" she asked, her voice tight with suspicion. She was clutching a briefcase in her lap. Over her right shoulder hung a tote bag, which rested on top of the briefcase. She guarded both as if he were a thief.

"I'm not sure," he said truthfully. "It was just a feeling." When she said nothing to that, he said, "Who was shooting at you?"

"You don't know?"

"Of course I don't know! What kind of question is that?"

She sighed. "I'm sorry." For a long moment she stared out the passenger window, as if trying to decide what to say, what not to say. Finally, she said, "It was Hakeem. He had the gun. And my ex-husband."

"Oh, my God." This was terrible news. Max had no idea what a crack shot Hakeem was, or how lucky she was to be alive.

But her *ex-husband*? What did *he* have to do with Hakeem?

Dominic said, "Max. You've got to let me help you."

"Then, tell me where my mom is."

"What are you talking about?"

"She left me a note. Said she went off on a so-called *romantic weekend* with Mr. Sharp. But she didn't say where. They could be anywhere." Her voice broke, and she turned the back of her head to him again.

Dominic thought rapidly. If Griswold was involved with Sharp, then that would explain a lot of things that had puzzled Dominic through the months. It would also raise the stakes considerably. To Max, he said, "The Boss has a log cabin up in Franklin county, by the Upper Saranac Lake. Sometimes he . . . takes women up there." He glanced over at her.

Max nodded. "Then, that's where they'll be holding Mom hostage."

"Don't you think you're overreacting?" he said, keeping his voice as gentle and non-accusatory as possible. "Your mom doesn't know anything. Why would they want to hold her hostage?"

"She may not know anything about CovertCom," said Max, "but she knows where Gaby is."

"Oh." Tightening his grip on the steering wheel, he said, "Oh, shit, Max."

"Yeah. Oh, shit." Her voice had assumed an otherworldly monotone, and Dominic wondered if she might be going into shock. It didn't appear, from just the cursory glance he'd been able to give it, that the gunshot wound was all that severe, but she'd suffered a trauma nonetheless.

He fretted with the car heater. "Are you warm enough?"

She stared at her hands. "My hands are cold." One of them was bloody from holding it clasped over the wounded arm.

Dominic turned up the heater and adjusted a vent to blow toward Max. He wasn't sure what to do. The arm needed attention and Max needed rest, but until she had discovered what had happened to her mother, she would do neither, of that he was certain.

Dominic didn't think Hakeem had been able to see who'd been driving the Mercedes. What he hadn't told Max was that the Boss had already ordered the Spy Squad up to the cabin. So it would be necessary for him to go there, but to show up with Max could put her in grave danger. The appearance of her ex-husband on the scene had changed everything.

As the car warmed up, Max laid her head against the car window and, almost against her will, dozed off.

Dominic took the New York State Thruway north. While he drove, he considered what to do next. He knew a safe place in Albany where he could leave Max while he went on to the cabin. Maybe he could salvage the situation after all. He'd have to make a couple of phone calls first. Dominic didn't want to make them from the car, however, not with Max sitting next to him.

The injection of Max's mom into the situation was a complication, no doubt about it, but Dominic thought he could handle it. As he drove, he considered and rejected several plans.

About fifty miles south of Albany, Max stirred, sat up, rubbed the back of her neck, extended her sore arm painfully, and peered out the window. "Saugerties," she said drowsily. "That's where the Woodstock rock festival really took place, wasn't it?" She yawned.

"Actually, it was outside Bethel," he said. "At Mr. Yasgar's farm." He smiled at her.

She did not return the smile. "Where are we going?"

"I know a place where you can be safe, Max," he said carefully. It was so ingrained in him not to reveal any more about himself than was absolutely necessary that he hesitated to say more just yet, even to Max. "Then I'm going on to the cabin."

As he carefully considered his words, casting about for the best way to explain himself, Max took care of the problem for him. He came up behind a Winnebago pulling a boat on a trailer, and was forced to slow down. While he was considering the best way to pass, Dominic registered the fact that Max had disengaged her seat belt, but his mind didn't seize upon it, because he assumed she was going to try and make herself more comfortable.

So he was completely unprepared when she yanked on the car door handle, kicked the door open, and dove into the wind-screaming night.

Chapter Twenty-seven

Although the tote bag and briefcase broke her fall somewhat, Max hit the pavement hard in a tumbling end-over-end roll that ripped open both knees of her jeans, peeling off the skin from her knees to her shins. She gripped the briefcase and her tote bag so tightly that the skin was also burned off her knuckles and the backs of her hands. The leather cap flew off her head and rolled into the ditch. Although the heavy goose-down coat offered some protection to her upper body, the wound to her arm tore open again with a searing pain.

The taillights of the Mercedes glowed bright as Dominic hit the brakes, fishtailing to a stop. Max staggered to her feet and limped as quickly as possible toward the line of trees pressed close to the road. By the time she heard the slam of a car door, she was huddled motionless in the brush.

"Max!" he shouted. *"Maaax!"*

Max couldn't see Dominic because she dared not lift her head and peer around, but she could hear him searching frantically for her up and down the roadside.

"For God's sake," he cried. "I would never hurt you! Please, you gotta trust me!"

Fierce pain set in from every open wound on her body. Max bit her lip to keep from groaning. Tears coursed down her face, but not from the physical pain.

It started to rain.

"Maaax!" he yelled, his voice growing hoarse. "Let me help you! Come on out, please!"

His cries grew louder as he approached her hiding place. "I can't leave you out here, Max! *Max!*" This time her name came out sounding like a sob.

Every fiber and sinew of her body tugged at her, begging her to crawl out, to trust this man to protect her, to help her, to do whatever it took to rescue her mother.

The temptation was overwhelming, and she almost gave in to it.

The only thing that kept Max still was that last remark he'd made, about leaving her someplace safe and going on to the cabin. What was that all about?

There were too many unanswered questions where Dominic Antonio was concerned, and Max could not risk the safety of her family as long as Dominic refused to trust her with those answers.

Leaves crunched underfoot as he drew near. There was a stumbling noise then, "Goddammit! Stupid worthless piece of shit flashlight batteries!"

He was close enough that Max could reach out and touch him. Heart thudding, aching with cold and miserable with burning pain, she waited. It would be so easy to get to her feet and fall into his arms. After all, he had saved her from Hakeem, hadn't he?

"Okay, *fine!*" he yelled, his voice surging with a frustrated burst of anger. "Stay out here and freeze to death, for all I care!"

She heard him stomping off through the leaves and getting into the car, but rather than driving away, he pulled over to the shoulder of the road and backed up slowly, slowly, as if giving her one more chance to reveal herself. At one point the light from his car headlights arced over her. Finally, reluctantly, the car pulled away.

A helpless sense of abandonment washed over Max. *What the hell have I gotten myself into?* she thought morosely as she struggled stiffly to her feet and began hobbling along the tree line in search of a gas station or truck stop, someplace warm and dry where she could clean herself up and make some semblance of a plan.

She knew that Dominic was heartsick with worry over her, and the thought upset her, but she tried to put it out of her mind. There were far more important things to think about at the moment. She needed help.

Once again, she considered calling Agent Underwood, but rejected the idea. He was too driven by his own agenda.

As she limped along, trying to ignore her screaming

body and the cold drizzle of rain working its way down the back of her collar, juggling the bags with her bleeding hands so that she could carry them more easily, Max realized who could help her.

She had to get to a phone. She had to call her brother. How foolish of her not to have thought of it before.

As soon as Brett Maxfield heard his sister's voice, he knew she was in serious trouble. He glanced over at his wife, who lay next to him in bed, watching late-night TV. "I'm going to take this call in the den," he told her. "Hang it up for me, would you?"

Once he had changed phones, he made sure he could hear the distinctive click of the phone being hung up in the bedroom before giving Max the go-ahead to talk. What she told him sounded incredible and kept getting worse. Finally, he interrupted her. "Have you called Clark?" he asked.

"No. I wanted to talk to you first."

"Okay. Listen, sis, don't call him. Not yet, anyway."

"Why not?"

"Because we're going to have to do some things that might not be entirely legal, if you know what I mean, and Clark would never be able to live with that. He'd call that FBI guy or something. You know how he is.

"Yeah."

He pursed his lips. "Where are you now?"

"I'm at a Holiday Inn at Saratoga Springs."

"Good. Did you use a credit card?"

"No. Cash."

"Did you register under your own name?"

"Linda Sullivan, from Boston. Brett, I know how to do this."

"Yeah. Okay. It's going to take me . . . let's see . . . from Fort Bragg . . . Max, it's going to take me at least twelve hours to get there, and I'll have to let my C.O. know and some other stuff, so you just sit tight and wait for me, okay?"

"You're driving?"

"Yeah.

"You could fly. I think commuter airlines land here."

"Think about it, Max. I'll be traveling with firearms.

Even renting a car at the airport would be a bitch, if I didn't get arrested by airport security first."

"Oh."

There was a yawning silence while his sister processed this information.

"If you want to do it some other way," he said, "then tell me now."

"I don't know any other way, Brett," she said. "That's why I called you. I figured if anybody in this family could get us out of this mess, it would be the Green Berets." She laughed weakly.

"The Green Berets won't be having a whole hell of a lot to do with this one, sis," he said. "This is about family."

"Yes," she said, and her voice was strong, so he said good-bye and they hung up.

After a moment of contemplation, he decided which weapons to take. His army-issue .45 and other regulation weapons were locked up securely in the Arms Room— nobody ever took out firearms without giving a damn good reason and signing them in and signing them out— unless, of course, they were on a mission.

He was on a mission, all right, but it wasn't army, so he had no intention of using his official firearms. Instead, he would take guns that he owned, personally. Brett walked over to the glass gun case against the den wall, took the key out of the desk drawer, and unlocked the cabinet.

Reaching up, he took down his dad's colt 1911-A1 .45 and held it for a moment in the palm of his hand. For his dad's sake, he would love nothing better than to be able to take it and use it to help his sister and rescue his mother; there would be a certain rightness to that. But the firing pin was worn, and he'd had some problems finding that and other replacement parts. He didn't dare run the risk of having a problem with it now. Besides, Brett knew that his dad would be far more interested in his getting the job done than in his taking any sentimental risks.

He replaced the gun on its hooks and stood for a moment with his arms crossed over his chest, thinking. He would want Max to be armed. There was no doubt that she was a crackerjack electronics whiz, all right, but she didn't know shit about guns. A .45 would have entirely too much kick in her inexperienced hands; in fact, he decided against even giving her a semiautomatic. Even a small risk that the ammo would jam up on her was too much.

A wheel gun would be better. Brett selected a Smith & Wesson .357/.38 double-action revolver, and got out a box of .38 wad cutter—target practice—ammunition to go with it. The wad-cutter bullets would cut down on the kick, and the four-inch barrel would help with accuracy. For the hell of it, he tossed in a speed loader. Nothing worse than trying to reload six individual bullets into the cylinder of a revolver with shaking hands, he reflected grimly.

Before closing and locking the gun cabinet, he took out his Mossberg M500 pump-action shotgun and a box of shells, plus an extra magazine for his own semiautomatic Colt Double-Eagle .45 and a box of Federal 230-grain Hydra-Shok ammo.

The worst part was yet to come: telling his wife.

"I don't feel well Garrett," said Liv. "I'd like to go to bed now."

"Fine." Nodding toward Ryder, he said, "Take her upstairs and see she gets settled in for the night. And Liv?"

"What?" She stopped, clutching her bags closely.

"Don't you even think about sneaking out. We're miles from the nearest house. You got that?"

"Oh, yes," she said. "I got it."

Taking her arm, Ryder helped her up the stairs. His touch was gentle, and Liv suspected he might feel sorry for her.

Good. Sympathy could come in useful later.

Liv had no idea what was going to happen next. But if Gabe was involved, then it didn't take very strong powers of deduction to know that Max would eventually be sucked into it, one way or the other. Right now, Gabe and Garrett had the odds stacked up pretty heavily in their favor.

Ryder deposited Liv in her room, pointed out the

bathroom and the closet where extra blankets were kept, and left. Liv was disconcerted to find that there was no door to the bedroom, but that it was a loft which opened up to the great room below. Still, it was set back deeply enough beneath the rafters of the house to afford some privacy.

She looked around. The furniture was unique; the mountain cedar lodgepole bed handmade, as was the birch-wood dressing table and bedside nightstand. Candles were placed throughout the room, colorful rag rugs, and in one corner, next to a twig rocker, sat a thick birch-wood container filled with tree boughs whose leaves glowed with autumn colors. Trees crowded close to the windows, and she could hear them whispering and creaking as if to warn her away.

Liv sat down on the bed. The sheets were warm flannel in dark forest-green; the comforter, a green-and-red tartan plaid similar to what Garrett had in his bedroom at the penthouse.

A stage setting, she thought. *Everything in Garrett's life is a set and costumes and props, all designed to enhance his performance.*

How could she, a grown woman not inexperienced in the ways of life, have missed the signals? How could she not have known that he was an actor, and she merely an extra in his little play?

Chapter Twenty-eight

Max slept very late. In the bathroom the next morning she examined herself. The gunshot wound, while merely a graze, was developing an infection and throbbed fiercely. The abrasions she had sustained while diving out of a moving car—though she had thoroughly cleaned them before bed—were in dire need of antibiotic ointment and gauze. Max feared venturing too far astray from the Holiday Inn, but there was a convenience store next to it and a gift shop downstairs.

Stuffing her hair up under the leather cap, which she had picked up where it had fallen on her way to the tree line to hide from Dominic, Max pulled a pair of dark sunglasses out of her bag, gathered up some cash, and crept out of the room. Unfortunately, her ragged clothes brought her more attention than she'd bargained for. The huge rips in the knees exposed the scrapes and sores beneath, and the gunshot wound had left the arm of her coat and the sweatshirt bloody and torn.

Max didn't see that she had much choice but to buy some new clothes, so she caught a cab and visited a Wal-Mart supercenter she'd passed on the way into town the night before. There she bought new jeans and sweatshirt and socks, as well as a pair of roomy sweatpants to wear in the motel room, a new goose-down coat and first-aid supplies. She even picked up a hamburger and fries at the McDonald's located at the rear of the store, called another cab, and limped furtively back to her room at the Holiday Inn like the fugitive she was.

The ointment and bandages helped to take some of the sting out of her wounds, and aspirin eased the pain from the gunshot wound and some of the inflammation from the arm. After that, there was nothing for her to do but wait. With the exception of a quick trip down the corridor for ice to put on her arm, she did not leave the room again.

She worried. She worried about her mom, and she worried about Dominic. Over and over in her mind, she could hear him calling for her in the rain-slashed night. What made her think she couldn't trust him?

In the end, she decided that it hadn't been *Dominic,* so much as it had been the entire situation from which she had fled. It was a matter of survival, pure and simple.

In the meantime, she had to keep her wits about her. This was a high-stakes game and she was under the gun, a cold player making a blind bet, sandbagged between two chiselers. When the time came for the showdown, she didn't want to be tapped out.

She wanted aces wired.

Max had just eaten dinner and stashed her room-service tray when she heard the sharp rap at the door that had to be Brett. Still, she peered through the peephole first before flinging back the door and throwing her arms around her brother. So overwhelming was her relief at finally seeing him that she actually grew light-headed and had to sit down.

He looked around the room. "You got a room with two beds?"

She shrugged. "I figured you might need some sleep after your trip and . . . well . . . I was too scared to be alone again at night."

He sat down next to her and put his arm around her shoulder. "Not to worry. The cavalry's here now."

"Ouch!"

"What?"

"Just my arm. Don't worry about it. I've been a big weenie all day long."

"Let me see. Max! I said let me see!"

Sheepishly, she turned her sore arm toward him, and he pushed up the sweatshirt sleeve, peeling back bandages for a peek.

"It's infected." He glanced at her accusingly.

"It's better now. I told you. It'll be all right."

He sighed. "You always were the biggest damn tomboy."

She grinned. "And whose fault was that?"

"Zane's, of course. We always blamed everything on Zane." He was grinning back at her.

After a moment Brett cleared his throat and said, "So what's the plan, Stan?"

Max got to her feet and limped over to the dresser, where she got down the briefcase. Though the leather surface was battered and dented, she'd checked the things inside and they seemed fine. She said, "When I realized that Mom was being followed and the apartment was bugged, I outfitted her with a WMTTX 4700 MD wireless mike and tracking transmitter."

"What the hell is that?"

She sat back down on the bed, cradling the briefcase in her lap. "It's illegal to sell in the U.S., and is only really available for use at the highest level of government intelligence operatives. I used my contacts at CovertCom to get hold of one. It's called 'the ghost,' and it's no wider than a credit card."

"Wow." Brett was no starry-eyed innocent where electronic surveillance and countersurveillance gear was concerned, but he did love to hear Max talk about her toys.

With an appreciative nod, she said, "It's equipped with a 'man-down' feature." Snapping open the briefcase to reveal, nestled in gray egg-carton foam, various dials, gadgets, and screens inside, Max added, "I've already narrowed down Mom's location, thanks to Dominic, to the Lake Placid area. With this we can trace her right down to the room in the house."

Brett nodded, as if it were a common thing for one's mother to carry a transmitter around with a "man-down" feature, but added, "She must have been really scared."

"Well, she'd been uneasy, really, the whole time we were in New York. This helped her feel safer, and since it's not any bigger than a credit card," Max pointed out, "she didn't really mind. Mom trusted me that it was state-of-the-art, even though she didn't completely understand how it worked or what it could do."

"That sounds like Mom."

"Yeah." Looking up from the briefcase, Max said, "The thing is . . ."

"What?"

"Well . . . it's not enough just to find Mom, you know?"

He nodded. "I copy."

"I've got to shut down my son-of-a-bitch ex-husband and Garrett Sharp once and for all."

"Agreed."

After a pause Max said, "We're going to need Zane's help, Brett."

"Aw, geez!" He got up and turned away from her, his hands on his lean waist. "That little twerp? He'll just fuck everything up, Max!"

"No he won't. I've thought it all out." She pleaded with her eyes. "C'mon, Brett. Don't be a butt-head about this."

"I'm not being a butt-head," he said, swinging back around to face her, light on his toes as a dancer. "I'm being an asshole."

She broke out laughing.

"It's just that you can't depend on him. Ever since we were kids—"

"We're not kids anymore."

"*I* know that and *you* know that, but has *Zane* figured it out?"

"Brett." She pursed her lips in exasperation. "Look, we all know that as a regular G.I. Joe, you are the unsurpassed king."

Her brother rolled his eyes and groaned.

"But Zane is a computer wizard, and I need his help to get all my plates in the air and keep them spinning."

"Max. Have you ever heard the expression, *crash and burn*? That's what'll happen to all your plates if you put Zane in charge."

She shrugged. "Who said anything about putting him in charge? I just need his help, is all. I'll tell him what to do, and he'll do it."

He quirked one eyebrow. "Are you sure about that?"

"I'm sure."

"Because this *is* our mother's safety we're talking about here, you know."

"Hey!" she flared, suddenly angry. "Who do you think's been taking care of her for the past eight months? I've been living with her since the day I got out of prison, so don't *you* try to remind *me* what's at stake here!"

Clownishly, Brett stuck both hands up in the air. "Don't shoot! I surrender!"

Max grabbed up a roll of gauze bandages and threw it at him.

He caught it one-handed. "You always did throw like a girl."

Groping around in one of his bags, she said, "Just tell me where you packed the guns, so I can shoot you now and be done with it."

But they were both laughing. It was the kind of wartime laughter soldiers know, the kind of soft lionhearted laughter that drifts over the camp just before they arm themselves and go roaring into battle.

Under the circumstances Jack Underwood could see only one way to salvage the Operation EAVESDROP case before it blew right up in his face—and maybe even track down Max before anybody else shot at her—and that was to pinpoint the exact connection between federal judge Gabe Griswold and Garrett Sharp and his CovertCom operation.

In classic cluster-fuck conditions, Underwood knew, there was never one single big thing that went wrong. Rather, a whole series of little things screwed up this way and that until the whole thing was a hopeless snarl. Several notable debacles involving government agencies in recent years had provided textbook scenarios of what *not* to do, and the FBI was nothing if not trainable. They had learned from their mistakes and had a few successes under their belts to show for it.

Underwood figured he could find Max with any of a number of given investigative methods, and call in HRT and go in with guns blazing, but something told him that was not the way to go with this one. Patience. Clear thought. Careful steps. Call it a hunch; call it being punch-drunk with too much coffee and too little sleep, but somehow Underwood knew that it would be far smarter in this case to make sure he had all his little ducks in a row before pulling out the popgun and taking aim.

The first thing he did was enlist the aid of Dirk or Pierce or—Lance, that was it—Lance the computer wonder boy, to help him dig up the information necessary to implicate the esteemed judge. They worked for twenty hours straight the first day, until Lance fell asleep at his keyboard and Underwood grew so tired he forgot his own password.

After a few hours' sleep and a shave to please the suits, they were back in full hacker mode, and it was some time after that that Underwood connected the dots. Using a printout obtained by the wonder boy and some files he dug up in WESTLAW, the scales fell from his eyes and Underwood saw.

Griswold was going light on certain select accused felons who funneled through his courtroom—not enough to draw attention to himself—but enough so that they had more than an even chance of being acquitted. Apparently, he favored those who possessed certain high-tech skills, who could be used most effectively by CovertCom. Once that was done the good judge would then channel the selected naughty boys into the worldwide spy shop enterprise run by his buddy, Garrett Sharp. Sharp would then use the newly freed felons now working for CovertCom to commit fraud and theft of information from their own clients, which they would then sell to the clients' competitors. In the meantime, Sharp and Griswold would invest in the stock of those rival companies— through blind trusts and DBA businesses—that they had themselves so smoothly set up for that very success.

Underwood had not just a strong case for theft and fraud, but a clear case for judicial corruption. He had no doubts that by the time this thing was over with, he'd also have some indictments for attempted murder.

And he'd be on the fast track for SAC at some plum field office.

Arms hanging straight down at his sides, he slumped in his chair for a moment, leaned his head straight back so that he was staring up at the ceiling, and let out a long, loud, and very un-FBI-like war whoop.

312 *Deanie Francis Mills*

Underwood's first impulse was a boyish desire to show off for Max, to call her up and tell her all the neat stuff he had found out. But, of course, he couldn't do that.

Still, in spite of the fact that Max was still missing and the case was far from resolved, Underwood couldn't help but feel as if he'd just glimpsed the Holy Grail in all its glory . . . and only had to kill one little old dragon to get to it.

Brett picked up Zane at the tiny local airport, where he had taken a commuter airline after flying nonstop from L.A. to New York. As usual, he was dressed like the same kind of junior high geeks that Brett and Brand used to beat up. He was sporting a heavy backpack that had to have come straight out of an Army/Navy surplus store, which irked Brett no end. Loping along with that flat-footed hippie-type gate of his, carrying a laptop computer in one skinny hand, Zane stuck out the other for his usual wimpy shake, and they walked to the car in silence.

As they got into the car, Brett said, "How's Gaby?"

"She's fine," said Zane as he grappled for his seat belt. "I've sent the heads-up, and everything's cool."

"Good."

"How's Max?"

"I've seen her better."

Zane was quiet for a moment, and then he said, "It's just eating you up, isn't it?"

"What?" Brett jiggled with the car heater.

"You can't stand it that Max needs my help. You wanted to come riding in on your big white horse and be the macho family hero, but lo and behold, who does little sister call but the liberal, Clinton-voting, gun-hating, tree-hugging, peacenik computer hacker nerd brother to come to the rescue." He chuckled.

Brett, glancing at his brother's lightweight windbreaker, flipped off the car heater and turned on the air conditioner full blast.

After another long uncomfortable moment, Zane crossed his arms over his chest and tried to suppress a shiver. "So how's Janice?"

"Fine."

"Good."

They rode in silence for the rest of the drive to the Holiday Inn, where Max greeted Zane with a warm hug and a warning glance in Brett's direction. Brett took a seat in a chair off in the corner and watched them chatter like a couple of girls for a few minutes, then they got down to business.

Max said, "First of all, I'll need to make some phone calls, but I don't want the calls traced—not even to this geographical area."

"No problem," said Zane, upending his backpack and dumping out several loose-leaf notebooks filled with meticulous notes, a cellular phone, and electronic doodads that he sorted through like toys.

Brett noticed that there was no change of clothing in the backpack. *Gross,* he thought. *Little twerp didn't even bring a change of underwear.*

Max was making admiring noises over Zane's laptop computer. "It's a Hewlett Packard palm top with custom interfacing that plugs into my modified Oki 900 cellular phone," he bragged lovingly.

"Brett and I have been working on a plan," said Max. "Let me bounce it off you and see what you think."

As she spoke, Zane was nodding, but he didn't seem to Brett to be paying any attention to their sister at all. One minute he'd be down on his hands and knees under the table groping around for the phone jack, the next he'd be rummaging through all the crap on the table until he found some little gadget, then he'd be plugging in this and clacking around on that. Brett wasn't exactly a computer illiterate; after all, he used computers at work every day and had a modem in his house, but he still had no idea what Zane was doing with all those wires and shit, and he was annoyed as hell that the little rodent was so busy showing off his electronic acumen that he'd probably long since lost the thread of Max's discussion.

"Zany!" he finally cried, deliberately using the childhood nickname he knew his brother despised. "Sit the fuck down and pay attention to Max. This is important!"

Zane stopped fidgeting and glared at Brett. "You can't

order me around like one of your little mindless robot troops, Colonel *Brasshole*," he said.

"Maybe not, but I can sure kick your ass all the way back to L.A." barked Brett.

"Oh! I'm so *scaaaared*," simpered Zane. "I'll remember that the next time I hack into the Pentagon. Maybe you could use a little *transfer*. I hear Bosnia's really nice this time of year."

"Your little pretend threats are so pathetic," said Brett.

"You think so? Fine then! *You* reroute Max's calls. I'm sure they teach you useful life skills like that in Killing 101."

"Fuck off, Zany!"

"You fuck off."

"I want both of you to SHUT UP!" screamed Max.

A guilty, tense silence blanketed the room.

Families, Brett thought. *They're like duty rosters in a wartime bivouac. Sometimes you walk point on patrol, and sometimes you burn shit. Either way, you could still get your head blown off.*

While Max and Zane worked, Brett settled himself on one of the beds to check over his weapons and ammunition, and started to plan his part of the mission.

Chapter Twenty-nine

"Okay," said Max, leaning closer to Zane and shoving aside several Ding Dongs wrappers and empty Mountain Dew cans. "I leave a message on Mr. Sharp's voice mail, to call me at—"

"My pager number."

"Right. But when I call him back, if he has some way of tracing my call—"

"He'll get the San Diego Zoo."

Max thought a moment. "It's risky. I could just leave a message on the voice mail—"

"But then you wouldn't get to talk to Mom and make sure she's okay."

She nodded, then glanced at Brett, where he sat on the bed, watching a football game. "Do it," he said, without looking up from the television.

She dialed the number and said, "Mr. Sharp, this is Max. I have some news about my ex-husband that should interest you. Call me at this number." She gave the number and hung up.

He must have been checking his voice mail frequently, because his return call came within a half hour's time.

"All right," he said. "What's this news you have to tell me about Gabe?"

"It's not that easy, Mr. Sharp," she said nervously. "For one thing, I'm not even going to speak to you until I find out if my mother is all right."

"Of course she's all right."

"Not good enough," said Max. "Let me speak to her."

There was a long pause, then, *"Rebekah?"*

"Mom!" cried Max. "Are you okay? Has anybody hurt you?"

"No, darling. I've been well treated."

"Mom—we're going to get you out of there. Brett is here, and Zane. Just sit tight."

"I have to go now, sweet girl. I love you."

"I love you, too, Mom," said Max, struggling mightily to maintain control.

"Very touching," said Sharp. His oily voice so soon after her mother's was like an unexpected splash of cold water to the face. "If you want to talk to your mother again, Max, I suggest you quit playing games. You give your daughter's whereabouts to Gabe, and we'll hand over Liv to you."

"I'm afraid it's not that simple, Mr. Sharp. Not when the FBI is involved."

"What are you talking about?" The words were sharp with shock and suspicion.

"I told you. It has to do with Gabe and the little game you two have been playing with CovertCom. Let's just say your trust in him has been misplaced."

"You don't know what you're talking about. This is all a bluff."

"Is it?" said Max slyly. "If we were playing poker right now, would you bet on it?"

There was a long, frustrated pause. "What do you want?"

"I want to meet with you at the lake house."

"Absolutely not. We can meet, if you wish, but not here."

"Then, I'm afraid we don't have anything to discuss," said Max as she abruptly hung up the phone. She was shaking. Looking at her brothers for support, she said, "What do I do now?"

Brett said, "Nothing. Let him stew in his own juices for a while. He will expect you to call back, and when you don't, he'll get worried."

She nodded. "Now Gabe." To Zane she said, "I don't have Gabe's pager number anymore. I think he may have changed it. I know his regular number is unpublished."

"No problem," he said. "All it takes is a little social engineering." Picking up the phone, he called Dallas information, got the number for Judge Griswold's answering service, and dialed it. Assuming a light, effeminate voice with a heavy Texas accent, he said, "May I please speak to Judge Griswold?" After a moment he covered the receiver, and in that same voice, said, "Oh, no! He's out of town."

Shaking her head, Max grinned and glanced over at Brett, who rolled his eyes.

Zane said, "Well, I just don't know what to do then, ma'am. You see, this is the Department of Motor Vehicles. It seems there has been a hit-and-run accident involving Judge Griswold's BMW, the one that was parked at the long-term parking lot at DFW and . . . what? Oh, yes, I'm afraid the damage was extensive, and the airport security people are trying to reach the judge to . . . yes, I'll hold." He winked at Max. After a moment he said, "Oh, thank you ever so much. Yes, this pager number will be fine, thank you. Have a nice day!"

He hung up and handed the phone number to Max, who immediately dialed it. She said, "Gabe, this is Max. I have some information about Garrett Sharp that should interest you. Call me at this number."

This time the wait was longer, and it got to Max. The room seemed to close in around her. It was like a nightmare for the claustrophobic, of being locked in an elevator plunging to the ground and there was no time to scream.

The ringing phone jazzed her like an electric shock. Heart pounding, she picked it up. "Hello?"

"Max. This is Gabe."

"Yes." She could feel her own pulse in her throat. Her ex-husband's voice sounded so familiar and yet so foreign.

"I'm sorry about what happened at the apartment."

"No, you're not," she said bitterly. "Did you think you could charm me with your lies?"

Fear, in the throb of a heartbeat, had turned to cold rage and a hatred beyond anything Max had ever experienced in her life. *I could kill him,* she thought. *I could take one of Brett's guns and blow his head off and never even look back.*

Struggling to regain her composure and keep her focus, she said, "I have some information about Mr. Sharp that could destroy you, Gabe. You know and I know that you don't give a shit about Gaby. If I give you this information, you will leave us both alone, or I will tell everything I know to the FBI, and you will be finished. Perhaps *you* would like to see what it's like inside a federal prison."

"Why should I believe anything you say?" he scoffed, though she could detect a slight vibration of doubt in his voice.

"You'd better believe me," she said. "After all, I'm holding all the cards."

After a long, tense moment, he said. "All right. Where and when do you want to meet?"

"I've got you a room reserved at the Lakeside Motel in Saranac Lake. That's in upstate New York. Be there by six p.m. tonight. I'll call you then and leave further instructions."

"I can't possibly get to upstate New York by then!" he protested.

Max hung up the phone, and although she was scared to death, she did permit herself a small high-five with her "social engineer" brother.

"Now," she said, "I've got one more phone call to make, and I know this one will be traced."

"I'll take care of it," Zane said. "Just give me a few minutes . . ."

When the phone rang at his desk, Jack Underwood was leaning far back in his chair, his glasses balanced on his stomach, guiding a Visine container over his eyeballs and bracing himself for the cold sting of the drops. He let the phone ring while the droplets oozed down the side of his face, fumbled for his glasses, and groped blearily for the receiver.

"Yeah? Jack Underwood."

"Underwood? This is Max."

Flinging aside the Visine bottle, Underwood leapt to his feet, signaled wildly for Lance's attention, and drew a rapid circle in the air with his index finger. Lance finally caught the signal, nodded importantly, and dashed off to make sure that the phone trace was underway. Sinking back into his chair, Underwood said, "Are you all right? Are you hurt? We know about the shooting, Max."

"Wow. I guess it took all the formidable resources of the FBI to figure that one out, huh?"

"Oh," he said. "And I was so hoping you might have sustained an injury to your mouth."

"No such luck, Underwood. Only a graze to the arm."

"Tell me where you are," said Underwood. "Let me help you."

"Now, now. That would just be entirely too easy, don't you think?"

"Max. This isn't a game."

"Everybody keeps telling me that."

"Who's everybody?" He quirked his eyebrows impatiently at Lance, who made a TV talk-show director's gesture for "stretch it out; use up time."

"Oh, my ex-husband, the Honorable Gabriel Griswold. And my boss, Garrett Sharp. Or are you my boss, Underwood? I keep getting confused on that point."

"Who shot at you?"

"I think we need to make a distinction here, don't you? They didn't just shoot at me. They tried to kill me."

"Who tried to kill you?"

"Bad guys."

It was utterly exasperating. He was getting absolutely nothing accomplished.

Like a big-footed puppy, Lance came galloping across the room. Underwood clamped his hand over the receiver just in the nick of time as the young man cried, "Disney World! They traced the call to Disney World! Do you want me to call the Tampa field office?"

Knocking his glasses askew, Underwood put his hand over his eyes and heaved a big sigh. Removing his other hand off the telephone receiver, he said loudly, "No, Lance, I do not want you to call the Tampa field office." He could hear Max chuckling. "Very funny," he said, a ghost of a smile playing across his face. "Disney World," he quipped. "That's a pretty Mickey Mouse thing to do, you know."

"Personally, I thought it was a stroke of genius."

"Well, are you going to help me out here, or not? I'm not getting any younger."

"I'm going to give you directions to a rural location in upstate New York," she said, her voice suddenly very serious. "And you better write them down, because I don't think anybody at Disney World is going to know where this place is."

"I'm ready," he said.

"And, Underwood?"

"Yeah?"

"Go gentle into that good night, will you? Sharp's got my mom."

Underwood didn't know what to say to that. He was painfully aware that Max had been worried about her mother's safety for some time, and he had assured her that she was in no particular danger. "Max—" he began.

"Just take down the directions," she said, her voice heavy with unsaid recriminations.

As soon as Underwood had taken down directions, he headed straight for the SAC's office. He was going to need some help from the Albany field office SWAT.

While he was at it, he may as well call Quantico and put the "Super-SWAT" boys, as the FBI's elite Hostage Rescue Team was called, on standby.

He had a feeling that by the time this was all over, they'd be needing all the help they could get.

"Stupid little bitch!" yelled Garrett, the veins standing out on his neck. Liv sat in the chair close by the phone where she'd last spoken to her daughter, and said nothing. What could she say? For the first time she realized how much the trappings of wealth could blind onlookers from the truth. *Even if your instincts were warning you, as mine had been,* she reflected, *you could get so easily distracted from those warnings by the dazzle and glitter of money.*

No wonder Rebekah had been so opposed to her dating Garrett. She must have known about the criminal practices of her boss, but couldn't quit her job because of his connection to Gabe.

All this time, thought Liv with great sadness, *my daughter must have been in hell.*

And what had she done to help? Flaunted the situation in her daughter's face every time she went out with Garrett Sharp, getting all prissy and "it's-none-of-your-business" huffy whenever Rebekah had tried to talk to her about it.

Why didn't she TELL me? thought Liv for the thousandth time. Now look at her. Here she was, held hostage by this despicable man and his cohorts, and Rebekah was out there somewhere, rallying her brother troops, trying to come up with a plan. Now Liv understood why Rebekah had spent so much time with Clark and Brett in Dallas. They must have been trying to figure a way out of the situation even then.

"She indicated that the FBI was somehow involved," Garrett was saying to Evan Ryder, "that maybe we've been implicated, and Gabe's planning to turn state's evidence against us." His voice had leveled off somewhat, and Liv had to strain to hear what he was saying as she pretended to examine an *Adirondack Life* magazine.

"No way," said Ryder. "Judge Griswold's too big a fish for the feds. They'd never let him loose to make a case on you."

"So it's a bluff," mused Garrett.

Ryder shrugged. "I've seen that woman play poker."

"So what's she up to, then?"

A sharp rap at the front door caused them all to jump.

"What the hell?" Ryder withdrew a gun from his shoulder holster, jogged across the great room to the front door, and stood to the side of it.

"Open up! It's me, Dominic!"

Liv was so relieved her whole body slumped.

Ryder glanced back at Garrett, who nodded. "Let him in," he said.

Gun still drawn, Ryder eased open the door. "Anybody follow you?"

"No," said Dominic, striding into the room and ignoring Ryder's drawn weapon as if that were a natural way for someone to be greeted. His gaze fell on Liv, and he immediately crossed the floor to where she was sitting. "Liv," he said, taking one of her hands. "How you doin', babe?"

"I'm well, thank you, Dominic." She said. An unexpected wave of confusion had struck her just as he bent down to speak to her. *Was Dominic involved? Did Rebekah know? Is that why she'd broken up with him?*

Just as he straightened up, Liv caught a glint of a gun beneath his open coat.

A great sense of betrayed trust washed over Liv at that moment. Suddenly angry and hurt—as much for her poor daughter as for herself—Liv thought, *Is there no one in this world you can trust?*

And in the next thought, *Family.*

Liv had not herself come from a trustworthy family. Her father had been an alcoholic who could never seem to hold a job. Her mother, in an attempt to shoulder the burden, had become bitterly resentful through the years and cold toward her own children, as if it had been their faults for coming into the world in the first place. Her brother had followed in their father's footsteps and become a drunk.

So Liv had reinvented the concept of family with her own marriage and children. She had built for her own children what she herself had never known as a child. Richard had truly been her knight on a white horse, whisking her away from the misery that was home and giving her the entire world in return. He'd been ten times the father to his own children that hers had been. In many ways, he had been a father to Liv.

But Richard was gone now. It was up to her. She would need to be brave and smart and watch for any gaps that she might exploit, any hints as to the enemy's weaknesses, any chinks in their armor.

Of one thing Liv was certain: Richard wasn't the only member of the family who was a fighter.

"About time you got here," scowled Garrett Sharp to Dominic. "What took you so damn long?"

"I got lost," lied Dominic.

"Then, why the hell didn't you call?"

"I tried! My car phone was all screwed up."

"We've got trouble," said Sharp, as though he hadn't spoken. "Big trouble."

Pulling off his leather driving gloves and stuffing them

in his coat pocket, Dominic said, "What kind of trouble?"

"Max. She's a loose cannon."

Dominic kept his expression bland and his voice steady. "You heard from her?"

"Damn right we heard from her. She's trying to set up a meeting here. Says she's got some information on Gabe that could bring the feds down on us big time."

"Her ex-husband?" asked Dominic innocently. "What's she talking about?"

Sharp waved his hands in the air irritably. "He's a partner in this business. What, you didn't know that?"

"No," said Dominic with slow care. "I didn't realize that."

Sharp shrugged. "No reason why you should. He's kind of a silent partner, right, Evan?"

Ryder smirked.

"So anyway. She's hinting around that Gabe might be willing to turn state's evidence in exchange for what he knows about CovertCom. What do you think?"

"I think he's a man who can't be trusted," said Dominic with a glance toward Liv. She was pretending to read an article in a magazine.

Sharp picked up a fireplace poker and jabbed savagely at the fire. "Max can't come here," he said. "It's out of the question. We've got to convince her to set up a meeting someplace else."

"What's wrong with bringing her here?" said Dominic. "It's your turf. Your advantage."

"You think this is some kind of sporting event, Antonio?" said Sharp, still holding the poker in a manner Dominic found menacing. "I've got no fucking security around here! I bought this house to impress women. Period. A place out of the city to bring women." He looked directly, insultingly, at Liv, who appeared not to have heard him.

Holding up one hand, he began to tick off the security deficits on his fingers. "I've got no perimeter security—not even a fucking fence. No security lighting. No CCTV," he said, referring to closed-circuit security cameras, "no PIRs," (passive infrared sensors), "no gates, no guards, *nothing*."

"Well, Jesus, Mr. Sharp, it's just Max! You expect her to come roaring in here in an APC and crash through the wall or something?"

Slamming down the poker onto the hearth, Sharp said, "I don't know what the fuck to expect! That's just the problem! For all I know, she's going to come blasting in here with the goddamned FBI HRT!"

Dominic shook his head. "I can't see Max bringing Hostage Rescue in on this, Mr. Sharp. She's made far too many sacrifices for her daughter up to this point for her to risk anything happening that could jeopardize the security of her little girl."

"Shit, Dom, we already know the kid's in Switzerland!"

Dominic sucked in his breath. He couldn't stop himself. "You told her that?" He glanced over at Liv, who seemed to be concentrating with unusual ferocity on the magazine.

"Max knows," said Sharp in a smug, tight little voice.

"If Max knows that Gabe is on to the fact that her child is in Switzerland," said Dominic, "then you can damn well bet the kid's not in Switzerland anymore."

Sharp pursed his lips. "Good point."

Dominic said, "I'm just curious, sir. How did Max's ex find out where her little girl is? She guarded that secret pretty fiercely."

"We don't know where she is, exactly," said Sharp, dropping the poker with a rattle. "Just that she's in, or was in, Switzerland." He grinned, and it was a nasty grin. "How did we find out? Gosh, Dom, you'll have to ask Dom. *Perignon*, that is!" Staring pointedly at Liv, he broke into an obscene little laugh.

With a sniff Liv groped around in the pocket of her sweater for a tissue and blew her nose. She did not look up from her magazine, but her face was blushing a furious rose.

At that moment Dominic wanted to kill the s.o.b. for humiliating such a great lady in such a degrading fashion. He was sorry he'd even brought it up.

"What did Max say, exactly?" he said, putting Liv out of his mind with some effort.

Sharp said, "She indicated that she would trade the information she possesses about Gabe for her mother."

Dominic nodded. "What did she say when you refused to meet here?"

Sharp turned away. "She hung up."

"Then, right now, I'd say it's dealer's choice, Mr. Sharp. You want to hear what she has to say, then you don't have a whole hell of a lot of choice as to where you will be when you hear it. It's her call." It gave him no small amount of satisfaction to point that out to his egotistical boss.

"And just take my chances that she'll bring the feds in with her," said Sharp angrily.

"For what it's worth, I don't think she will," said Dominic. "But it's a risk. How big a gambler are you?" he pointed out reasonably. "How valuable is that information to you?"

Sharp, staring into the fire, said in a slow hypnotic voice, "I'd kill for it." Turning his cold blue eyes toward Dominic, he added, "And that's a fact."

Dominic Antonio had known many bad men in his life, but this was the first time that he had ever felt as if he were gazing into the face of pure evil.

At that moment he realized that before the night was over . . . someone was going to die.

Chapter Thirty

They moved through the trees as quietly as possible, step by step, in the traveling over-watch formation, with the lead fire team about twenty yards ahead of the rear fire team. Each team was positioned roughly into the figure of a capital letter A. One SWAT agent traveled point a few yards ahead of the agent who made up the apex of the A. Two agents on each side made up the slanted lines of the A, while one other agent formed the crossbar of the A.

This was the position given to Underwood, the crossbar, in the rear team. SWAT didn't like normal mortal human beings interfering with their glory-boy jobs, but Underwood had prevailed because the truth was that nobody knew any more about this case and what to expect than he did. As they neared their objective, a log cabin located in a clearing in the trees, the bounding overwatch team spread out into a straight line, approaching roughly at an angle to the building and finding cover behind trees.

From his radio earphones, Underwood heard that the building appeared to be deserted except for one vehicle which was parked outside in plain view. "That doesn't sound right," he murmured into his mike. "There should be more than one car outside. Over."

"Maybe they're not all here yet," said the agent in charge through his earphones. "We'll send a recon team up to check it out. Over."

As Underwood's team began to spread out in support of the lead team, he took his position behind a tree. Somewhere in the shadow-flickering, tree-rustling night, steel-nerved snipers perched still as death, with starlight scopes on their .308 sniper rifles, and waited like the grim reaper.

Even though Underwood was armed and flanked by crack federal agents, he was still spooked down to his toes.

It was freezing. Snow lay powdered on the ground like flour dusting, and the trees groaned as if in complaint. *The thrill seekers can have this job,* decided Underwood. *Give me a desk and a hot cup of coffee any day.*

Unlike the SWATs, who were outfitted with night vision goggles that left their hands free, Underwood had to rely on starlight binoculars. Taking off his glasses, he focused through the sights and watched as a couple of agents crept up to the building and fanned out to the rear.

He waited.

When next the agent in charge spoke, Underwood was startled. He'd been letting his thoughts drift. The man's voice sounded like it was whispering right over the back of his ear.

"Recon says there appears to be only one guy in there, but there's a sophisticated setup of electronic audio monitoring devices. What's your take on it, over."

"Oh, *noooo,*" moaned Underwood aloud. At just that moment the front door of the cabin swung open, and it seemed to Underwood as if the entire forest tensed up. Through his starlight binoculars Underwood could see a skinny guy who didn't appear to be armed. The light from inside the cabin, which spilled out and haloed the guy in a green glow, only confused everyone's NVG's. Underwood replaced his glasses and squinted toward the cabin. He could make out the young man cupping his hands over his mouth.

Into the night the man shouted, "Halloooo! Is there a Jack Underwood anywhere out there?"

As Underwood buried his face in his hands, he heard, "Agent Underwood, if you're out there . . . I'm Zane Maxfield. I've been expecting you guys. Come on in!"

When Max drove up to the cabin, the first car she spotted was Dominic's. There was a Range Rover she didn't recognize, and cars belonging to the other Spy Squad members. There was also a rental car that had to be Gabe's.

Hail, hail, the gang's all here, she thought.

She tried to remember everything Brett had told her. He'd insisted that she wear the .357 in a special holster designed to be concealed underneath her jeans, and it was miserably uncomfortable. She'd left the top button undone and the grip of the gun protruding slightly, hidden by her coat. This was just in case she were separated from her tote bag. The shotgun was lying across the front seat of the car with a blanket tossed over it.

Several events had transpired that had made their job easier. For one thing, Sharp had relented and agreed to a meeting at the cabin, which necessitated his giving her directions. This enabled them to come within range of the WMTTX 4500 MD transmitter's "man-down" signal. Fortuitously, her mother had thought to activate the signal, which was the luckiest break of all. Brett, using the multi-channel receiver housed in the briefcase Max had taken from her apartment, was making his way through the surrounding woods now. It was Max's job to distract the other people in the cabin and somehow separate them from her mother, if necessary, so that Brett could find her and get her to safety.

With shaking hands Max checked the little BW-4000 body transmitter tucked in her coat pocket, made sure everything was in order, took a deep breath, and got out of the car, leaving it unlocked and the keys in it. Then, creeping with great stealth up the split-log steps to the wide front porch, she took care of one final piece of business before knocking timidly at the front door.

The door opened quickly, and Max recoiled to find Hakeem standing there. Brushing past him, she glanced around the room. She could see everyone but her mother and Sebastian Taylor gathered here and there around the handsome hearth, which meant that Sharp had assigned the bodybuilder to act as her mom's guard.

The room was magnificent, but then, so were most of the things with which Garrett Sharp surrounded himself. It was easier that way for people to be seduced by the succulent fruit and not notice the rotten pit at the core. She'd gotten about halfway across the room, trying with all her might not to be drawn in by Dominic's compelling stare or Gabe's searing glare, when Hakeem barked, "Stop!"

He approached her, holding in his hand a VL-5000-P portable countersurveillance receiver. He reached for her.

Almost instinctively and with no real thought, Max's arm shot out and she slapped his hand with a loud *smack* that reverberated to the rafters of the room. "Don't touch me!" she cried.

Grabbing her wrist in a vicious grip, he snarled, "You little cunt—"

"Hakeem!" Sharp's voice whip-cracked through the tense room. "You can scan her without touching her. Is that clear?"

Reluctantly, Hakeem dropped Max's wrist and began running the portable scanner inches from her body. He was not using headphones. Almost immediately, the scanner let out a piercing alarm beep from the vicinity of her coat pocket. Before she could move, Hakeem had reached into the pocket and yanked out the transmitter, holding it high over his head in triumph. The glance he gave her was soul-burning.

"You see?" he cried. "The bitch is a jackal! She has betrayed us!"

"Give it to me," said Sharp. He took the transmitter from Hakeem and flung it into the fire.

"Perhaps she is armed," said Hakeem loudly. "I will gladly search her body for you." He turned toward Max, curling his lip at her as though she were a putrid stench.

"Don't be ridiculous," said Dominic. "Max knows nothing about weapons. I don't think she's ever even fired a gun."

Cursing in Arabic, Hakeem grabbed Max and began running his hands over her body.

Before anyone other than Max could protest, his hand landed squarely on the holster hidden beneath her jeans. "She's armed!" he cried.

"Then, take the weapon, Hakeem," said Sharp.

To Max's mortification, Hakeem immediately unzipped her jeans and gave them a yank. She slapped him.

As he withdrew the .357 from the holster, he backhanded her.

"That's enough!" bellowed Sharp, and Hakeem stepped back with the weapon.

Dropping the empty holster on the floor Max pulled up her pants with as much dignity as she could muster. She avoided looking at anyone.

Sharp said, "So. We are all gathered together, just as you wished. Your little plan to record this meeting has been foiled. But by all means, speak. We eagerly await hearing what you have to say."

Max said, "You've been double-crossed, Mr. Sharp. By my ex-husband. And you, Gabe, have been double-crossed by Mr. Sharp."

Tension collected in the shadowy corners like cats crouching before the pounce. In the eerie silence that followed Max's statement, she said, "Both of you have offered to turn state's evidence against the other. I know this because I was approached by an agent with the FBI to see if there was any truth to the allegations each man had made."

"That's preposterous!" shouted her ex-husband. "Turn state's evidence for what? I've done nothing wrong." He turned toward Sharp. "Is this true? Have you been talking to the feds?"

"Of course not!"

"Well, neither have I."

"So you say."

"What's that supposed to mean?" He looked back at Max. "Don't you see what my pretty little ex-wife is doing?"

"Think what you want," interjected Max. "But the feds are, shall we say . . . very interested in what I know."

"You little bitch," began Sharp.

Gabe held up a hand. "Don't worry. They'd need evidence to make their case."

"I can provide that, too," said Max.

A tense silence stretched across the room as both men considered that. Silently, Max prayed that she could keep them occupied long enough for Brett to get her mother out.

"What do you want?" said her ex-husband.

"I want my daughter back," she said truthfully. "And I want you out of our lives."

"Forget it."

"Listen to her!" snapped Sharp.

"And I want enough money for us to live comfortably."

"I knew it," said Sharp.

"You know," said Gabe with a smirk. "This is extortion. Blackmail. And you're an ex-con."

"And you're a son of a bitch," she said. "So what?"

They glared at one another across the room.

After a long silence Gabe said, "How much money?"

"That's it!" yelled Underwood, flinging down the headphones. "Let's go."

Swiveling in the other direction, he caught up Zane Maxfield by the collar of his shirt and dragged him straight up in the air. Pushing his face so close his breath lifted the man's hair, Underwood said, "You tell me *this instant* where we can find these guys or so help me God, your sister's blood will be on your head!"

"Chill out, Mr. G-Man," said Zane. "Everything's cool. Max wanted me to wait until you guys had heard the drill. Just hand me that map over there, man, and I'll show you. It's not but a couple of miles away. Don't get your underwear all twisted. Geez."

Brett almost laughed at the incredibly lax security around the cabin. He'd expected all kinds of paranoid bells and whistles, but was not all that surprised at finding the opposite. Men who held the kind of power and position as Garrett Sharp were also usually possessed of an ego that knew no bounds. In spite of what the man did for a living, he apparently believed that nobody would ever dare to spy on *him.* The "it-won't-happen-to-me" attitude was common in the security business.

Once Brett had reached the house, he crept around and checked to make sure that the suction mike Max had intended to attach to the front window before going into the house was indeed in place.

It was. *Good girl,* he thought.

Then he eased around to the side of the building. A door led to the kitchen. Brett tried it. It was unlocked.

With a slow shake of his head, he eased the door open and slid into the kitchen. The open arrangement of the place was appalling. The kitchen led to the great room where, around the corner, Brett could hear voices. Darkened back stairs led to the loft area where he'd ascertained from the transmitter receiver in Max's briefcase that his mother was staying. Carrying his .45 cocked and locked, Brett traversed the stairs one at a time, silent as a shadow.

The stairs opened into a narrow hallway that led like an L to the loft rooms. Brett intended to stay as far back from the balcony area as possible, to avoid being seen by the people down below. He could hear voices raised in argument. Good. That meant that the plan was underway; it also meant that anybody gathered downstairs would be focused on the fight and would not be looking up.

Nevertheless, Brett felt hideously exposed as he reached the end of the hallway and took a quick-fire look around the corner. A large, muscle-bound man sat in a twig rocker, thumbing through a comic book. Their mom sat on the bed, propped fully dressed on pillows, her hands in her lap, listening intently to the argument that echoed from the great room below.

There was no way to enter his mother's room without attracting the man's attention, and as soon as he did so, the guy would be sure to raise the alarm to the men down below. Max had told Brett that the men were all armed, and judging from what she'd told him about that guy Hakeem Abdul, Brett figured they knew how to shoot. One thing was for sure, though, he couldn't stay out here. Already he felt like a target.

Easing his face around once more, Brett froze. His mother was staring straight at him. It was like getting caught with his hand in the cookie jar when he was a kid. Brett didn't know any more what to do now than he had when he'd gotten caught stealing cookies.

Suddenly, his mother placed her hand over her chest and said, "Oh, Sebastian! I'm having a chest pain. Oh!"

The man immediately got to his feet and bent over the bed toward Brett's mother.

Hurtling into the room like a big cat, Brett brought the grip of the .45 down on the man's head with all his strength. The guy dropped like a rock, facedown on the bed.

Brett glanced at his mother. She was smiling, and tears had welled up in her eyes. She mouthed the words, "Thank you," and blew him a silent kiss.

Tough ole gal.

Backing up as far from the balcony as possible, Brett gestured to her and she sprang from the bed like a girl. And before he could even think, Hi Mom, she was burrowed into his chest and was squeezing the living daylights out of him. As he nuzzled her fragrant hair and patted her narrow, delicate shoulders, Brett was filled with murderous rage at the men who had hurt his family.

Revenge, however, would have to wait. Right now, he had to get his mother away from this place.

Taking her arm in a gentle, but firm, grip, he led her toward the hallway.

Just then all bloody hell broke loose.

The SWAT boys had a welcoming party awaiting them at Garrett Sharp's log cabin. As they crept through the forest toward the cabin, a shot rang out. Immediately, one of the agents returned fire.

"*Hold your fire!*" screamed Underwood at the top of his lungs. *"FBI! Hold your fire! FBI"*

And in response came an answering shout, "Hold *your* fire, asshole! *U.S. Customs Service!*"

At the sound of gunfire outside, the inside of the cabin erupted into chaos.

Dominic, Hakeem, and Evan Ryder all drew weapons at once, diving for cover as they did so. Max, thunderstruck by what was happening and frozen in place, saw Hakeem shove Gabe to the floor. Sharp ducked down behind a couch, shouting, "What's happening? What's happening?"

It was a bizarre ballet of confusion, made all the more stunning when Max heard Dominic bellow at the top of his lungs, *"U.S. Customs Agent! Everybody drop your weapons! NOW!"*

Max thought, *Huh?*

Somebody fired, and the room exploded into a nightmare mélange of gun smoke and earsplitting gunshots.

Max crouched down and put her arms over her head, as if making herself smaller would somehow put up a protective shield over her body. Her reactions were too slow; she didn't know she was in shock.

She was hit by a staggering blow to her body.

At first she thought she'd been shot, but then she realized she'd only been tackled. Dragging her arm almost out of its socket, Brett yanked her into the kitchen and shoved her down behind the heavy pinewood table, which he had overturned even as she heard another explosion just beside her face.

Someone touched Max and she jumped, but it was merely her mom. They grappled for one another's hands and squeezed tight.

Brett turned to Max and yelled, "I thought Zane was supposed to send the SWAT guys over here!"

"He is!" she hollered.

In that split second, her brother's attention was focused on Max. It was a fatal lapse.

Like a satanic apparition out of the mists, a keening, screeching form flew from around the corner and hit Brett broadside before he even had time to react, knocking his gun out of his hand. It skittered across the hardwood floor far out of reach.

Hakeem Abdul, his face twisted with demonic fury, had his hands around Brett's throat in a death grip. The two men grappled and rolled.

Max sprang to her feet and grabbed her brother's .45. She flung herself spread-eagled onto Abdul's back, cocked the pistol, and shoved it under his jaw.

Max heard herself screaming, *"Let my brother go or I'll blow your face into the next room, MOTHERFUCKER!"*

In that instant, time seemed to stop.

A familiar voice yelled, *"Max! No!"*

It would be so easy to pull the trigger. So easy.

And then she heard Dominic's voice in her ear, saying, "Give me the gun, honey. I'll take care of it."

But she wouldn't loosen her grip. "I want to kill him," she said. "I want to kill them all."

"I know. And I don't blame you. But this is not the way to help your brother or Gaby."

At the mention of her little girl's name, Max eased up somewhat on her grip. Still, Dominic had to pry the gun out of her hands. She tried to get off Hakeem, but she was feeling suddenly weak-kneed. She felt her mother's gentle touch, and it gave her strength. She stepped aside.

Dominic said, "Hakeem, I am Judson Heath, a U.S. Customs agent, and you are busted. Get facedown on the floor now, or I guarantee I will kill you."

Just then the front door and the back door crashed open simultaneously, and heavily armed men, dressed in black from head to foot, swarmed into the house, filling the air with banshee shrieks that Max would never forget for as long as she lived. One of the men pounced into the kitchen on legs like coils, holding one of the meanest-looking weapons Max had ever seen and screaming at Dominic to drop his gun.

"Wait!" spoke another man in a deep voice. "He's one of ours."

Somebody dragged Hakeem away. Still in shock, Max stared at Dominic as though she'd never seen him before in her life.

Suddenly, her mother said, "See? Didn't I tell you he was a nice boy?"

Max stared at her. Liv was smiling. Max rolled her eyes.

Brett got up and rubbed his throat. He grinned at Max and said, "Thanks, sis."

"My pleasure."

As they grinned at each other, he added, "Of course, I'd have felt a whole lot better if you'd released the safety."

"What?" She glanced at Dominic. He was grinning, too. He held up the gun to show her.

She sighed. "Oh, brother."

"So you kicked ole Hakeem's ass, huh?" said a familiar voice. "You go, girl." Underwood stepped beaming into the kitchen. With a gesture toward Max, he said, "My informant."

Dominic—or was it Judson?—looked over at Max

then, and gave her the sweetest smile she'd ever seen on any other human being. He said, "Informant, huh? I might have known."

To Underwood, he said, "Special Agent Judson Heath, U.S. Customs. I've been working undercover on this case for over a year, following that charming fellow over there." He pointed at Hakeem, who was prostrate, face-down, on the floor in the great room, his hands behind his neck, under the watchful guard of three scowling feds.

Underwood said, "*Customs?* It would have been nice if you guys had let somebody know what the hell you were doing."

Dominic—or Judson—said dryly, "I could say the same thing about you feebies. If I'd known Max was an informant for you guys, it would have made my job a hell of a lot easier."

"Still. I can't believe this! Two investigations going at the same time?"

"And neither one of us knew about the other. Figures." With a sigh he added, "We've just got to stop meeting like this."

To Underwood, Max said, "Agent Underwood, I'd like you to meet my other brother, Major Brett Max-field, U.S. Army Special Forces. He came along to help us out. We'd be dead without him."

Underwood smiled. Extending his hand toward Brett, he said, "Nice to meet you." As he and Brett shook hands, he glanced over at Max. "Yet another brother? Hell of a family you got here."

And she said, "Underwood, you don't know the half of it." But her voice was distracted, her attention caught by a sight Max never thought she'd live to see: the Honorable Judge Griswold, being escorted in handcuffs by two federal agents.

"Wait a minute!" she cried. They ignored her.

"Hold it!" yelled Underwood. The men stopped.

Max walked over to them and gazed up into her ex-husband's eyes for a long, exquisite moment. She was trembling, every nerve ending in her body electrified.

Then she spat full in his face.

When they led him out, Max's contempt was still dripping from him.

PART V

JACKPOT

In a really just cause the weak conquers the
strong.

——Sophocles

Chapter Thirty-one

The feds moved in on CovertCom and removed truck-loads of evidence. Within a few days, the heart-stricken Rose Peterson, Garrett Sharp's secretary, had been cleared of any wrongdoing, due, for the most part, to Judson's intervention.

Judson.

The name was going to take some getting used to.

In the weeks following, Max saw very little of her former lover. Jack Underwood whisked her away like a federal tornado, and she had spent days and days and days being debriefed by the FBI concerning her part of the investigation.

Underwood had already become something of a legend in the Bureau for his handling of Operation EAVESDROP. He was due to be transferred to the criminal investigative division of the FBI at the headquarters in Washington, D.C., an assignment that, he told her, very often led to a choice posting later as special agent in charge of a major field office.

Max knew that Underwood had lost his family because of his dedication to his job. The job would always come first. Max hoped it was worth it to him. She wished him well.

Thanksgiving had come and gone in a colorful blur, and Christmas didn't look much more promising. Although Max and her mom had much to celebrate and be thankful for, there was still much more to wrap up.

There was one more detail to take care of. A gigantic, crucial detail. Everything, but everything, hinged on it. If Max lost on this hand, she knew, she would lose everything.

And if she won, she would gain the whole world.

But if there was one thing Max had learned through the years, it was this: that in order to gain everything, sometimes it was necessary in life to risk losing everything. And nothing in life was ever worth the risk more than love.

January in Dallas could be bleak and miserable at times, reflected Liv, but on this day, the gods had conspired to make everything perfect: from the sparkling blue skies to the mild temperatures in the sixties.

Everything was as it had been on the day Max returned from prison—at least, on the surface, everything was the same. The whole family was congregated at Clark's lakeside home, but oh, what a difference nearly a year had made!

This time every time Liv and Max met one another's quiet gaze, they would tear up. It was ridiculous, really, but they couldn't help it. They couldn't believe it, either, were afraid to believe it, really, that it was *finally happening*.

Liv didn't know who was more nervous today, herself or her daughter. Any minute now, Brett would be returning from DFW, and the wait was almost unbearable. Suddenly, Max jumped up and paced over to the sliding glass door, let herself out, and took off in a brisk walk through the backyard toward the lake. Nobody inquired after her. They were all nervous, too.

For the hundredth time, Liv hurried to the front window, parted the drapes, and peered up and down the streets. Brett, who had flown in yesterday from Fort Bragg with his pretty little wife, Janice, had taken Clark's Cherokee Jeep to the airport to pick up their precious cargo.

Then she saw the car, and her heart leapt to her throat. For a long dreamlike moment, she watched as the Jeep slowed, then turned into the curved driveway in front of the house. When the car door opened and Brett unfolded himself from behind the wheel, Liv came unstuck. Screaming, *"They're heeeeere!"* at the top of her lungs, she flung back the front door and ran on the legs of a young deer out the door, across the grass, and into the arms of her son.

He was crying; she was crying; everybody was crying. "Mom," he whispered. "Oh, Mom."

"My darling boy," she sobbed. "My sweet boy Brand. Welcome home. Welcome home."

"Mom! Mom!"

Max thought the reedy voice calling from the direction of Clark's house was Hannah, calling for her mother. Immediately, she turned around to see if anything was wrong.

She stood on the edge of the lawn behind Clark's house, thin and tall and graceful as a gazelle, her straw-blond hair streaming behind her like golden rays of sunshine. She looked like a dream, like all the dreams that had tormented Max in the predawn hours of her years in prison.

And, as in those dreams, Max thought, *This isn't a dream after all. This is really happening.* And she thought her heart would burst with joy.

Because this time it *was* happening. This time it was a living dream.

Max started out at a walk, then broke into a jog, then ran all-out.

She didn't have to go far. Her daughter was running toward her, too.

At ten years of age, and tall to boot, Gaby was too big to pick up, but Max did it anyway, swinging her into the air, laughing and crying and kissing her child.

Gaby whispered, "I missed you, Mom."

But Max couldn't speak. There were no words.

Because *this* was real.

After a moment she looked up and saw Brett striding toward her across the grass. Or *was* it Brett?

He said, "Guess which twin I am and I won't give you a noogie."

Still sobbing and laughing at the same time, Max said, "No fair. If it's Brand, you'll give me a noogie anyway!" She threw one arm around her brother's waist in a fierce embrace, but only one arm, because nothing would ever, ever make her let go of her little girl again.

Judson Heath waited all the way until both trials were completed and both Garrett Sharp and Gabe Griswold

sentenced to federal prison before he visited Max. She
was still living at her apartment in New York, with her
daughter. Her mother, Liv, had returned to Texas to
live, and her brother Brand was sharing the apartment
with her for the time being, in order to make Gaby's
transition to her new living arrangements as smooth as
possible.

He was more than a little nervous. He'd seen very
little of Max in the six months since the CovertCom
bust. Judson hoped she understood.

Hell, he just hoped she'd talk to him.

He'd done some quiet behind-the-scenes checking,
and had learned that Max had been living mostly on
savings and the investments she'd made while CovertCom was going strong, but that she'd had trouble
finding work and might soon wind up at a Radio Shack
over on Sixth. Brand was apparently doing night-guard
security for the apartment building. Between the two of
them, they were barely eking out rent and might soon
have to move to a lower-rent neighborhood, something
Max dreaded doing, apparently, because Gaby was so
happy at her school.

So all that amazing talent between the two of them—
the crackerjack electronics expert and her Green Berets
brother—was apparently being squandered. Judson
hoped to change all that, if she would let him. He took
the elevator up.

To his surprise, she was waiting for him in the corridor. She'd left the door to her apartment ajar and was
standing there in blue jeans and a white UT sweatshirt
with the sleeves pushed up around her elbows. She
wasn't wearing any makeup, but her translucent complexion was glowing, her tousled blond hair shining, and
she looked more relaxed and beautiful than he had ever
even imagined possible in his wildest fantasies.

"Hi," she said in a shy little voice. Stepping up to him,
she lifted her face and kissed him softly on the cheek.
She smelled like a springtime garden.

She made his knees weak.

"Come and meet my family," she said, taking his hand
in her warm long fingers.

In the apartment, a man who looked exactly like her

brother Brett got to his feet and extended his hand to
Judson. He stood tall and physically fit, and his handshake was firm and strong, his gaze direct. Judson instinctively liked him.

"This is my brother Brand," said Max. "He took care
of Gaby and kept her safe when I went to prison."

"It's an honor to meet you," said Judson.

Max disappeared into the hall, and Judson heard her
calling to someone. Max came back into the room with
a skinny, spindly-legged little girl who was the mirror
image of her mother. Judson had no trouble imagining
that this must have been what Max had looked like as
a kid.

"I'd like you to meet my daughter, Gaby."

Judson walked over to them and squatted down to
eye level with Gaby. She gazed at him with intelligent,
honest eyes. "It's a pleasure to meet such a brave young
person," said Judson solemnly. He took her hand in his
and kissed the back of it, which provoked a gale of
giggles.

"You look just like Tom Selleck," she said. "I love to
watch *Magnum, P.I.* reruns. Do you like that show?"

"Yes, I do," he said.

"Maybe we can watch it together sometime," she said.

"I'd like that very much."

"Okay," she said. "Uncle Brand? Can we go to Central Park today, please? It's so pretty outside."

"You bet, honey. I'm going to visit with your mom
and her friend for just a few minutes first, all right? Go
back to your room and get your homework completely
done—even the math—and then we'll go."

With a gleeful little skip, she pirouetted and danced
off to her room.

"I think I'm in love," said Judson with a smile.

"You and half the boys in her class," said Brand.

They sat down in the living room.

"You're dying to know, aren't you?" teased Max.

"Dying to know what?"

"How Brand came back from the dead. I know you.
You can't stand it, but you're too polite to pry."

He grinned. "I'm never too polite to pry."

Max and her brother exchanged glances. He shrugged. "You go this time. It's your turn."

She smiled. "Okay. The truth is, Brand really was killed in Desert Storm in a helicopter crash. At least, we *thought* he was."

"But you know," Brand inserted, "Special Forces goes into a mission without dog tags or any other ID."

"What happened?" Judson asked Brand.

"Well, we were on a special-ops mission, and the chopper went down over enemy territory. Everybody on board was killed except me, but I was busted up pretty bad. Iraqi troops were rapidly approaching the scene, which means I'd have been history anyway, probably, but I was picked up by a sympathetic Bedouin." With a sigh he said, "I found out later that the Iraqis blew the crash site to smithereens—for no real reason, you understand, other than to cause anguish to the families."

Max said, "All they had to send anybody was pieces, just pieces of bodies." She grew quiet.

Judson gently prodded, "The Bedouin?"

With a nod Brand said, "That man saved my life. He hid me from the Iraqi soldiers and kept me alive, and at some time while I was laying there in his tent, I got to thinking about Max and Gaby. Her situation was truly desperate at the time, just hopeless, really. I had just called my mom not two weeks before the crash, and she was crying about it. It tore my heart out, I tell you, and just the thought of that bastard getting his hands on my niece made me homicidal."

"So he did it," said Max. "He let the army think he was dead, and let me tell you, it was no small sacrifice."

"It wasn't that big a deal," said Brand.

"Oh, yes, it was," she said with a glance toward Judson. "Don't listen to him."

"Well, my closest buddies all died in the chopper crash anyway, to tell you the truth," said Brand.

Max touched his hand.

"So you called home, then?" prompted Judson after a respectful silence.

"I did. I called home, and when the general hysteria had died down—I mean man, they had just gone to my *funeral*—"

"So once everybody calmed down," said Max, "Brand made the proposition to Mom that we send Gaby out of the country, and that he could take care of her at least until she was old enough to legally decide for herself whether she wanted to have anything to do with her father."

"Incredible." Judson turned an openly admiring gaze toward Brand. "Just plain heroic."

Brand shrugged.

Max touched her brother's arm affectionately. "Of course, Brand had to assume a new identity. And just to be on the safe side, Zane set up the electronic dead drops so that we could keep up with them with no fear of leaving any sort of phone bills or other evidence of where Gaby might be."

"And we all made the decision, up front," added Brand, "to think of me, Brand, as being dead. I made them promise that, even within just the family, they refer to me in the past tense. I was scared to death that, with everything I'd gone through, one of my own family would accidentally betray me. There were to be no letters, no snapshots, no communication of any kind."

Max nodded. "He was dead to us. From that point on. Even in private. And he was right, too. I mean, it would be just like Gabe to hire a P.I. to snoop through the garbage or bug Mom's home or whatever, and even one little slip would have betrayed Brand." She sighed. "God, it was hard."

"Tell me about it," said Brand.

Everyone was quiet for a moment.

Judson said, "I understand Senator Kane pulled a few strings to get Brand back into the country?"

Max nodded. "A few. But Mom had put Brand's death benefits into a trust fund and hadn't touched them. She returned the money to the government as soon as the senator intervened, so there would be no question of impropriety. Mainly, Senator Kane had to do some big-time talking over at the Pentagon, I think, but he's apparently got a lot of friends over there, since he fought so hard to keep several army bases in Texas open through all the military downsizing. He convinced them that, due to the special, extenuating circumstances, they should quietly give Brand an honorable discharge, rather than charging him with desertion and throwing him in jail. Senator Kane also helped to get Brand and Gaby back into the country."

"Once he got the door open," added Brand, "it happened pretty quickly after that. Gaby never really liked the American school in Geneva. She always said the kids there were rich and snooty, so we couldn't get our bags packed fast enough."

"And, boy, did the senator get some *major* brownie points with Mom!" laughed Max.

"No kidding," said Brand.

"Are they seeing each other?" asked Judson innocently.

"Boy are *you* out of the loop!" cried Max with another happy laugh. Judson stared at her. In all the days they'd spent together, he'd never even seen this side of her.

He ached for her, literally ached.

He cleared his throat. "Well, one reason I've come is that I have a proposition to make to the both of you."

Brand and Max glanced at one another and back at Judson.

"You know, I took early retirement from Customs."

"No," said Max. "I didn't know."

"I'd been undercover so damn many years, I was starting to forget who I was," he said.

Max blushed and dropped her gaze.

"I'm starting up my own spy shop now," he went on, "and I've already acquired some clients, just from all the publicity the CovertCom case generated."

He paused. When nobody spoke, he went on. "In fact, I've got so much business that I need some help. A partner. Or two."

Max glanced up sharply.

"I mean, it would be business on a shoestring at first. I don't have all the resources that CovertCom had—after all, this is an honest business."

Brand said, "Judson, I don't know anything about electronic countersurveillance."

Judson said, "Well, that's just the thing, see. I'm wanting to branch out a little and offer overall corporate security consulting as well. I would need someone capable of handling that end of the business."

Brand looked at his sister, but spoke to Judson. "We've been trying to think of some way that I could remain close by and continue to play a part in Gaby's life."

"Then, this would be perfect," hazarded Judson.

Both men turned toward Max.

When she didn't speak for a while, Brand got to his feet. "Tell you what. I'll take Gaby on to the park, and you two can talk about this. Sis?" Max looked up. "Whatever you decide to do is cool with me."

"I know." She jumped up and impulsively kissed his cheek. The two of them fussed with getting Gaby out the door, and Judson shook Brand's hand again.

"Brand, I'd love to have you on board. I think we'd make a hell of a team."

Max's brother gave him another firm handshake, thanked him, and bustled Gaby out the door, who was already chattering like a little starling.

Max closed the door behind them and waited until the chirping young voice vanished.

Judson stood across from her. Technically, they were only separated by a few feet, but it may as well have been several miles.

"There were so many lies between us, *Dominic*," she said finally. "So many secrets."

"Yes."

"How can we ever get past that? How can we ever learn to trust each other?"

"Easy," he said. "We just start over."

"That's ridiculous! You can't—"

He took a step closer. "My name is Judson Heath," he said. "I'm from Evanston, Illinois. I grew up close to Lake Michigan. My dad died when I was in college, and my brother, Tom, was killed in the Vietnam War. My mom still lives in the same house, and I try to go see her a couple times a year. She's way different from your mom, but I think they'd like each other. And I know she would love you."

"C'mon . . ."

He took another step closer. "I served in the Marine

Corps for three years, and then I joined the U.S. Customs Service. I've been working undercover for six or seven years; too long, really, mostly in the organized crime underworld. It was getting to me. Making me forget who I was. Keeping me from having any kind of real life."

"But—"

He stepped very close, close enough to smell her perfume. "Until last year, I had never been in love or had a serious relationship with anybody. I couldn't, you see, because of my work, but mainly that was just an excuse. I just never did meet anybody I wanted to fall in love with."

"What happened last year?" she whispered.

"I met you and, baby, all bets were off."

"Pretty risky, you know," she murmured, gazing up at him from beneath her lashes. "Starting a new business. Starting a new life. Stuff. You know."

"You think I'm bluffing?" he said with a slow grin.

"There's only one way to find out," she said. "And that's to play the hand to the end."

"I'll show you my cards if you'll show me yours," he said. "We've got a real two-way action going here."

She put her arms around his neck. "Jokers wild?"

He pulled her close. "In this game? Hell, they're *all* wild."

"In that case, I fold. Let's put the cards to bed."

Acknowledgments

So many people generously donated their time and expertise to ensure that *Tightrope* was absolutely accurate in its technical detail that I hardly know where to begin to thank everybody.

For technical assistance on electronic countersurveillance, I am most deeply grateful to Jeff Spivack of Data Security Group, Norcross, Georgia, for reading the manuscript page by page and stopping me before I made a complete idiot of myself. Our weekly telephone exchanges were a sheer delight, and I am sure glad I can now call Jeff my friend.

Once again, I am thankful for the friendship, technical guidance, and overall general cheerleading that I get from my good friend, John Bailey of the Interagency Task Force, Klamath Falls, Oregon. Any technical mistakes that may appear in this book are strictly mine—Lord knows these two men did their best to help me get it right.

Many, many thanks also go to everybody at the Federal Prison Camp, Bryan, Texas, for answering all my questions, giving me a tour, and reading the manuscript to check for technical accuracy, especially Warden Ann Beasley and her executive assistant, Greg Thompson.

Thanks, too, to my friend, police officer Craig Andersen of Nyack, New York, for helping me to navigate the highways and byways of upstate New York. Craig and all the other great folks I hang out with over on the Police forum at CompuServe are more dear to me than I can say. Stay safe, guys, and keep laughing.

Once again, my friends in the Federal Bureau of Investigation have requested that I not publish their names, and I am happy to oblige, but I want them to know how very much I appreciate their insight, expertise, guidance, and humor.

I would also like to thank my lifelong friend and brother-in-law, Colonel Richard W. Mills, U.S. Army Special Forces, who has always demonstrated, by his life and his character, just what the slogan, "Be the best that you can be," means.

Tightrope is a book, first and foremost, about family, and the importance of always knowing that there is somebody, somewhere you can count on to be there for you when you're in trouble. This book is my gift to my parents, my brother and sisters, and my in-laws. It's my way of saying thanks for always being there for me.

My husband, Kent, my love and my life for the past twenty-four years, and my two terrific kids, Dustin and Jessica, have always been my rock, my inspiration, and my strength. Much love and many thanks, once again, to you all.